A Dangerous Dress

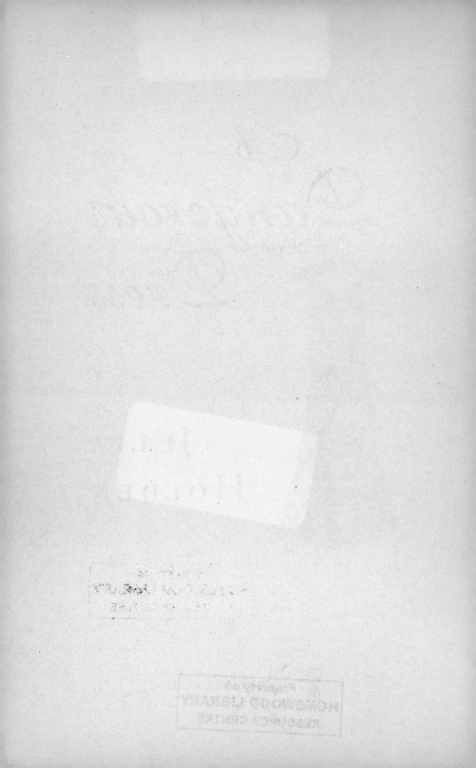

A Dangerous Dress

JULIA HOLDEN

New American Library

New American Library
Published by New American Library, a division of Penguin Group (USA) Inc.,
375 Hudson Street, New York, New York 10014, USA • Penguin Group (Canada),
90 Eglinton Avenue East, Suite 700, Toronto, Ontario M4P 2Y3, Canada (a division of Pearson Penguin Canada Inc.) • Penguin Books Ltd., 80 Strand, London WC2R 0RL, England • Penguin Ireland, 25 St. Stephen's Green, Dublin 2, Ireland (a division of Penguin Books Ltd.) • Penguin Group (Australia), 250 Camberwell Road, Camberwell, Victoria 3124, Australia (a division of Pearson Australia Group Pty. Ltd.) • Penguin Books India Pvt. Ltd., 11 Community Centre, Panchsheel Park, New Delhi - 110 017, India • Penguin Group (NZ), cnr Airborne and Rosedale Roads, Albany, Auckland 1310, New Zealand (a division of Pearson New Zealand Ltd.) • Penguin Books (South Africa) (Pty.) Ltd., 24 Sturdee Avenue, Rosebank, Johannesburg 2196, South Africa

Penguin Books Ltd., Registered Offices:
80 Strand, London WC2R 0RL, England

First published by New American Library,
a division of Penguin Group (USA) Inc.

First Printing, July 2006
1 3 5 7 9 10 8 6 4 2

Grateful acknowledgment is made for permission to reprint the following copyrighted material:

"Bewitched," words by Lorenz Hart, music by Richard Rodgers. Copyright 1941 (renewed) Chappell & Co. All Rights for Extended Renewal Term in U.S. controlled by WB Music Corp. and Williamson Music. All Rights Reserved. Used by Permission.

REGISTERED TRADEMARK — MARCA REGISTRADA

LIBRARY OF CONGRESS CATALOGING-IN-PUBLICATION DATA:

Holden, Julia, 1959–
A dangerous dress / Julia Holden.
p. cm.
ISBN 0-451-21864-7
1. Young women—Fiction. 2. Dresses—Fiction. 3. Americans—France—Fiction. 4. Fashion shows. 5. Paris (France)—Fiction. 6. Manhattan—Fiction. I. Title.
PS3608.O4832D36 2006
813'.6—dc22 2006000202

Set in Granjon • Designed by Elke Sigal

Printed in the United States of America

For my daughter Rachel

and

the Jane in all of us

Acknowledgments

Warmest thanks to Bill Contardi, Kara Cesare, Claire Zion, Mom and Dad, Grandma Mary, Gianluca, Carolyn, Mary Jane, and, of course, Milan. To my dear Parisian inspirations: Françoise; Flavien, Céline, and all my friends at Hotel d'Aubusson; Loredana; Colin at the Bar Hemingway; and Valerie at Armani Collezioni. Finally, deepest gratitude to Laura, and, always, Mitch.

1

This is the story of a dress. A dangerous dress. A magical dress, I think. My Grandma's dress. And it is a true story.

Essentially.

I know, just because I went and qualified *true* with *essentially,* now you're going to think this story is *not* essentially true. But it is. For example, here are some of the things that are one hundred percent true.

I go to the glamour capitals of the world, Paris and New York, where I do incredible (but true) things. Like selling the most exclusive designer clothes on the planet to the most radiant human beings on the planet. And attending an ultra elite private fashion show on a yacht, surrounded by the most gorgeous partygoers in the universe. And debuting on live TV as the fresh new voice of a major network news program. But in spite of all that fabulousness, this story starts—and may even end—in a town that everybody under the age of forty whose opinion I value, including me, more often than not calls Bumfuck. Even though its real name is Kirland, Indiana. If I were making this up, I wouldn't start—and I certainly wouldn't end—in Bumfuck.

The town is named for Hap Kirland, who was an engineer. The railroad type. Probably nobody would've ever named anything for him, except that in 1887 he was driving a train out of Chicago, and right after he crossed the state line into Indiana, he ran off the tracks. The place he derailed, people started calling Kirland Siding. Which over time got shortened to Kirland. That's what they taught us in school. Although why anybody would name a town after a guy who couldn't keep his train on the tracks is beyond me. And what kind of a name is Hap, anyway?

A sign at the town line says, WELCOME TO KIRLAND, INDIANA, POPULATION 5,120. The number is wrong. Nobody's sure which way it's wrong, but everybody agrees it's not wrong by much, so it's just easier to leave it the way it is. What matters, and what we can all agree on, is that Kirland is a small town.

If you only talked to people from Paris and New York, you'd never guess that genuinely dramatic things happen in small towns. Because those big cities are made up of two kinds of people: those who never lived in a small town, and those who fled small towns to move to more exciting places like Paris and New York. And now I am about to perpetuate this problem. Because even though I'm from a small town, most of this story happens in Paris and New York. But I don't want you to think that nothing of interest has ever happened in Kirland, Indiana.

The interesting events began in 1986. I did not actually observe those events, as I was only five at the time. But everybody in Kirland knows what happened. Every last detail. Not a day passes without somebody telling the story like it happened yesterday. Each time somebody tells it, everybody stops and listens to what Nick Timko did to Mary Kovach.

Back in 1986, everybody in Kirland loved Nick Timko. My mom insists I loved him just like everybody else did, even though I was five. Nick was a huge baseball star at Roger Wells Kent High School, which is the public high school. Nick was a senior, and he went steady with my cousin Mary, who was a junior. Mary's mom, Rose, my mom's sister, died about eight years ago. Mary's dad, my Uncle John, is president of the Independence Savings and Loan Association of Northwest Indiana.

Nick couldn't decide between a baseball scholarship at Purdue and an offer to play single-A ball for the Cleveland Indians organization, even though Mary wanted him to go to Purdue so he could come home on weekends. But Nick couldn't decide, and they had a fight about it at the senior prom at Reinhardt's restaurant, and Mary ran off crying. Only before he could run after her, the prom committee announced the selection of the Prom King and Prom Queen. Of course Nick was crowned King, and of course Tina Kaminski, who everybody says was hot enough to peel paint off a Pontiac, was crowned Queen. So Nick and Tina had to dance together. Even though Tina was dating Greg Deegan, I guess she was always a little hot for Nick just like everybody else was, and for all I know maybe he was a little hot for her too. Or maybe it was just that night. But the consensus is that when they danced the ceremonial first dance, they danced very very close. And I guess they didn't stick around for the second dance, because they ended up in the back seat of Nick's old Dodge Dart in the parking lot. Which is where Mary found them.

Before the sun was up the next day, Nick beat it out of town and started playing minor league baseball. He eventually made it to the major leagues for about twenty minutes. He never showed his face in Kirland again. We have an expression—when other people say *It'll be a cold day in Hell* or *When pigs fly,* folks in Kirland say *That'll be the day Nick Timko comes home.* And to this day, unless you ask her point blank, my cousin Mary never even mentions his name. Other people do, but not Mary. Which I think is entirely understandable, given what he did.

Incidentally, I do not want to suggest that every small-town romance is as dramatic as Nick and Mary's. My point is simply that interesting things do happen in small towns—not that they happen all the time. They do not.

Anyway, enough about Nick, because the part where he's relevant is done. But Mary is very relevant. With Nick gone, she had to figure out what she was going to do next. Uncle John always wanted her to go to work at Independence Savings. A lot of people assumed he would want Mary's younger brother Johnny to work there, what with Johnny being a boy and all. But Uncle John figured that since Mary was born first, she should work at the bank, and maybe even take it over someday. I think if Nick had behaved and not gotten all sticky with Tina, he and Mary would've gotten married, and even though Mary wouldn't have loved it, I think she'd have been willing to go to work at Independence the way Uncle John always hoped.

As things worked out, though, Mary decided that if she was going to be unhappy about love, she sure wasn't willing to be unhappy about work, too. So after high school she went off to Indiana University in Bloomington, where she drank way too much but still graduated with a teaching credential. Then she moved back to Kirland and started teaching third grade, which she still does. She also convinced herself she was in love with George Boba, whose sole redeeming quality was that he wasn't Nick Timko, and they got married. Only George turned out to be a shit. Six years ago Mary and George had a baby girl who had Down syndrome. George must've done or said something awful about that, because two weeks after the baby was born, Mary broke his nose and she and Paris moved back in with Uncle John that same day. Paris is Mary's daughter. She is the most amazing cute *smart* adorable six-year-old child ever, and since that day, George Boba has never seen her, doesn't want to, and I hope he dies.

As I said, Mary named her baby Paris. I always thought that was the best name I ever heard for a girl. So one day I asked Mary why she picked that name. First she said because nobody in Kirland ever named their baby Paris, which is true but not relevant. So I kept asking her, until finally Mary told me that she and Nick always talked about going to Paris together. Paris, France. Which I guess is maybe a little relevant. Or at least very romantic.

Even though Mary never wanted to work at the bank, my cousin Johnny was happy to. Johnny had his whole life figured out. The day he turned eighteen he enlisted in the Army, just like Uncle John had done. But Johnny had seen his dad limp around with a cane on account of the shrapnel in his hip from the Korean War. So he joined the Quartermaster Corps, which he figured would be about as safe as an Army job could be. Plus he might learn some accounting that'd come in handy when he finished his tour and went to work at Independence.

Only a year after he enlisted, along came Desert Storm, and Johnny got shipped out. I mention that not because now it's topical to talk about Iraq. I mention it because Johnny died in an Iraqi Scud missile attack. He and twenty-seven other soldiers in the Quartermaster Corps. After Johnny's funeral, my Uncle John stopped flying the American flag in front of the bank, even though he is the most patriotic man I know. But that's really not the point. The point is that Uncle John was never the easiest-going man. Johnny's dying made him even more difficult. And on top of everything, now there was nobody to go to work at Independence and follow in his footsteps.

I knew he wouldn't ask Mary again. She'd have said no anyway. But he knew she'd made up her mind, and even if he didn't agree with her decision, he respected her, and he wasn't going to use Johnny to pressure her into taking the job.

He did not, however, have any such qualms about *me.*

So when I graduated from high school, Uncle John paid for me to go to Purdue. Where I had an inordinate amount of fun. (Stupid Nick. Stupid stupid stupid.) And where I also earned a BS in Management. Which, I'm sorry, was not the fun part. It was the Uncle John part. It was all this accounting. And statistics and probabilities and economics and policy and—

Ohmygod, somebody please pour me another beer.

Wait. That's not entirely fair. If I hadn't studied Management at Purdue, I never would have gotten sick of all the Management courses. I never would have browsed the course catalog looking for something, *anything* else to take as an elective, to keep my brain from turning into an Excel spreadsheet. I never would have found the Consumer Sciences and Retailing department.

Maybe you cannot tell from the name, but the Consumer Sciences and Retailing department is all courses about, well, clothes and shopping. I am not kidding. Did you know such a thing existed in college? I didn't. If I had known when I started, I'm not sure I ever would have made it to that job at Independence.

Not that I was any kind of a fashion expert when I went to college. Frankly I don't know how anyone could grow up in Kirland, Indiana and be one. Except for Susie Anderson, whose mom used to take her to Paris twice a year just to shop for clothes. What such people were doing living in Kirland, I don't know. Needless to say I hated Susie Anderson. And wanted to be her. Desperately.

On the other hand, I bet Susie never met Mister Giorgio Armani in Paris, the way I did.

But I am getting ahead.

The point is that while I was growing up, I was not Susie Anderson. I did not shop in Paris, or anyplace else glamorous, or even fun. I shopped in JC Penney at River Oaks Mall. At best. When it came to fashion, all I could do was watch Cindy Crawford and Elsa Klensch on cable after my parents finally got cable, read the occasional *Vogue* or *Elle,* and dream about someday shopping in glamorous, fun places and wearing glamorous, fun clothes.

Then second semester of my junior year, just to give my brain a break, I took CSR 327. History of Fashion. Which was great fun, not too hard, and there was no accounting involved.

Then came the week we covered the 1920s. And here we are getting *extremely* relevant.

Because that was the week I saw my Grandma's dress projected on the big screen at the front of the lecture hall.

2

My Grandma's dress is, quite simply, the most amazing dress I have ever seen.

I am not saying that because I am biased, but because it is true. And that is no small statement coming from me. I have personally visited every vintage clothing store in the entire city of Paris. Which, as you probably know, is a place where they make some pretty nice dresses. So when I say Grandma's dress is special, I know what I am talking about.

Before I tell you about the dress, I need to say just a little about my Grandma. First, and forgive me I know this sounds like an acceptance speech, but without her none of this would have been possible. And second, because the more you know about my Grandma, the more amazing the dress becomes.

Grandma used to give me neck rubs, and even when she got very old, she had very strong hands. She did WordFinder puzzles using a magnifying glass that looked like a tiny telescope, which she needed because by the end she was legally blind. Legally blind, sure, I guess, but you never saw anybody clean a house like that. Don't ask me how she knew where the dirt was. She passed away in 1998, just two weeks shy of her ninetieth birthday.

Why do people say *passed away?* She died. She weighed eighty-five pounds at the end, and she died. And I still miss her.

Grandma did not always weigh eighty-five pounds. When I was born she weighed a hundred and ninety-four. That's what she told me. For all I know it was more. But she was big. She told me she got to where she wore a size twenty-two. Maybe the hundred and ninety-four pounds is true, because she told the truth about the size twenty-two. When she died she left me her clothes, and even though there wasn't much, there were several of these huge old size twenty-two housecoats.

If you didn't grow up in a small town, or in the Midwest, or you just don't know, a housecoat is like a robe, only made of a much thinner fabric. Which makes no sense, because in a place like Kirland, which is not a mile off Lake Michigan and that wind, what good it does to wear a robe made of such thin fabric, I don't know. But there they were. Housecoats. Size twenty-two.

I could speculate about how Grandma got to be so big, but I don't have to, because she told me. Before I tell you, first you need to know about people in Kirland. There are mostly two kinds: Steel people and Oil people. Historically, those were the only industries in town: the U.S. Steel steel mill, and the Standard Oil oil refinery. Since most folks worked for one or the other, you came from either a Steel family or an Oil family, I guess because they were different unions, but partly it seemed to be a personality thing, too. At least, that's how it struck me, based on my own family.

When I was born I had all four grandparents alive. My dad's family was a Steel family, and my dad's parents were Steel people. They were tall and skinny and kind of cold, and they didn't give you a lot of hugs, even when you were at that really cute age. So my grandmother on my father's side was always just a grandmother.

My mother's family was an Oil family. They were short and round and loud, and I always wanted to go to Grandma's house, where there were always great old songs playing on the cabinet phonograph. Even if I went there every day, I got more hugs than you can imagine, even when I reached an age we can all agree is not terribly adorable. At Grandma's, everybody was always in the kitchen, and somebody was always frying up pierogies, or baking nut roll, or kneading the dough for amazing homemade bread.

Incidentally, Kirland is a very high-cholesterol environment.

I have seen Grandma's wedding pictures, and she was a slender young thing. So I just assumed she got to be so big eating all the pierogies and nut roll and amazing bread. But one day, I guess when she figured I was old enough to handle it, she told me the truth. She said all that weight came from the Boilermakers.

A Boilermaker is a drink. It comes from a time before fruity drinks, when mixed drinks meant things like Manhattans and Stingers, which are now fashionable again. Boilermakers are not fashionable again. They were probably never fashionable. A Boilermaker is:

One shot of whiskey. And one mug of beer. That's it.

Some people shoot the whiskey straight and drink the beer as a chaser. Other people pour the whiskey into the beer and drink them together. Still other people drop the shot glass of whiskey *into* the beer mug, then drink it like that. The first method is certainly the most efficient. The second is kind of putrid. The third is putrid and also inefficient, because if your beer mug starts out full, dropping the shot glass in makes you lose some of the beer. Personally I went for shooting the whiskey and then chugging the beer.

I have a little experience of my own with Boilermakers. You know how at Notre Dame the football team is the Fighting Irish, and if you play football at USC you're the Trojans? At Purdue, you're a Boilermaker. So, at least at Purdue, Boilermakers never really went out of style. Which on occasion led to certain events that are none of your business.

Anyway, according to Grandma, that was where all her weight came from—Boilermakers. She told me that one day she just got tired of being a size twenty-two, so she gave up the Boilermakers, cold. I was about ten at the time. Let me tell you, she must have been drinking an awful lot of boilermakers. Because when she gave them up, she started to drop those pounds. Until she weighed eighty-five pounds, and then she died.

She made my Grandpa give them up, too. Maybe he shouldn't have quit the Boilermakers, because about six weeks after he did, he had a stroke and died. It probably had nothing to do with the Boilermakers, but you never know. I haven't said much about Grandpa, which really isn't fair. He was short and round and loud and huggy. He always gave me the spare change from his pockets. I loved him a whole lot. I hope wherever he is—and yes, I believe in that kind of stuff—wherever he is I hope Grandpa won't be mad, but he's just not all that important. Not to this story.

Because, as far as I could learn in my research, Grandma got the dangerous dress when she was nineteen years old, but she only started dating Grandpa when they were twenty-one and married him when they were twenty-two. So you see, the dress came from somebody else. Which made it even more dangerous. And far more mysterious.

Just like her house was perfectly clean even when she couldn't see, Grandma was perfectly organized when she was dying. She didn't have a will. I suspect most people in Kirland don't have a will. That may cause problems for people who are not as organized as Grandma was. It did not create any problems for Grandma. Two weeks before she died, she went around her house Scotch-taping little tags to everything, saying who got what. She didn't have a lot of things. But she made sure everybody she cared about got something.

After the funeral, I didn't want to go look right away. Grandma had just died, and I was very upset. Because she was extremely special to me. I was very sad, and I didn't think looking through her empty house would be much fun. But my mom said that if Grandma could be so organized for everybody, at least we could all go see what she gave us. So I went.

Mom got Grandma's framed picture of the Pope. Cousin Mary got a lamp I always thought looked like an old-fashioned hair dryer. Mary's daughter Paris got Grandma's collection of WordFinder puzzle books. Like I said, I got her clothes. Which, I must admit, initially I wasn't too excited about. Because there were all those housecoats. Size twenty-two. Size sixteen. Size ten. Down and down, the housecoats documented Grandma's slow disappearing act.

There were other things, too. Skirts, blouses, and a few dresses. Church clothes. Shoes. None of which fit me and—sorry, Grandma—none of which I would even consider wearing.

Then there was Grandma's wedding dress. Which was a pretty dress in Grandma's wedding picture. Unfortunately the silk had turned all yellow and brittle with age. So even if I ever have the occasion to wear a wedding dress, and even if I want to wear a traditional one, and even if for sentimental reasons I want to wear my Grandma's dress—I can't. It's all stained and mildewed and cracked, so it smells . . . well, not good enough to wear to your wedding.

I finished going through the closets, and that was pretty much it. Because after all, where else would you keep clothes? Just for the heck of it, I wandered down to the basement. For most people, a basement is like a grease trap. Things accumulate there, and unless it gets so clogged that you absolutely have to clean it, you don't. Not Grandma, though. Her basement was this big empty room. Besides the furnace and some plumbing, there was mostly a lot of nothing there. Except a table with a lamp, a couple of pieces of Depression glass, and a bunch of rosaries with the beads worn down to almost nothing. All the Scotch-taped tags on those things had other people's names on them. Next to the table was an old suitcase.

A suitcase? Grandma never went anywhere that I knew of. Or that anyone else in the family knew of. I mean anywhere. Ever.

It was a very old suitcase. The frame was made of wood, and the side and top and end panels were rattan. The handle was crumbly old leather. If it had been new, the suitcase would have looked at home in a Fred Astaire–Ginger Rogers movie. Which made me wonder a couple of things.

First, what was Grandma doing with it?

And second, where had she been hiding it all these years? Because let me tell you, I spent a lot of time in Grandma's house. It's not very big. And I've been through all of it, including the basement.

At least, I thought I'd been through all of it. Only here was this suitcase that I'd never seen.

The suitcase had a name tag on it—not an old luggage tag, but one of Grandma's Scotch-taped bequests. She had been really careful with this one, though. She had doubled up the tape, sticky side to sticky side, and made a loop, so the adhesive wouldn't touch the bag. Which made it seem extremely important. I was very excited when I looked at the tag.

Only it said, *Suitcase for Uncle Joe.* Not for me. In just a few seconds I'd decided this was something special, and it must've been for me. Now it wasn't. I was so disappointed.

I don't know what made me turn the tag over. None of the other tags had writing on both sides. But I did. And the other side said, *Contents for Jane.*

Which was how I found the dress.

3

I need to be very careful about how I describe the dress. Because it is *completely* relevant. More than just relevant. Essential.

The bodice of the dress was made of two layers of this amazing sheer pearl-blue silk satin. If the dressmaker had used only one layer, the dress would have been indecent in 1928, and maybe even today. Because you could see right through a single layer of the silk. But with another layer added, the dress became translucent rather than transparent. You could *almost* see through it, but not quite. Which made it *incredibly* provocative.

The fabric was cut on a diagonal, what fashion design people call "on the bias," which makes the fabric cling to the body much more intimately than if the weave was simply vertical and horizontal. The bodice was sleeveless, and the neckline plunged modestly in the front and so immodestly in the back that it would be daring even now. I can only imagine what a fuss it would have caused when first worn. The front of the bodice was sewn with an elaborate Art Deco pattern of dark blue glass beads so iridescent you'd think Tiffany made every single bead. I am talking about Mr. Louis Comfort Tiffany, not the store with the turquoise gift boxes.

The pearl-blue tulle skirt flirted with transparency, and it was also sewn with the amazing blue beads, but fewer of them, so they did not weigh down the skirt. The hemline looked as if it would fall just below the knee in front and to about midcalf in back.

I could not have written that description when I first saw

the dress. I needed to get quite an education first. At the time, all I could think was *Wow.*

Once I got past *wow,* I realized it was the kind of dress you'd picture the women in F. Scott Fitzgerald novels wearing. The young, pretty ones. The ones who make the men and boys gasp for breath. The careless, reckless, gorgeous, sexual ones. The *dangerous* ones.

There was something else in the suitcase, too. An old menu. From a restaurant called La Tour d'Argent. Which is French for The Tower of Silver. I know because I looked it up on the Internet. The name is in French because the restaurant is in France. In Paris, to be precise. In fact, it has been there for four hundred years. The fact that one restaurant has been in business in the same place for four hundred years is pretty amazing, but not nearly as amazing as the fact that, as far as I could tell, *my Grandma* had been there. Not to mention that she had apparently been there wearing this reckless, gorgeous, sexual, dangerous dress.

I asked my mom why she never told me Grandma went to Paris.

"As far as I know, she didn't," my mom said.

"Then where did she get the menu?"

"I don't know anything about it," she said.

"What about the suitcase? Where was that?"

"I have no idea," she said.

"But you grew up in this house," I said. "How could you not know anything about it?"

"Because I don't."

"What about the dress? Did Grandpa give it to her?"

"I have no idea," she said.

"Did Grandma ever go *anywhere?*"

"Not that I know of," she said. Then she stopped and thought for a while. "I wonder." She sat down and frowned, which is what she does when she is trying to remember something. Finally she said, "I was only eighteen. Almost nineteen. I was helping Grandma and Ginny Anderson cook chickens over at Sacred Heart. I asked

Grandma where she thought I should go for my birthday. I just meant, What restaurant? Only she gave me this stare and said, 'You're not going anywhere. Not for the next six months.' Then Ginny asked Grandma, 'What's wrong, you think it runs in the family?' And then the two of them laughed until they cried. I asked Grandma what was so funny, but she never told me."

"You think she went to Paris?"

My mom and I both looked at the dress, and the menu, and the suitcase. She didn't have to say anything. I had the answer.

From what my mom said, Ginny Anderson seemed to know something about it. Maybe she even went with Grandma. Ginny was Susie Anderson's grandma, and if I had heard this story years ago, I could have asked her. Only Ginny died two years before Grandma, and Susie and her family moved away after that, so all I had was the suitcase, the dress, and the menu. In other words, a mystery. Which I vowed I would solve.

As it turns out, vows are easy to make. But mysteries are not necessarily easy to solve.

In fact, for a long time, the only thing I had besides the suitcase, the dress, and the menu was the vow. For four whole years, in fact. I wish I could tell you that I immediately knew what to make of it. But I didn't. In fact, I didn't have a clue what to do. So I did something practical: I took the dress to Chicago. Which I should mention is only about a half-hour drive from Kirland. Twenty minutes if there's no traffic, although there's always traffic. So half an hour.

Here's another thing you need to know about Kirland: A lot of people who live there *have never been to Chicago*. Like I said—Bumfuck.

I folded the dress very carefully, wrapped it in white tissue paper, and gently placed it in a big shopping bag, which I seat-belted into the front seat of my Tercel. I drove into downtown Chicago to find a dry cleaner. And no, it did not occur to me to take the dress to a dry cleaner in Kirland. If I have to explain why, you have not been paying attention.

I parked at the Chicago Place Mall on North Michigan Avenue and found the public phones. The mall is modern, but the phones still had phone books hanging from them. I looked in the Yellow Pages under *Dry Cleaners,* and wrote down a couple in the most expensive neighborhoods. Then I drove until I found one I liked the look of.

I guess I picked the right dry cleaner. When the ladies behind the counter saw Grandma's dress, their eyes got big. They oohed and aahed, and they handled it very carefully, like they knew immediately it was something special. They did a very nice job cleaning it, too. When I picked it up, it was packed like it would survive a nuclear war.

They charged me fifty-two dollars. I almost fainted. But I didn't. I paid, took the dress home, and put it—and the mystery—away in my closet. Where they both stayed.

For four years. Until my junior year at Purdue. Second semester. History of Fashion.

We were looking at slides. Which we saw a lot of. Which was when Grandma's dress came up on the screen.

The picture wasn't *like* Grandma's dress. It *was* Grandma's dress. Actually, the very first thing that occurred to me was that somebody must've stolen the dress from my closet back home in Kirland and taken a picture of it, although why anybody would do such a thing I couldn't imagine. Then right away I decided that was silly. Which didn't stop me from going back to my dorm room and calling Mom and having her check, and of course the dress was still hanging where it was supposed to be.

Before I called my mom, I went up to the professor at the end of class. Her name was Professor Singer. She was tall and thin and looked like she had almost been a model when she was younger. I say almost, because her eyes were a little too close together. But she was very nice when I told her I had a question about a dress. The one with the very sheer skirt. With the blue-black glass beads. Did she know anything about it?

She checked her notes. "It just says 'Collection of Flapper Dresses, 1920s, Paris.'"

"Nothing else?" I asked.

"Nothing else." I guess she could see that I was unusually interested. "Why?"

"Because . . ." For a moment I wasn't sure if I should tell her. Like it was my big secret. The thing that made me feel special, different from everybody else in that big lecture hall, even if I hadn't earned the right to feel special, since the dress was really my Grandma's, after all, and I only got it because she died. But even if I hadn't earned it, just having the dress in my closet back at home made me feel like I had some little spark of magic that was all mine. And I was afraid the magic might go away if I told.

Then I thought, *If you can't tell your History of Fashion professor about this dress, who can you tell?* So I told her Grandma had a dress exactly like that, which she left to me.

"It's a very unusual dress," she said. "For there to be two identical dresses would be . . . unusual."

"It is unusual," I said.

"Where are you from?"

"Kirland," I said. I almost said *Bumfuck,* but I didn't think I should call it that to a professor, so I didn't.

"That would be . . . *very* unusual," she said.

"I *know,*" I said.

"You're sure it's exactly the same?"

"Absolutely." I was.

"Hmmm," she said. Then she thought a little. I was afraid her eyes would cross. But they didn't. "What do you know about its provenance?" she asked. *Provenance* is a fancy art word that means where something came from and where it's been.

"Absolutely nothing."

"Well," she said. "Well." And I thought that was that. But then she said, "We can't lose an opportunity like this, can we?"

I didn't know what opportunity, but I shook my head no anyway.

"You're required to write a paper for my class," she said. "The dress can be your paper!"

"But I don't know anything about it. And"—I tried to say this part very diplomatically, and I even pointed at her notes to back me up—"neither do you."

"But you can *research,*" she said. "I'll help you. Oh, this is going to be fun!"

Up to that moment it never occurred to me that you could research a dress. I knew you could research the building of the Sears Tower, or the history of space exploration, or even—yuck—the savings and loan industry in northern Indiana. I knew you could, because at one sorry time or another in my so-called education, I'd actually had to research those things. But I didn't know you could research a dress. Much less an old dress. Much less an old dress you knew nothing about.

Only now I did know something. Two things, in fact. First, it was really from the 1920s. And second, it—or they—had been made in Paris.

"Paris?" I asked.

"Paris," Professor Singer said.

"Paris, *France?*" I asked.

"Of course," she said. I guess if you are a professor of Fashion History, then of course it's Paris, France.

Not only did my Grandma apparently go to Paris and dine at some fabulous famous four-hundred-year-old restaurant, she also apparently got her reckless, gorgeous, dangerous dress in Paris. All of which made me wonder where else my Grandma might have been, and what else she'd done, that I knew nothing about.

"There are really ways to research a dress?" I asked.

"Oh, yes," she said.

And do you know, there are. It was quite a lot of work. I had to read articles, and even a couple of books, about specific French designers. Like Madeleine Vionnet. Today she is pretty much only a perfume. But in the 1920s she was a very influential Parisian designer. She was the one who pioneered cutting fabrics on the bias. So at first I thought maybe Grandma's dress was a Vionnet. Except for the split-level hemline. And the fabric choices. So I came up with a theory. That somebody who worked for Vionnet then went to work for another designer named Louiseboulanger, and borrowed elements from both, then added some of her own.

I was sure the person who designed this dress was a woman.

Anyway, that was my theory. And I was pretty well able to pinpoint 1928 as the year it was made. Probably late 1928. Because hemlines dropped in 1929, along with the stock market, although I don't think the two things were necessarily related.

Professor Singer was right about it being fun. Plus I learned an enormous amount, although *not* how Grandma came to own such a dress.

I put everything I'd learned into my paper. Which took a really long time. It ended up being thirty pages long, and it had ninety-seven footnotes. I am not a big fan of footnotes. If I could have written this paper with even one footnote less, I would have. But I couldn't. It all belonged.

I will not quote much from the paper. It would take up too much space, and a lot of it is pretty technical, about fabrics and stitches and beads and such. And I have already told you most of my conclusions. But one part of the paper was my favorite, and apparently it was Professor Singer's favorite part too, because she wrote *Yes!* and *Wonderful!* in big letters in the margin. It was the final paragraph:

> I started researching this paper because I had questions. Why did my grandmother go to Paris? Did she buy the dress herself, or if not, who gave it to her? What amazing adventure must she have been embarked on? I did not find the answers to those questions. But I still think I can draw some conclusions from the dress, and what it must have meant to my grandmother. Everyone knows that dresses can be powerful

things. For example, Cinderella's fairy godmother gave her a beautiful dress, which empowered her to go to the ball, meet her Prince Charming, etc. My grandmother's dress is also very powerful, and with all due respect to Cinderella, it must have given my nineteen-year-old grandmother powers that would make a fairy godmother blush. Obviously, it gave her the power to show her skin, and to make men swoon. But I think it also gave her the power to think for herself. To vote. To drink. To smoke. To shop. The power to make her own choices, and her own mistakes. And last, but most certainly not least, the power to have great sex. I do not know if my grandmother did all of those things, and frankly, it is a little strange to think about your grandmother that way (at least it is strange for me). But the fact that she had this amazing, adult, *dangerous dress* I never knew about makes me hope that once upon a time, she lived an amazing, adult, *dangerous life* that nobody in Kirland ever knew about either.

In case you are wondering, that part did not have any footnotes.

I guess Professor Singer liked the paper. She gave me an A-plus on it, and another A-plus for the whole course, even though Purdue actually only recognizes grades up to A. What made me feel even better than the pluses was that she submitted it for some kind of fashion industry competition, and it won third prize. The fact that it won anything at all came as a total shock to me, because she didn't even tell me she was entering it. I didn't feel bad that it was only third prize, either. Because Professor Singer told me most of the entries came from places like the Fashion Institute of Technology in New York, and were written by people who are making fashion their entire careers. So third place was pretty good, if you ask me.

The five hundred dollar prize was even better.

To be honest, I felt like a little bit of a fake. Because I was not a real fashion student. And besides, all I had done was write about my grandmother's dress. Which, as I have said, I just inherited one day without ever earning it. Feeling like a fake did not stop me from accepting the five hundred dollar prize, though. Or from spending a little too much of it on Boilermakers and related events that, like I said, are none of your business.

I have to tell you one more thing about my paper—the very best thing about it. The title.

The title was "A Dangerous Dress." Which was perfect.

And which, it turns out, was also *very* relevant.

4

I hope I have convinced you that small towns are complicated, interesting places. Even if you personally wouldn't choose to live in one.

In any event, here's where the glamorous part of the story starts. But you'll have to bear with me just a bit longer, because it begins with me still in Kirland, sitting behind my desk at Independence Savings and Loan. Doing the job my cousin Mary wouldn't take, and my cousin Johnny would've taken, only he died. Working for my Uncle John, who, as I mentioned, is not the very easiest person in the world to get along with. And that is as my *uncle.* As my *boss,* he was . . . well, how shall I put it?

Most days he made me want a Boilermaker. Some days a whole bunch of Boilermakers.

This was a multiple-Boilermaker day. Uncle John had just finished being mean to me. He wasn't a yeller, but he sure knew how to make you feel small. Even if he came over to compliment your work, he managed to point out that it took you too long, it should have been neater, and it would've been a lot less bother if he had done it himself. And most of the time, when he came to talk to you, it was not to compliment your work.

He and I had just finished having one of those you-did-something-wrong chats. I felt about as smart—and about the same size—as the brick on my desk.

I didn't put the brick on my desk. It came with the job. It's a very small brick, as bricks go. Kind of a dull yellow-brown color, instead of your traditional red. Even among bricks, it's below average. And that's just how I felt.

Then the phone rang. I picked it up. "What?" I said. If I sounded cranky, well, how would you sound if you were a stubby stupid brick?

"Oh," said the man on the other end of the line. My whole brick attitude seemed to throw him a little off balance. "I'm . . . I'm looking for Jane Stuart."

"What?" I said again.

"Is this Jane Stuart?"

He was really going to make me say it again, wasn't he. *"What?"* I said.

"I'm looking for the author of 'A Dangerous Dress,'" he said.

All of a sudden I couldn't even say *what.* I was too confused. He said the *author* of "A Dangerous Dress," as if it was a book, instead of just a paper for my History of Fashion course.

"I'm sorry to bother you," he said. "I had a hard enough time getting the alumni office at Purdue to give me this number. But if you aren't Jane—"

Suddenly I wasn't a brick anymore. "But I *am* Jane."

Only now he apparently didn't believe me. "I'm looking for the author of a monograph about a very special dress," he said.

Although I am a graduate of Sacred Heart Catholic School, Roger Wells Kent High School, and Purdue University, I had never heard anyone call anybody's college term paper a monograph. But he did say the dress was very special. "It's my Grandma's dress," I assured him. "Or was. She left it to me. It's in my closet," I said. Then I took a deep breath. In through my nose, out through my mouth. A boyfriend taught me that. He was wrong. It didn't help the sex. But it seemed useful right now. I said, "I am the author of 'A Dangerous Dress.'"

Then the man on the phone began quizzing me with questions that only the author of "A Dangerous Dress" would know. Fortunately I knew the answers. I say *fortunately* because he'd obviously read my paper much more recently than I had. "All right then," the man finally said. "You *are* the person I have been looking for."

"Excuse me," I said. I lowered my voice, because Uncle John had just opened his office door and was looking around the bank. He does that sometimes, for no apparent reason—just opens the door and gives the bank a long, slow look. "But who are you?" I whispered. Then Uncle John closed his door, the way he always does after one of his long, slow looks.

"My name is Elliot Schiffter," said the man on the phone. Then he paused. I swear he did it for dramatic effect. "I'm calling from Reliable Pictures."

I have a confession to make—and I hope you won't be mad or disappointed, because I told you on the first page that everything I was writing is true. Essentially. And so far everything has been not just essentially true, but completely true. Only now I have to tell you that Reliable Pictures is not the real name of the movie studio that Elliot Schiffter works for. Although Elliot Schiffter is his real name. I will tell you this: You would know the studio's name if I told you.

"I need your help," Elliot Schiffter said to me. "Reliable Pictures needs your help. A great creative enterprise needs your help."

He really said that. I would never have made up that "great creative enterprise" stuff.

"What kind of help?" I asked.

"Creative help," he said. "Costume design help. For a major motion picture." He paused again. Then he said, "A major motion picture that may never get made. Unless you help us."

I suggested a minute ago that I thought this Elliot Schiffter person was being perhaps a little melodramatic. Now, though, I was forming a different impression.

"Please," he said, "give me your e-mail address."

Now I was starting to think that he sounded . . .

"So I can send you your plane ticket."

. . . desperate.

5

Desperate or not, Elliot Schiffter had my full attention. Because he was offering to send me a plane ticket. He hadn't mentioned where I was supposed to be going, but as far as I was concerned, if you're from Kirland, anywhere else you go is up.

"Reliable's art house subsidiary is making a movie," he said. "They're about to start production. A lot of the story takes place in 1928. And the first scene they're going to shoot is the climactic twenties party scene."

You may not know this—I didn't—but as Elliot explained to me, when they make movies, they do not film the scenes in order. So the last thing in a movie may be the first thing they film. Which is a little counterintuitive, but that's how they do it.

"Only there's . . . an obstacle," Elliot said. Then the phone line got quiet.

"An obstacle?"

"Look at your e-mail," Elliot said.

I looked. I had a new message with an attachment. This is what the attachment said:

```
THE MURPHYS' APARTMENT - INT - NIGHT.

MOVING SHOT through the huge apartment. In the
ballroom, JOSEPHINE BAKER, 21, a stunning black
woman wearing very little, sings, backed by a
```

small orchestra. Guests dance on the parquet floor. Waiters carry trays piled with shrimp, and champagne in glasses bigger than finger bowls.

Hemingway and Catherine enter. She is wearing a diaphanous beaded dress—a grown-up, sexual, dangerous dress. The Murphys greet them.

SARA
(dry as a martini)
It appears Pauline has had her baby early. And shed a few years.

HEMINGWAY
Pauline's pooped. She thought her friend Catherine might like the party, though.

SARA
(even dryer)
Her friend is wearing a lovely dress.

GERALD
Charming.

As Catherine passes him, Gerald looks at Hemingway and raises his eyebrows approvingly.

"I don't understand," I said.

"The *dress,*" Elliot said. "Catherine's diaphanous beaded dress. The grown-up, sexual, dangerous dress."

"I don't understand," I said again.

"The movie's director is Gerard Duclos," Elliot said, like that should mean something to me. It didn't. "Gerard is very particular about details. He insists the dress actually be from 1928. And that it be *perfect.* So far, the costume people haven't found anything that satisfies him. Until they do, Gerard won't shoot the scene. This picture has an all-star cast. It took two years to get everybody's schedules to dovetail. But if Gerard won't shoot the scene, the schedule slides. If it slides two days, we lose Kathy. Which means we also can't shoot the scene in Gertrude and Alice's apartment. If we can't shoot that scene on time, we lose Elijah. And if we lose Elijah, we lose the whole movie," said Elliot. Grimly.

I promise you, I will tell you who those names are, and I will use their real names.

"We cannot lose the movie," said Elliot. "So."

"So?" I asked.

"So," said Elliot. "We need a dress. *The* dress. And it seems Gerard Duclos is a big fan of Google. He went looking, and found your monograph. 'A Dangerous Dress.'"

I confess, when I read that scene from the script, I missed it. But when Elliot said the name of my paper, it finally struck me. They needed . . . *a dangerous dress.* Made in 1928.

"Monsieur Duclos insists we fly you and your grandmother's dress to Paris immediately."

Paris??? The words *oh yes please thank you* were almost out of my mouth—only something he said stopped me cold.

They wanted Grandma's dress. And I most certainly could not hand Grandma's dress over to a total stranger. Not even a total stranger who was the Senior Executive Vice President for Motion Picture Production of Reliable Pictures. Not even if it meant passing up my ticket out of Bumfuck. Before I could figure out what to say, though, Elliot continued.

"Monsieur Duclos wants you to be a consultant. He said his costume designer doesn't understand his vision and doesn't know what he's looking for. He said you will understand. I think he wants you to show them your grandmother's dress and tell them what they need."

I felt so relieved I almost slid out of my chair. I didn't have to *give* them Grandma's dress. I could just *show* it to them.

"Monsieur Duclos insists that only you can help him," Elliot said. "He won't even consider using anyone else. And he's the director. What he wants, he gets. So, will you help us?"

"When do I start?" I asked.

"They're scheduled to start filming the party scene in four days. That doesn't leave us much time. I'll e-mail you the script and your ticket." Then he paused. And this time I am absolutely, positively sure he did it for dramatic effect.

Finally he said, "You'll leave . . . tonight."

6

"Come in," said Uncle John.

I walked into his office. Actually I didn't walk in very far, in case I decided I needed to get out of there in a hurry.

He was behind his desk, which you would call cluttered if you weren't mad at him, and a godawful mess if you were. Every inch was crammed with Sacred Heart stuff and Knights of Columbus stuff and American Legion stuff. Not to mention genuine work-related stuff. Oh, and about fifty pictures of his granddaughter Paris, plus a couple of my cousin Mary, and even one of me. Uncle John was reading something, or pretending to, and he didn't look up. I knew from experience that if I waited for him to look up, I could be standing there a very long time.

"I'm taking a vacation," I said.

"No you're not," he said. He still didn't look up.

"Yes I am," I said. "I have been working here almost three years, and the most I've taken off in a row is three days when cousin Mikey got married in Bloomington."

"You took off four days in January."

"I had the flu," I said. Boy, was I sick. I should have gotten a flu shot. This year I am definitely getting a flu shot.

"When are you going?" he asked. Still not looking up.

"Tonight," I said.

Uncle John looked up at that. "No you're not."

"Yes I am. I have a plane ticket."

"Since when?"

"Since five minutes from now. They're e-mailing me the ticket." Uncle John tolerates the computer as a necessary evil. I hoped that things like e-tickets would intimidate him.

"You can't go," he said.

"Sure I can," I said. Now this probably sounds very bold on my part, especially considering that Uncle John can be a pretty tough guy. But he is also my uncle, and one of the relatively few advantages to working for a family member who you've known forever is that you have a pretty good sense of where you can push them and where you can't. Besides, it was a really slow time, and I knew that and he knew that. "Plus I'll just be gone a couple of days," I said. Which was completely true when I said it, because that was what I believed at the time.

Reluctantly, Uncle John said okay. *Woohoo!*

I went back to my desk. An e-mail came in from Elliot, with the script as an attachment. I printed it out. Here is what the cover page said:

THE IMPORTANCE OF BEATING ERNEST
an original screenplay

The bottom of the page said Copyright J. Thomas, and there was an address on King Street in New York, NY.

I was about to start reading, when another e-mail came in. I opened it, and *woohoo* turned into *ohmygod.* I immediately called Elliot Schiffter. "There's a problem," I said.

"Didn't you get the e-mail?" he asked.

"Yes, I got the e-mail," I said.

"You don't like the seat? You're in First Class. You want a window instead of an aisle?"

"The seat is fine," I said.

"Then what's the problem?"

"You're sending me to Paris," I said.

"And?"

"Paris, *France,*" I said.

"I already told you that," Elliot said. "That's where they're making the movie. So?"

"So I just realized: I don't have a passport."

There was a prolonged silence. So long, I thought we might have been cut off. Finally Elliot said, "Sure you do. Everybody has a passport."

"I don't. I live in Kirland, Indiana. I'm twenty-five. I never needed a passport."

"I'll call you right back," Elliot said. Then he hung up on me.

Thirty seconds later, the phone rang again. Forty-five seconds, max.

"We're putting you on a later flight," Elliot said. "Go home. Pack. Be ready to leave in half an hour. A car will take you to the passport office in Chicago. They will process your passport on an emergency expedited basis. Then the car will take you to O'Hare Airport. Your flight will leave at . . ." I could just picture some little assistant whispering information into his ear—"six-oh-five," he said. "Any questions?"

"No," I said.

"Then why are you still talking to me?" Elliot asked. Before I could answer, he hung up again.

Two thoughts immediately collided in my head. The first was, *I am going to Paris. I. Am. Going. To* Paris. *Paris,* France. Which was amazing. Incredible. Unbelievable.

The second thought was, *I have to leave in twenty-nine minutes.* Which was impossible.

I am not speaking figuratively. I am not the very fastest person in the world when it comes to picking clothes. And, as you probably know, picking clothes is a fairly important part of packing a suitcase. Especially when you're going to Paris, France. I had no idea how I could possibly do it in twenty-nine minutes.

I ran home, which is only two blocks away. When I got there I pulled out a suitcase—my mom's, because I don't exactly have my own luggage. I do have some duffel baggy kind of things, but to go to Paris, I thought I should at least have an actual suitcase. Not that it was the suitcase I would have picked for Paris. It's made of this pink carpet-bag fabric. But it was big. Then I proceeded to pull absolutely every piece of clothing out of my closet. No exaggeration. Every single thing. Then I just grabbed and tossed. Here are a few of the things I took:

Everything I own that is black.

A Miracle Bra. Not that I have anything to apologize for in that department, thank you, but every girl can use a little help now and then.

A teeny tiny thong. Just in case an appropriate occasion presented itself.

Every hopelessly ripped, shredded-at-the-heels pair of jeans I have ever refused to throw away no matter what my mom said.

The most perfect little black Dolce & Gabbana skirt and top, which Celestine gave me. Celestine is my best friend from college, and she lives in Paris. I need to tell you considerably more about her. But first let me finish about my packing.

A fiercely painful pair of Stephane Kélian pumps. Also from Celestine.

All told, I packed enough clothes for a week. Or two. I had no reason to think anybody would need me in Paris for that long. But I could hope, couldn't I? Let's face it: If somebody offered you the chance to get out of Kirland, even for a day, you'd grab it. If you got the chance to stay away longer than you planned, you would. If staying away longer meant, oh, forever? Sign me up. And that's if I was going just anyplace. But Paris? Oh, *please* let it be forever.

I also took a copy of my "A Dangerous Dress" paper. Actually I packed that in my carry-on. Which I guess to the uninitiated might look like a small duffel baggy kind of thing. I figured I'd better reread the paper. Because that was why Elliot Schiffter was flying me to Paris.

And, of course, I packed my Grandma's dress: wrapped up in

white acid-free tissue paper, folded very gently, and surrounded by a protective wall of Tampax boxes and Stayfree packages—which I packed for that express purpose.

Looking at the dress, all wrapped and protected in my mom's suitcase, I wondered if I would ever have the nerve to wear it.

I suppose I should make this clear: I had never worn it. Ever.

I didn't even know if it fit. Sure, I had held it up in front of me, lots of times. It *looked* like it would fit. But I never put it on. The thought of me wearing Grandma's dress has always seemed . . . how do I say this? . . . almost sacrilegious. Like if you were invited to a Christmas party and somebody offered to let you wear the Shroud of Turin, you wouldn't, would you?

Okay maybe that is not a perfect comparison. But you get the idea.

So the fact that I was packing my own personal Shroud of Turin and taking it with me to Paris was somewhat terrifying. At the same time, though, it was . . . inspiring. Liberating.

You read the part of my paper about the transformative powers I believed the dress must have had to be able to turn my small-town Grandma into a sophisticated, enchanting, *dangerous* woman of the world. Even though the dress was almost eighty years old, it still felt pretty powerful to me. Maybe the dress wasn't the Shroud of Turin after all. Maybe it was a magic wand—not a fairy godmother's, but my very own Grandma's. And if I was lucky, it might have enough magical powers left to transform me, too.

7

Just as I zipped the suitcase shut, a car horn honked.

I looked out the front window. A big black Lincoln Town Car was outside. I stuffed the screenplay into my carry-on duffel baggy, together with my "A Dangerous Dress" paper. I grabbed the suitcase and the duffel, and ran for the car.

In three minutes we were out of Kirland and onto the toll road to Chicago. I took out my cell phone and called my mom, who had gone to Mrs. Holupki's house for an early lunch. I couldn't think of a clever or subtle way to introduce the subject, so I just said, "I'm going to Paris!"

"Paris is in school, dear." I swear I heard my mom *tsk-tsk* at me. "Please don't disturb her."

I guess I hadn't been entirely clear. "Not Mary's Paris. *Paris* Paris."

"Paris, *France?*"

"Of course Paris, France." I gave her the two-minute version of events. I must say she took it pretty calmly. My parents are very steady people.

"You will be careful," she finally said.

"Of course, Mom."

"Then . . . have a wonderful time." She giggled. *"Paris?"*

"Paris, Mom."

"But you don't have a passport," she observed.

At that moment the driver pulled up in front of the Federal

Building on Dearborn Street. "Eighteenth floor," he said. "They're waiting for you."

"I will in a few minutes," I said. "Anyway, I'll be fine. And I'll be back in a couple of days. Tell Daddy I love him. Bye!"

The driver was right: I got off the elevator, found the passport office—and the instant I walked in the door, a nice young woman greeted me by name. Then a nice young man took my picture with a special digital camera that printed out two identical photos for the application. The nice young woman handed me forms, filled out except for my signature. It was becoming quite clear that there are real advantages to being in the movie business. That made me think, *If I do a really great job and find this dress and save this movie, maybe I can get an actual permanent movie business job. One where you fly First Class, get driven around in Lincoln Town Cars, and drink sparkling water while the nice people at the passport office set a new land speed record processing your paperwork. A job in Hollywood. Or Paris. Anywhere but Kirland, Indiana.*

Whether my goal of leaving Indiana behind and getting a First Class-flying Hollywood job was realistic or not, it motivated me to pull out my "A Dangerous Dress" paper. While I waited, I read the whole thing. Including all those footnotes. Because Elliot Schiffter had not been very specific on the phone, and who knew what that director might ask me? I wanted to make a good impression. No—a perfect impression.

A First Class impression.

I never gave much thought to how long it takes to get a passport—or any thought, for that matter. But if you had asked, Is it possible to get a passport in under three hours? I would have said no. A week, maybe. Don't ask me how they did it. But it is possible: two hours and forty-two minutes. I have the passport to prove it.

We got to O'Hare Airport at about five ten. My flight was scheduled for six-oh-five. As you probably know, that is not necessarily a safe margin if you want to be sure you make your flight nowadays. Especially an international flight. Except that the advantages of being in the movie business do not end at the passport office. You also get to have somebody meet your car at the airport, check your suitcase at the curb, escort you directly to security, and put you into the short, fast line for the X-ray machine and the metal detector. I had always wondered who those people are who get to go in that short fast line. Now I know.

I did hesitate for a minute when they were checking in my mom's suitcase. Remember, my Grandma's dress was in that bag. I was really nervous about being separated from it, even for the length of the flight. It was from 1928, which by definition made it irreplaceable. And it was my Grandma's. I did not want to take the slightest chance of Grandma's dress being lost. Let's face it: Airlines have been known to lose things on occasion. In fact, I was so anxious I actually started to tell the skycap the whole story about the dress.

"Do you want to buy extra insurance?" he asked.

"No," I said.

"So . . . ?"

"So . . . I just don't want you to . . . lose it," I said.

"We'll try hard," he said, and flashed me a paternal smile.

I got to my gate in plenty of time, even after stopping to buy a couple of magazines. I bought *Premiere*—because, after all, I was in the movie business. Also *Daily Variety,* for the same reason. Although $3.25 for a magazine that is only about twenty pages long seemed a bit much.

Preboarding for the flight was announced: First Class passengers only. I walked up and handed the attendant my ticket and my brand-new passport. "I'm sorry," the flight attendant said. "We are seating First Class passengers only."

"But I'm—"

In row forty-two. I hadn't looked at my ticket before this moment. The first ticket Elliot Schiffter sent me was for a First Class seat. I know they had to put me on a later flight because of the passport thing, but I had just assumed I'd still be in First Class.

Obviously there was some mistake. I would have to talk to Elliot about this. Meanwhile, though, all I could do was blush and slink off and wait with the crowd until they called everybody sitting in the back of the plane.

That is where I was. The last row, to be precise—where the seat doesn't recline all the way back, because the bathroom is right behind you. In the middle seat.

I guess because of the delay from the passport, I had missed all the nonstops from Chicago to Paris, so I was flying through Atlanta of all places. Thank goodness it only takes two hours to fly from Chicago to Atlanta. I don't think I could have sat in that awful seat for ten hours nonstop, hemmed in by people who only spoke French and who promptly fell asleep, so that when I needed to use the restroom I had to climb over them.

About an hour into the flight I noticed a woman who kept walking past me down the aisle, then forward, then toward the back of the plane again. Finally she stopped and leaned over the sleeping Frenchmen.

"I can't believe they didn't put you in First Class," she said to me.

On the one hand, I agreed with her completely. On the other hand, I wondered how she possibly could have known about Elliot Schiffter and the tickets.

She leaned down toward me again. "I don't mean to bother you," she said. "But I just had to say, I *loved* you in *Lost in Translation.* Working with Bill Murray must have been so much fun."

"Oh," I said. My brain hadn't fully caught up to what she just said. But I said "Thank you" anyway. Because I knew she had paid me a compliment.

Before I could figure out what else to say, or not say, the man in the seat next to me woke up. He looked up at the woman, who was hovering about four inches over his nose, and made a huge noise clearing his throat, *arrrrughh-ughh.* Which in any language plainly meant, *Please move before you fall on me.* So the woman just said "Bye," gave me a little wave with her fingertips, and walked back to her seat.

Now the man sitting next to me was looking at me. "I am *not* Scarlett Johansson," I said.

I have no idea if he understood me or not. He just closed his eyes and went back to sleep.

Notwithstanding what that lady said, I do not look like Scarlett Johansson. I mean, maybe a teeny tiny bit. She and I are probably about the same height, maybe even around the same weight. And we are both blonde. At least, I am. She changes her hair so much now, it's hard to tell. And I guess the shape of my face is kind of like hers. But that's it. If you had three or four Boilermakers, you might look at me and say, "You look a little like Scarlett Johansson." Then after you sobered up, if you remembered saying it at all, you'd say, "No, you don't."

But that's what she said. Maybe she had a few Boilermakers before boarding. Anyway that was the best thing that happened on the flight, which tells you it was a pretty rotten flight.

After what seemed like forever, we landed in Atlanta. I had to change to an Air France flight, but I didn't care. Because I got to get out of that terrible seat.

My flight came in at Terminal T. My Air France flight was leaving in half an hour from Terminal E. And by the way, Terminals A, B, C, and D are between Terminal T and Terminal E. So I ran the whole way. But I did get there in time. And no, I did not have the middle seat again.

I had the seat next to the middle seat. In the same back row.

8

The flight from Atlanta to Paris was long. But in spite of my excruciating seat, the awful food, and the overpriced screw-top wine, it was okay, because I was so excited. About going to Paris, and about my new movie job, of course. But also about seeing Celestine. Who is my best friend, who lives in Paris, and who becomes extremely relevant. So it is high time I told you about her.

For reasons that are not very interesting, there was nobody from my freshman year at Purdue that I particularly wanted to room with. When I put in my housing request for sophomore year, I figured I'd take my chances. And taking my chances, I got Samantha.

She was much shorter than me, so we would not be able to share clothes, which was too bad. She was an Engineering major, pretty, and Asian. And oh, by the way, Samantha was a lesbian. She told me so in about the first five minutes. She said, "I should probably tell you, I'm a lesbian." Which, by the way, was fine with me. Although please don't go getting any ideas. Because I didn't. It just didn't bother me.

It bothered *her*.

She immediately decided we were not going to have a good healthy roommate relationship. She asked for a transfer, and they gave it to her in two seconds flat.

Leaving me without a roommate. Which could be a problem. If I waited for the housing office to assign me somebody, I was at severe risk of getting a person with major issues. So I took matters into my own hands. If I was going to get a bad roommate, at least let her be a bad roommate I picked for myself.

But I didn't get a bad roommate at all: I got a best friend. I got Celestine. Here's how.

In my desperate search for a roommate without major issues, I combed the virtual message boards on the university's web site. But I also looked at physical bulletin boards, the old-fashioned kind with cork and thumbtacks. On one board there was a pale lavender piece of paper. It was handwritten in writing different from any I had ever seen.

The notice was Celestine's. The handwriting was different because Celestine is from Paris, France. Even though people in Europe are writing the same letters and numbers as us, they write very differently. I didn't know that then. I only knew I'd never seen handwriting like that.

The only thing the notice said was: *Who is my roommate?* Plus a cell phone number.

I called. I don't know why. She could have been awful.

But she was Celestine.

I arranged to meet her in one of the lounges. As soon as she walked in I thought, *Oh please let that be her.* I admit, my immediate reaction was selfish. Because I could see right away that Celestine is the type of girl who attracts a lot of boys, and high-caliber boys at that. And they can't all get her, so that would give me a shot at one or two.

Celestine is the second-prettiest girl I have ever known. In fact, she is almost beautiful. But only almost. It's as if she was born with an absolutely perfect face. Only then somebody gave her nose the tiniest twist while everything was still soft, and it stayed that way. She is very sensitive about it, which I have tried forever to convince her is nonsense. And I am right. I have known a girl who is even prettier than Celestine. Movie-star-perfect gorgeous, in fact. But in my view, no guy who qualifies as a human being would date her.

Because girls like that know they are movie-star gorgeous, which gives them an attitude that, to say the least, is not lovable.

Celestine is exactly the opposite. Because she's so ridiculously insecure about her looks, she is totally approachable and lovable, and she does not intimidate boys. So she has more dates than she knows what to do with, and she always will. At least until she settles down, which she swears she will, but I'll believe that when I see it.

When we first met, Celestine told me she was from Paris. She said her mother was a poet. I never met anybody whose mother was a poet before. I asked what her father did. She said he was a cad, and that was all she ever told me about him. Then she said she was a student at the Sorbonne. I didn't know then what the Sorbonne was, but it sounded so sophisticated it made me wish I was a student there myself. Just as I was starting to wonder what this amazing sophisticated French girl was doing at Purdue, she explained that there was an exchange program between the Sorbonne and Purdue, and she was here for the year.

I am going to let you in on a little secret. First, the not-secret part: Americans have a thing for Europeans. American men melt if a woman has a French accent, and American women melt if a man has a French accent. Italian, too. And British. And Spanish. German, not so much. Anyway, here is the secret: *Europeans—including Celestine—have that same thing with Americans.* That was why she decided to come to the United States for a year and immerse herself in, well, Americans. If she ever does settle down, I guarantee you it'll be with some white-bread Boilermaker boy from Indiana or Ohio or Wisconsin.

Anyway, Celestine and I went straight to the housing office and told them we had done their work for them. We instantly became best friends, and we still are. Thank goodness for e-mail and the occasional very expensive phone call, because even though she lives in a time zone far far away, I would be lost without her. And did I mention that we are almost exactly the same size? Which girl roommates should absolutely always be. Celestine got to wear my sturdy nondescript middle-America wardrobe from Marshall Field's in Chicago, which she loved, for reasons I cannot fathom. And I got to wear her fabulous European designer clothes with labels like agnes b and Versace, which I loved wearing, for reasons I trust are obvious. At the end of the year, after we cried and hugged and cried and she finally flew back to Paris, I opened the closet and found she had left me a fabulous little black Dolce & Gabbana top and skirt, and a gorgeous but fiercely painful pair of Stephane Kélian pumps. Which is how those things ended up in my mom's pink carpet-bag suitcase.

I left for Paris in such a hurry, I didn't even have time to e-mail Celestine to tell her I was coming. So it would be a big surprise. Although maybe not. When I wrote my "Dangerous Dress" paper, she had already moved back to Paris. I sent her a copy because I was very proud of it, and because, in a way, it was about Paris. After she read it she called me. I told her I thought it was a funny coincidence that she was from Paris, and now, out of the blue, I ended up writing this whole long paper about Paris.

"But it's not a coincidence at all," she said.

"What do you mean?"

"The dress called to your Grandma. It made her come all the way to Paris to get it. Now she has given the dress to you, and it is telling you to go to Paris, just like your Grandma did. Someday it will bring you here."

I laughed. Celestine didn't. "You're serious," I said.

"I'm a mystic," she said. Then she laughed, too.

I had forgotten all about that conversation. I only remembered it sitting on the plane. The plane to Paris.

Maybe Celestine actually was a mystic—because Grandma's dress really was bringing me to Paris.

9

Thinking about that conversation, and Grandma's dress, gave me goose bumps.

Although perhaps they just had the air-conditioning in Coach turned up too high.

Once my goose bumps went down, I unzipped my little duffel baggy carry-on and took out the screenplay. *The Importance of Beating Ernest.* Since Elliot Schiffter and Reliable Pictures were flying me all the way to Paris to help them find a dress for this movie, I figured I'd better at least read the script.

The Ernest in the title is Ernest Hemingway.

I don't know about you. But when I was a junior in high school, I had to read some book by Ernest Hemingway. I don't remember which one. All I remember is that I hated it, hated having to read it, hated everything about it. So when I saw that the screenplay had to do with Ernest Hemingway, I thought, *Uh-oh.*

Silly me. I *loved* the screenplay.

Maybe because it's actually not mostly about Hemingway. The main character is this old college professor named Harold Klein. He teaches literature, and he's an expert on Hemingway. Which is really ironic, because when Harold was a very young man he went to Paris and fell in love with a beautiful French girl named Catherine. She fell in love with him, too. Only rat bastard Hemingway stole her away, even though he was married at the time.

So you see, Ernest Hemingway is the *villain.* Maybe that's why I liked it so much.

Anyway, old Harold Klein is dying. And a young student convinces him to go back to Paris. To try to find Catherine, who was the love of his life. He goes, and he sees an old woman who is maybe Catherine. Only before he can find out, Harold gets run over by a guy on a Vespa.

This is not a sad story.

Because Harold wakes up, it's 1928, and he's nineteen again. Only this time he knows everything he learned in his whole life. He and Catherine fall in love all over again. And here comes rat bastard Ernest Hemingway all over again. But this time Harold has the chance to get it right. Of course it's not easy. If love came easy, it would be a very short movie. Harold has run-ins with Gertrude Stein and Alice Toklas, and Scott and Zelda Fitzgerald, who apparently were pretty funny in real life, although probably not intentionally. Even though Harold should know better, having lived through it all before, he does something stupid and Catherine gets really mad at him. So in swoops Hemingway. He invites Catherine to a glamorous soiree *and buys her a dangerous dress,* which she wears to the party. Only Hemingway's wife sneaks Harold in, and Harold steals Catherine right back.

But Hemingway chases them down. There is a big fight, where scrappy little Harold actually beats up big drunk thug Ernest Hemingway. Only Harold takes a terrible beating too, and he passes out, and we don't know if he's alive or dead.

Wait, it's happy.

He's alive. But when he wakes up, he's old again, and he's in a hospital in Paris. The old lady at his bedside *is* Catherine, who has never fallen out of love with him. And the best part is, Harold is *not* dying after all. Which the doctor can't explain, but hey, it's a movie. Harold and Catherine get married in the same Paris café where they first met. They dance, they kiss, and—

"I *love* this!"

Then I realized I had said it out loud.

Fortunately the people sitting on both sides of me were asleep.

I don't usually rave out loud about things I read. But I *did* love it. It was so romantic. Funny, too. But mostly romantic.

I put the screenplay back in my duffel baggy. Then I looked at my watch. I still had another four and a half hours till Paris. So I decided to take a nap.

I guess what with all the rushing around and the excitement I was pretty tired, because in just a few seconds I felt myself drifting off. Before I fell asleep, though, I thought, *Look where I was only twenty-four hours ago. Look where I am right this minute. And just imagine where I could be twenty-four hours from now.*

Only I didn't have to imagine. I was going to Paris. Paris, *France.*

Where absolutely anything could happen.

10

Finally we landed at Charles de Gaulle airport. I was one of the last people off the plane. I looked around, but there was no one waiting to greet me. I followed everybody to passport control. Where there was no line. I do not mean there was nobody waiting. On the contrary: There were about six thousand people waiting. There was just no line. So it took quite a while until the passport control guy scanned my passport and let me into the country. Actually he was very handsome, but there was only one of him. Then it was off to baggage claim.

Baggage claim at CDG is a lot like passport control. Which is to say it is not the most organized place. They give out luggage carts for free, so everybody takes one. Many people take two. It's like a big game of bumper cars, only played in about sixteen different languages.

Given the crummy seat I got on the planes, it will come as no great surprise to you that my bag was one of the very last ones out. At least I had no trouble spotting it. Let us say that not everyone flying to Paris has a big pink carpet-bag suitcase.

I hauled my bag into the main terminal, which is even less organized than passport control and baggage claim. Then I really started to worry. Fret. Panic. Not just in little flashes, either. Full-blown panic. Because somebody was supposed to be meeting me—only there was nobody. Instead of saving a movie, I was in the middle of mayhem, without a clue how I might actually get to Paris on my own if I had to, or where I was even going. I was beginning to feel like Kiefer Sutherland on *24,* with a big digital clock ticking away my time. Okay Kiefer Sutherland faces somewhat weightier matters on *24,* but you get what I mean. To make matters worse, everything was in French.

And I do not speak French.

Just when I was trying to decide whether to cry or scream, I found the driver. He was standing off to the side smoking a cigarette. Lots of people in the terminal were smoking. Which right away told me I was not in Kansas anymore. Anyway, the driver was wearing a Niketown sweatshirt and big hip hop sneakers. I thought they looked silly on this somewhat middle-aged little Frenchman. Still, he was my savior.

I am not suggesting any religious connotation when I say he was my savior. Although it did seem pretty miraculous to me. In the midst of all that bedlam, I found him. And he had a sign with my name on it.

Even if it was the *tiniest* little sign.

"Excuse me," I said. He looked up from his cigarette. I pointed to the sign. "That's me."

"Zat's you?" he asked. I'm not making fun. He really said it that way.

"That's me."

I guess he believed me. Because he immediately grabbed the handle of my mother's big suitcase, and off he went, running madly through the airport, weaving in and out of the huge crowds. Only he obviously knew his way around this airport, and I didn't. Plus he already knew where he parked his car, and I didn't. So in about ten seconds he was gone, my suitcase was gone, and may I remind you that *my Grandma's dress was in that suitcase.*

Now I was absolutely sure I wanted to cry. But I didn't. I heard somewhere that if you are lost, you should stay put so they know where to look for you. I probably heard that on a news story about hikers lost in the Himalayas or some such. I'm not sure the same rules apply when you're in the middle of a million people in

Charles de Gaulle airport. But I stayed where I was anyway. Finally the driver came back and found me. He looked annoyed, but I didn't care. Because he still had my suitcase. Grandma's dress was back. I was rescued. Saved.

We got to his car. Which was not a big Lincoln Continental. It was just a car. A Renault, which is a French car. Not a very large one, either. It's a good thing my Mom's suitcase was not one inch bigger. Because the suitcase would've had to ride in the back seat and I would've been in the trunk.

The instant we were out of the airport, the driver started to drive very fast. I do not generally mind driving fast. But this car was very small. And it sure felt like we were going extremely fast. Some people always look at the speedometer to see how fast the car is going. I am not usually one of those people. But I looked.

The speedometer said we were going 145. Which made me very anxious.

Then I remembered: That was not 145 miles per hour. We were going fast, but not *that* fast. That was kilometers per hour. Okay, how many miles is 145 kilometers? I couldn't remember.

I now know the answer, because I looked it up. We were going 89.5 miles an hour. Which in that tiny little car seemed awfully fast. Especially zooming in and out around the other slowpoke cars that were only going, say, 85 miles an hour.

I was about to ask the driver to slow down. But all of a sudden the traffic got quite awful, and we went from flying to crawling just like that.

After an hour, the traffic was making me even more nervous than the speeding had done. First because I kept imagining that big *24* digital clock pounding away at me. Second because I really needed to pee.

Fortunately, right about then traffic started to move. And all of a sudden I could see.

I was in Paris.

For all I know, we had probably been in Paris for quite some time. But now it looked the way somebody who has never been to Paris expects it to look.

The driver turned left, onto a pretty old bridge across a river that even I knew must be the Seine. On an island in the middle of the river, up soared a huge ancient cathedral with wings that seemed to fly everywhere, and two enormous towers, and even I knew that was Notre Dame. I recognized it from the Walt Disney movie, which I watch with my cousin Paris sometimes when I babysit. Every time we see that movie, I tell her that someday I will take her there, and then she will be Paris in Paris. Which she finds extremely amusing. Of course, every time I ever said that, it was just silly talk. Only now it wasn't so silly. Because there was the real Notre Dame—and here I was.

And do you know? Even though I was tired and stiff, and desperately needed to pee . . . even with all that, being in Paris felt pretty good.

Who am I kidding? I was in Paris, *France.* It was amazing.

Remember, I grew up in Kirland, Indiana. And growing up in Kirland does not give you the very broadest horizons. So I never *really* believed I would find myself in Paris. Although the thought had occurred to me—probably starting six years ago, when my cousin Mary named her daughter Paris. Which she picked on account of her and Nick planning to go to Paris, France, someday. Which never happened. The whole tragic aspect of it—that Nick and Mary would never get there—made it seem like Paris must be this perfect place where everything worked out. Romantically, anyway. And if things worked out for you romantically, everything else just fell into place, right?

I was only nineteen years old when I got that notion about Paris. Everything about life and love seemed very straightforward to me then. Whereas now I am a jaded twenty-five-year-old cynic. Only perhaps I am not totally jaded. Because suddenly I was in Paris, France. And just being there made me feel like I was glowing. Even better, I had Grandma's dress with me. Grandma's dress, which came from Paris all those years ago, had come back—and it was bringing me along on a wild and wonderful ride. At that moment, I felt like absolutely anything and everything was possible.

The car turned right, onto a big street that paralleled the river. It was a bright sunny afternoon, just the way you would want your first day in Paris to be. There were hundreds of people out walking. Maybe thousands. All just strolling along the Seine, holding hands, laughing, smiling. Not one of them looked like they had a care in the world.

I thought, *I could be one of those people. I could be anyone I felt like being. I could eat, and drink, and shop. I could find romance. Real romance, too, nothing like Jimmy Krasna fumbling at me with his clammy cold hands in the back seat of his mom's Chrysler in the parking lot at Kirland Park.*

I was in *Paris.* Happiness would be so easy.

11

Except. I am willing to bet that not one of those happy free romantic people strolling along the Seine had just two days to find the perfect antique dress to save a movie. Suddenly I wasn't glowing anymore: I was panicking.

The driver turned left, onto a tiny narrow little street. Then he made kind of a right turn, and a couple of kind of lefts, which took us to an even tinier street. I say *kind of* because these streets did not run at right angles. Like maybe the guy who drew the plan for this part of town had too much to drink first.

Then the driver stopped. "I am too far," he said, looking over his shoulder. He put the car in reverse and backed up—fast. Down this narrow little street. For a whole block.

So when he stopped the car, yanked my suitcase out of the trunk, and dropped it unceremoniously onto the sidewalk, that was fine with me. All that mattered was that I had survived the ride and gotten to my hotel. It is called the Hotel Jacob, I guess because it's on Rue Jacob. It's an old building, four stories high. The lobby is dark old wood, and it makes you feel like you just walked into the 1920s.

When I checked in, the desk clerk asked me for a credit card. I thought that was a little strange, since I was here working on the movie. The clerk told me my room number, 302, handed me the key, and pointed to the elevator.

Nobody carried my suitcase upstairs. Which is actually a good thing. Because the elevator was small. You may have been in small elevators before. But you only *think* you have been in small elevators. This elevator was big enough for my mom's suitcase. And my little duffel baggy carry-on. And me. And that is all. In fact, the elevator had one of those old-fashioned gates you pull closed before it will go, and if for instance I had been wearing my Miracle Bra, I'm not sure it would have closed.

The room was clean. Not fancy, but nice, although it was definitely on the small side. The bed was a double, not even a queen. The closet was little, the bathroom was little, and the only dresser in the room had two teeny drawers that I knew wouldn't be enough for my clothes. So I unpacked things in odd places. My panties, including the little wedgie thong, went into the nightstand drawer. My socks went into the desk drawer, right on top of the stationery. You get the idea.

Before I unpacked, though, the first thing I did was pee. Forgive me if this is an unladylike observation, but taking a pee when you really desperately need to is highly underrated.

I did not hang Grandma's dress in the closet. I wanted to, but I couldn't. There was no place to put it. The closet was just too small.

I was thinking what a huge coincidence it would be if Grandma had stayed in this exact same hotel. Although I am not really much of a believer in coincidence. Anyway I hoped she had. I wondered for about the millionth time how Grandma had come to own her dress. I hoped she had gotten it under the most adventurous, reckless, dangerously passionate circumstances possible.

These are odd thoughts to think about your grandma. At least, they were about mine. Because, except for her sophisticated taste in music, absolutely nothing about the Grandma I knew suggested she had ever done anything adventurous, much less reckless, much less dangerously passionate. But I knew she had to have. The dress and that old menu proved it. And she had given the dress to me. If Grandma could do and be all those things, maybe she thought I could, too.

After my clothes were stowed, I took a shower. And taking a shower in a Paris hotel, at least judging by this hotel, is highly overrated. First, there is no shower curtain, just a little glass panel that looks like somebody changed his mind midway about putting in a stall shower. The rest of the shower is wide open. Instead of a showerhead, there is a handheld spray-nozzle thing that you put in a bracket on the wall if you want to use it like a real showerhead. A word of advice: Put the nozzle thing in the bracket *before* you turn the water on. Because, what with there being no shower curtain, let me tell you, I sprayed water everywhere.

Needless to say, there was no bathrobe. There were towels, but not many, and I had to use most of them to mop all the water off the floor. I ended up drying myself with a hand towel and a washcloth. Which was not very satisfying. But at least I wasn't wet.

So there I stood. I was totally, well, you know, naked. I looked around my hotel room. Sure, it was tiny. But it was a tiny hotel room in Paris, France. Which made the whole situation seem exciting. Dangerous. Sexy, even.

Then I got a crazy idea. Only standing there naked, in my Paris hotel room, feeling dangerous and sexy, it didn't seem so crazy.

Very carefully, I took the white tissue paper off Grandma's dress, and took the dress off its padded hanger. Then I held the dress right up against my bare skin. Which by the way is pretty much how you would wear this dress, with absolutely nothing between you and it, since there is no way to hide a bra in the bodice. Panties, yes, because as I have told you, the tulle skirt was almost transparent, and you would not want to get arrested or anything. But definitely just a thong. Like for example the teeny one I had just unpacked.

I will try to describe to you how the dress felt against my skin, although words really do not do it justice. If you have never worn silk, you must. If you have never worn old silk, which is hard to find, you should try. And if your skin has never felt a double layer of gorgeous old sheer silk satin cut on the bias to really hug your body, I feel sorry for you. I was right about the dress having magical powers: All at the same time, it made me feel hot and cold, strong and weak . . . careless, reckless, gorgeous, sexual. *Dangerous.*

And I hadn't even put it on yet.

Do not ask me where I was going to go in that dress. Or what I was going to do when I got there.

But I was about to slip it on and find out.

12

Then the phone rang. Which, I am afraid, broke the mood.

It was a loud double ring, kind of a *brrrr brrrr* sound. Quite an obnoxious sound, actually. I picked it up quickly, before it could assault me again.

"We need you down in the breakfast room right now," said a woman's voice. Before I could say anything, she hung up.

It was not breakfast time. In fact, it was past four o'clock.

I pulled on a pair of jeans—black, of course—and a cute black T top that leaves just a little belly showing—not enough to be crass, just a little—and a pair of black Skechers. Then I put Grandma's dress away, locked the door, and ran down a steep staircase to the lobby. Off the lobby I found the breakfast room.

Which, at least during nonbreakfast hours, had clearly been turned into The Movie Room. Among other things, that means it was full of Movie People. Not movie stars—I will tell you about them soon. You know how at the end of movies, the credits go on for about six miles? Every one of those names is an actual person. The room was full of them.

It was also full of smoke. As far as I can tell, all Movie People smoke. They are also very carefully careless about how they dress and how they look. Everybody looked as if they just pulled on the first thing their hands touched that morning, and had put styling gel in their hair three days ago and hadn't shampooed since. Except if you looked closely, you got the feeling they'd actually spent a lot of time planning that morning, just so they would look so unplanned.

A tall thin pretty blonde girl whose clothes and hair looked extremely unplanned came up to me. "I'm Jamie," she said. "I'm the PA. But you can just call me Jamie."

Here is another thing you need to know about Movie People: As I quickly learned, they are very big on initials. Jamie explained that PA is short for production assistant. PAs appear to do everything on a movie production that nobody else wants to do. To me, it looks like a shitty job, although it seems like they all had to graduate magna from places like Brown and UCLA to get such a shitty job.

Jamie the PA said, "Now, this is very important." She sat down. So I sat down. And I waited. But the instant I sat down she stopped looking at me. More precisely, she started looking at a spot somewhere just above and behind my right shoulder. I turned around and looked. There were other Movie People back there, but they all seemed to be busy doing other things, and none of them were looking at Jamie. "Uh-huh," Jamie said. "Uh-huh."

Then I noticed she was wearing one of those tiny little bug-in-your-ear, wire-in-front-of-your-mouth mobile phones. The kind that is so small, you can't tell when somebody's on the phone as opposed to, say, just talking to the voices in their head the old-fashioned schizophrenic way. You also can't tell when somebody on one of those phones hangs up. Because all of a sudden Jamie was looking at me again.

"So you're the dress girl," she said. Then without waiting for me to respond, she said, "Uh-huh." Not to me, though. She was looking over my shoulder again.

For what seemed like a long time, she said nothing at all. Finally I said, "So I'm the dress girl."

Jamie was holding a clipboard. She looked down at it, then up at me. "Yes, you are," she said. And with that, she got up and walked away. Leaving me sitting there. Without a clue about what I should do first.

Right about then was when this homeless man walked up to me. At least, he looked like a homeless man.

The man looked like he had not shaved or had a haircut in months. I do not just mean he had a beard. He had not shaved his cheeks, or his neck, or anything. Plus he was wearing a ratty old blazer that was way too big on him. The blazer had a big check pattern, which looked hideous against his pants, which were striped. Not to mention dirty. It was as if he picked his whole outfit at Goodwill. On a very bad day at Goodwill. Then worn those clothes a lot. And not washed them. Ever.

The homeless man came up and gave me a big hug. Honestly. The first thing I thought was, *This cannot be happening.* The second thing I thought was, *At least he doesn't smell.* Then he kissed me on the cheeks. Right cheek, left cheek. The French really do that. That is not just in the movies.

Then he said the most unusual thing: "My daughter has told me the most wonderful things about you." He stepped back and looked me up and down. "But she did not tell me how very attractive you are. Shame on her."

He smiled. Even under all that hair on his face, I could see he had a very charming smile. And nice blue eyes. It occurred to me that if somebody cleaned him up, there might actually be a handsome man under there. I also noticed that there was something the littlest bit off about the angle of his smile. In fact, the angle of his whole face. Like somebody had given it a little twist, and it stuck. It seemed familiar. I was still trying to figure it out when he said,

"I am Gerard Duclos."

Gerard Duclos. This homeless man was the *director.* The *great* director.

"By the way," he said, "Celestine says to send you her love. She is in Barcelona for a few days, but she will come by and visit as soon as she is back."

Ohmygod. This homeless man was Celestine's *father.*

As I told you, the only thing Celestine ever said about her father was that he was a cad. She certainly never said he was a big-shot movie director. Not to mention that Celestine's last name is not

Duclos. But between the resemblance and what this man had just said, I was convinced it was true.

I said, "It's very nice to meet you." I held out my hand to shake hands. He laughed when he saw that, and gave me another big hug. Actually, I thought he held that hug a little longer than you would expect from your best friend's father. But that was probably my imagination. And if it wasn't, I figured it must just be a cultural difference.

"It is destiny," Gerard Duclos said, when he finally stopped hugging me.

"Destiny?"

"Your *grandmère* gives you the beautiful dress," he said. "You write the magnificent paper, and send it to your best friend. My daughter. Years pass. Now I am making the movie. No matter what I do, I cannot find the dress. I weep, I moan, I complain to everyone. Celestine says to me, 'You must read my friend's paper.' I do, and I say, 'This is the girl. The girl who can bring me Catherine's dress. The perfect dress.' So you see, destiny has brought you to me."

And I thought it was Google. Then again, here I was in Paris. I remembered my conversation with Celestine after she read my paper. Maybe it really was destiny.

Gerard Duclos led me around the room. He introduced me to the UPM (unit production manager) and the line producer, and the first AD and second AD, which in both cases stands for assistant director. Then he took me to a big table covered with fashion sketches, where a nice-looking middle-aged woman was sitting. Her hair was very gray, but she wore it long and straight. I thought that was actually quite impressive of her. Most women would have dyed it and cut it years and years ago, but it looked very nice on her. Even before I met her, I liked her.

"This is Irene Malraux," said Gerard. He pronounced it *ee-REN mahl-ROW,* only with the *r* sounds way at the back of his throat. I can only make that sound when I have a bad cold, but then it's not attractive. "She is our costume designer."

Right away I was terrified. This woman was a professional, not to mention a real grown-up. And here I was, a total amateur, not to mention just twenty-five. I had never designed costumes for a movie. In fact, I had never designed anything for anything. I just wrote a college paper about my Grandma's dress. I figured Irene probably hated me.

"I *loved* your paper," Irene said, smiling. If she was lying, she should have been an actress instead of a costume designer. "I am very happy you are here to help us." She actually *looked* happy. *Oh thank you Irene. Thank you thank you.* "Gerard and I have made many movies," she said. "But in this period, I am not such an expert as you." Which made me blush. "I have many ideas," she said, and waved at the sketches. "But Gerard does not like."

"We cannot make the new dress," Gerard Duclos said. "We need the old dress. The perfect dress." He smiled and nodded, as if he had said something profoundly wise. "So," he finally said. "Give me the dress."

"What?"

"The dress. Your *grandmère*'s dress. This is why I brought you here. *Give it to me.*"

Now wait just a second. I thought back to what Elliot Schiffter had said. He did not say I had to give them Grandma's dress. He said I had to *show* it to them. But now Gerard most certainly wanted me to *give* it to him. And, forgive me if I state the obvious, but the difference is crucial.

I spoke without even thinking. "I didn't bring it."

Irene Malraux gasped, and her eyes got wide.

"What did you say?" In an instant, Gerard's expression had turned to stone.

Which only made me more certain that I did not want to hand Grandma's dress over to these people. Who knew what they would do with it? The way Gerard kept demanding it gave me a very bad feeling. So I said, "Elliot Schiffter didn't say you wanted to use Grandma's dress. He only said you wanted me to help you find a dress." Which was what Elliot said. Sort of.

I guess that was not what the great director Gerard Duclos wanted to hear. "Send her away," he instructed Irene, and turned to leave.

"No!"

Irene did not say that. I did. In fact I fairly shouted it. Anyway it worked. Gerard stopped and turned back to look at me. He still looked pretty stony.

"No," I said more calmly. I straightened up as tall as I could. "I am an expert. I am the author of 'A Dangerous Dress.' "

"She is," Irene urged Gerard.

"I will find your dress," I said to Gerard in my most expert-like tone. Then for good measure I added, "I will find you . . . the *perfect* dress."

Gerard leaned close and looked in my eyes, as if he could see right inside my head. I held my breath. Irene held her breath.

I was probably starting to turn blue when Gerard turned to Irene and said, "She will know it. She will see it, and she will know. She will find it."

And with that he strode away. Irene scurried after him.

"You're going to need a lot of help from the French," said a voice behind my back. I spun around to find PA Jamie scrutinizing her clipboard.

"What?"

She looked up. "The French. You're going to need their help. So you need to know how to speak to them."

Which right away got me worried about not speaking French.

"They all speak English now," said Jamie. "Anybody who says they don't, they're just pretending to give you a hard time. But if they give you a hard time, you probably started the conversation wrong."

"How do I start the conversation right?"

"Always start politely. After that you can be as rude and demanding as you want."

"How do I start politely?"

"Always say *'Bonjour.'* Unless it's evening, then say *'Bonsoir.'* Unless you're interrupting somebody. Which could be even if they're not doing anything or talking to anybody. If *they* think you're interrupting them, you are. Then you say *'Excusez-moi.'* "

"How will I know if *they* think I'm interrupting?"

Jamie sighed and rolled her eyes. "You just have to figure it out. It's very, very important."

And with that she walked away. Leaving me there without a clue. Again.

"Why is she still here?" demanded a voice behind me.

I spun around again. As I spun, I wondered if Movie People always sneak up behind you.

Gerard Duclos was back. Irene, too. Gerard turned to Irene. "Well?"

Just then a tall thin pretty young blonde woman came up to the table. At least she didn't sneak up behind us. I thought she was PA Jamie until I took a second look. In fact, she was somebody else. PA Allison, to be exact. Movies have lots of PAs. "Kathy doesn't like her room," said PA Allison.

"She will learn to love it," Gerard Duclos said.

"She doesn't even *like* it," PA Allison said.

"All right," he said, "she will only learn to like it. She must find the spirit." And with that, he shooed the young woman away. I guess I looked curious. "Kathy Bates," he said to me. "She is our Gertrude Stein. It is quite brilliant."

So now you know. The Kathy who Elliot Schiffter was talking about is Kathy Bates.

I was trying to get my brain around the notion that Kathy Bates, who is a big movie star, was in this movie. *My* movie. And staying in this hotel. *My* hotel. Only then Irene spoke up.

"If she is going to find the dress," Irene said to Gerard Duclos, "she must first see the body that will wear it."

13

"The body that will wear it." That is exactly what Irene said. Not "the person who will wear it." It sounded odd to me. Like she was talking about a thing, not a woman. But I figured it was probably a translation glitch. Although both of them spoke English extremely well.

"Of course," said Gerard. He stood up, Irene and I stood up, and I followed them out of the breakfast room, through the lobby, and up the stairs to the second floor, which in Paris they call the first floor. Do not ask me why.

We walked to room 111, and Gerard knocked. When he didn't hear anybody inside say anything, he opened the door anyway. There *was* somebody inside. Boy, was there ever.

"This is our star," Gerard Duclos said. "Nathalie Gauloise."

I feel obligated to say something about Nathalie Gauloise, because I have been scrupulously honest about when something is only essentially true versus one hundred percent true. Gerard Duclos introduced her as Nathalie Gauloise. So that is true. But I am absolutely certain it is not her real name. First, because so many actors and actresses change their names. Like Winona Ryder is really Winona Horowitz, which is apparently not a movie-star name. And second, because of what Celestine later told me Gauloise means. In Roman times, France was called Gaul, so Gauloise kind of means "French." It would be like an American actress whose last name was "American." You wouldn't think that was *her* real name, right?

Gauloise is also the name of a French brand of cigarettes—nasty-smelling unfiltered cigarettes. So personally, even though I suspect Nathalie changed her name to Gauloise so people will think *Ooh, she is so French,* I hope that people will see her name and think of the horrible cigarettes. Actually, I hope nobody will ever see her name, period.

Gerard gave Nathalie a big hug, which again I thought he held too long for a man his age. Because if anything, Nathalie was even younger than me. Maybe twenty-two. She was playing Catherine, the girl young Harold Klein falls madly in love with. The character is only eighteen. But I guess in the French movie business, just like in America, older actors and actresses play younger parts all the time. Whatever. Gerard was definitely past fifty, and the way he hugged her made me squirm.

She didn't seem to mind, though. In fact, when Gerard was finally through hugging her, Nathalie draped herself over him and rubbed, like a cat rubbing up against a scratching post.

I do not care much for cats. I also do not care much for Nathalie Gauloise.

The truth is that when I first met Nathalie, I did not have any opinion of her one way or another. Of course, I am human just like anybody else, and I started forming impressions.

The very first one she made was that she is the prettiest girl I have ever seen. Really. And she still is—even though I am talking about someone you know I do not like.

You may remember I told you that Celestine was not the prettiest girl I ever saw because I have seen a girl who is drop-dead movie-star perfect gorgeous. Well, that girl was Nathalie. What's more, all of her is real, although it grieves me to say it. I wish I could tell you all that perfect gorgeousness is manufactured. But I can't. I have seen Nathalie up close—much closer than I would have liked, in fact. And I do mean all of her. Including parts that tend not to be real when they look so perfect. But everything about her is real. *And* perfect. She has perfect black hair. Perfect pale skin.

Perfect eyes, nose, cheekbones, teeth. Perfect tits. Waist. Butt. Legs. Even ankles and feet. So that was my very first impression.

Then Nathalie immediately started rubbing up against Gerard Duclos like a cat in heat. Which contributed significantly to my second impression.

Slut.

That was the first word that popped into my head. Followed by Cheap whore slut bitch.

Okay, maybe some of those words I thought of later, after everything happened. But that very first time, I distinctly remember. Slut.

Nathalie and Gerard Duclos were murmuring to each other in French. Then they stopped murmuring. Nathalie looked at me. She blinked those big black eyes. Needless to say, she has very long eyelashes.

"You are pretty," she said.

That was a surprise, coming from her. I said, "Thank you."

"But not so pretty as me."

"No," I said. Which was quite true. But having her say it like that turned her compliment into an insult.

"She did not bring the dress," Gerard apologized to Nathalie.

"She did not bring the dress?" Nathalie's eyes narrowed, and for an instant I thought she resembled a very pretty poisonous snake.

"She is an expert," Gerard assured her. "She will find the dress."

Nathalie's eyes unnarrowed, and the snake went away. "Find me the most good dress," she instructed me.

"Okay," I said. I was happy Grandma's dress was safely locked away in my mom's suitcase in my room. Cheap whore slut bitch Nathalie Gauloise didn't even deserve to *look* at it.

I didn't wait for her to say anything else. I walked out of the room. Irene followed me, shaking her head. "Nathalie will never accept the dress from me," she said. "She is jealous."

"Jealous?" With all due respect, Nathalie was at least thirty years younger than Irene, and thirty years prettier.

Irene shrugged. "Gerard and I have the history. The *ancient* history. And Nathalie is a stupid girl." Then she immediately corrected herself. "But she is the star. Of course she is right. So you must find the dress for her." Irene gave me a paper with Nathalie's measurements on it—a French thirty-six, which is like an American size four. The paper had a long list of other measurements, in centimeters and inches. Like her neck. Inseam. Bust, thirty-four inches. And her waist, which I will not tell you because it is so small that just thinking about it depresses me.

"You will also need this," Irene said, handing me a cell phone.

I own a cell phone. I can text-message, play games, all those things. My ringtone is programmed to play "Play That Funky Music White Boy," which is an inside joke with an old boyfriend who is not my boyfriend anymore, and the inside joke is none of your business. In short, I am not cell phone illiterate. But I did not know that not all cell phones work everyplace.

Here is what I mean. While I was stuck on my way in from the airport, I took out my cell phone to call home and tell my parents I had arrived safely. Only my phone didn't work. The little picture on the screen of the antenna searching for a signal just kept searching and searching. It never found one. Finally I gave up trying.

PA Jamie told me most American and European phones are on different frequencies, America versus Europe. So of course it didn't work. Irene was giving me a phone that worked.

It was a picture phone. She showed me how to use the camera, and how to dial Gerard's preprogrammed number. "Call when you find something," she said. "That way Gerard can just look and say no."

Then she gave me a list of vintage clothing stores, and a map of Paris, indicating the locations and addresses of the stores. There were an awful lot of them.

"I am sorry I cannot go with you," Irene said. "But the whole movie . . . everybody wears the 1920s clothes. I have much work. Everything else, Gerard is happy. But this dress . . ."

"I'll find it," I said. I had a flicker of self-doubt. Then I remembered Grandma's dress. The magic would not have brought me this far only to let me down now.

"I think the chance is more good in the stores here in the Sixth, and in the Fourth."

"The sixth and fourth what?" I asked.

For a second, Irene stared at me like I was a Neanderthal. Then I guess she remembered where I was from, because she patiently showed me on the map. Paris is made up of twenty districts called *arrondissements.* Which I now know how to spell but still can't pronounce, so I will just say *districts.* Anyway the districts are laid out in a spiral. The Fourth is on the Right Bank of the Seine, and the Sixth is on the Left Bank. Do not ask me who thought this was a sensible way to lay out a city.

Also do not ask me why one side of the Seine is called the Right Bank, and the other side is called the Left Bank. If you turned around, what was the Right Bank to you a minute ago would now be the Left Bank, if you see what I mean.

Irene looked at me, and I was pretty sure I saw panic in her eyes. I wondered how much trouble she'd be in if I didn't find the dress. Probably plenty. Because clearly I was the dangerous dress hunter of last resort.

She gave me a hug and kissed me on my cheeks—right cheek, left cheek. Then she said *"Bonne chance,"* and escaped.

She did not give me any money. In fact, nobody gave me money or a credit card or anything like that. So I did not know what I would do if I found a dress.

No, not *if.* This was the main event. *When. When* I found a dress.

The dress.

I even knew how I would recognize it. It would be the dress that was almost as dangerous as Grandma's—but not quite.

14

I did not immediately start looking for the dress.

Instead I took out the cell phone Irene gave me. First I called home, where I got the answering machine. I said the flights were great, which wasn't true, but I didn't want my parents to fret. Then I said Paris was great, which was true so far. Finally I said I would call again after I found the dress, which I hoped would be soon.

Then I called Celestine. Because Celestine is my best friend, she lives in Paris, and I was suddenly in Paris too, for the first and maybe only time ever. Not to mention that her lecher of a father was now my boss. So even though I had a perfect dress to find, and even though Gerard Duclos had said Celestine was in Barcelona, I called her anyway.

I do not know what she said on her answering machine, because she said it all in French. At the end of her message there were four funny beeps, then a very mechanical-sounding French man's voice said something I was pretty sure meant Celestine's machine was full. Some things do not need translation.

I put the phone away and got to work searching for the dress. I spent the next three hours shuttling from one vintage clothing store to the next. In fact, I made it through seven different shops.

It turned out that how I would buy *the* dress without money was not an immediate concern. Because I did not find the dress.

That isn't to say I didn't see anything gorgeous. I did. Paris is the home of haute couture. You can find all kinds of glorious used clothes from Givenchy and Yves St. Laurent and Chanel. There is even more stuff that doesn't actually have one of those superstar labels, but the couture is just as haute—if not hauter. Like for example Grandma's dress, which had no label at all, but which was the hautest dress I had ever seen.

Unfortunately, the wonderful garments I saw in those seven shops were mostly from the forties and fifties and sixties. They were not from the 1920s. You could find the best, most diaphanous, most dangerous dress from 1948, and it would look absolutely nothing like the best, most diaphanous, most dangerous dress from 1928.

I did find several evening dresses from the 1920s. A few were in pretty good shape, and a couple might have fit Nathalie. But one of those wasn't remotely diaphanous, and the other one *was* diaphanous—and orange. I could just picture her declaring it "*'orrible*."

By eight P.M., the shops were closing, so my hunting was done for the day. I suppressed a flash of panic. I would find the dress tomorrow. I *would.* Anyway, I was extremely hungry. And it occurred to me, What better place in the world to be hungry than in Paris? Now all I had to do was find the perfect Parisian spot to eat perfect French food and drink perfect French wine.

I turned a corner and, as fate would have it, found myself on a little street lined with carts selling sandwiches with meats and cheeses, stands selling pastries that looked so good it made my stomach hurt, and one place that had this rotisserie thing right there on the sidewalk, with chickens rotating over the grill. The smell was just amazing. It struck me that I needed to eat immediately or I would not live long enough to find the perfect dress. Okay that is a little bit of an overstatement. But I was famished.

I tried to buy one of the sandwiches. Only the woman at that cart did not take credit cards. Or dollars. "Euros," she said.

I had no euros. My perfect French-food moment would have to wait until I got some. So I hurried back to the hotel with my stomach aching. I didn't even go upstairs. I took eighty-seven dollars out of my wallet, which was all the cash I had, went to the front desk and asked to change it.

"Of course," said the desk clerk. He started to count out euros for me.

"What do you think you're doing?" said a voice behind me. A man's voice. Which I didn't recognize.

I spun around and found myself face to face with an American man. He had his arms folded across his chest, the way people do when they disapprove of what you're doing. It is a posture I saw a lot on my grade school nuns and my high school principal, Mr. Demjanich.

This man did not look old enough to be a high school principal. He was maybe twenty-seven or twenty-eight. He was also kind of cute, and I do not think of high school principals as cute. But cute or not, the man did have that stern principal look about him.

I knew the guy was American for two reasons. First, he sounded American. Second, he was wearing a baseball cap. I had not seen a single French person wearing a baseball cap. His hair, at least what wasn't covered by the cap, was sandy brown. Nice hair. Not all men have nice, thick hair. He did.

"I'm changing money," I said.

"No you're not," he said.

"Yes I am," I said. The desk clerk had finished counting out the euros and was handing them to me.

"No you're not," said the American. He may have been cute, but boy was he pushy. He actually reached across the desk, picked up my eighty-seven dollars, handed it back to me, and said to the desk clerk, "She's not changing anything." What's more, he took me by the elbow and steered me out of the lobby and onto the sidewalk.

"How dare you?" I said. Which is a phrase I had heard in old romantic black-and-white movies, but I'd never actually said before. Then again, this was the first time I had been forcibly escorted out of a Paris hotel by a handsome but pushy American man.

"Don't you know anything about money?" he asked. From the

way he asked, I could tell he thought I didn't. Which was pretty insulting, considering that I work at Independence Savings and Loan Association of Northwest Indiana. Although in the interest of full disclosure, I should admit that I had very little experience dealing with foreign currency. Actually no experience. But it was rude of this man to rub my nose in it. I resented him quite a lot. Which was too bad, because he was quite handsome, in an intellectual sort of way. Like somehow I knew he wasn't wearing those glasses because they were fashionable, but because he had worn his eyes out studying. Although they were very attractive frames. Which accentuated his very attractive eyes.

"What do you mean, I don't know anything? I know lots of things." Which even I thought was pretty lame. Frankly I think I would have done better just repeating *How dare you?*

"Not about changing money. I assume you have a wallet." He started to walk away.

Do not ask me why, but I followed him. He was terribly obnoxious. But very attractive, too. "Of course I have a wallet," I said. He had seen me take it out, so his question confused me.

"And in that wallet you have a cash card," he said. Still walking.

"Well of course I have a cash card," I said. Still following.

"So," he said. He stopped so suddenly I almost plowed into him. The absence of personal space between us made me notice that he was only three or four inches taller than me, which made him about five-nine, or maybe five-ten if he was thinking tall thoughts when they measured him. And I swear, it's not my fault, but the thought just popped into my head that he was a very convenient height for kissing.

"What is this?" He pointed to something.

I looked. "A cash machine." Incidentally, there are no cash machines at Independence Savings, because Uncle John thinks people will take out more money than they put in.

"Try opening your wallet. Taking out your cash card. Putting the card in the cash machine. And asking for money." He did not say any of this in a particularly nice way, which made me totally forget about kissing him. But I did all those things anyway.

I had seen cash machines while I was running from one vintage clothing store to another. But I assumed they wouldn't work. If my American cell phone didn't work in France, why should my American ATM card?

My ATM card worked.

As I was thinking about how much to ask for, he said, "The euro is a buck twenty-five. So a hundred euros is a hundred twenty-five dollars."

I got a hundred euros: four twenties and two tens. The bills were much prettier than our money, lovely blue and peach, with pictures of stained-glass windows, bridges, and a map of Europe. I put the euros in my wallet. "Tell me why I had to do that," I said.

"Because the euro is a buck fifty at the hotel."

"Oh." I didn't take the time to do the math, but I knew he had just saved me money. But why did he have to act so superior?

At that moment my stomach growled. Not grumbled—growled. Practically roared.

Maybe I did it because he had saved me money. Or because I wanted him to lose that attitude. Or because I wanted to spend my first evening in Paris dining with a handsome, kissable man. Whatever the reason, I asked him:

"Are you hungry?"

15

"Where would you like to eat?" he asked.

Since he seemed to think I didn't know anything, I couldn't imagine why he was asking me where to eat. I didn't want to look ignorant, but I didn't know any restaurants in Paris.

Then I remembered the menu I had found in the suitcase with Grandma's dress. "How about La Tour d'Argent?" I asked.

He actually laughed out loud.

Had I said something stupid? Maybe after four hundred years, the restaurant had finally closed, and I was the last one to know. "What's so funny?"

"La Tour d'Argent is probably the most expensive restaurant in Paris," he explained.

"Oh." *Great.* I *had* said something stupid. I waited for him to rub my nose in it.

Only he didn't. Instead he asked, "Do you like Italian?"

"Why would you eat Italian food in Paris?"

"Have you ever eaten real Italian food?"

Real Italian food? Maybe it was a trick question. "I've eaten at the Como Inn," I said. "It's this big place on the north end of Chicago."

"In other words, you haven't eaten real Italian food. So do you like Italian?"

"Sure," I said.

"Okay, let's go." He started to walk, so I followed him. Without missing a step, he flipped open a cell phone and punched in a number. "Hello, Sebastien? Can you get us a reservation for eight thirty at Il Vicolo? Terrific." He snapped his phone shut.

I looked at my watch. "That's in five minutes."

"Which will give us just enough time to get there," he said.

"If they have a table open in five minutes, why do we need a reservation?"

"Because this is Paris," he said.

He was a very fast walker, which meant that he kept getting ahead of me, and I had to run to catch up. It wasn't very thoughtful of him, walking so fast that I kept falling behind.

On the other hand, I learned that he has a very nice butt.

We walked another half a block when something occurred to me. "Should I change?"

He stopped and looked at me. "No. You look nice the way you are." Then he started walking again.

Ooh. He thought I looked nice. Which gave me a warm little feeling. I realized, *I am not just anywhere, I am in* Paris. *Going to dinner with a handsome stranger I just met.* That warm feeling started to grow, and in a few seconds I felt like I was glowing again.

Only then I thought, *He could've said "You look* great" *or "You look* fantastic." Saying "You look *nice*" wasn't all that much more than saying "You look fine." And saying "You look fine" would be about the same as saying "You don't look embarrassing." Kissing was officially off the table.

He wasn't much taller than me, but boy could he walk fast. I was starting to get out of breath. "Hey," I said.

"Uh-huh?"

"I don't know your name."

He stopped again. "I'm sorry," he said. "You're right. I'm Josh." He shook my hand. He had a nice handshake. Solid. Not too hard, but definitely not too soft either. Just right.

"I'm Jane," I said.

We kept walking. We turned down a quiet block with not a restaurant in sight. I started to think maybe Josh didn't actually know where he was going. Then there it was, an adorable little place, kind of tucked back from the street.

The hostess kissed Josh on both cheeks and said, "*Buona sera, Signore* Tomahs." She seated us, then came back thirty seconds later with big glasses of champagne, or whatever it is that real Italian restaurants serve that looks and tastes just like champagne.

Josh set his baseball cap on the table. It was my first chance to take a good look at him, so I did. I told you that he had nice hair. But now, without the hat, I could see that his hair was *really* nice: sandy brown, the perfect length, with a little bit of a wave that I bet just happens without his working on it. Which is totally unfair, given how much time I have to spend on mine.

I also told you his eyes were attractive. But what color were they? Green, maybe. Or blue. But not exactly. *Hmm.* Josh was the first person I ever met where I couldn't figure out the color of his eyes. Eyes tell you a lot. And he had the eyes of a very complex, intriguing person.

"What?" Josh asked all of a sudden.

"I didn't say anything," I said.

"You were looking at me," he said.

"No I wasn't," I said.

"Yes you were," he said.

Well of course I was, but I didn't want to admit it. So I said, "No, I was looking at"—I glanced around—"your hat."

"My hat," he said. Skeptically.

The waiter arrived. He was a friendly young man in a white shirt and black pants, and he had an Italian accent that I bet even Italian girls would think was sexy. If I hadn't been with Josh, I am positive I would have flirted with him.

I was trying to decide whether I had formed a wrong first impression of Josh. He really had been obnoxious with the cash machine thing. Then again, he'd saved me money. Now he had taken me to this lovely restaurant, and he was being very nice. He offered to let me pick the wine, and only chose it after I insisted. He also helped me with the menu. He suggested we share a buffalo mozzarella appetizer, risotto with black truffles for him, and for me something called pappardelle ai funghi, which he said was a wonderful pasta with wild mushrooms. Although it is really unfortunate that the Italian word for mushrooms is *funghi,* because, well, *funghi* is . . . fungus. *Ew.*

After the waiter left, Josh smiled at me. He had a very nice smile. A real-person smile. I smiled back.

"So," Josh said.

"So," I said.

"My hat," Josh said.

Oops. I thought he forgot. I had to say something about the hat. It was black, with a white *H* over a gold star. I tried to think of an *H* city with a baseball team. "Houston?" I asked.

"Astros," he said. "Very good."

"Texas," I said.

"The Houston Astros are undeniably from Texas," he said.

"I meant you," I said. Although I certainly didn't hear an accent.

"No," he said.

"But you're a Houston Astros fan," I said.

"No," he said.

"I'm confused," I said.

Josh leaned close to me. Even though he was confusing me, I liked him leaning close. He lowered his voice. "Let me tell you," he said, "about the worst night of my life."

16

That may not sound like a promising subject for conversation on a first date. But I was intrigued. Plus it didn't hurt that Josh was so cute and intelligent.

Okay, maybe it wasn't officially a date. He did not ask me to dinner, I asked him. But this was turning into a date. Which was just fine.

"October fifteenth, 1986." Josh said it so ominously that I half expected him to say "A date which will live in infamy," but he didn't.

"You must have been . . ."

"Nine years old."

Oh, great, I thought. I was about to hear some deeply disturbing story of childhood trauma that would keep me up at night.

"National League championship series. Game six." Josh said. "The Astros and the Mets."

Whew. We were going to talk about baseball, not child abuse. I could handle baseball.

"I thought you weren't an Astros fan," I said. I wanted him to see I was paying attention.

"I'm not," he said. "But I was then. I grew up in Bridgeport, Connecticut."

"Connecticut doesn't have a baseball team," I said. I am not a huge baseball fan, but I know a little. If a girl wants to go on dates, or at least if she wants to go on second dates, she'd better know a little about baseball. And football. Basketball. Hockey. NASCAR. Beach volleyball. Australian rugby. Thanks a lot, ESPN2.

Anyway, I think Josh liked that I knew Connecticut doesn't have a baseball team. "Exactly," he said. "So you had to pick a team from someplace else. Where I grew up, pretty much everybody picked the Yankees."

"But you picked the Astros," I said.

"Looking back, I can't imagine why. They had the worst uniforms in the history of baseball. They had *AstroTurf,* for God's sake. But I thought they were cool." He shrugged. "I guess I have this character flaw. Something about rooting for the underdog. The Astros never won the World Series. Back then, they had never even won the pennant."

"They sound like the Cubs," I said. "Do they have a curse?" In case you don't know, the Chicago Cubs have a curse involving a billy goat. Which seems like an odd thing to have a curse about, but that is neither here nor there.

"No curse," Josh said. "Nothing supernatural or glamorous. They just never won." He got this little-boy look in his eyes. "Only 1986 is different. The Astros win the National League West. They're playing the New York Mets for the pennant. The Mets are up three games to two, but the last two games are in Houston, in the Astrodome. And Tony Scott is pitching game seven. Tony Scott *owns* the Mets. So if they can win game six, the pennant is a lock."

Maybe it was the jet lag. Or the Chianti. Or the fact that I am genuinely just not all that interested in baseball. But the more he talked about this very important baseball game, the more my eyes started to swim.

"Bottom of the fourteenth, it's like magic: The Astros tie it."

I willed myself to pay attention. Because through the haze, I could sense that Josh was getting to the point that really mattered to him.

"So when the Mets score three more in the top of the sixteenth, it's okay. Because we're going to win. I'm positive. And sure enough, bottom of the sixteenth, Houston scores two. We've got the tying run on first. The winning run at the plate. Jesse Orosco is on the mound for the Mets. Kevin Bass is at bat for the Astros. Two outs. And the count goes full, three and two."

Honestly, I did not come all the way to Paris to listen to a guy talk about baseball—no matter how cute and complex and kissable he was. But Josh wanted me to care, so I tried. As hard as I could. Only I wished he would *please* get to the point.

"Bass strikes out. The Astros lose. The Mets go to the World Series."

"Oh," I said. I hoped I sounded really disappointed. "So what about the hat?"

"When the Astros lost that game, I promised myself I'd wear the cap until they won the World Series. I was a kid. I figured they'd win it the next year. I didn't know I'd still be wearing it twenty years later."

"But you're not a fan anymore."

He shrugged. Wistfully. "I grew up. Went away to college. Law school. Moved to New York. Baseball didn't seem to matter as much. Plus there were the strikes. Salaries. Steroids. Eventually it didn't feel like the same game I loved when I was nine years old."

"But why do you still wear the hat?"

Josh looked me right in the eye. Do not ask me why, but when he spoke, I had the very distinct feeling that he was talking about more than baseball. "I made a promise," he said. "That *has* to count for something. Don't you think so?"

"Yes," I said. "When you say you're going to do something, you should do it."

"Besides," Josh said, "I think somebody has to stick up for lost causes." He looked at the Astros cap and shook his head. "No matter how lost they are."

I had an idea. "Have you tried Saint Jude?"

"What?"

"Saint Jude. You could light a candle." Josh looked at me blankly. "Saint Jude is the patron saint of lost causes." My grade school nuns would've been proud. Not that I necessarily believe in that stuff. But if the Astros had never won the World Series, it wouldn't hurt for Josh to light a candle to Saint Jude, would it?

"I'm not Catholic," Josh said.

"Oh." I tried to remember whether that mattered or not. I wasn't sure. "I don't think that matters," I said. I wanted to be encouraging. Plus it really *shouldn't* matter. In my opinion.

Right about then the food came. And let me tell you, it was amazing. Josh was absolutely right: I had never eaten real Italian food before.

"Anyway," Josh said, somewhere near the end of the buffalo mozzarella—which by the way means the cheese is made from buffalo milk, not that it comes from Buffalo, New York—"if I were going to ask Saint Jude to help me with a lost cause, I wouldn't waste it on the Astros."

"But then you could stop wearing that hat," I said. Let's facc it: Keeping your promises is terribly important, but it was a real pity for him to cover up such nice hair.

"That's true," he said. "But I could ask for something that means even more to me."

"Like what?"

"Like getting my movie made."

17

I almost dropped my fork. Which would've been a shame, because those wild mushrooms were unimaginably delicious, even if they were *funghi.* But the point is, did you ever see in the movies where somebody has a flashback to ten different scenes in two seconds, and all of a sudden they put the pieces together and figure something out? I had one of those moments.

Flash. I meet a man in my hotel, which is full of Movie People for my movie.

Flash. We're on the street, and he tells me his name. "I'm Josh," he says.

Flash. I start to read the screenplay Elliot Schiffter sent to me. The bottom of the cover page says `Copyright J. Thomas.`

Flash. Josh and I walk into the restaurant. The hostess kisses his cheeks and says "*Buona sera, Signore* Tomahs." *Tomahs* must be how an Italian person says Thomas.

Flash. Josh says maybe he'll ask Saint Jude for something that really means a lot to him. "Like getting my movie made," he says.

Flash.

First name, J. Last name, Thomas. J. Thomas. *Josh Thomas.* Who wrote *The Importance of Beating Ernest.*

My movie was Josh's movie.

Only wait a second. "You said you went to law school," I said.

"That's right," Josh said.

"So . . . are you a lawyer?" I asked.

"Well, yes," he said.

No no no! That was the wrong answer. He had to be a writer, not a lawyer. People who have those flash moments in the movies and put all the pieces together never get it wrong.

"Actually," he said, "I'm kind of a *recovering* lawyer." He took another drink of Chianti. "These days, I'm really more of a . . . screenwriter."

Yes yes yes! He was the right Josh Thomas. The man who wrote the screenplay that had brought me to Paris. The wonderful, funny, romantic screenplay I loved. I had come all the way from Kirland, Indiana to Paris, France, and who wound up saving me from a hostile exchange rate and taking me to dinner at the most adorable, authentic Italian restaurant but screenwriter Josh Thomas. It was an incredible coincidence. Except as I have told you, I am not much of a believer in coincidence. Coincidence or not, though, the romantic potential of the whole encounter seemed, well . . . unlimited.

Suddenly I saw him in a whole new light. I had already started to like him quite a bit. But now he practically glowed. I wondered what to say next. Because I did not want to say the wrong thing to this handsome, romantic, glowing man.

I decided not to let on that I had any idea who he was, or that I had anything to do with the movie. Although I had to control myself, because my first impulse was to tell him how much I loved his screenplay, and that I was going to find the perfect dress so Gerard Duclos could film the climactic party scene and make the movie.

The reason I did not tell Josh those things is quite simple: I was *really* starting to like him. And I sensed that he might feel the same way about me. Maybe it was fate, or karma—or magic, I thought, remembering Grandma's dress. Whatever it was, it was a completely new feeling for me, and I wanted to make it last. So I figured, *Let me save this for that very magical moment of the evening, when I would know the time was right.* Then I'd say, "We have something very special in common." And when I told him, he'd say, "That's wonderful!" He would be so grateful I was helping his movie, he'd give me a big hug, maybe even a kiss, and of course I'd kiss him back, and after that . . . Well, just thinking about it made me tingly.

It was too early to tell him. It might be a nice moment, but not *the* moment. That's why, when Josh told me he was a screenwriter, I just said, "Really?"

"Really. Although if you ask my mother, she's hoping this is temporary. She says, 'You'll get it out of your system.' Like it's the flu. She says writers starve, and people in the movie business are bums."

"Do writers starve?" Well excuse me, but I was curious. Because the clothes he was wearing were pretty nice. Expensive nice. John Varvatos, maybe. Nice shoes, too. Most guys don't bother spending the money on nice shoes. Let me also say this: I would not date a man solely because he makes a lot of money. On the other hand, if he is already a man I wanted to date, the fact that he makes a lot of money certainly wouldn't be a deal breaker.

"Starve? Not so far. You would not believe how much producers and movie studios will pay just to option a script." I guess I looked blank, because he explained. " 'Optioning' means they pay you just for the right to decide whether to make a movie. If they actually go ahead and make it, they pay you a whole lot more."

"So you get paid for writing movies that nobody makes?"

"Ouch," he said.

The last thing I wanted to do was be mean to this very special, creative, romantic man, who I was liking more every minute. But I guess maybe it came out that way.

Anyway, he said, "Yes. You can make a very good living writing movies that nobody makes. Only you don't feel like you're *really* a writer until you get your first movie made. At least, I don't. And you wouldn't believe the stupid reasons movies don't get made." He winced, and I got the feeling I had opened an old wound. "My last script came within three days of the start of principal photography. *Three days.*"

"What happened?"

"The director read the script."

"Hadn't he already read it?"

Josh looked at me like I was from Mars. Or Venus. Anyway, some other planet. "Of course not."

"So . . . when he read it, I guess he didn't like it?"

"Are you kidding? He *loved* it. In fact, he told the studio it was so good, they had to dump the guy who was supposed to star, and give it to George Clooney."

"So . . . I guess George Clooney didn't like it?"

"Don't be ridiculous. He cleared his schedule immediately. In fact, George thought it was so good, he told the studio to double the budget."

"So . . . I guess the studio wouldn't do it?"

"Are you nuts? They won't offend George Clooney. They wrote a check on the spot."

I was so confused. None of this sounded like a reason a movie *wouldn't* get made. "So . . . what happened?"

"They had a bigger budget, so they hired a new cinematographer. A buddy of George's. They play basketball at George's villa. Anyway, three days before they start filming, George and the guys are playing three-on-three. George steps on his friend's foot. The cinematographer calls a foul. George says, 'That's no foul. I stepped on your foot; it was an accident, and even if it was on purpose, don't be such a wuss.' The cinematographer says, 'I'm no wuss, but even if I am, at least I'm no pretty-boy prima donna.' To which George says, 'Oh yeah, well, if I'm a pretty-boy prima donna, then you're fired!' To which the cinematographer says, 'You can't fire me; I quit!' "

"So . . . no cinematographer, no movie."

Josh scowled at me. "No no no. Those two guys have been friends forever. They calmed down, poured a couple of single malts, lit up a couple of Cohibas, and agreed they weren't going to let any stupid movie spoil their friendship. They *both* quit. End of movie."

I felt like I had just witnessed a train wreck. I felt so bad for Josh. "That's incredible. I mean, that all those things would go wrong."

"Nothing incredible about it. Stuff like that happens all the time. It's a miracle anybody's movie ever *does* get made." Then a smile crept over his face. A very attractive smile, I might add. "But this time it's my turn. That's why I'm in Paris. They're making my movie."

"So that's why you're staying at that hotel," I said.

"I'm not," he said. "I'm a couple of blocks away, in this great little four-star I read about in the *New York Times.* I can't believe they're putting all that talent in a three-star hotel."

"But everybody working on the movie is staying there. Why aren't you?"

He shrugged. "I'm not exactly . . . *working* on the movie. Movie studios don't pay writers to watch their scripts get made. I'm here in Paris on my own dime. But I've waited a long time for this. I wouldn't miss it for anything."

He looked awfully happy for a guy whose movie wouldn't get made if the girl from Bumfuck—namely me—couldn't find the perfect dress. I guessed he was trying to be optimistic.

Josh poured us both some more Chianti. He clinked my glass and took a big drink. "Everybody's flying in. Kathy Bates is already here." Then his eyes opened wide. He looked like a kid opening presents. I adored his enthusiasm. I could just tell he was the sweetest man. "Kirk Douglas is coming. *Kirk Douglas* is in my movie. How cool is that?"

I knew right away that Kirk Douglas must be playing old Harold Klein. Which was absolutely perfect. And by the way: *Oh. My. God.* I know he is an old man, but I *love* Kirk Douglas. Did you see him when he got that special Oscar? I cried.

"As soon as Kirk Douglas attached to the project, all these big names came running," Josh said. "Jude Law is playing Scott Fitzgerald. Can you believe it?" He still had that endearing little-boy look on his face. He was not obnoxious or arrogant at all. He was smart and humble and, as I may have mentioned, very attractive, and I found myself wondering how I could have thought anything bad about him at that cash machine. In fact, he seemed quite perfect. "They're all doing it for scale." He was still talking about the movie. "That's, like, next to nothing. Which is a good thing, because the budget is next to nothing. In fact, if it weren't for that obnoxious slut, the movie wouldn't be getting made at all."

Slut? I knew he must've been talking about Nathalie. Totally independently, he and I had formed the exact same opinion of her. Our minds worked alike. We were compatible in every respect. Destiny—and magic—were very clearly at work here.

That was when the Chianti ran out. We talked about getting another bottle, but I wanted to get an early start the next day. I said maybe we should stop drinking. Then I looked at him. He looked at me. Both of us just looked at each other. Then he smiled. An intimate smile. An I-want-to-get-to-know-you-very-well-starting-right-this-minute smile. It was the perfect smile. Suddenly I felt so warm, my fingertips started to sweat.

We switched to drinking grappa.

We also shared a tiramisu. And let me tell you. If you think you have eaten tiramisu, like at the Olive Garden? You have not.

Even in the middle of what was rapidly turning into the most romantic night of my life, I reminded myself that I was in Paris on business. I had to find a dress. So I steered the conversation back to the body that would wear it. "What obnoxious slut?"

"Nathalie Gauloise. She's this . . . actress." Josh said the word as though it pained him to say it. "She's this little French . . . well, bitch." I giggled. "She *is*. She's the director's girlfriend. She's probably the only reason he's doing the movie. The thing is, in France the TV networks subsidize the movie industry, so it's cheaper to make a French movie. The studio in LA figured out they can qualify if one of the stars is from here, and she'll say a bunch of her lines in French."

Okay that part was not all that conducive to romance. But you have to remember, Josh was a recovering lawyer.

Right about then a piece of tiramisu fell off my fork and onto the table. Perhaps all that Chianti and grappa had made me a little sloppy. Whatever the reason, I did something I pretty much never do: I picked up the piece I dropped. Picked it off the table with my fingers. Intending to put it right into my mouth, because it was too sinfully good to waste.

It never got to my mouth. Josh reached over and took hold of my wrist. Which stopped me cold. For just a second I thought, *Oh no, my manners are so bad, I have offended him.* Silly me. Gently, but still firmly, Josh pulled my wrist toward him. Until my hand was right in front of his mouth. Then he ate the tiramisu out of my hand.

Then he licked my fingers.

Oooooooooh.

"Let's get out of here," he said.

18

Here is how perfect Josh Thomas was that night.

We did not go running off to his hotel room. Or my hotel room. Or anybody's hotel room. Even though—and I am being terribly honest with you here—if he had asked me to, I think there is an *extremely* good chance I would have.

But he didn't ask. Even though he was interested. A girl can tell. He just wasn't going to rush. And not rushing is, in my opinion, the most perfect thing a man can do under such fairy-tale circumstances. I mean, the prince did not even *try* to kiss Cinderella at the ball.

So not only did we not rush, we strolled. Along the Seine river. We just walked along, on that very same broad sidewalk where only eight hours earlier I had seen all those happy couples walking and smiling and holding hands. Do not ask me what kind of romantic time warp exists in Paris, because how could it possibly have been only eight hours? Eight hours, and forever ago. Now, together with Josh, I was one of those couples.

His hand even fit perfectly with mine.

The night sky wasn't black, not even when we walked past the endlessly long, endlessly lovely Musée d'Orsay, where the huge illuminated clocks told Parisians it was five to eleven. No, the Paris sky was a deep purple blue, a color I'd certainly never seen in Indiana.

We had already passed three bridges, all bright and noisy with traffic. Now, though, we came to a narrow, pedestrians-only bridge, which was quiet and dark.

"Come on," Josh said.

As we reached the midpoint of the bridge, a sightseeing barge crowded with tourists glided below. The barge's spotlights seeped up through the spaces in the bridge's wooden planking, and for a few seconds the whole span seemed to glow under our feet. Then the barge passed, and we were in darkness again.

Josh stopped walking. So I stopped, too. "Wait," he said. I waited.

Then he kissed me.

Oh my.

I have had many first kisses. My *first* first kiss was Bobby Sterbavy. Up in the balcony of the old Hoosier Theatre on One Hundred and Nineteenth Street. And he really should have done something with that gum. But every boy you have ever kissed the first time is a first kiss. And I have had my share.

But I never had a first kiss like when Josh Thomas kissed me that night on the Pont Solférino in Paris.

Part of it is just that Josh is a very good kisser. Better. Excellent. That is not an opinion, it is a fact. Josh knew exactly how to kiss *me.* And the wonderful thing was, the way he kissed told me exactly how to kiss him back.

We kissed for quite a long time. It is simply amazing that I did not melt right through the bridge into the river.

Finally we stopped kissing and I opened my eyes.

I saw fireworks. I mean, the sky was literally sparkling, like a thousand tiny silent fireworks flashing and dancing just for me. "The sky is sparkling," I said.

"I know," he said.

"Why?" I asked.

"The Tower," Josh said.

"What?"

"The Eiffel Tower," he said. "After dark it sparkles like that every hour on the hour for about ten minutes."

I looked at the lights, and he was right: The sparkles were very clearly in the shape of the top of the Tower.

Up to that point, the kiss plus the sparkles added up to the single most wonderful moment in my entire life.

"I wanted to kiss you at the perfect time, in the perfect place," he said. "So you'd open your eyes and see"—he pointed at the sparkling Tower—"that."

My first thought was, *How wonderful of him. How romantic.*

Unfortunately, my first thought was interrupted by my second thought, which was: *Hmmm. He knew the schedule. He timed it on purpose.*

Which made me wonder how many other girls he had kissed on this very spot, just before the lights on the Tower began to dance.

I thought maybe we would head back now, but Josh said no, he wanted to take me to one of his favorite places in the whole world. I tried not to think about who the last Miss Fireworks had been. Between the restaurant and this bridge, his judgment had been pretty good so far. Besides, I much preferred to focus on my first thought than my second. So I said "Sure."

We stepped off the bridge and onto the Right Bank. Then we walked through a park. There were tall hedges and enormous bushes of flowers. The smell was so sweet that I thought for a minute this was the place Josh was taking me. But we kept walking, out of the garden, across a busy avenue, and two blocks farther.

Suddenly a plaza opened up in front of us. It was as if someone had cleared an entire city block except for one lonely column right in the middle, then lined the sides of the empty square with the longest, grandest uninterrupted facade I had ever seen. Josh told me this was the Place Vendôme, home of Cartier, Van Cleef & Arpels, Boucheron, and Giorgio Armani.

"Where are we going?" I asked.

"My favorite bar," Josh said.

Hmph. Did he take every Miss Fireworks to his favorite bar? That would be an awfully good reason *not* to go. Plus I still had that whole dress issue to deal with in the morning.

"You'll love it," Josh said, giving my hand a squeeze. I thought about the way we had kissed, and, at least for the moment, all my doubts faded away.

Josh's favorite bar is at the Hotel Ritz. Which, in case you don't know, is where the word *ritzy* comes from. Walking into the Ritz was like walking back into another century. And I don't mean the one six years ago. A century with lots of money. Pretty good taste, too. I liked everything about the place, from the old revolving door to the bellboy with his round little hat.

The bar was called, of all things, the Bar Hemingway. I thought that was fairly ironic, given that Hemingway is the villain of Josh's screenplay. Anyway, I guess when the allies liberated Paris in World War II, Ernest Hemingway himself liberated the Hotel Ritz. Or at least the wine cellar. So they renamed the bar for him.

That's what the bartender told us. His name is Colin, and he is the nicest man. Not to mention that by global consensus he is the world's best bartender. He is particularly famous for mixing the perfect drink to fit the mood of you and your companion. I must say he read us pretty well. He made us something he called a Lemon Charlie, which doesn't sound all that alluring, except the name is actually from a liqueur called Limoncello something or other. There is also some very special vodka in it. So we are not talking about a lightweight drink.

Josh and I sat down in heavy old leather armchairs, and Colin brought us our drinks and set them on a round leather-topped table. The walls were old wood paneling, and there were black-and-white photos all around, and books on shelves. It felt more like a library than a bar.

A library full of famous and important people. Everybody was somebody. There was a model I recognized, although I have never known her name, so I am not cheating by not telling you. And two men in the corner arguing, who Josh said were from the *New York Times* and the *Herald Tribune.* And some old man Colin said was France's minister of something or other. Those sorts of people. And us.

Josh and Colin traded a few Hemingway trivia questions, on which they were both quite expert, and I tried to eavesdrop on the French minister, who was clearly trying to hit on the model even though she must have been a third his age. Then Colin went back to the bar and left Josh and me alone.

We just sat, and—oh my gosh—held hands, and talked. I seem to recall that everything he said was fascinating, witty, and romantic, but for the life of me I can't remember a word. Perhaps because of how much alcohol we had consumed, how attractive Josh was, and how perfectly my hand fit in his. Anyway we sat for a while, talking about I don't know what, coughing at the *New York Times* guy's cigar smoke, and drinking our Lemon Charlies. All four of them. Four total, that is. Two each. The whole time, I barely thought about the last Miss Fireworks.

Incidentally, the Bar Hemingway at the Ritz may be Josh's favorite bar in the world, but it is not the kind of place you could drink at every night. At least I could not. Because the drinks cost twenty-three euros. Which, I know from the exchange rate lesson Josh gave me, is twenty-nine dollars. Each.

At some point, Josh started to chuckle.

"What's so funny?" I asked.

"Nothing. I'm just . . . happy. Ecstatic. Everything is working out. I'm here with you. And *they're making my movie.*"

He was really sounding overconfident about the movie thing, given that I hadn't found a dress yet. I tried to bring him back down to earth, just a little. "The movie isn't *that* big a deal, is it? I mean, if this one doesn't work out, you can always write another one."

"You don't understand," he said. "Till now, it's like I was cursed. I've had five scripts optioned. Every time, the producer and the studio swore it would get made. And every time . . . nothing. I told you about the last one. Three days before the start of principal photography." Then he shook off the memory like a dog shaking off water. "Not this time, though. This one is absolutely, positively going to happen. Guaranteed. Starting day after tomorrow."

"If . . ." I said. It just popped out. I swear the fact that I couldn't stop wondering about who the last Miss Fireworks had been had nothing to do with it.

Josh went pale. He took hold of both my hands. "If what?"

"If they find the dress."

"What dress?"

How dense could he be? "*The* dress. Catherine's diaphanous beaded dress. The grown-up, sexual, dangerous dress they don't have yet. The dress Gerard Duclos won't shoot the climactic party scene without. The dress they flew in some girl all the way from Bumfuck to find."

Josh stared at me like I was the Angel of Death. When he spoke, I could barely hear him. "What are you talking about?"

Ohmygod.

He didn't know.

19

I drank the rest of my Lemon Charlie in one gulp. At that moment, I think I knew exactly how old Hap Kirland felt, the minute before his train ran off the tracks. "Never mind," I said.

"What do you mean, *'never mind'*? How do you know all these things?"

I probably should've kept my mouth shut, but I couldn't. "I'm the girl they flew in all the way from Bumfuck to find your dress."

Josh let go of my hands. "No you're not."

"Yes I am."

He stood up and backed away slowly, as if I was contagious. "It's happening again," he muttered. "They're not going to make my movie. All because of you."

"No."

"Yes. You did this. *You.* You turned me into a lost cause."

Help me Saint Jude.

Perhaps Saint Jude was not listening at that precise moment. Although it is not fair of me to pin it on Saint Jude. Josh is the one who did it. Maybe if he hadn't drunk all that wine and grappa and those Lemon Charlies he wouldn't have done what he did next. Maybe if George Clooney hadn't called a foul on the cinematographer just three days before the start of principal photography Josh wouldn't have done it. But here is what he did.

Colin walked over with the check. He looked at Josh questioningly. Josh looked at the check, then at me. He said to Colin, "She's buying." Then he walked out.

I stood up. I wanted to run after Josh.

Only there was Colin, with the check. He is a very nice man, but a check is a check.

"Did you see what he did?" I asked Colin.

He nodded. "Filthy brute," he said. It was really quite nice of him to take my side.

"He is not!" I said. "He's just . . . upset." I sat back down. Then I stood up. And sat down again. I didn't know what to do. At the exact special perfect romantic moment, I was supposed to tell Josh that I was in Paris to find the dress for his movie because I fell in love with his script on page one. He was supposed to hug me, I was supposed to hug him back, then there would be all the tingly stuff. Only I told him at the exact awful horrible moment, in the worst possible way. And it was even worse, because he left me with the check. Which just lay there on the table. Mocking me.

Okay checks do not mock you. Not even when an almost-perfect moment goes drastically catastrophically wrong. But if checks could mock, this one would have.

I closed my eyes. I am pretty sure I would not have cried with my eyes open. But not absolutely sure. Anyway I counted. To ten. Twenty. Thirty. I opened my eyes. Josh was still gone. The mocking check was still there.

I had single-handedly shattered Josh's dream. He thought he was cursed, and I was now officially his high priestess of doom. And any man superstitious enough to still wear a stupid Houston Astros cap after twenty years would undoubtedly never forgive his high priestess of doom.

But I could try. I could find him, apologize, and tell him I would find the perfect dress so they would make his movie after all.

I realized I was wasting time sitting there. I stood up. At least I had my wallet with me. The bad news was that the check was for ninety-six euros. I had the hundred euros I got from the cash machine, but I didn't want to leave myself with only four euros. I also had my MasterCard, which I was sure had enough room on it. Pretty sure. Depending on the exchange rate.

I put the MasterCard away and took out my ATM card. Which is also a Visa card that draws money from my checking account. I have my paychecks direct-deposited, so I knew there was enough money in there.

Incidentally, my checking account is not at Independence Savings. Which makes Uncle John mad, but it's his own fault, because he refuses to put in ATM machines. So I opened my checking account at Bank of America, and they were happy to give me a Visa ATM card.

I handed Colin my card. He swiped it. The receipt chugged out: approved. No problem.

I ran out of the bar, and out of the hotel, but Josh was nowhere in sight.

Right there on the empty street, I made myself a promise. Not something silly like an Astros cap either. I promised myself I was going to find that dress. The right dress, the perfect dress. No matter what. I was going to save Josh Thomas's lost cause. I was going to become his guardian angel, not his kiss of death. I was going to hand the dress to him and say "Here, now they can make your movie."

Then I was going to slap him for sticking me with the check like that.

Then after I slapped him, I thought maybe we could kiss and make up.

All in all, I thought it was a pretty good plan. In fact I only saw one immediate obstacle: finding my way back to the hotel.

One of the things that makes the Place Vendôme so beautiful is that it is very symmetrical. Which, I discovered, means it looks pretty much the same whichever way you are facing. On my way into the Ritz, I wasn't paying all that much attention to directions, as I was rather distracted by Josh. On my way out, ditto, and ditto.

Only after I had *left* the Place Vendôme did I realize I had no idea where I was.

When I looked at the map the next day, I saw that I mistakenly exited the north end of the plaza, instead of the south end. Which meant I was going away from the Seine, when I needed to be going toward it. It should've been no big deal. I just needed to find a cab. Only at one thirty A.M. on a weeknight, there are not a lot of taxis on the streets of Paris. So I had to walk. And I guess I took the long way. My life would have been considerably easier if I had just taken out my map then. But what with all the wine, grappa, and Lemon Charlies, not to mention that perfect kiss, and then getting unceremoniously dumped by the very romantic man who gave me that perfect kiss, suffice to say I was distracted.

Finally, at two forty in the morning, drunk and miserable, I got back to the hotel.

I went straight to the front desk to get an early wake-up call. Only the clerk was busy talking to Marty, the movie's unit production manager—the UPM. Gerard Duclos had introduced us when he took me around the dressing room. Marty was a little man who wore his hair big, like Elvis's. He wasn't exactly talking to the desk clerk. More like arguing.

"Part of my job," Marty scolded, "is to make sure all the little unexpected bills don't turn into big unexpected bills. And this"—he waved a piece of paper under the clerk's nose—"is a big unexpected bill. Which I am not going to pay."

"I am sorry," said the clerk, "but that is what they cost."

"No way," said Marty.

It looked like it might take a while. And I was afraid to go to sleep without the wake-up call. So I said, "Excuse me."

I could tell Marty recognized my face, but couldn't remember who I was. I guess UPMs deal with a lot of people. "Can you believe it?" he said to me.

"I just want a wake-up call," I said.

"Sure, but can you believe it?" asked Marty.

"For what hour?" asked the desk clerk.

"Six o'clock," I said to the clerk. "Believe what?" I asked Marty.

"What they're charging me for Snickers bars," said Marty. He shoved an invoice in front of me. It was for eight hundred Snickers bars.

"Six P.M.," said the desk clerk.

"That looks like a lot," I said to Marty.

"See?" Marty said to the desk clerk.

"What?" I said to the desk clerk.

"Six P.M.," said the clerk.

"Six *A.M.,*" I said to the clerk.

"See?" Marty said to the clerk again.

"Why do you need eight hundred Snickers bars?" I asked Marty.

"Six A.M.," said the clerk to me.

"Oh, sure," said Marty to the clerk. "When *she* asks you to change something, you change it." Then Marty looked at me. "Haven't you ever made a movie before?"

"No," I said.

"Then why did I hire you?" he asked.

"You didn't hire me," I said. "I'm the dress girl."

"Ohhhh," said Marty. Then he gave me a suspicious look. "You should be shopping."

"It's almost three A.M.," I said.

"The candy drawer," Marty said.

"What?"

"On the set. I always have a big drawer full of candy. It keeps the crew happy. Especially Snickers bars. They say, 'We're hungry. We need to break for lunch.' But you've got two more setups you need to put in the can before lunch. So you say, 'Have a Snickers bar.'" He gave the desk clerk a nasty look. "But never in my life have I paid so much for Snickers bars!"

"Did you ever buy Snickers bars in Paris before?" I asked.

"No," Marty said.

"Maybe Snickers bars just cost more in Paris," I said.

"This is *exactly* what I am trying to say," said the desk clerk.

"It makes more sense when she says it," Marty said. He turned back to me. "You *really* never made a movie before?"

"Never."

He looked genuinely amazed. "Where are you from, anyway?" Marty asked.

"Indiana," I said.

"Wow," he said.

Nobody has ever said "wow" when I told them I was from Indiana.

"A small town?" he asked.

"Really small," I said.

"Wow," he said again. Then he said, "I always wanted to be from a small town."

"You're kidding," I said. Only I could tell he wasn't.

Suddenly Marty's eyes opened wide, and a look came over his face like he had just seen the burning bush or something. "I have a question," he said.

"Okay," I said.

"What's a Hoosier?"

20

I will make this quick. It was already almost three A.M. I was desperate to get to bed. I had a wake-up call at six. Then I had a dress to find to save Josh's movie.

I told Marty a Hoosier is something you call anybody from Indiana. That was not the answer he was looking for. He wanted to know, what exactly *is* a Hoosier?

I did not waste Marty's time, and I will not waste yours. I told Marty, and I will tell you: I don't know.

He was disappointed. But he remained impressed, and even envious, that I was actually from a small town in Indiana. "Someday I'm going to get out of the movie business," he said.

"Okay," I said.

"My piety consultant tells me I need to be reborn," he said.

"Okay," I said.

"Spiritually, not literally. Maybe I'll move to a small town in Indiana and be reborn as a Hoosier."

"Sure," I said, although what I thought to myself was, *You'll be reborn as a Hoosier the day Nick Timko comes home to Kirland.*

I said good night, walked upstairs, and went to bed. Where I tossed and turned, trying hard to forget about Josh Thomas. How much I liked him. How mad I was at him. How much I just plain didn't *get* him. I wondered if I would ever get him. If anybody from Kirland, Indiana could ever get him. I did not do a wonderfully good job of forgetting. But I was so tired, I fell asleep anyway.

Next comes my obnoxious wake-up call. Only to get a sense of my complete wake-up experience, you must remember that three days ago I was minding my own business—on Indiana time. That two days ago I flew to Paris. Which is on, well, Paris time, which to say the least is radically different from Indiana time. The day I arrived, I stayed up until three A.M., falling in and out of love and winding up stuck somewhere in the middle, then got only three hours of sleep. Now I had to wake up and find a dress like I promised myself, or they wouldn't save Josh Thomas's movie. And oh, yes, I'd had all that Chianti and grappa and those Lemon Charlies.

Now you can appreciate how I felt when the phone went *brrrr brrrr.*

To my credit, I actually did get up, but it was even harder than I had expected. It was still dark in the room, even though I had left the curtains wide open. It was dark outside, because it was raining. No. Pouring.

I checked that Grandma's dress was still in my mom's suitcase, exactly where I left it. I had been through a lot in the last few hours—the last few days, for that matter. Grandma's dress is extremely powerful, but I cannot imagine any dress in the world, no matter how special and dangerous, that could have made me feel all that much better at that moment. But knowing the dress would be waiting for me when I got back to the hotel certainly helped.

I closed the suitcase. Then I put on my most disposable clothes and stumbled to the breakfast room. Where they were, in fact, serving breakfast. There were all these wonderful French breads with crunchy crusts, about six different cheeses, at least three of which I'd never seen before, two kinds of ham, and very strong coffee.

None of the actors and actresses were there yet. Nobody I recognized, anyway. Of course, you would not expect the famous glamorous people to be at breakfast at six thirty in the morning. At least I would not. Because they were probably all out late last night. Doing the kinds of things famous glamorous people do in Paris. I had been out late last night too, but I was not famous or glamorous. Plus, they did not have to find a dress, and I did.

I finished the butteriest croissant I ever ate, with the best strawberry jam I ever ate, and made myself drink the rest of my cup of brutally strong coffee. It tasted burnt to me, but I figured I would need the caffeine. I was just starting to wonder where I was going to find an umbrella at a quarter to seven in the morning, when a voice behind me said, "Umbrella?"

I turned around. It was Marty, offering me a big black umbrella. I am pretty sure he was wearing the same clothes he had on during the Snickers and Hoosier debate.

Before I could even ask him how he knew, he said, "It's my job."

Off I went. The umbrella was great, although it must have been made in the United States. Because it was very wide. Too wide for the sidewalks in Paris, some of which are walk-the-plank narrow. But a too-wide umbrella was better than none. Unfortunately the umbrella didn't help my feet. Stepping off the curbs was like going whitewater rafting. Before I had gone two blocks, my Skechers were soaked. I went *squish squish* as I walked. Only it did not sound like *squish squish* to me. It seemed as if my sneakers were saying *Josh Josh.* Like I needed the reminder.

According to the map Irene gave me, there was a big cluster of vintage clothing stores in the Fourth district, so I figured I'd try those first. The Fourth is across the Seine. On the Right Bank, for those of you to whom that Right-Left business makes sense. I estimated it was only a mile or so from the hotel to the shops. That probably does not feel very far when it's not pouring buckets. I thought about taking a cab, but I didn't see any. Besides, even though it was only seven A.M., the streets were full of cars, none of which seemed to be getting anywhere. So I walked, *Josh Josh Josh Josh,* until I could feel my toes getting all pruney inside my sneakers.

You may wonder what I expected to accomplish at seven in the morning, since the stores weren't open yet. But Irene had given me a long list, and based on the seven I had covered the day before, I figured I could eliminate a bunch just by looking in their windows. It was always possible that the one perfect 1928 dress might be stuck randomly in the middle of a vintage shop full of sixties Mod, but I didn't have time to look in every one, so I decided to follow my best guesses.

Shops started to open around ten or eleven o'clock. Some of them never opened at all. By eleven I had crossed a bunch off the list as not promising enough to waste time with. That gave me a more manageable list.

I actually started to think I might find a dress. *The* dress. Especially when, around five thirty, Irene's list led me down a little alley and I discovered a tiny store that was all Art Deco. It wasn't just a clothing store. There were some small tables and a few chairs, and cigarette lighters shaped like skyscrapers and desk lamps in the form of airplanes. But there was also lots of clothing, and it was all Art Deco. Technically, most Art Deco stuff is from the 1930s, as opposed to the 1920s. In case you are wondering what's the big deal if a dress is from 1928 as opposed to 1930, remember we are talking about fashion. Two years can be forever. For example, look at the difference between clothes in 1966 and 1968.

I know I was not born in 1966 or 1968, but I took that History of Fashion course. We spent two whole lectures on what Professor Singer called the Transformative Sixties. And I will tell you, I am glad I was not around in the Transformative Sixties, because I would be ashamed if I had to admit I wore any of those clothes.

Anyway. A dress from even 1929 would be no good, because hemlines dropped way down that year. But dresses in 1928 were already pretty Deco, so I was confident this store would have a lot for me to look at. And it did.

In fact, there were even two dresses that got me kind of excited. I can't say that either of them quite struck me as perfect. But they were very, very good. And what was perfect, anyway? I mean, *perfect* is a highly subjective standard, don't you think? So I actually pulled out the picture phone and called Gerard Duclos. Some American person answered, but she found Gerard right away when I said who I was.

"Is it perfect?" he asked. He sounded excited.

"I think so," I said. Which was only lying a little bit.

"You are not sure," he said.

"I'm sure," I said. Which was lying more than a little bit.

I took a picture of the first dress. It was red satin, and it had a gypsy girdle, which is a rather provocative wide sash over the hips, and it ended in an asymmetrical pleated skirt. It was really stunning, and I would bet money it was from 1928. I even thought maybe it was by a designer named Jacques Doucet, although there was no label.

If you are wondering how I know all this, please remember that paper I wrote, and all those footnotes.

I put the phone up to my ear. "So?" I asked.

"No no no!" Gerard Duclos said. He sounded furious. "This is *red,*" he said. "Catherine's dress is not *red.* Nathalie will *never* wear red." He sighed. "I have lost confidence in you."

Nowhere did the script say Catherine's dress was not red. But he was the director. "I'm sorry," I said. I took a picture of the other dress.

This one was a pale, very sexy opalescent pink. The pink was quite close to the color of skin, so when you first looked, you wouldn't be sure where the dress ended and the woman began. The illusion was accentuated by the neckline, which plunged low in front and even lower in back. And the hemline was daringly high in the front and longer on the sides and back. Maybe an Augustabernard. Whoever made it, it was a very provocative dress.

I put the phone back to my ear. Nothing. "Hello?" I said.

"This dress," Gerard said slowly. "This dress." Then he said nothing for a while. Finally, he again said, "This dress." Then he said, "You should buy this dress."

Yes. *Yes yes yes yes yes*

"No," he said.

"What?" I said.

"No," he said. "No, I am wrong. This is a very good dress.

Now I have confidence in you again. But this is not the right dress. Nathalie requires not the very good dress. Not the almost perfect dress. Nathalie must wear the perfect dress. So you must keep looking."

Then he hung up.

21

I was defeated. Totally utterly miserably defeated.

I didn't care if Gerard Duclos' confidence in me was lost or found. I had been kidding myself. I had been kidding everybody. Now there would be no movie—on account of me.

I was going to break my promise to myself. I was not going to save Josh's lost cause. I felt terrible. Not for me. For Josh. Even if he had been a jerk, walking out and sticking me with the check, that was outweighed by how bad I felt for him, and all the other things I felt for him. If I saw him right now, I would tell him that I had read his script, it was fantastic, it would make a wonderful movie, and I was so sorry I couldn't find the dress. I might even kiss him, if he would let me.

But he wasn't there. All I could do was head back to the hotel and admit my defeat. I suppose I could have just called Gerard on the cell phone. But if I was going to ruin their movie, I ought to do it in person. Face up to your failures—that's what Mom and Dad and Uncle John have always taught me. Especially Uncle John.

The walk back seemed endless. I trudged. Sloshed. *Squish*ed. *Josh*ed. Slogged my way back across the Seine, over an old bridge that a plaque said was the Pont de la Tournelle.

I felt so completely vanquished, I literally could not lift my eyes. All I could do was stare at the pavement as I made myself put one foot in front of the other.

If I hadn't been so downcast, I might not have seen it at all. But suddenly, on the sidewalk in front of me, there it was: a coat of arms. Like you see on the shield of a knight. Okay I have not met any knights. But I have seen *A Knight's Tale.* Which is quite a bad movie, but let's be honest, Heath Ledger is *extremely* good-looking. And as I recall, all the knights had coats of arms on their shields.

The coat of arms on the sidewalk was made of metal. Silver, I think. It had a castle on it. A little castle, like the chess piece. A rook. But the rook is not important. The words are.

The words on the coat of arms said: LA TOUR D'ARGENT. Which was the name on the menu I had found in the suitcase, along with Grandma's dress.

I looked up from the sidewalk. I was standing in front of a restaurant. *The* restaurant. *Grandma's* restaurant.

At that instant, no matter how defeated I felt, a little spark lit up inside of me. Through coincidence, or fate, or magic, I had stumbled across the very place where Grandma had . . . well, I don't know what. But the very place where Grandma had *something.* Eaten dinner, I'm sure, because after all it was a restaurant. There must have been much more to it than that, though. If it had just been a meal, no matter how fabulously delicious, I don't think she would have taken the menu, brought it all the way back to Kirland, and stashed it away in that suitcase for decades. No, I knew somehow that the restaurant and the dress were linked together. Something special had happened here. Something careless, reckless, gorgeous, sexual. Something *dangerous.*

I looked at the restaurant for a long time. Then I turned around and looked back across the Seine. Right there was Notre Dame, soaring up through the rain, the tops of the towers disappearing into mist. Even in my half-drowned state, it was an enchanted view. I could only imagine how magical it must have been for my Grandma when she was a young woman, a girl really.

As I have told you, I learned pretty much everything I could about Grandma's dangerous dress, and I put all those facts in the paper for my History of Fashion course. But I was never able to learn how she got the dress, where she wore it, and for whom. At this moment, though, I was closer to those events than I had ever been. Maybe they had all happened almost eighty years ago, but they had all happened *right here.* Despite my despair, despite the rain, I felt an incredible connection to Grandma and her wild past, like somebody had just plugged me into an electrical socket. I closed my eyes and let that electricity flow through me.

And, behind my eyelids, here is what I saw.

The rain was gone. The dark purple night sky was clear and the breeze was scented with roses. There was a full moon, which reflected across the Seine and lit up Notre Dame like a floodlight. There were only a few cars on the street, and they were all long luxurious antique things with swirling chrome fenders and polished wood running boards and cut-crystal hood ornaments. The longest, most luxurious sedan of all swooshed to the curb, and a chauffeur wearing an elegant black uniform opened the passenger door with a flourish. A man emerged. He was perhaps twenty-five years old, wearing perfect black tie and tails, and he was devastatingly handsome. When he spoke, it was with a British accent that caressed the words sensuously. "Come, my dear," he said, reaching a hand into the car. "Destiny awaits us."

A delicate female hand took the man's hand—and I knew it was my Grandma's hand. A perfect small female foot, wearing a graceful rhinestone-adorned slipper, emerged from the dark interior—and I knew it was my Grandma's foot. I saw the hem of her dress—*my* dress. I held my breath and waited for her to appear.

She started to step out of the car.

22

That is when the lightning struck.

I am not speaking figuratively here.

I do not know how close to me the lightning bolt hit. Remember, I had my eyes closed. But even through my eyelids, I was suddenly dazzled by the brightness. And just a second later there was a clap of thunder that left my ears ringing.

Grandma, the handsome man, the gorgeous old car—they all vanished. I opened my eyes, then closed them again, but the romantic figures didn't reappear. The scent of roses had been replaced by ozone, and the clear moonlit sky was once again a torrent of rain.

I wondered if any of it had been real. I think it was. I think, somehow, it was another gift from Grandma. I hoped so.

Real or not, though, seeing that moment from the past fueled the little spark inside of me. Now it was a bigger spark. Although it certainly wasn't a bonfire of hope. After all, I was still feeling quite completely defeated about the dress, I was out of time, I had nowhere else to look, and my lower half had crossed the line from merely soaked to downright sodden. Not to mention that my sneakers still insisted on *Josh*ing as I walked. But there was a definite midsized spark nonetheless. One that gave me the energy to keep walking.

The Hotel Jacob is only about five blocks off the river, but because the streets in Paris seem to have been laid out by a drunk, I couldn't walk the five blocks in a straight line. I had to walk two blocks straight, then a short block to the right, then half a block on this little diagonal street, then back toward the river for a block, then turn left. And that would have been the short way. But the sewers had backed up, and the intersection of the little diagonal street and the jog back toward the river had turned into a lake. No matter how drowned and demoralized I already felt, I could not bring myself to wade through it. So I improvised: I kept walking up the little diagonal street another block.

I walked past an open doorway and caught a whiff of food. Suddenly I was so hungry I almost fainted. I realized I hadn't eaten a thing since breakfast. I didn't want to stop. I was so depressed I didn't feel like eating. But I felt as if somebody had drilled a hole through my middle, so I went in. It was a bakery. I bought a muffin and handed the girl behind the counter a ten-euro note. She gave me back a five euro-note and change, which I stuffed in my pocket. Then I devoured the muffin. I probably didn't look very dignified. Sorry. I was really hungry.

I went back out into the rain and continued down the little diagonal street. At the corner I turned right and walked a block. Then I turned back toward the river. I figured I needed to go two blocks in that direction to get back to my regular route. After one block, though, the street I was on split into a fork, two little streets that were almost parallel. In my waterlogged state, choosing between the street on my left and the one on my right was almost more than I could handle. Two roads diverged in a wood. This one or that one. The lady or the tiger.

I chose the street on my left.

Halfway down the block, I saw it: a little vintage clothing store called Jazz. I pulled out Irene Malraux's list. Jazz was not on it. I almost didn't go in.

I looked in the window. The display was very 1950s Givenchy. Very Audrey Hepburn. Lovely clothes, but nothing from the 1920s. Nothing that said "Come inside." But still.

I leaned closer, and tried to look *past* the display to the clothes on the racks. I saw something sparkly. Maybe an old 1920s beaded dress. Or not. But what was one more store? I opened the door and stepped inside.

The place was maybe twenty feet across and twenty feet back, crammed with racks and racks of clothes. Plus there was an old wrought-iron spiral staircase right smack in the middle of the space, running all the way up to the ceiling, with even more clothes hanging from the railing. The only person in the store was a round old woman sitting right behind the window display on a wooden chair behind a little oak desk that was cluttered with ribbons, bolts of silk, pincushions, a huge square glass ashtray overflowing with cigarette butts and ashes, and a little black-and-white TV with a flickering picture but no sound.

I looked at my watch. Almost seven. It was still light out, so I wasn't sure if almost seven fell into the *bonjour* or *bonsoir* category. I decided on "Bonsoir."

The old lady looked at me, took a drag on her cigarette, and said, "*Bon*jour." She turned her attention back to the little TV screen.

Since the old lady did not seem at all interested in helping me, I found the beaded dress I had glimpsed through the window by myself. I concluded I had wasted my time, because it was clearly from the 1940s. Pretty, though. And I thought, *Well, if my entire trip here has been a total failure, maybe I could at least buy something fun for* me. So I pulled the dress out to see if it was my size, which it wasn't. It didn't matter, though. Hiding on the rack, *next* to the first dress, was another beaded dress, which I hadn't seen because it was smooshed in. My heart did a little tumble. It was almost definitely from 1928. It was extremely simple. And breathtaking. A veil of black beading over a luminous gray silk slip. Very carefully, I took it off the rack.

My hopes crashed.

It was tiny. I mean *tiny.* You will remember that I said Nathalie Gauloise was a thirty-six, which is the French equivalent of a perfect size four. But this dress was not a four. It was not even a two. It was a size zero. And there was no extra fabric to make it bigger. None. Which meant, not the slightest possibility that this fabulous dress would ever fit Nathalie Gauloise. I almost cried. But only almost. Instead, I took the dress over to the old lady and said, *"Excusez-moi?"*

She reached over and turned off the TV. Then she smiled. "You have need help?"

"Yes. Oh, yes. Please." Then I took a deep breath. I held the gorgeous little dress up in front of me. "Do you have any more like this?"

"This is pretty," she said.

"It's very pretty. But it's too small."

She took a long breath through her cigarette, then asked, "Is for the film, yes?"

Which as you can imagine took me by surprise. "The film?"

"The film. Duclos." She narrowed her eyes. "Irene did not send you to see me?"

"No. You know Irene?"

"I am named Françoise." The old lady squeezed out from behind the little desk, walked up to me and held out her hand, very formally, and we shook hands. "I am the mother of Irene."

"You're kidding," I said. Which I know was not polite. But you never saw two women who looked less alike.

Françoise looked around the little store, then back at me. "This shop have belonged to *ma mère.* My mother. She sold the special things to the special people. Now this shop belongs to me. I sell the special things to the special people. But I am not so young anymore. I tell Irene, if she want, the shop next belongs to her. So she can carry on what we do." She lowered her voice. "What we do, is very important. It is like . . . a mission." Then she leaned close and scrutinized my face. Finally she asked, "You have been to this shop before?"

"No."

That answer seemed to puzzle her. "Your mother have been to this shop before?"

"No." Then a wild idea occurred to me. "How long has the shop been here?"

She smiled. A little mysteriously, I thought. "A long time," she said. "Long enough."

Long enough for Grandma to have gotten her dangerous dress here?

Then Françoise waved her hand, as if to chase away the past. Or maybe she was just shooing away her cigarette smoke. "Irene does not want the shop. She prefers the films. Duclos. *Pwui.*" I am happy to say she only made that sound, but did not actually spit. "She is stubborn, though. This film, I could help her. But she does not call me. She says, 'I do myself.'" Then she patted me on the cheek and smiled warmly. "But you are different. You have the *politesse.*" She sized me up again, then came to a conclusion. "Yes. You are special. So . . . come."

With that, Françoise hauled herself up the wrought-iron spiral staircase, and I followed. At the top was a door. She shoved it open with her shoulders and disappeared into the ceiling. Then she flipped a light switch, and I saw there was a tiny room up there. Françoise and I took up pretty much all the open space. Everything else, all around us, was clothes.

"Here are . . . the nice things." She squeezed past me and back down the spiral staircase. Leaving me alone.

With the nice things.

23

Françoise was not kidding. We are talking *nice*.

Up in the little room with the nice things, it became clear to me that Grandma's dress is not the only powerful dress in the world. On the contrary. Clothes are powerful in general. Dresses in particular. And dangerous dresses most especially. Now I felt like I had stepped into a nuclear reactor that was positively pulsating with clothes. It was as if I had chugged about six Red Bulls in the space of a minute. Which by the way you absolutely should not do. Trust me.

Once my head stopped spinning, I took a more careful look around and saw that no matter how nice everything was, I still had not gone to perfect-dress heaven. Most of the dresses weren't from the 1920s, and even when they were, the year was wrong, and as I have explained, even a dress from 1929 will not pass as a dress from 1928. Plus I still had to deal with things like size, and color, and condition. But . . . I found a dress. No. I found *the* dress.

It was a silver silk satin, cut on the bias, which meant it would cling to Nathalie Gauloise and show her perfect little shape. The fabric just glowed, and it was very sheer, so even though you couldn't actually see through it, the fit would leave absolutely nothing to the imagination. It had the deepest plunging back I had ever seen on a dress from the 1920s, and a slightly higher hemline than usual, just above the knee, which at the time was extremely daring. A gather of fabric at the left hip was accented by a starburst of rhinestones, which may not sound particularly sexy, but it drew your eye down to the hips. And if I have to explain what is sexy about looking at the hips of a woman with a perfect size-four body who is wearing this clinging shining miracle of a dress with a back that plunges all the way down to that really sensitive spot at the base of the spine, well, there is no hope for you. It was unquestionably a dangerous dress.

In fact, it was the perfect dress. When I carried it downstairs, Françoise smiled.

I took out the cell phone and dialed Gerard Duclos' number, but I couldn't get a signal. I looked outside. It was still pouring. I looked at the dress. It was still perfect.

"How much is it?" I asked. There was no price tag on it.

"This dress is . . ." She thought about it for a while. "Four hundred euro."

That is when I remembered that nobody had given me any money or a credit card. I figured I could put it on my Visa ATM card and have the money come out of my checking account, but the idea of laying out so much annoyed me, which I guess showed on my face.

"But," said Françoise, "I give you . . . three hundred euro."

"Okay," I said immediately, because this dress was worth a lot more than three hundred and seventy-five dollars. I handed over my card, Françoise swiped it, handed it back to me, and then we waited.

Finally a paper slip sputtered out of the machine. Françoise frowned. "I am sorry."

I knew there was more than enough money in the account to cover this. Not a vast fortune or anything. But more than enough.

"We do again?" Françoise asked. I handed her the card. She swiped. We waited. Finally she shook her head. Sadly. She showed me the receipt. It was in French, but whatever it said, it was clear in any language that the card had been declined.

I tried to think what I could do. I needed this dress. *Needed* it. For my movie. For Josh's movie. For Josh.

Françoise looked at her watch and said, "I am leaving . . . now."

"Okay," I said, and dug out my MasterCard. I did this extremely reluctantly. Because I had very real doubts about whether there was enough room on this card. There wasn't. Then I remembered the euros in my wallet. I could put most of it on the card, and pay the rest with euros. "Try two hundred."

She did. "I am sorry," she said again.

I was getting desperate. "Try a hundred." Don't ask how I expected to make up the rest.

We waited. Then Françoise smiled. The little slip chugged out of her credit card machine. She handed it to me, and I signed.

"You have two hundred euro?"

"No," I said. Because I didn't.

Françoise looked annoyed for just a second, then shrugged. "You have how much?"

I handed her my wallet. She removed all the euros: four twenties and a ten. Ninety. Then she took out my eighty-seven American dollars, which was worth about seventy euros. One hundred plus ninety plus seventy equals two hundred and sixty.

I was about to dig into my pocket for the change I got back from the muffin. Only Françoise said, "No. That is enough." She smiled mysteriously again, and I swear her eyes twinkled. "You and I, we carry on the tradition, yes?"

She packed up the dress—*the* dress—like the pro she was, even found a plastic bag to shield it from the rain. As she packed it, I couldn't help but think that maybe my Grandma had stood in this very spot and watched Françoise's mother pack up *her* perfect dress. The thought made me tingle.

When the bundle was complete, Françoise handed it to me, got up on her toes, and kissed me on my cheeks, right and left.

"Tell Irene I say . . . hello."

Before I could even say *thank you,* she shut the lights and shooed me outside. We opened our umbrellas, then she waddled away.

I had done it. Incredibly, impossibly, I had done it. I had found the perfect dress.

But I still needed one more thing.

I needed Gerard Duclos to agree with me that it was perfect.

24

I ran back to the hotel. Even though I knew I must look like a drowned rat, I went straight to the breakfast room. Gerard was there. Marty. Irene. Pretty much everybody else I had met, but nobody seemed to be doing anything. They were all just sitting and smoking. I think every single person in the room was smoking. Except me.

I walked up to Gerard and announced, "I found it."

"You found it?"

"I found it."

"You did not call."

"It doesn't matter."

He frowned. "The first dress was very bad."

"I'm sure about this one." And I was. "I'm absolutely sure."

Gerard stood up and looked into my eyes, then turned to Marty and said, "She found it."

"So what are we waiting for?" asked Marty. "I'll go get her." He scurried off. About two minutes later he came back. "She's coming."

It took another minute. But finally, she came. Nathalie. You'd have thought the room was full of photographers, the way she posed and preened on her way in. When she got to where Gerard and Marty and I were standing, she glanced at me, then tossed her hair and put her arms around Gerard and started nibbling on his earlobe. "You have found my dress?" she purred.

I opened the bag and took out the tissue paper–wrapped bundle.

Carefully I unfolded it and took off the paper. I held the dress up. The light in the breakfast room was not great. Even in that dim light, though, even without anybody wearing it, the dress shimmered like it was alive.

Everybody looked at the dress. I think I even heard a few people gasp. Then everybody looked at Gerard. Everybody except me. Because all of a sudden I saw Josh—my Josh.

If you are wondering why I was suddenly thinking of him as *my Josh,* go back and read again about him kissing me. Sure, there was that other stuff, like him sticking me with the check for those expensive drinks, but when I saw him in the doorway of the breakfast room, all I could think was, *I kept my promise. I found the perfect dress. I saved Josh's lost cause. Now everything will be all right. Now he will be happy. With me. We will be happy together.*

Then Gerard did the most unusual thing. He started to cry. Which I did not necessarily take as a good sign. "This dress," he said. He wiped his eyes with the ratty sleeve of his ratty sport jacket. "This is . . . the dress. The perfect dress. *Catherine's* dress."

Everybody in the room breathed again. Several people applauded. I tried to catch Josh's eye, but I couldn't see him. Because suddenly Gerard was grabbing me. Kissing me. It did not feel like a you-found-the-perfect-dress-and-saved-my-movie kiss. It felt like an I-am-horny-and-want-to-have-sex-with-you kiss. I did not kiss him back. In fact I gave him a pretty good shove.

I looked for Josh in the doorway, but he was gone.

My skin felt hot. Inside, my stomach did a little flip-flop.

Gerard just laughed and put his arm around Nathalie. "So the dress is perfect, yes?"

Nathalie was looking at me in a way I did not care for.

"Yes?" Gerard asked her again.

"Maybe."

Everybody in the room stopped breathing again.

"What do you mean, 'maybe'?" Gerard demanded. "The dress is perfect."

"Maybe," Nathalie said. "I must wear it first."

With that, she peeled off her little black T-shirt. She was not wearing anything underneath. Then she unzipped her tight hippy-hugger jeans and stepped out of them. She was not wearing anything underneath them, either.

She raised her arms up and posed. "The dress," she said. I felt like an idiot. But I did exactly what she wanted. Like I was her personal maid. I positioned the dress over her head and let it slide down onto her body.

"It *is* perfect," said Irene.

It was. It fit Nathalie as though it had been made for her, clung to her like it wanted to have sex with her. Which was what all the men in the room wanted. Probably some of the women, too.

"Mirror," Nathalie said.

There was no mirror in the breakfast room. One wall of the lobby was a big mirror, though. So we all followed Nathalie as she slunk out of the breakfast room and through the lobby to the mirror. Watching her move in it was quite incredible. It was a *very* dangerous dress.

She looked in the mirror. Posed. Pouted. Posed. Frowned.

Then she turned to Gerard and said, "I hate it."

I was stunned. Gerard was stunned. I am pretty sure everybody was stunned.

"But why?" Gerard asked. "It is *perfect.*"

"It is not perfect," Nathalie said, like it was obvious. "You cannot see my tits."

Which, by the way, she pronounced *teets.*

Let me stop right here and be very clear about this. The way that dress clung to her, you most certainly could see her tits. Every curve. Every . . . everything. You could practically watch her heart beat. But if she meant the dress was not *transparent* . . . well, that's true. It wasn't. By the way, if you ask me, this dress was much sexier than if it *had* been transparent.

Nathalie wasn't asking me. She wasn't asking anybody.

"My fans," Nathalie said. "I cannot disappoint my fans. They must see my *teets.*"

Gerard Duclos looked at me. "She says her fans must see her *teets.*" Do not ask me how he said that with a straight face. Incidentally, although I did not know this at the time, I later learned that before being cast in this movie, the only thing Nathalie had ever done was pose for a magazine that is kind of a French version of *Maxim*. Because it is French, the models wear even less than they do in *Maxim*. Apparently Nathalie did not want to disappoint the fourteen-year-old boys who bought that magazine and looked at her pictures while they . . . well, you know. *Ew*.

"I will not wear this dress," Nathalie said.

"She will not wear it," Gerard said to me. He looked back at Nathalie.

"Tell her she must find another dress," Nathalie said to Gerard.

He turned to me. "She says you must—"

"I heard what she said! But she's wrong. There is no other dress."

"There must be other dresses," Gerard said.

"No. Not like she wants. They didn't make see-through dresses in 1928."

"What does she know?" Nathalie sneered.

I stood up as tall as I could, which made me a couple of inches taller than Nathalie. I got right up close to her, inches away, and looked down into her pretty little face. "I beg your pardon," I said. "I know. I am the author of the monograph 'A Dangerous Dress.' "

"She is," Gerard said.

"Words," Nathalie said. "Stupid words. Anybody can make up words."

I wanted to slap her. Instead I said, "I most certainly did not make anything up."

"Hmph," said Nathalie.

I looked around for help. Surely *someone* must see that I was right.

I spotted Irene, and for just a second I caught her glance. Then she turned away. I remembered what Françoise had said about her daughter, and I felt as if a delicate thread between the past and the future had snapped, right before my eyes.

Then I spotted Marty. He looked at me. I gave him my Hoosierest pout.

I guess Marty really did want to be a Hoosier. Because he tapped Gerard on the shoulder, cleared his throat, and said, "Maybe she's right."

The room went deathly silent.

Gerard swiveled slowly to face Marty. The top of Marty's pompadour only came up to Gerard's nose. Gerard stared down his nose. When he spoke, each word dropped out of his mouth like a stone. "Is . . . it . . . *your* film?"

"No," Marty admitted.

"Whose . . . film . . . *is* it?"

"The director's film." Marty recited it by rote, as if it were the Pledge of Allegiance.

"And who . . . is . . . the director?"

"You are." Marty's eyes shifted to the floor, and he shuffled back into the crowd.

Gerard turned back to me. "So. You are wrong. You will find another dress. And you must do it quickly." He smiled. Nastily, I thought. "Because filming begins in the morning."

This was insane. How could I convince them I was right? Then I knew the answer. "You stay here," I told Gerard. "I'll be right back. I'll show you." I ran upstairs to my room. I unlocked the door and shoved it open.

On the bed was a single, perfect, long-stemmed, delicate pink rose, and a note. It said:

> *You are wonderful. Whereas I am a stupid jerk. I am also very, very sorry. Dinner at La Tour d'Argent? My treat. (I promise.)*

Josh
P.S. I know another spot where the lights are even prettier.

When I read that last line, all I could think of was Josh kissing me again, and for a second I wanted to drop everything and try to find him. Then I remembered why I came up to the room. Maybe I could still convince them I knew what I was talking about. Maybe Gerard would insist that Nathalie wear the dress. That way they would make Josh's movie. Otherwise the movie was doomed, because it would be impossible to find another perfect dress by morning.

I opened my mom's suitcase and took off the white tissue paper.

I walked down the stairs carrying Grandma's dress. In fact, I took my sweet time coming down those stairs. I had a point to prove, and if it involved making a dramatic entrance, so be it.

Everybody was still waiting in the lobby.

I paraded past Nathalie and held up Grandma's dress for Gerard. "Here," I said. "Do you see? This is the dress I wrote about. Look at the fabric." I slid my hand between the two layers of pearl-blue silk satin. Looking through just one layer of the fabric, you could see my hand. "See? If they wanted it to be transparent, they would have made it with just one layer. But they didn't. You weren't supposed to see through it. The dress she wants doesn't exist."

As if in slow motion, Nathalie raised her right arm to her left shoulder and took hold of the perfect dress I had found for her. Slowly, sinuously, she removed it, until she was stark naked again.

Then she ripped the dress in two. She let the two halves slip out of her fingers and onto the floor. I felt like I had just watched somebody commit a murder.

The room was totally silent for maybe ten seconds. Maybe a minute. It felt like an hour. Then Nathalie turned to me, pointed at Grandma's dress, and said, "This dress is pretty."

I unfroze. "Of course it is," I said stupidly. I really could not see where she was going.

"I am not talking to you." She shifted her attention to Gerard. "I like *this* dress."

"Don't you understand?" I asked. "You can't see your *teets* in this, either."

"But you *could,*" suggested Irene. "I could cut out the inside layer of the fabric. Then everyone can see everything."

"Yes." Nathalie looked awfully pleased with herself. "You cut it. Then I will wear it."

"No!" I believe I shrieked when I said that. "You can't cut it," I told Irene. "You can't touch it." Then I turned to face Nathalie again. "And you. You most certainly cannot wear it." I headed for the stairs. I did not even want my Grandma's dress in the same room as these people.

"Fine," Nathalie called after me. "Then there is no dress."

As I walked past Irene, I stopped. "Your mother says hello," I said. "She's very nice. You should call her." Irene flinched as if I had slapped her. Served her right.

Then I kept walking. I knew they were all looking at me. But I didn't stop. I just walked up the stairs and didn't look back.

I knew what it all meant. Nathalie had ruined the dress I found, and I wouldn't let them destroy Grandma's dress to suit Nathalie. So there was no dress. They couldn't shoot the party scene. The schedule would slip. They would lose Kathy Bates. They would lose Elijah. If they lost Elijah, they lost the movie. Elijah Wood, by the way. He was playing young Harold Klein.

I had found a dress. The perfect dress. And none of it mattered, because they weren't going to make the movie. Josh's lost cause was finished, even before it started.

All because of me.

25

Once I got to my floor, I ran straight to my room and locked the door behind me. Then I saw that pink rose from Josh, and I burst into tears.

My mom's suitcase was still open on the bed. I started packing, because I knew I would be leaving soon. I wasn't sure when they would kick me out, but it wouldn't be long.

I left a big space in the suitcase and built my little protective wall out of tampon boxes and sanitary-pad packages again. Then I took Grandma's dress and laid it out, very carefully, on the white tissue paper. I wrapped it and folded it and put it into the suitcase. Finally I zipped the suitcase closed, locked the combination lock, and put the bag near the door.

When I was finished, I realized I was shivering. I had spent all day walking in the pouring rain. I was still running around in wet clothes, and I guess it was catching up to me.

I peeled off the soggy clothes, draped them over a chair, and got an extra blanket from the closet, even though it was May. I pulled the drapes closed, turned off the light, crawled into bed, and wrapped myself as tight as I could in the sheets and blankets. I don't know what time it was. I shivered and cried in the dark for a while. Finally I fell asleep, although it is hard to sleep well when you know something bad is coming in the morning. If I dreamed, I don't remember what.

I do remember what woke me. There was a knock on the door. It was still dark. Then I realized I had my head under the covers, so of course it was dark. I pulled off the covers. It was still dark. The clock radio read five thirty. I thought that was awfully early for a visit. But if somebody is firing you and kicking you out of your hotel room, they probably don't care very much about being polite. I was guessing it was Marty. Poor Marty got all the delightful jobs.

Whoever it was knocked again.

I thought about not answering, until it occurred to me that if they had a key and I didn't answer, they would open the door anyway. As I mentioned, I was not wearing any clothes, because I had just peeled off my wet things and gotten straight into bed.

So I asked, "Who is it?"

"Gerard," said Gerard Duclos. Even through the door, I recognized his voice. I was surprised that he had come himself to fire me.

"Just a minute," I said.

I switched on the little lamp over the bed and found my clothes. My shirt and panties were dry, although my pants were still damp, and my socks and sneakers were sopping wet. I got into my clothes as fast as I could, but I left the socks and sneakers off. And let me tell you, pulling on a pair of wet jeans in a hurry, especially when you are panicking, is not so easy.

"Open the door, please," said Gerard. So I did.

I have already told you that I recognized the voice as Gerard Duclos'. But that was all I recognized. The man who stepped into my room had a perfect haircut, and was so clean-shaven the skin of his face glowed. He was wearing a very dashing slender pinstriped suit, and a lovely pink button-down shirt open at the collar. I think I even caught a whiff of cologne.

I took another look at his face. I have told you that even with the long hair and that awful overgrown beard, Gerard Duclos could not hide his resemblance to Celestine. Seeing him clean-shaven, I was struck even more by how much he looked like her. He had cut his hair, shaved his beard, and now he looked like something out of the French equivalent of *GQ*.

I guess I was staring, because he explained. "I have a superstition.

The very first movie I made, it is"—and he paused to think—"thirty-three years ago. I was maybe your age. Very poor. All the money I had, I bought film stock and rented a camera. There was no money for clothes or haircuts. And no time. I did everything. I wrote the movie. I was the cameraman. I was the editor. I did not sleep. By the time the movie was finished, I looked . . . the way you saw me." He smiled a dazzling smile. "That movie was the big success, made me famous, gave me money. So now, every movie, from before production starts until the movie is finished, I do not shave. I do not cut my hair. And I wear the clothes people throw away, the way I did that first time."

"But . . ."

"But this movie is over now. Nathalie has destroyed the dress. You will not give us the other dress. We cannot shoot the scene. The schedule moves. The actors must leave. The movie becomes impossible. There is no movie." He smiled. "I think I look better like this, yes?"

He was really very handsome, but I was quite preoccupied with other things. "Did you come here to fire me?"

"Of course not."

"I'm sorry I ruined your movie."

"I can always make another movie." He sounded awfully cavalier. Not at all like Josh. Poor Josh. Getting this movie made meant everything to him, and now there was no movie.

There was a perfectly good chair over by the desk, but Gerard sat down on the bed, which brought him very close to me. "You look lovely," he told me.

I had just woken up. I had terrible sleep breath, and I'm sure I had terrible sleep hair. I was wearing the same clothes I had worn all day yesterday traipsing around in the rain. Consequently, what he just said sounded quite stupid to me. I guess maybe that justifies my answering him by saying something equally stupid. "My pants are wet," I said.

"Yes they are." I believe he leered. I say "I believe" because frankly I have not had much experience with men leering. In any event, it was not a smile, not a sneer, and there was a large dose of sex in it. So I think I am correct in saying he leered.

"I couldn't let them cut up my Grandma's dress," I said.

"Of course not." He scooted himself a little closer to me on the bed.

"I really thought the other dress was perfect," I said.

"But it *was* perfect. Don't you know why Nathalie refused to wear the dress you found? Because *you* found it."

"I don't understand."

"Don't you? I think every girl understands these things. In here," he said, tapping me on the chest. "Nathalie does not like you because she knows I *do* like you."

"That's silly."

"Is it? Nathalie has the sex with me. She does not want me to have the sex with you."

"But you and I aren't having the sex," I said.

He moved even closer to me. Any closer and he would be in my lap. "Not yet," he purred. Then he tried to kiss me.

Even though he had left me very little room to maneuver, I jumped up and scooted away. So his lips probably hit me about at the waist. I suspect I gave him a denim burn across the mouth. At least I hope so. Now, though, I had a real problem: I was in the corner of the room. There was no place else for me to go. And Gerard Duclos was quite a lot bigger than me.

Looking back at it, I should have been scared. But I wasn't. Things were moving too fast. Gerard stood up, putting one hand on one wall and the other hand on the other wall, blocking my way. I was really trapped.

Just then, somebody else knocked on the door. Mind you, it was five forty-five in the morning.

I probably should have yelled "Help" or "Rape" or something, but the fact is, I just said "Yes?" The door swung open.

It was Josh. He saw me. He saw Gerard.

Of course, I saw him too. My heart leaped. Practically somersaulted.

And right then, it was *really* time for me to say something clever, like "Save me." But I was so stunned to see him, not to mention thrilled, that for a second I couldn't say anything at all.

Then I actually did open my mouth to say something. Only before I could, Josh slammed the door shut.

Gerard had seen Josh, too, over his shoulder. He hadn't moved his arms, though, so I was still stuck in the corner. When Josh slammed the door, Gerard turned back to face me. Now he was leering. This time I am quite positive. He stopped leering, though, because I kicked him. As hard as I could. I aimed for his balls, and judging from how he reacted, I scored a direct hit.

In case you have never seen a man who has actually been kicked in the balls, they behave exactly the way men do in the movies when they are kicked in the balls. They fall onto the floor. Their knees draw up to their chests. And they have trouble breathing for a while. Only in the movies it is just pretend. Here it was entirely real.

The next logical thing would have been for me to call the police. Or the hotel manager. But it is hard to be logical when you are being sexually harassed and then assaulted by your best friend's father. So here is what I did. I yelled, "Get out of my room!"

He was still lying on the floor gasping, so I got down on my knees and kind of rolled him across the room. I stood up and opened the door, then bent down and shoved him until he was out in the hallway, where he lay on his back, eyes closed, still trying to catch his breath. Finally he opened his eyes and looked at me.

And do you know what he did? He *smiled.*

"Now," he croaked. "Now you are fired."

26

So. I had just been fired from this amazing movie job because I wouldn't let them hack my Grandma's dress to shreds so some oversexed nicotine-stained French movie slut could show off her tits. I had just kicked my best friend's father, who also happened to be a famous French film director, in the balls. I was wondering how on earth I was going to get to the airport, and if I got there, whether I'd find that my return plane ticket was no good because they cashed it in so the crew could eat Snickers bars. I didn't know what to do. I just stood there, waiting for them to break down the door of my hotel room and drag me out.

I was terribly upset. And broke, and afraid. So in spite of the whole thing with her father, I decided to call Celestine. The cell phone they gave me had already been disconnected. But when I picked up the phone in my room, there was a dial tone. So I called her.

She answered the phone. "Allo?" Then she listened while I told her everything. I might have left out a couple of bits about Gerard, but I told her enough. "Pile everything in a cab and come stay with me," she said when I was finished.

"I don't think I can afford a cab."

"It's not very expensive. I'm sure you have enough." When I didn't say anything, she asked, "How much *do* you have?"

All I had was the change from that muffin. The only paper money was a five-euro note. The rest was coins. A two-euro coin. A one-euro coin. Four coins with 20 on them—20 I don't know what you call them, euro-cents? A copper-colored coin with a 5 on it, and two littler coppers marked with 1s. Eight euros and eighty-seven whatevers.

Before I could even tell Celestine how much—or rather how little—I had, I think she knew I was really in trouble. Maybe she heard the jingle and figured out I was counting change. "Never mind," she said. "It's not far. You can walk."

"My suitcase doesn't have wheels."

"Oh," Celestine said. "All right. Just put what you need right now into a little bag you can carry, and check everything else with the desk clerk. We can pick it up later."

"If they don't throw it away."

"They wouldn't do that." She chuckled.

I didn't know how long I had before I got evicted from my room. Deciding what to put in my little duffel bag is the sort of process that ordinarily might take me ten or twenty minutes. Or an hour. But I thought I might not even have ten minutes. I unlocked the suitcase, unzipped it, and grabbed my clean panties, Miracle Bra, a T-shirt, fresh socks, and a dry pair of sneakers. Oh, and a box of tampons. I put those things in my duffel baggy. I also took Josh's note. And the rose. I had to break the stem, but that was the only way it would fit in my little bag.

I looked at Grandma's dress. There was no way it would fit. And Gerard probably told the hotel staff to be on the lookout for the dress girl, so I couldn't escape detection if I walked out carrying the dress. I had to leave it. Which scared me. The dress was the only reason anybody had flown me to Paris. The dress was my passport. And you can't walk around in a strange country without your passport.

But then I thought, *It will be okay. They can't do anything to my luggage. That would be illegal.* Anyway, I had no choice. So I zipped the suitcase up and carried it to the lobby. I did not tell the man at the front desk that I was checking out. In fact I told him I was *not* checking out. I also might have made a mistake about what room I was in. I figured Gerard Duclos would tell them to throw the girl in 302 out into the street. If I said I was in 309, maybe they wouldn't make the connection. I guess they didn't. The clerk gave me a claim ticket. He carried my mom's suitcase to a storage room, and said just be sure to pick it up by seven P.M.

When I got outside I could see it was going to be a beautiful day. Thank goodness.

I walked toward the river and didn't stop until I was halfway across the Pont Neuf. Which by the way means "New Bridge." Even though Celestine told me the Pont Neuf is the oldest bridge in Paris. I simply do not understand the French.

I sat down on a semicircular stone bench and took out the map Irene gave me. I figured out that Celestine lived in the Fourth, probably only four or five blocks from where I had been desperately searching through vintage clothing shops yesterday. At least I knew the way there.

I got to Celestine's building at about a quarter to eight. She had said she needed to run a few early errands, then go straight to work, so she wouldn't be there to let me in, but she gave me the buzzer number for her landlady, who she said would give me the key.

I found the address and buzzed apartment number one. There was a little intercom speaker next to the buzzer, and I expected a voice to come out of it. Instead, a window opened right over my head, from which an old lady leaned out and looked down. She was quite round, and bore a strong resemblance to Françoise. Do not ask me why so many young Frenchwomen are tall and slender, while so many old Frenchwomen are short and round.

Celestine's landlady leaned so far out her window, I was genuinely afraid she would fall out and land on me, but she didn't. She just said "Aaaahhh." Then she disappeared back inside.

After a few seconds I heard a click. The door swung open.

Doors in Paris are quite different from doors in the United States. They are enormous, probably eight feet high and four feet wide. They must weigh a ton, and you wonder how on earth you are going to open them, since the huge doorknobs, which by the way are stuck right smack in the middle of the doors, don't even turn. But the secret is, the doors are mechanical. You punch an access code, or somebody buzzes you in, and the door swings open for you. Do not ask me how they opened their doors before electricity.

I walked through the doorway, into a passage paved with old cobblestones that led to a courtyard. On the far side of the courtyard was a short flight of steps leading to another door, which was made of glass panes and had a real handle. That door opened into a hallway, where I found the door to apartment one. Actually I found the old lady standing in front of the door to apartment one. I later learned her name is Madame Cluny, although she did not introduce herself then. She handed me a key and pointed up the sweeping curve of a stairway.

I walked up the stairs and found apartment seven. I let myself in, put down my little duffel baggy, and looked around.

The apartment was on about six different levels. When you walked in, immediately in front of you, three steps led up to a landing. At that landing, if you turned left, you were in a tiny kitchenette. If you turned right, there were four more steps to the bathroom. If you didn't turn left or right, just went straight, there was a short hall, then two steps *down* to the living room. It had an enormous arched window that took up the whole far wall. On the left side of the room was a wall of closets. On the right, a stepladder climbed up to a sleeping loft. The ceilings in the kitchenette and bathroom were quite low, but the living room must have been twenty feet high.

I walked into the living room and looked at the huge arched window. It must have been thirty feet across and twelve feet high, and it was really quite dramatic. I guess Celestine must know from experience that people always look at that window. Because right in the middle of it, she had Scotch-taped a note. I took it down and read it.

J,
I am so sorry G behaved so badly.
Food in fridge if you are brave.

Fresh towels in the bathroom. Shampoo you like is in the pink bottle.
Come see me at work. Armani, 41 Ave. George V, 8e. Take the Vespa—key on hook by door. Wear anything you want.
C

Since breakfast the day before, I had only eaten that one little muffin, so the first thing I did was raid the refrigerator. I probably would have eaten anything in there as long as it didn't come running out when I opened the door. Do not ask me how Celestine stays a perfect size six consuming all that milk and yogurt and all those amazing cheeses. I probably maxed out my saturated fats for the week in ten minutes. At least when I was finished, I wasn't starving anymore.

Then I took a shower. A really long hot shower. Although the hot water was a little indecisive. About whether or not it was hot. I should also mention that Celestine has a shower curtain. Her bathroom was not designed for one, but her year at Purdue must have opened her eyes to the joy of shower curtains. Celestine is none too handy, and she had tacked her curtain up in an extremely amateurish way. Still, an amateurish shower curtain is much better than none.

After the shower I put on a white robe Celestine had left hanging for me. I'd almost swear it was linen, not cotton, although why anybody would make a bathrobe out of linen I don't know. Plus it didn't wrinkle like linen. In any event it was lovely.

I felt like a human being again. Even better—being in my best friend's apartment, enjoying the things she left for me, I felt like at least somebody loved me. Even if I had broken my promise to myself. Even if I had not saved Josh's lost cause. Even if I had ruined the movie.

27

Deciding what to wear may not sound important or challenging to you. But it's both.

I have already told you how powerful I think clothes can be. Grandma's dress is the ultimate example, but clothes in general are powerful things. And here is a concrete example.

At that moment, my self-esteem was more than a little wobbly. What with me having totally failed both myself and Josh Thomas. At such times, making the right decision about what to wear is crucial. If you don't believe me, try this: The next time you are feeling really down and worthless, put on the ugliest, least fashionable thing you own—probably something you got from an immediate family member. Now look at yourself in the mirror, and tell me you don't feel even worse. Of course you do.

Now rip off those awful clothes and, fast as you can, put on the thing you own that you would be most likely to see in a photo spread in *Elle.* If you don't own anything like that, I recommend you go buy such an outfit. But do it *before* trying this experiment.

Look in the mirror again. If you don't feel glamorous, gorgeous, and like an entirely different being from the toad in the JC Penney jumper your brother gave you for your birthday, you're hopeless.

So I knew I was about to revitalize myself. But I also knew I faced a serious challenge, because Celestine had instructed me, *Wear anything you want.*

That would be a kind offer coming from anybody. Coming

from Celestine, though, it was incredibly generous. Celestine does not have just any old wardrobe.

Let us put aside for a moment that Gerard Duclos is a sexual predator. He is also a big important French film director, and he is a celebrity. He gets invited to all the right parties, given by all the right people. Who, in Paris, just happen to include people like Thierry Mugler and Karl Lagerfeld and Jean Paul Gaultier.

All these people *give* clothes to Celestine. Which is perfectly understandable. She is sweet and beautiful, and if I were a fashion designer I'd give her clothes too. The fact that her father is who he is probably doesn't hurt either. Maybe the designers figure that if they're nice to Celestine her father will use their clothes in his movies.

Anyway. Celestine's closet looks like somebody died and went to *Vogue* heaven.

Wear anything you want.

You might think that being turned loose in *Vogue* heaven would be every girl's dream. Especially a girl from Bumfuck—a girl who, I quickly ascertained, was still the same clothing size as Celestine.

Instead, standing there looking at all those amazing clothes, I felt anxious. Some of my anxiety was probably left over from the grand finale of my glamorous career in the movie business. But some of it had to do with going to see Celestine at work. Celestine does not work at just any old place. She works at Armani. Armani is the perfect place for her to work, but it only made me more anxious. I couldn't walk into Giorgio Armani wearing any old thing, now could I?

Then I spotted two identical navy-blue pantsuits right next to each other. It was a little warm out to be wearing a jacket, but they were made of a lightweight tropical wool. The deciding factor was that there were two of them. Even if for instance I perspired all over the first one, Celestine would have another one to wear while she got the first one cleaned.

Next to the suits were two perfect little white scoop-necked short-sleeve tops. I picked one of the suits, one of the tops, and a simple pair of flats. As soon as I had decided about the clothes I started feeling less anxious. I did get a little twinge when I saw that the labels on the suits and the tops said ARMANI COLLEZIONI. Then I realized, nobody could possibly fault me for walking into Giorgio Armani wearing, well, Giorgio Armani.

Now I just had to figure out how to *get* to Giorgio Armani.

I was so focused on the *Wear whatever you want* part of Celestine's note that I had glossed over the rest. I went back and reread the part that said *41 Ave. George V, 8e* and *Take the Vespa—key on hook by door.*

I started to get anxious again.

Finding Avenue George V on the map was easy. The Vespa was the problem. A Vespa is not a motorcycle. With all due respect to Vespas, which are perfectly cute, they are hardly even scooters. They are very Audrey Hepburn, and if you don't know what I mean, then stop right here, run out and rent *Roman Holiday.*

But getting back to my point, there is nothing whatsoever intimidating about Vespas. Which is exactly what I found so intimidating. I had just spent the last two days walking around Paris, and I had observed several things about the traffic.

First, there are so many cars. And even more motorcycles and scooters.

Second, people drive very fast.

Third, the cars are very small, so people zip into the tiniest openings in moving traffic, regardless of the size of the opening, the speed of the traffic, or the color of the light.

Fourth, there are the lane lines, which for the most part *do not exist.* Why Parisians think lane lines are a bad idea, I don't know.

Finally, there are the street signs. Which *do* exist, on every corner. It is just impossible to read them. Because in Paris they do not mount street signs on poles like everyplace else. They attach blue plaques with the street names printed in white letters to whatever building is on the corner. The longer the street name, the more letters they squeeze in. It's easy to read RUE DE BAC. But you try to read BOULEVARD BEAUMARCHAIS, stuck on a little sign twenty feet up the side of a building, while you're whizzing by on a Vespa, with six thousand cars and ten thousand motorcycles racing past you at hundreds of kilometers an hour, without lane lines. That is why I was anxious.

Then again, everybody else seemed to survive out there, so I guessed I would too. I didn't even let myself get hung up on whether my Indiana driver's license would let me drive legally in Paris. Nobody else seems to worry about driving legally in Paris.

I checked my map, figured out the route, picked up the key to the Vespa, and studied the bright cobalt-blue helmet, which I decided not to wear. Who wants to make a grand entrance at Giorgio Armani with helmet hair? Then I thought again about the traffic. Maybe a little helmet hair wouldn't be so bad. I took it with me.

Down in the courtyard I found a shiny, gorgeous, perfectly adorable cobalt-blue Vespa parked among several other scooters. It had to be Celestine's. It was perfect, the gorgeous color matched the helmet, and it was the only Vespa there.

I had never driven any kind of motorcycle or scooter before, but driving the Vespa was easy. Even if I did miss the first turn I was supposed to make. Then almost turned the wrong way down a one-way street. Many Parisians will ride scooters the wrong way down one-way streets, but I am not brave enough to do that. At least not intentionally.

I finally got headed the right way, and turned onto a big street called Rue de Rivoli, which I got to stay on for three kilometers, which is about two miles. Now all I had to do was sort of curve around the Place de la Concorde and turn right onto the Champs-Elysées.

The Place de la Concorde has beautiful fountains, green and bright gold, and in the middle is an Egyptian obelisk called Cleopatra's Needle, which looks like the Washington Monument, only covered with hieroglyphics. I learned those things from picture postcards. Although I drove through the Place de la Concorde, I did not get a very good look at it. To be precise, I drove around it. And around and around. Like in *National Lampoon's European Vacation,* where Chevy Chase gets stuck driving around a traffic circle. It was funny in the movie.

Ha ha.

I made the mistake of approaching the Place de la Concorde in the left lane, which becomes the inside lane of a huge traffic circle. Actually more like a traffic oval. You will recall that I am from Indiana, the home of the Indianapolis 500, which some people call "eight hundred left turns." That was what I felt like, going around and around the Place de la Concorde, stuck in the inside lane.

There are no lane lines at the Indy 500, either.

Finally—*finally*—I scooted to the right lane without injuring myself or others. I turned onto the wide Boulevard des Champs-Elysées and went straight for a while. When I had to turn left onto Avenue George V, I couldn't bring myself to cut across all those lanes. I wimped out, waited for the pedestrian green light, then waddled the Vespa across the crosswalk and turned onto George V. Finally, ahead of me, I saw the Armani store. All I had to do was park.

The rules about parking in Paris, if there are any rules at all, are different from anyplace else I've ever been. People park cars with two of the wheels on the sidewalk, or even all four on the sidewalk. They just ride up over the curb and park scooters and motorcycles right in the middle of busy sidewalks. So in theory, my choice of parking spaces was unlimited.

Parking on the sidewalk looked easy enough. I now suspect there is a trick to it. Like slowing down first, and using your foot to ease the scooter up over the curb. At the time, though, I didn't give it much thought. When the front tire hit the curb, I bounced about two feet up in the air, then landed on the seat, hard. I looked up, and the Armani store window was getting awfully close in a hurry. So I braked kind of suddenly, and almost but not quite got thrown over the handlebars. I did stop. With at least an inch between my front tire and the store window.

I know the Vespa has a kickstand. But at that moment I was more focused on getting down and kissing the sidewalk. So I got off the Vespa without putting the kickstand down. Gravity being what it is, the Vespa fell on its side. For a second it looked to me like a cobalt-blue horse that was sick and keeled over, and I had the irrational thought that somebody would have to put it out of its misery. Then I remembered it was a Vespa, and not my Vespa, either. I picked it up, figured out how the kickstand worked, and parked it properly. By Paris standards.

When my knees had mostly stopped shaking, I went inside the store.

28

When you walk into Armani on Avenue George V, there is a little branch of the store on your right, which displays men's sweaters, shirts, ties, and accessories. On your left are the sales desk, men's dressing rooms, and the bathroom. Most of the store stretches in front of you like a corridor. You walk past mannequins with fancy women's clothes on your left, and racks of men's suits, coats, and jackets on your right. There's a comfy chair for customers, then a row of sweaters, shoes, bags and accessories down the middle. In the back is the promised land—women's clothing: pants and blouses and jackets and suits and dresses and gowns and beaded gowns and oh my. In the very back are the ladies' dressing rooms, the tailoring room, and the stockroom. Not that I took everything in the first time I walked into the store. I didn't. I was distracted by the fact that as I was walking in, Lucy Liu was walking out.

I am not absolutely sure it was Lucy Liu. But I think so. Besides, it seems like the kind of place she would shop.

After my brush with Lucy, I started looking in earnest for Celestine. Of course, I did my best to look at the clothes too. It was my first time in an Armani store. For all I knew then, it would also be my last time, so I wasn't going to miss anything. And if you are wondering what is the big deal with Giorgio Armani, I guess you have never watched the Oscars, the Emmys, the Golden Globes, or Joan and Melissa Rivers.

There were just a few people shopping. Most of the people in the store looked like they worked there. Even though they were all wearing different outfits, all the outfits were navy blue, and all the people wearing them were slim and cool and oh so fashionable.

At that moment Celestine came out from the ladies' dressing room area at the back of the store. She was probably fifty feet away, but she spotted me immediately and her face lit up.

She broke into a run, then planted her feet flat, held her arms out like a surfer, and *slid* all the way up to me. She gave me a big hug and kissed my cheeks, right, left, right, left. Wow. Four was a new record for me. Then she looked at me, and all the blood drained out of her face. "Oh my God." She gasped. "What are you wearing?"

I was wearing a navy pantsuit and a perfect little scoop-necked white top under the jacket. Just like Celestine.

All of a sudden I realized why she had two of the exact same outfit in her closet. I was wearing the Armani salesgirl uniform. "I didn't know," I said. "But . . . it's not so bad, is it? I mean, it's kind of funny."

She didn't look like she thought it was funny. In fact, I never saw Celestine look so serious. "You don't understand," she said. "He may be coming to the store today."

"He who?"

She looked around and lowered her voice. *"Signore Armani."*

Giorgio Armani the person lives in Italy, and spends most of his time in Milan. When he comes to Paris it is mostly for fashion shows, not to visit his stores. And if by chance he goes to one of the stores, it tends to be the store at the Place Vendôme—the very same Place Vendôme where Josh Thomas took me to his favorite bar in the world and then walked out on me, and where I subsequently got lost coming out of the Ritz. Everything in that store is Giorgio Armani black label, the most expensive. So the news that he might actually be coming here, to the Armani Collezioni white-label store, which is only the second most expensive, had everybody who worked here excited. Thrilled. Terrified. Like if you went to church one Sunday the same as always and somebody mentioned to you, "Oh, by the way, the Pope is stopping by today."

"Là! Il est là!" A handsome young man who stood halfway out the door was pointing urgently down the street.

All the navy-suited people ran for the door, even Celestine. She ran right out with the rest of them. Leaving me alone in the store. Me and the three customers. Fortunately, nobody seemed to be actually *shopping.*

You know what I mean. I don't care what or where the store is, some people only ever walk into a store to *look,* even if it's a Wal-Mart in Valpo, Indiana. Furthermore, I have found that the higher the prices in a store, the higher the percentage of just-lookers. So I hoped that the man and the two women were just browsing.

Sure enough, the man wandered out, and about half a minute later one of the women left. The other lady was strolling through the men's clothes up at the front, so I figured I was safe, at least as long as nobody else came in.

For the first time since I walked in, I looked at the floor. It's made of tan-colored stone, very soothing. And very smooth. I remembered the way Celestine slid up to me. We used to do that at home, when I was little. Kirland is very cold in the winter, so there's always plenty of ice. Before I learned to skate, I used to run and slide, just the way Celestine had on the stone floor.

I looked around. The browsing lady was still in men's, so I took a little run, planted my feet, and slid. Then I did it again. Took a longer run, and slid even farther. And farther. And—

"Excuse me."

In midslide, I looked up to see the browsing lady holding a blouse.

"How much is this. . . ."

I opened my mouth to say something, although I had no idea what. But she put her hand up, right in front of my face, and stopped me.

"No, wait," she said. She dug into her purse, a brand-new Louis Vuitton shopping bag. Not the nice classic Vuitton, but that new print in those obnoxious candy colors. She pulled out a palm-sized gadget, typed something on the little chicklet keys, then looked up. "Chemise," she said, with a huge smile. Only she said "*Ch*emise." Pronouncing the *ch* like channel.

I couldn't help myself. "Chemise," I said. Pronouncing the *ch* like Chanel. Bear in mind, I think I have made this clear already, but I do not speak French. It just so happens that *chemise* is a perfectly good English word. But the *ch* is pronounced *sh.* Even in English.

All of a sudden two things occurred to me. First, I probably shouldn't be saying anything at all to the customers. And second, I probably shouldn't be *correcting* the customers.

"Do you know," the lady said, "that is just like you French people."

I wondered if impersonating an Armani salesgirl is a criminal offense in Paris.

"First ignoring me while you slide around like you were a child, then correcting me like *I* was a child. I have only one thing to say to you," she said.

Our Father who art in Heaven.

"Thank you." She grabbed my hand and shook it. Her long fingernails dug into my skin. "Thank you so much. Everybody in Atlanta told me the French are just bossy and rude and condescending. Especially in stores. But do you know, since I have been here, everybody has just been so"—she struggled to find the right word—*"nice,"* she finally said, and made a face like it tasted bad in her mouth. "I don't know why, but they have been depriving me of a genuine French experience. So God bless you, child." She smiled a big smile. For a second I thought about telling her that bright red lipstick was so not her, but I figured maybe that would be a little too much genuineness all at once. "Now tell me," she

said, holding up the blouse. "How much is this . . . *chemise?*" Pronounced right.

I looked at the tag. Which she could have done just as easily. But she wanted me to be French. I didn't want to disappoint her, so I tried to remember how French people speak English.

"Sree hundred and twenty." It sounded really fake to me, but she didn't blink.

Instead, she held the blouse up in front of herself. "What do you think?"

I didn't like it on her. But I did see one on the same rack that I thought would be nice. Several, actually. I picked one of them up. "Zees one," I said. "Zees eez, for you . . . more good."

"Ooh," she said. "This is going to be fun. Well, dear, let's get me into a dressing room."

I got her size pretty much right away just from holding the clothes up and eyeballing. Even though I had some experience with Nathalie Gauloise, all I knew was that a thirty-six was a size four. Dottie—that was her name—was no size four. She looked like a ten to me, which it turned out was a forty-two. Fortunately there were lots of those on the rack.

She was a very easy fit, and a very fast shopper. If she put something on, it fit. If I told her it looked good, she wanted it. So in about ten minutes she was ready to pay for a pile of clothes.

"Don't let me forget to fill out that form to get my tax back," she said.

I started to perspire. I could help somebody pick clothes, and I could tell them if something looked good or not, but cash registers? Credit cards? Tax forms?

Dottie walked out of the dressing room and I followed her, carrying a huge stack of stuff. I did a quick count in my head. About 5,600 euros. With the crappy exchange rate, over seven thousand dollars.

As we walked toward the front of the store, a man appeared.

He wasn't very tall—maybe five-nine, tops. And he was an older man. But just because I use the word *older,* do not think one single negative thing about his looks. Because he was . . . well, gorgeous. He was tan, and he had the most gorgeous white hair and gorgeous blue eyes. He was wearing blue jeans that were faded just the right amount and that fit him perfectly, and a navy blue T-shirt—wool, I think, maybe even cashmere—that fit him even better than the jeans. And he had the most amazingly gorgeous muscled arms.

If that seems like a lot to notice while you're walking from the back of the Armani store to the front, did I mention he was gorgeous?

As Dottie and I got close to the front of the store, I saw that all the blue-suited men and women who worked there were gathered in the doorway. There were more of them than fit in the doorway, so some of them were outside looking through the window. They weren't looking at Dottie, or at me, or at the pile of clothes I was carrying. They were looking at the gorgeous man.

He, however, *was* looking at Dottie. And at me. And most of all, at the pile of clothes, which I put down on the counter next to the register.

The man turned to the blue suits crowded into the doorway. *"Dagli un lavoro,"* he said.

Nobody moved.

When he spoke again, he sure sounded annoyed. "*Porco Giuda,*" he said, "*ma non c'e nessuno qui che parli italiano?*"

He smiled at Dottie and me. He had the most dazzling white teeth, and the most charming smile. When he turned toward the door, I somehow knew he wasn't smiling.

"Hire her," he said. In English. Then he walked straight out the door. Right through the blue suits, as if they weren't there. They might as well not have been. They parted for him like he was Moses and they were the Red Sea. He was not Moses. He was Mister Giorgio Armani.

Although you have probably figured that out by now.

Then he was gone, and the spell was broken. All the employees rushed into the store.

I turned to Dottie. "Sank you." At that instant my best friend appeared next to me. "Celestine weel help you now," I said.

29

It was amazing how fast the day went by. I guess I never had a job I liked so much before. No offense, Uncle John. Anyway, before I knew it, it was seven o'clock.

Seven o'clock. Now why did that ring a bell?

Uh-oh. The clerk at the Hotel Jacob told me to pick up my suitcase by seven. "We have to leave," I said to Celestine. "Right away." Suddenly I had a very bad feeling.

"I will drive," Celestine said. If she saw my look of terror as we approached the Vespa, or noticed the scrapes on her scooter from my parking job, she didn't mention it.

"Please hurry," I said. I didn't know if seven o'clock was some kind of deadline, if I was already too late, or what it was I was too late for.

We pulled to a stop directly across from the hotel. "Go claim the bag," Celestine said. "Have them call you a taxi, and put the suitcase in the trunk. I'll give you the fare."

Even though it was a quarter past seven, I hesitated. I was afraid to go into the hotel, which was full of Movie People I had just put out of work. I was about to ask Celestine to get the bag for me—only at that moment, across the street, I saw a man turn the corner and come running in our direction. A man I knew. All of a sudden my face felt hot. I ducked down behind the Vespa, which didn't provide a lot of cover, but was better than nothing.

"What are you doing?" Celestine asked.

"I can't let him see me," I said as the man rushed into the hotel.

"Him who?" she asked.

"Josh."

"Who is Josh?"

"I'll tell you later."

Celestine gave me a look. "Oh yes you will."

A whole minute went by. My legs were starting to hurt from squatting behind the Vespa, so I asked, "What's he doing?"

"Talking to the desk clerk."

"What's he saying?"

"How should I know? He's across the street. And inside."

"Does he look mad?"

Celestine looked back toward the hotel. "I think he's yelling."

"How can you tell if you can't hear him?"

"He's pounding on the desk."

Just then, a beat-up little gray pickup truck pulled in front of the hotel. The sides of the cargo section were unpainted plywood. Even though I couldn't see very well, it looked like there was trash in the flatbed.

"What color is your bag?" asked Celestine.

"Pink."

"Pink??"

"It's my mom's bag. I wouldn't buy a pink suitcase."

"Okay." Then she looked across the street again and frowned. "This is not good." The way she said it, it sounded so much worse than not good that I stood up to see.

A bellman walked out of the hotel and tossed my mom's suitcase into the back of the pickup truck like a sack of garbage. Then the truck barreled away. Before we could even move, it was gone.

I was just starting to comprehend what had happened when I saw Josh step out of the hotel. I ducked back behind the Vespa so he didn't see me. "That's great," he said to the bellman. "Thank you very much." Then he walked down the block, reached the corner, turned, and vanished.

I stood up. My knees were shaking, and not because I had been crouching down for so long. "Did you see what he did?"

Celestine nodded.

"He told them to get rid of my stuff."

She nodded again.

It is very difficult for me to describe how I felt at that moment. I was crushed. Shattered. Any word that describes being smashed into tiny little pieces. Because Josh Thomas had done this to me. My Josh.

Only it was very clear now: If he had ever been my Josh, even for a second, he wasn't now. And he never would be. Never could be. Not ever again.

I still felt terrible that I was personally responsible for his movie falling apart, even though, as I think I have shown, you would have to be a pretty mean person to really think it was my fault. But how could he have done what he just did? After the way he kissed me? After he left that perfect rose in my room?

He must really have been bitter to get them to throw away my things like that.

Then ohmygod, the full force of the disaster hit me. "My Grandma's dress was in that bag."

"We'll find it." Celestine said it because she is my friend, but I knew she didn't believe it. There was no logo on the truck. We didn't get a license plate. We had no way to trace it. It was just gone.

I knew I would never forgive Josh for sacrificing Grandma's dress to get back at me. But there was so much more. Even though we'd practically just met, we had been on the verge of something. Something perfect. Only now, right before my eyes, he had killed that something.

Celestine and I got on the Vespa and rode away without another word. On the way back to the apartment, she stopped for Japanese takeout even though I told her I wasn't hungry.

Back at her place, she pulled two big bottles out of the refrigerator. "Sake," she said.

I always thought you were supposed to drink sake hot, but I knew better than to question Celestine's judgment about such things, so we drank cold sake. I didn't feel very hungry, but I ate the sushi anyway. It was yummy. It seemed only mildly strange to me that in three days in Paris, other than breakfast, I had yet to eat anything you'd actually call French food.

By the way, sushi is something you should not order in Kirland. I don't even think there's anyplace that sells sushi, but if there is, don't buy it.

I finished a very delicious California roll. I don't know if they call it that in Paris. But in any event, I finished it. Then the next thing I knew I was crying. For Grandma's dress. For Grandma. For Josh. For me. For losing everything in the world that mattered to me.

Except my best friend. Thank goodness Celestine was there. She knew when to let me cry. And, when I had pretty much cried myself out, she knew exactly the right moment to take two more big bottles of sake out of the fridge. I should mention, it was quite good cold. We got pretty toasted. Celestine asked about Josh, like she said she would. I told her all about him, like I said I would. I told her pretty much everything, starting from when I met him. She thought he was obnoxious, like I did at first, then kind of fell for him, like I did next, then *really* fell for him after the kiss on the bridge, then felt awful for him, like I did after the dress fiasco, and finally hated him along with me for the way he made them throw away my mom's suitcase and Grandma's dress. "I hate him," I said when I was finished.

"So do I," Celestine said.

"Don't you think I should hate him?"

"Of course you should."

"Good," I said. "I do."

"Then to hell with him." We clinked bottles and drank. I'm not sure drinking good sake out of the bottle is exactly the classy thing to do, but we were both past worrying about classy.

"To hell with him," I said. When I heard those words come out of my mouth, they sounded like somebody else was saying them. But I attribute that entirely to the sake.

"And to hell with Gerard," Celestine said.

"Yeah," I said. Then I said, "Who is Gerard?"

"My father."

"You call him Gerard?"

"What should I call him?" she asked. "Father? Papa? *Dad?*" she asked, in her best imitation of a nasal Midwesterner. "He does not act like a father. He acts like a Gerard. Like a badly behaved boy. To hell with him."

"Yeah."

"I'm so sorry he did what he did to you," she said.

"It's not your fault," I said.

"Of course not," said Celestine. "But I am still terribly sorry. To hell with him."

Sometime around midnight, Celestine reminded me that we both had to go to work in the morning. She tried to convince me to take the sleeping loft, but I said no way. I was perfectly happy to sack out on the couch. Which I was, actually. It is soft cozy old red leather, as comfortable as any bed.

As soon as she turned out the lights, I found myself thinking about Josh. And promises. Lost causes. The Astros. His movie. My Grandma's dress.

If I kept thinking about those things, I would never get to sleep. So I made a conscious decision to think about something else. Like for example my amazing new job. Just four days ago I was working at Independence Savings and Loan in Kirland, Indiana, feeling like I had about as much of a future as the dull little yellow brick on my desk. Today, Mister Giorgio Armani himself had hired me to sell his fabulous clothes at his glamorous Paris boutique.

I couldn't wait to tell my mom. My dad, too, but especially my mom. She and I always watch the Oscars and the Emmys and the Golden Globes together, especially the red carpet preshows, and we love to be catty about who is wearing what awful dress. But neither one of us has ever had anything bad to say about any Armani dress, so she would be particularly impressed with my new job.

Of course, if I called my mom, I would have to admit that I lost Grandma's dress. And I was not sure how I could possibly bring myself to tell her that, since Grandma was my mom's mother. So even though I had this amazing new job to brag about, maybe I would not call home after all.

Ever.

30

Celestine and I got up very early the next morning. Which was complicated somewhat by all that sake. But headaches did not stop us. We were on a mission.

Before I describe our mission, you need to know that Paris is a very, very clean city. Big cities are typically not very clean. And Paris is certainly a big city. But the streets are clean. The sidewalks are clean. The little public trash receptacles always seem to be empty. All this cleanliness is so remarkable, you would think that the average Parisian would know who is responsible for it. But you would be wrong.

Our mission was to find my suitcase. Since we did not get a name or a license off that evil little pickup truck, we figured our only hope was to find where trash goes in Paris. I asked Celestine who picks up the trash.

"I don't know."

"But you have lived here your whole life."

"And the trash has always gone away without my help. I don't know."

Celestine tried to figure it out online. But the French government web sites seem to have been created by videogame designers. The kind of games where you are lost in a maze with only a magic sponge and a hiccuping eunuch to help you find the treasure. We did not have six years to figure out the maze, so she logged off and started calling people. She knows a lot of people in Paris. Including some very important ones. Although most of them are not the type of people who are awake, much less in the mood to answer questions about trash, at seven A.M. In any event, none of them knew anything about who picks up the trash.

Then she remembered Didier. Who is apparently a minor pop music star in France. And who she seemed to recall was the son of some kind of deputy minister. She did not remember him right away because she said he was a very bad kisser—Didier, not the deputy minister. But Didier must have thought Celestine was a fine kisser, because he did not mind at all that she woke him up. He immediately put us in touch with his father.

So at eight fifteen in the morning, there we were, Celestine and I, in our matching Armani salesgirl outfits, in a very regal government building that Celestine said was built in 1763. A very good-looking soldier with a very big gun walked us down about two miles of corridors, then finally showed us into a bland little office that looked like it was built in 1963. Behind the desk sat a very small man with a very big mustache who introduced himself, first in French and then in English, as Monsieur Lebecq, deputy undersecretary of the Department of Facilities and Utilities. It rhymed in French, too.

Briefly, I told him what happened.

"I see." He shook his head sympathetically. Then he thought for a while. Finally Monsieur Lebecq asked, "Is it a sewer matter?"

"I don't think so. It's a suitcase. It wouldn't fit down a sewer drain. A little truck picked it up."

"If it was a sewer matter, I might be able to help you. Public inquiry into sewer matters is permitted. For nonsewer matters, public inquiry is *not* permitted."

"It's not a sewer matter."

"That is a pity."

"Where does nonsewer trash go?"

"I don't know."

"Are you saying you don't know because you don't know, or because it's a nonsewer matter, and public inquiry is not permitted?"

"Both."

At that point, Celestine jumped in. The two of them talked in French for about five minutes. I understood not one word. Finally Monsieur Lebecq opened a desk drawer and extracted several pieces of different-colored paper and handed them to me. I could tell they were forms. There were eleven of them, all in French. All different.

Celestine stood up. So I stood up. Then she started to swear. I don't know what she said, but Monsieur Lebecq turned red, then redder, then almost purple.

"Let's go," Celestine said to me. So we left.

Outside, Celestine snatched the forms from me. "Do you want to fill out all these forms, or do you want to throw them away?"

"Why would I throw them away?"

"Because you will stand a better chance of finding your suitcase if you take the forms to the nearest trash bin, climb in, and wait to see where they take you."

31

I did not climb into the trash. And we did fill out all those forms and file them. "But only because you want to," Celestine said. "Your chances of getting help because you file forms are none and none."

"You mean slim and none."

"I mean none and none."

"Why?"

"Because you are in Paris," she said. "And because you are in France."

If any French person is reading this, please do not be mad at me. I didn't say it, Celestine did. And she is, after all, a French person.

Celestine made some more phone calls. But very quickly, we ran out of ideas about how to find the suitcase. It was just gone.

I did not care about the actual suitcase. Or about the lovely D&G outfit and Stephane Kélian shoes that Celestine had given me. Okay I cared about them just a little bit. But really, I only cared—I mean *cared*—about Grandma's dress.

It was so many things to me. It was my inheritance from Grandma. It was my inspiration. It was the thing that made people think I was special, the thing that got me out of Kirland. It was the source of my power, to the extent that, for about ten minutes, I had any power. And now it was gone. I felt lost.

Being with Celestine helped, of course. And, oddly enough, so did my new job. New jobs are scary things. When I started at Independence Savings, even though I had been there probably thousands of times in my life, and even though Uncle John was my uncle as opposed to just my boss, it was scary. So starting a new job in a foreign country surrounded by people speaking several languages I don't understand should have been even scarier. Only it wasn't.

The first day, things were a little awkward, because nobody at Armani Collezioni knew quite how to treat me. Except for Celestine, they weren't exactly thrilled I was there. After all, the sales staff was complete before they were told to hire me. On the other hand, nobody got fired on my account. And given how I got my job, even if they didn't like it, they didn't say so. I guess they were afraid word might get back to Mister Armani.

By the second day, though, everybody figured out that I was actually good for business. We developed a tag-team system. In case you don't know, that is a wrestling term. Except for Celestine, nobody at Armani Collezioni had ever heard of tag team.

Not that Celestine or I ever watched professional wrestling. Of course we agree that Dwayne Johnson is awfully good-looking. But we know that just from seeing him in movies. Not from watching The Rock kick Stone Cold Steve Austin's ass.

Anyway when you're a professional tag team wrestler, you wrestle with a teammate, and the person you're wrestling against has a teammate. When you get tired, or you've already done all your big signature phony moves and it's time for somebody else to show off, you tag your teammate. Then the new person jumps into the ring and you jump out. Hopefully before somebody hits you in the back of the head with a chair.

Tag team at Armani Collezioni was a lot safer, but the basic concept was the same. Somebody would walk into the store. The sales staff would size up whether they were a real shopper, or a just-looker. If they seemed like a shopper, one of the other salesboys or -girls would offer to help them. If the shopper spoke French, I stayed out of it. If the shopper spoke English, but there was even the littlest hint that they *might* speak French, I stayed out of it. But if the shopper spoke only English, and no French whatsoever—and let me tell you, it is pretty much a cinch to spot those people, 99.9 percent of the time—then it was my turn.

"Excusez-moi," Celestine would say. Or Jacques. Or Yves. Or Madeline, or Severine, or Pauline, or Jacqueline. Then they would look toward the front of the store, toward the little room behind the checkout, which is where I would sit and wait. And they would call, "Jeanne?"

Tag.

That was me. Jeanne. Which is not pronounced *Jean,* like blue jeans. More like *zhahn.* It's the closest French name to Jane. Anyway, they'd call "Jeanne," and I'd come running. In my best French-English, I would say, "I can . . . asseest you?" I asseested a lot of English-only Americans, and not one of them ever had a clue.

I was *really* good at my new job.

That is not just me saying that. Or Celestine. All my coworkers said so. They were very impressed. They wanted to know where I worked back in the United States. Calvin Klein, maybe? They refused to believe I had an accounting job at a savings and loan in Indiana. Not that they knew what a savings and loan was, or where Indiana was, for that matter.

On the one hand, I don't know why it was such a big deal. I can think of harder jobs than showing fabulous clothes to people who have a lot of disposable income. On the other hand, not everybody can do it. For example, take shirts and ties. Almost anybody can pick a suit—but for most people, picking the right shirt for the suit, then the right tie for the suit and the shirt, might as well be brain surgery. But it was easy for me. And it's not a skill anybody else in my family had, so this wasn't something I *got* from somebody. It was just something I *had.* It was all mine.

After my second day at Armani, I decided to call home after all. I had been gone five days, and I didn't want my parents to worry.

I got the answering machine again. I left a message saying my movie job was over, and now I was selling clothes for Armani. I said the new job was great, Paris was great, Celestine was great, everything was great. I said I still didn't know when I was coming home, and asked my mom to tell Uncle John I'd be gone a little while longer. Then I hung up.

I guess I forgot to mention about losing Grandma's dress.

Next, I called Bank of America to find out what was wrong with my Visa ATM card. They passed me around for a while, but eventually I reached a man who told me my account was frozen because of suspicious charges from Paris, France.

"That's because I'm *in* Paris, France. I'm the one making the charges."

"Well, how are we supposed to know that, ma'am?"

"Because I *am,*" I said. "Don't you have security questions that prove I'm me?"

"Absolutely," he said. He asked me my birthday, the mailing address on my account, and my social security number. All of which I knew. "Name of the first street you lived on."

"Wespark," I said. Which by the way is where I have lived my whole life. And where I still live. *"W-E-S-P-A-R-K."*

There was a pause. Finally the man said, "I'm sorry, ma'am."

"What do you mean, you're sorry?"

"That's not the answer I have here." With that, he hung up.

Oh shit. He was right. Because my parents lived in another house till I was six months old. When I originally gave the bank all this security information, my mom made me change my answer to be completely accurate. What was the name of that street? I couldn't remember.

I had no money. Which meant I was stuck in Paris.

32

Being stuck in Paris didn't seem too bad, until I found out that Josh Thomas was stalking me.

"Josh Thomas is stalking me," I told Celestine when I came back to the apartment the evening of my fifth day in Paris.

"That's ridiculous."

"I saw him."

"Where?"

"At our *patisserie*."

People in Paris do not grocery shop like you and I do. In Kirland, you drive to Sterk's market every two weeks, roll a huge cart with one wobbly wheel through the aisles, and fill it until you can't see over the top. In Paris, you only buy things the day you need them. Because you have to buy everything when it is totally fresh. From the way people act in Paris, I suspect there is a law that actually requires this. Also a law that says you cannot shop for different food groups in the same store. You buy meat at a *charcuterie,* bread at a *boulangerie,* and cheese at a *fromagerie.* If you need pastry—and trust me, if you are living in Paris, you need pastry—you go to a *patisserie*. Okay, maybe bread and pastry are technically in the same food group, but they have separate stores anyway.

So everybody in Paris makes like a dozen shopping stops every day on their way home, at the shops they think are the best ones in Paris. People go far out of their way to buy the best baguette, which is that long skinny French bread. Which French people really do eat, and really do walk down the street holding under their arms. Anyway, Parisians have very strong opinions about all these little stores, and I imagine that disagreements on who makes the best baguette are probably grounds for divorce.

Celestine believes that the best desserts in Paris come from a *patisserie* that is literally one block from her apartment. So she was shocked when I told her we would have to buy our *mille feuilles* someplace else from now on. The combination of perfect pastry and perfect convenience is not something one gives up lightly. "Why should we do that?" she demanded.

"Because I saw him at our *patisserie*."

"Josh? You did not."

"I did so. I was right behind him."

"From behind, you could not see if it was him."

"He was wearing his Astros cap." I had told her all about the Astros, and promises, and lost causes.

"Well," Celestine said, "that could be a coincidence." Although she did not sound very convinced. Because let's face it, there are not a lot of Astros caps walking around Paris. "What was he doing?"

"He was buying pastry."

"What kind of pastry?"

Do not ask me why Celestine thought that was relevant. "A Paris-Brest," I said. Which is a pastry that, according to the French, is shaped like a bicycle wheel. To me it looks more like a bagel, only a bagel topped with almond slivers and sprinkled with powdered sugar, and instead of being spread with cream cheese, the inside is stuffed with yummy almond cream.

"I guess if you were close enough to see that he was buying a Paris-Brest," Celestine said, "you were close enough to know if it was really him." *Oh. That's* why it was relevant.

In fact, before I had realized it was Josh, I was practically right behind him, with just one person between us. Then I saw him. Which immediately made me feel nauseous. Which is a very unusual way for me to feel, standing in the *patisserie* that Celestine says is the best in Paris. Fortunately I was able to run out of the pastry shop before he saw me.

For the past two days, I had done an excellent job of forgetting all about Josh. Okay maybe *excellent* is a little bit of an overstatement. Pretty good. Or at least fair. Under the circumstances, I mean. But in any event, seeing him brought everything rushing back. How I was starting to feel about him. Until he betrayed me, making them throw away my things like that. Grandma's dress.

Then it occurred to me that maybe Grandma's dress was paying me back for losing it. I have already told you how powerful Grandma's dress was, and so far, that power had always worked in my favor—but maybe, like the Force in the *Star Wars* movies, Grandma's dress had a dark side. Maybe now I was cursed.

"If they are not making the film, why would he still be in Paris?" Celestine asked.

"Because he's looking for me. He's stalking me, and he's planning to wreak some awful vengeance on me for destroying his movie." Okay that sounds a little overheated, I admit. But seeing him upset me terribly.

"Let's go out," I said to Celestine.

"You're joking," she said. But I guess I didn't look like I was joking, because then she said, "You're not joking!"

You must understand: Celestine goes out pretty much all the time, to fashion parties and artsy parties and who knows what other kind of parties. Since I moved in, she had been hinting around that we should go out to take my mind off things. And every time she hinted, I said thanks, but no. I told her I didn't want to go, because wherever she was going, I was sure everybody would only speak French, and, as you know, I do not. That was part of the reason. But the main reason was that I was so scarred and traumatized by the whole Gerard-and-Nathalie-and-movie-and-Josh experience, I just did not feel like going to parties.

Even though I did not tell Celestine the real reason, I'm pretty sure she knew. Because she knows me very very well. So when I said,

"Let's go out," she was surprised. And delighted. "It will be the best thing for you," she said.

At that particular moment, I did not care whether it was the best thing for me. I was just feeling spooked by seeing Josh only a block away, and in case he had tracked me down and planned to knock on our door that evening, I did not want to be home.

It so happened Celestine was invited to an ultra exclusive private fashion show that night. Actually she was invited to three different ultra exclusive private something-or-others that night, but she thought the fashion show would be the most fun.

Of course we had to dress perfectly. Which you might think would be complicated and time-consuming given the depth and breadth of Celestine's closet and the fact that there were two of us. But Celestine and I can tell each other immediately what looks fat and what looks perfect, so we always pick outfits faster when we're together.

With my help, she chose a Balenciaga leather jacket that was mostly biker chick with just a dash of S&M, a low-cut Michael Kors tank top, and vintage jeans, which means somebody worked very hard last week to make them look old and shredded. And with her help, I chose an Andrew Marc jacket over a gauzy white Helmut Lang crisscross top and ivory silk skirt. Needless to say we both had to wear radically high heels, which is totally impractical, especially in Paris, where every other street is cobblestones. The impracticality only made doing it more fun. To be even goofier, I wore the Balenciaga stilettos and Celestine wore the Helmut Langs, even though she was wearing the Balenciaga jacket and I was wearing the Lang outfit. Okay maybe that does not sound goofy to you, but it seemed pretty crazy at the time.

Celestine made a phone call, and a car came and picked us up. It was not exactly a limo, but for Paris it was a pretty big car. "Where is this fashion show thing?" I asked.

"I have no idea. That's part of the fun."

Another part of the fun was that somebody had shoved a cold

bottle of Perrier Jouët into the netting behind the driver's seat. By the time the car stopped, we had pretty much killed the bottle, and consequently we were in a pretty good mood. Until Celestine looked out the car window.

"Uh-oh," she said.

33

I did not see anything that looked terribly *uh-oh* to me.

The driver had stopped right in the middle of the Pont Neuf. Traffic was piling up behind us. People were honking horns and yelling. But that is all run-of-the-mill in Paris.

We had stopped next to a little stone plaza. Standing in the plaza was a man wearing all black, including black sunglasses, even though the sun had already set. Like a traffic cop moving in slow motion, he made a sweeping gesture with his arm, steering us out of the car and down a steep flight of stone steps. The steps were not a lot of fun in spike heels. But they led down to a very adorable park, which juts out into the river like the prow of a ship. There are no railings between you and the river, just stone walls that angle down into the green water.

Alongside the park, several boats were docked. Most of them were for sightseeing tourists. But one boat had a private mooring with its own boarding ramp.

On the first page of this story, I called this boat a yacht. Which is somewhat, but not entirely, accurate. To explain, I must tell you what Celestine told me about the barges of the Seine.

One of the things that make the Seine so beautiful and picturesque is the boats that always line its banks. Most of them are very old, and started life as working barges. They are all pretty much the same size, which Celestine said is seventeen feet wide and 128 feet long, so they can fit through the canals that run through France.

This particular boat may have started life as a barge, but along the way it had developed pretensions toward being a yacht. The decking was gorgeous tan wood waxed to a shine, all the fixtures were polished brass and heavy dark bronze, and the handrail that led downstairs was ebony carved to look and feel like braided rope.

Celestine gave our names to a man guarding the boarding ramp. She looked a little queasy, which is not how she typically looks when going to a party.

"Are you afraid of boats?" I asked.

"Not exactly."

We crossed the ramp. On the deck, there was a woman sitting in a chair. She had black hair cut above her shoulders, and she was playing a cello. Not very well, if you ask me. But I suspect her musicianship was not the main point. Because except for the cello, she was completely naked.

"Wait a minute," Celestine said. She walked around until she was behind the woman. "I thought so." Celestine motioned for me to come see. On the woman's back, somebody had painted two mirror-image *S* shapes, so she looked like a cello, too.

"I don't understand," I said.

"She is Kiki de Montparnasse. It is a famous photograph from the 1920s. By a very great photographer named Man Ray."

"Why?" We walked away from the naked woman and climbed downstairs.

"Who knows? It is a fashion show."

The boat's interior was dimly lit, but there were little spinning spotlights mounted on the ceiling, down the length of the cabin, and they sent beams of blue and purple and pink slashing across the crowd. At one end was a curtained area, then a small stage, and between us and the stage were two galleries of chairs separated by a raised runway. Most of the chairs were filled, but two next to the runway had fuchsia pillows on them. "Those are ours," Celestine said.

On the other end of the cabin, the bar was surrounded by a

crowd of Beautiful People. The type who populate the party pictures in every glamour magazine you have ever read, who would make you feel inferior even if they weren't royalty, or heirs, or movie stars, only they are.

Celestine must have read my mind. "You are the prettiest girl here," she assured me. It wasn't true, but hearing her say so made me feel good anyway.

"Let's get something to drink," I proposed.

She took a long look toward the bar. "You go. I will hold our seats."

I thought those fuchsia pillows were doing fine holding our seats without help. And I had a flash of panic at the thought of ordering drinks in a language I do not speak. But something about Celestine's expression made me just say "Sure."

The bartenders were two women. The first was very large, with short gray hair clipped close to her head, and she wore a formless dress that fit her like a burlap sack. The second woman was small and dressed all in black, jacket and trousers.

"Two martinis?" I asked the big woman.

"Gertrude," she said.

"Gertrude?"

"Stein."

Gertrude Stein—I remembered from Josh's screenplay. Just what I needed, a reminder of Josh. I looked at the little woman in black. "So you must be Alice Toklas."

"Don't talk to her," Gertrude snapped, handing me two drinks. She gave me such a scary look I scurried straight back to the seats. Even though the drinks were plainly not martinis. At least they were big. There was plenty of alcohol in them. And they were free.

As you have probably guessed, Celestine does not travel with a cash-bar crowd.

When I got to our seats, Celestine was not there. I spotted her a few feet away, talking with someone who looked like Marlene Dietrich. The person wore a black tuxedo jacket, a black top hat, black high heels, black fishnet stockings, and red lipstick, and had blond hair styled just like Marlene Dietrich's. Only Marlene Dietrich was a woman. And the person talking to Celestine was not.

An electronic beat started to pulse through the boat. At the same moment, through the soles of my feet and the seat of my skirt, I felt the engine rev to life, and we began to move. Celestine finished her conversation and sat down next to me. "Who was that?" I asked.

"Cherie Mouffetard. This show is her new collection. Cherie thought having her show on a boat would be very radical. Only Karl Lagerfeld did it two months ago. She was extremely annoyed, because the boat was already paid for. So she added the theme: famous women in Paris in the 1920s."

That explained Kiki de Montparnasse. And Gertrude, and Alice. Even Marlene. But it did not explain everything. "Cherie . . . looks like a man," I said.

"She is." Celestine's lips kept moving, but I couldn't hear her anymore because the music kicked in, loud. It was a mix of techno and house and Cole Porter. It is a good thing Cole Porter is dead, because if he was alive, what they did to his music that night surely would have killed him.

By the way, Cole Porter came from Indiana. I find the fact that somebody so witty and urbane came from Indiana to be quite inexplicable. Then again, my own presence in Paris—at Cherie Mouffetard's private exclusive fashion show, no less—was pretty inexplicable too. So maybe there is hope for all of us.

The curtained entrance of the little tent behind the stage parted, and the models started to strut down the catwalk. Actually, *strut* is the wrong word for the models who came out first. The men came out first, and they did not strut.

Shawn led the pack. Then Nick, Benn, Stavros, and Christian: Celestine told me their names. They all sulked and glowered and sneered their way down the runway. Their expressions were completely at odds with their classic white tie and tails. I hoped Cherie was not claiming credit for designing those, because the clothes were oh so Fred Astaire, even if the men and boys wearing them were oh so Eminem.

Watching them, I had the strangest thought: They reminded me of Josh. Which was the last thing I wanted, given that I had gone out that night specifically to avoid him.

What was so strange, though, was that not one of them actually resembled Josh. They were all tall, at least six feet, and Josh is not. They were all blond-haired and blue-eyed, which Josh is not. They all had cheekbones so sharp that you would cut yourself giving them the old French kiss-kiss, and Josh does not. So why every single one of them reminded me of Josh, I really cannot explain. But they did. It made me more than a little uncomfortable.

Fortunately, then the women came out. Daria was there, and Eva, and Gisele, and several other women whose faces I knew, and you would too, even if I didn't know their names and you wouldn't either. They were wearing the Collection.

As soon as I saw the Collection, I gulped my entire drink. Here is what I saw: Bias-cut bodices. Necklines scooping low in front and even lower in back. Gypsy girdle sashes. Hemlines cut high in front and lower in back. Instead of silks, the fabrics were twenty-first-century microfibers. Iridescent glass beads were replaced by holographic synthetics. And instead of being knee-length in front and midcalf in back, the hemlines were higher. Much higher. Still, the whole collection screamed *Deco Deco Deco*—and late 1920s Deco at that.

The dresses were beautiful. But I hated them. *Hated* them. Every time a pencil-thin mannequin came strutting down the runway—and *mannequin* is actually the French word for model, and yes, they strutted—all I could see was my Grandma's dress.

So there I was, on a gorgeous boat you could almost fairly call a yacht, sailing on the Seine in Paris, getting an ultra exclusive first look at the most gorgeous clothing you've ever seen being modeled by the most gorgeous human beings you've ever seen, surrounded by enough Euro-glam to fill a double issue of *Vanity Fair.* Not to mention Kiki, Gertrude, Alice, and Marlene. And I was totally, hopelessly miserable. All I could think about were the last two things in the world I wanted to think about: Grandma's dress. And Josh.

The Collection went on forever, with models who weren't Josh torturing me, dresses that weren't Grandma's torturing me, and the blaring sound system torturing poor Cole Porter. Not to mention so many photographers popping their flashes that I thought my head would explode.

At least if my head exploded, I would stop thinking about Grandma's dress and Josh.

34

My head did not explode.

Finally the fashion show ended. Celestine stood up and looked around. She had stayed calm throughout the runway parade. Now, though, a strange expression took possession of her face. I recognized the expression immediately.

When I was little, my parents bought me a tactile-defensive guinea pig. That means it did not like to be touched. Which is not a good thing if you are a guinea pig. When you reached into its cage, it shrank away and got this desperate look on its little guinea pig face. That was how Celestine looked. "Now you must help me," she said.

"Okay." I would do anything for Celestine, and she knows it.

"My boyfriend is here."

Ah.

You should understand that, by certain standards, Celestine does not have a boyfriend. And, by certain other standards, she has several. None of this makes me think the slightest bit less of her as either a friend or a human being. But these varying standards do make for some interesting times. Like this party, for example.

"Shawn," Celestine said. "He was the first model."

"Okay."

"And Benn. He was the third model."

"Okay."

"And Omar."

"Which model was he?"

She scowled. "Omar is not a model. He is a photographer."

"Okay."

"I did not know the fashion show was on a boat."

"I see," I said. Because I did see. The whole boat was only seventeen feet wide by 128 feet long. Inside was even smaller—maybe twelve feet wide by a hundred feet long. Twelve hundred square feet. Divided by three boyfriends equals four hundred square feet per boyfriend. Which is not a lot of space, if your goal in life is to keep each boyfriend from knowing that the other two exist.

For a while, things went surprisingly well, aided by the darkness and the crowd. In turn, Celestine found, hugged, and kiss-kissed—but didn't *kiss,* if you know what I mean—Shawn, Benn, and Omar, introduced each of them to me, then moved through the crowd without each boyfriend thinking he was being dumped, or avoided, or shuffled like the tunes on an iPod.

The trouble started when Stavros and Christian cornered Celestine. They didn't mean to corner her. They just both decided to ask her out at the very same time. Which was a little awkward, but not terribly, because fortunately neither of them had ever actually dated Celestine. Yet.

But while Stavros and Christian were haggling about who asked first, I spotted Shawn. He was at the front of the boat, which I guess is fore. Then I spotted Omar at the rear of the boat, which is aft. They were both heading toward Celestine, who was in the middle, which presumably is amidships. I didn't see Benn, but life being what it is, I had no doubt whatsoever that he would arrive at exactly the same time as the other two.

I squeezed between Stavros and Christian. And, I am not kidding, I whispered in Celestine's ear, "Abandon ship."

I grabbed her hand and pulled. Moving was not easy. We were fighting the crowd, the swaying boat, the high heels, and the effects of a considerable amount of alcohol. But we were both highly motivated. So in seconds we were up on deck.

Unfortunately, we were still in the middle of the Seine. And you cannot just step off a moving boat in the middle of a river. "I am so dead," Celestine lamented.

Omar poked his head out of the hatch. He hadn't spotted Celestine yet, but the deck wasn't crowded, so I had to agree with Celestine: She was so dead.

Then we sailed past a big green buoy. I do not know a lot about boats or rivers. But my general sense is that buoys exist to tell people in boats that something is coming which they need to steer around. Sure enough, just ahead and to our left was the little park we departed from. I thought the boat was docking, and we could escape—only then I realized we were on the wrong side of the park. We were not stopping, just sailing by. Close by. Close enough to see the glowing tips of the cigarettes in the mouths of the couples who sat at the edge of the park and dangled their feet down the steep stone walls.

I pushed a woman wearing a jeweled Egyptian bra and skirt and headdress out of my way.

"Colette as Cleopatra," Celestine said to me.

"We're jumping," I said to Celestine.

"What??"

Left to her own devices, Celestine would have done no such thing. But I did not leave it up to her. When we were as close as we were going to get, I jumped.

I reached my left hand toward the top of the stone wall that sloped from the park down into the river. I would have reached with both hands, only my right hand was holding on to Celestine. So like it or not, when I jumped, she jumped.

Fortunately, my left hand caught the edge of the walkway.

Unfortunately, when Celestine landed on top of me, I lost my grip.

Fortunately, Celestine managed to clamber up over me and grab onto the walkway.

Unfortunately, I discovered that Helmut Lang stilettos are

extremely pointy, at least when somebody wearing them is clambering over your head.

Fortunately, I nonetheless managed to grab hold of Celestine's Helmut Langs, which, also fortunately, stayed on her feet.

Unfortunately, my bottom half, including my Balenciaga heels and that lovely Lang silk skirt, got quite a soaking in the Seine. Which is not the very cleanest waterway in the world.

Finally, and most fortunately of all, Celestine, together with several considerably inebriated denizens of the little park, pulled me up out of the river and to safety.

"You are a crazy person," Celestine observed when we had finally stopped laughing.

"I think so."

"You are the only person in the world who would do such a thing for me."

"I hope so."

Later, in the taxi we finally convinced to take us home, notwithstanding my soaking-wet bottom half, she told me, "You are the best friend I ever had." And I knew she meant it.

"You too." And I meant it, too.

"I would do the same thing for you," she said. "You know that, don't you?"

The thought of Celestine sloshing around the Seine in her Balenciaga and Kors and vintage and Langs made me giggle. "You don't have to do that."

"Oh, good."

"But there is something you can do for me."

"What?"

"If you see Josh Thomas in our neighborhood, kill him for me."

To which Celestine said, "I will."

She said it so solemnly, I worried that maybe she would. I suspect the French authorities are fairly understanding when it comes to crimes of the heart, but I'm not sure killing the man who kissed your best friend and then threw away her Grandma's dress falls in that category. So I said, "Well, maybe don't actually kill him. But slap him."

She smiled at that. "I will."

I smiled too. Because I knew she would.

35

Then again, maybe slapping Josh was not the very best idea. He was possibly the only person in Paris who might know where Grandma's dress was. I decided that if I saw him again, even if he was stalking me, I would be brave and demand that he tell me how to find it.

Only I never saw Josh in our neighborhood again, and neither did Celestine.

To try to take my mind off the dress, I focused as much attention as I could on my fabulous job. Which, it turned out, was remarkably educational. In only my first four days at Armani Collezioni, I learned quite a lot. For example:

1. The more a man thinks that buying a woman a dress will impress her enough that she will take that dress *off,* the more he will spend on the dress.
2. You would not believe how many people go shopping for expensive clothes without wearing any underwear. Okay maybe you would believe it. But I couldn't.
3. Despite rumors to the contrary, European women shave under their arms like everybody else.

I loved my new job. I loved being good at it. Even though I was still in mourning over Grandma's dress, I was having fun. I couldn't help it.

Until late on my fourth day at Armani, when this American

man came in, followed by his American girlfriend. Maybe it had nothing to do with his being American. Maybe if I spoke French and was helping French customers, the same thing would have happened. But I doubt it.

The man was not what you'd call a fashion type by a long shot. He was wearing tan Dockers and an ivory cotton crewneck sweater. Maybe J. Crew. And loafers.

Then his girlfriend teetered in. She must've been walking twenty or thirty feet behind him. Which was completely understandable, considering the pair of Fuck Me boots she was wearing.

I hope I am not shocking anyone. But if you do not know this about women's shoes, you have led a very sheltered life, and it is about time you learn. There is a whole species of women's shoes called Fuck Me shoes. They all have two things in common: First, they all have very high heels. Second, they all send a certain very clear message.

Not all high-heeled shoes are Fuck Me shoes, but all Fuck Me shoes have high heels. There are no such things as Fuck Me flats.

Incidentally, I should make this clear: As I mentioned, Celestine and I both wore extreme high heels to that very exclusive fashion show. Balenciagas and Helmut Langs. The heels on those shoes were radically high and dangerously sharp. They made our legs look . . . well, it would be immodest for me to say, but suffice it to say there is a reason women wear such painful shoes, and in our case it was an awfully good reason. But they most certainly were not Fuck Me shoes.

Fuck Me shoes come in many different breeds. One of the rarest breeds is Fuck Me boots. Most boots don't have high heels. Most high-heeled boots don't send that certain message. But every so often a pair of boots just cries out for . . . well, you know.

The girlfriend's boots cried out.

I feel bad for just calling her "the girlfriend." She deserves to be called by name, but I can't do it. Because it doesn't matter that they were in the Armani Collezioni store for two hours. It doesn't matter that the man made her try on sixteen different dresses. All that time, he never once called her by name. So I can't, either.

The man's name is George.

The girlfriend's boots looked brand-new. In fact, I felt sure George bought them for her just the day before, and now he insisted she wear them.

To be fair, they were flattering. Sexy. In a Mistress Eva dominatrix tie-me-up web site kind of way.

Not that I have ever looked at any such web site.

Here's how I know the boots were the man's idea: The girlfriend told me she had been wearing them for four hours already, and it was only two in the afternoon. Now you must understand: Sometimes women will choose to wear Fuck Me shoes, without being asked. But wearing extreme heels is a very strategic exercise. You have to balance *How great will I look?* against *How long can I stand the pain?* Nobody, and I do mean nobody, would voluntarily put on these boots at ten A.M. and plan to wear them walking around Paris all day.

Because they hurt. High heels hurt, in general. And these boots hurt this woman's feet, specifically. They hurt her a lot. I was in and out of her dressing room at least sixteen times. She had to take the boots off for almost every outfit. Every time she took them off, she sat down, rubbed her feet, and said, "Ooooooohhh."

Typing "ooooooohhh" only conveys so much. I do not mean oh yeah baby that feels so good oh more yeah oh yeah ooooooohhh. No. I mean, oh God help me these boots hurt, let me get them off before they kill me . . . ooooooohhh.

Every man—especially George—should be required to put on a pair of four-inch Jimmy Choos. And then walk, say, from the Eiffel Tower to Notre Dame cathedral. Which is only about three miles. Hee hee.

There is no reason George should have put his girlfriend through bondage boot hell, because she didn't need the boots to look sexy. She was probably five-eight in bare feet, slender without being skinny. In fact, she was a thirty-six, which you will remember is the same as an American size four. Even though she was so slender, she had nice round tits, not at all saggy. They were so nice, I assumed that George had bought them for her, just like he bought those boots.

In case you are wondering, I am not telling you about her tits to be prurient. I am telling you because it is highly relevant.

The girlfriend wore her hair long and straight, the way men like. Bleached blonde, which was the only thing about her appearance I would have changed. I assumed he made her bleach it for him.

You can tell, I did not like George very much. Here is why.

His girlfriend tried on sixteen different outfits over the course of two hours, for no other reason than because he wanted her to. He did not care one whit what she liked, or didn't like. He was buying her a dress to make *him* look good.

Number six was the most flattering. It was a fitted jacket and matching short skirt in an extremely dramatic black-and-white diagonal print. Very powerful. Even though I would not have picked those boots for her to wear, or that color blonde for her hair, the combination of her hair, that outfit, her body in that outfit, and those boots . . . well, she could have walked out of the store and had her pick of the richest, handsomest, most fashionable men in Paris.

Come to think of it, maybe that was why her boyfriend did not like outfit number six.

He did not like much of anything, which pretty much made him an idiot. We are not talking about the Salvation Army thrift shop here. We are talking about Armani Collezioni. Plus, he was having her try on the top stuff. The cheapest thing she put on was 1,600 euros, and the most expensive was about 3,800. Two thousand to almost 4,800 dollars. Boyfriend George didn't like any of it. Until we got to number sixteen.

What happened next was partly my fault. But you really can't blame me. Because I had been working with these people for two whole hours. Nonstop.

At some point, a human being just has to . . . well, you know.

Pee.

So I showed the girlfriend outfit sixteen. It was a gorgeous iridescent blue silk dress, with a high neck in front and an asymmetrical cutout back, the cutout dropping diagonally from left to right, so the woman's left shoulder would be covered but her right shoulder blade would be totally bare.

Then I went to pee.

Oh, one more extremely relevant detail about the dress: The zipper was *on the side.* Not just the zipper, in fact. The label, too.

I came out of the bathroom feeling much better. Until I saw the girlfriend, walking out of the dressing room.

She had the dress on backward.

This actually happens every so often. Particularly with dresses where the zipper is on the side. Usually it does not have serious consequences. But remember how I told you about the asymmetrical cutout in the back? Because she was wearing the dress backward, that asymmetrical cutout was *in the front.* Which meant that the woman's left tit was where her right shoulder blade should have been in the dress.

Which left this perfect, round, not-at-all-saggy tit just hanging out there in all its glory, for the world to see.

I changed my opinion. The girlfriend's tits were real. At least she didn't do that for him.

She was not entirely comfortable with her tit hanging out. I mean how would you feel? She kept tugging at the dress, trying to hike it up to cover herself. But the dress wouldn't cooperate. It wasn't cut that way. For which you can't blame the dress. When the girlfriend looked around for help, I broke into a run. I reached her and started to say, "Eet eez—"

Only George cut me off. "Perfect."

"But," she said, "I'm all—"

"Perfect."

"You do not understand," I said. "Zee dress eez—"

"Perfect," he repeated, making it perfectly clear he did not want my opinion.

He was already lecturing her about how the Riviera and Cannes—he pronounced it *cans*—are filled with topless Frenchwomen who don't think twice about modesty, so for once she should stop being small-minded.

He had made up his mind: This was the dress he was going to buy. The dress he expected her to wear that way. Asshole.

Even if George wouldn't let me tell him the dress was backward, I could still tell the girlfriend. I hurried her off the sales floor and back to the dressing room, so she would not have to spend one more second exposed.

When I got back there, I was trying to figure out how to tell her. Remember, I was still playing French salesgirl. If I was going to break the bad news that she had just been flashing her tit at the whole store for absolutely no reason, I didn't want to choose that moment to come out of the closet, as it were, about not actually being French.

I was going to say "Eet eez wrong." Only I was pretty sure that wasn't specific enough. So then I thought about "Eet eez backward." But *backward* seemed like a very English word, and I didn't know if a French person speaking English, which was what I was supposed to be, would say that. I was trying out "Zees eez zee front" in my head, when she said:

"He is just the best."

"Excuse me?" I know, I should have said *"Excusez-moi?,"* but she didn't notice. Unfortunately, she kept going.

"George. Isn't he just the best? He is just the *best,*" she said. She unzipped the dress and stepped out of it. Now she was standing there almost naked, with *both* of her tits just staring at me—hi, how are you—and wearing nothing but a G-string that would make a stripper blush.

And those tie-me-up, tie-me-down boots.

I was embarrassed. She sure wasn't, though. She just kept talking the way you would chat with people in a crowded elevator. "He buys me these amazing things," she said. She smiled. "He bought me these boots, you know." Like those boots were the one thing in the world that every girl wished for. Then she sighed. *Sighed.* "He is the best," she said.

Let me be clear: There is absolutely, positively no excuse for the way George treated that woman. None. Period.

But in my personal opinion, there is also no excuse for her loving him for treating her that way. I had helped her try on sixteen different outfits, but suddenly I could not even stand being in the dressing room with her. I left, and never told her about the dress.

I asked Madeline to help good old George pay, because I knew I might say something that could get me fired. So I let him pay, and let them leave. I was so disgusted with the whole episode, I could only think of one positive result of the encounter.

I would never see either of them again.

36

Now kindly tell me this.

How was I supposed to know that stupid obnoxious George worked for the State Department?

Of the United States.

Or that the fancy party he bought his girlfriend that backward dress for was a formal dinner with the President of France?

Simply put, there was absolutely no way I could have known.

First, stupid George never said so. Second, stupid George's girlfriend never said so. Third, nothing about stupid George's Dockers looked like State Department issue. Fourth, what on earth was somebody on a government salary doing buying his girlfriend a 3,800-euro Armani dress—which, with the crappy exchange rate, equals almost 4,800 American dollars? Or those Fuck Me boots, for that matter. I mean, is that what we are paying our tax dollars for? I think not. I think somebody at the old IRS ought to be taking a very close look at stupid George's Form 1040. And finally, a very big fifth, what kind of bonehead representative of our very own United States government thinks it's socially proper, much less a good idea, to take his extremely attractive doormat of a girlfriend to a formal state dinner with her left tit hanging out of her dress? Would you have known? I rest my case.

I should also mention that, according to French news reports which Celestine told me about later, President Chirac was actually very happy with stupid George's girlfriend's dress. Which, if you consider the abysmal state of relations between the United States and France these days, was something of a diplomatic coup, which should count in my favor.

But not according to George. The asshole.

By now you have probably figured out that I did in fact see control freak George and his pushover girlfriend again. In fact, they came in the very next morning, after the state dinner.

George was mad. Actually, he was way beyond mad. Crazed. Insane. Ranting and spitting and flailing his arms. I will not lower myself to his level and tell you the things he said about me. People should not talk like that, and do not deserve to have such vile insults preserved in print if they do.

At one point I thought I was going to hit him. I didn't, though. I was sure Mister Giorgio Armani would not approve. So I just stood there while jerkoff George sputtered all over me.

The entire time, his girlfriend never said a word. Not one word.

In the thick of George's tirade, I glanced over at her and actually caught her eye. We looked at each other for a good ten seconds—long enough for me to be sure she knew the whole mess was George's fault. He had insisted she buy that dress. He had made her humiliate herself. Now he just needed to shift the blame to somebody else.

When she couldn't look me in the eye anymore, she stared at the floor instead.

Even though I hadn't done a thing, I felt mortified. It wasn't enough that George had made a fool of his girlfriend in public; now he had to humiliate me, too. In front of all my coworkers. In front of my best friend. In front of all the customers in the store. Including a very tall, good-looking man who was browsing through the ties.

Well excuse me for noticing him from the depths of my despair, but he was *extremely* good-looking.

Then I forgot about him. Because I heard George saying that if I wasn't fired, he was going to get the store closed down. I doubt he would have tried that. And if he had tried, I doubt he could have done it, State Department or no. But it was perfectly clear that he would keep on making a huge stink until he got his way. Huge stinks are bad for business. So they fired me.

Just like that. On the spot. Old George wasn't satisfied until the rest of the sales staff literally marched me out the door. Every single one of them. Including Celestine. For a minute, I was afraid *she* was going to hit George. There was no reason for both of us to get fired, so I caught her eye and shook my head no.

Ten seconds later, I was standing on the sidewalk on Avenue George V. Unemployed. Stunned. I felt like I had run full speed into a wall. The curse of Grandma's dress had struck again. I was so distracted, I didn't even hear it when a man's voice behind me asked, "What just happened?" I just kept staring at the store.

Then all of a sudden I couldn't see the store anymore. Because a man had stepped in front of me. A very tall man. A very good-looking very tall man. I was stunned, but I wasn't blind. He was the man I had seen in the store, buying a tie while George spewed invective.

"I'm sorry," he said, with a distinctly American accent. He was at least six-foot-four, and he had to bend down a little to talk to me. He had curly black hair and dark brown eyes, and he spoke softly, like he wanted to be sure his words didn't hurt me the way George's had. It was awfully considerate of him. "I saw you in the store."

"I know. You were buying a tie." In fact, he was holding the small package.

He looked down at it, and I swear, he got this guilty expression on his face.

"No I wasn't." He quickly put his hands—and the package—behind his back. Which I thought was odd. Although frankly I had more important things on my mind—like for example, that I had just gotten fired. For the second time in five days.

"I only came in near the end," he said. "What happened?"

To the very best of my recollection, here is exactly how I answered him.

"This stupid American man bought a very expensive dress for his girlfriend. I tried to tell him he was making a terrible mistake. But he didn't want to listen. So he paid a small fortune, she wore it, and they both got totally humiliated in front of Jacques Chirac. He needed to blame somebody else, so I got fired."

"You're kidding," said the good-looking tall man. He wasn't just good-looking: He was also pretty young. Maybe twenty-nine. Maybe thirty.

"I would not kid about something like that." I looked back at the store. "Fashion morons," I muttered, thinking about George and, I'm sorry to say, his doormat girlfriend.

"What did you say?"

"I said, fashion morons. Who would believe you'd find them at Armani?"

He glanced at the storefront. Then he turned back to me. "Fashion morons?" he asked, and I nodded, yes. "At Giorgio Armani?"

"Armani Collezioni, actually." I may have just gotten fired, but if there is one thing my Uncle John has taught me, it is to be precise about your work.

"Stick with Giorgio Armani," he advised. "We don't want to confuse people."

Huh? The only person he was confusing was me. Which he then continued to do. He pulled a little pad and a pen out of his pocket. He furiously scribbled something on the pad. When he was finished scribbling, he looked at the store, looked at me, and said, "This is great!"

"I don't see how this is so great."

"But it is. Don't you see? You're *perfect.*"

"Well, thank you," I said. I still didn't know what he was talking about. But never turn down a compliment. Especially not one from such a nice-looking man.

"You told that American he was making a mistake buying that dress."

"I *tried* to tell him, but he wouldn't listen."

"And he was sorry later."

"Of course. They made a ridiculous mistake."

"This is too good to be true." He beamed.

"What are you talking about?" I can only take being confused for just so long.

"You don't know." At first he sounded puzzled. Then he shook himself, like a big dog shaking off water. "Of course you don't. Sorry. Silly me." He was charming and good-looking and a little goofy at the same time. He reminded me of a Labrador. Incidentally, I like dogs. Particularly Labradors. "I'm Reed," he said. "Reed James. I'm a TV producer."

Without even thinking, I said, "You're kidding." I guess maybe I had kind of a suspicious look on my face. It had nothing to do with Reed. Just a few days before, I had been thoroughly abused by those awful Movie People. And the movies and TV are pretty much the same thing, right? So my first impulse was to assume the worst about Reed.

He misunderstood why I looked suspicious. "No, really," he said. "I know that sounds like a pickup line. But I really am. I'm a television news producer."

"News?" That didn't sound much like the movies at all. I thought maybe I should give the television news producer a chance. So I smiled at him.

"Fox News," he announced proudly.

At the time, I did not know a great deal about Fox News. I don't watch a lot of news, but I did have some slight idea what Fox News was about. For example, I knew that it was quite popular in Kirland, because people talked about such things. When you saw them in the market, or at a funeral, or at lunch in the Panel Room after church on Sunday. In fact, I specifically remembered something old Annie Dobash said. Annie is the oldest living person in Kirland, Indiana. She is only going to appear in the story just this once, because she is really not relevant. Except for the fact that

I remember her saying she watches Fox News, and she loves seeing Bill O'Reilly give those Hollywood fancy boys hell.

I continued smiling at Reed. "Really," I said, sounding very interested. "Fox News?" The fact is, I was at least a little interested. Plus, it's God's honest truth that men like it when you sound interested in what they do. And Reed was quite adorable.

Reed smiled down at me. "So you know Fox News?"

"Who doesn't?"

"And you still want to talk to me?"

I laughed. Charmingly, I hope.

By the way, Reed had very long eyelashes.

"All I know," I said, "is that I love seeing Bill O'Reilly give those Hollywood fancy boys hell."

37

"I can't believe it," said Reed.

"Believe what?"

"You don't understand," he said. "This is just too great. I mean, it's too perfect. I'm here in France *specifically* looking for a fresh new American voice. A real American in Europe who has a real American point of view."

I have a point of view. In fact I have lots of them. I figured that whatever point of view Reed was looking for in somebody, I must have one in there someplace. I said, "I have a point of view."

"So I see," he said. "Plus you're a girl." When an attractive, age-appropriate man is talking to me, I ordinarily insist on being called a woman. Nowadays you really cannot let men diminish you by calling you a girl. At least, as a general rule you cannot. But Reed was being so enthusiastic about me that I didn't want to interrupt him. "We have a little trouble with the female eighteen-to-thirty-five demographic," he explained. "So your being a girl is a huge plus. And you're a really cute girl." *Oooh. He thinks I'm really cute.* "Which is obviously even better. I mean, with radio, who cares what Rush Limbaugh looks like? But we're on TV." He crossed his fingers, as if hoping his next question would have a particular answer. "Where are you from?"

"Indiana."

"Yes!" He began jumping up and down. Then he stopped, bent toward me, and crossed his fingers again. "Big city or small town?"

"*Very* small town."

"Yes!" He got so excited, I swear I thought he was going to hurt himself. He was literally dancing in the street. He wasn't a wonderful dancer, but hey, nobody's perfect.

Then he stopped and looked at me again. Finally he asked, "You aren't a lesbian, are you?"

Let me just say, if he was asking me that question because it had something to do with Fox News and fresh new American voices, it would be bad. Maybe even against the law. But if he was asking me because he was trying to figure out . . . oh, for instance, whether to ask me to dinner, then I thought it was a perfectly fair question.

"No."

"Yes!" He took a step back, held his hands out at arm's length, made a frame with his thumbs and forefingers, and looked at me through the frame, the way people do in the movies. Incidentally, I could not help noticing that he had very large hands. Instinctively I looked down at his shoes. He had big feet too. And you know what they say.

"Do you know who I am?" he asked.

I wondered if he had caught me looking at his feet. I think I blushed. "Reed James," I said. I wasn't sure if this was a test, but at least I could show him that I was paying attention. I don't care how traumatic a situation you find yourself in: When a man that handsome introduces himself, you make good and sure you remember his name.

"That's right. But I'm also your knight in shining armor."

"You are?"

"I am." Then he got a worried look on his face. "Although knights in shining armor are pretty much a European thing, now that I think about it." He seemed to be talking more to himself than to me. "Maybe I'm the cavalry coming over the hill. Or the Marines. More American." Then he remembered I was there. "You pick," he said to me. "Would you rather I was a knight, the cavalry, or the Marines?"

Out of the three, personally I would have to go with the knight.

Fairy-tale stuff, you know. And I am sorry, but girls love princess stories. At least I do. For example, since Grandma died, I had invented a thousand stories about how she got her dress, and in every one Grandma was the princess.

On the other hand, it was clear Reed wanted me to go for the cavalry or the Marines. I compromised. "You can be all of them."

"Excellent. Perfect. I am your knight in shining armor. And the cavalry coming over the hill to save you. And the United States Marines. All rolled into one."

"Okay," I said.

I realize that was a pretty noncommittal response. But to tell you the truth, I was still confused. As I have said, he was very good-looking. He was being very nice to me. He thought I was cute. He was happy I wasn't a lesbian. He had some vague ideas about me being a fresh new American voice with a point of view. And he wanted to be some kind of action-figure hero for me. All fine and good. Only I had not the slightest idea what he was talking about.

I guess my confusion showed on my face. Because he explained. "I'm sorry," he said. "You don't understand." He paused—quite dramatically, I might add—until finally he said,

"I am going to make you a star."

38

Let me go on record: I have heard a lot of lines from guys. But this was the first time any man ever said he was going to make me a star.

My very first thought was of that scene in the movie *Fame*. Where the creepy greasy photographer convinces the girl to go to his studio and he takes nasty pictures of her. Well she certainly should have known better. Because he looked like a creepy greasy photographer. Whereas Reed looked like somebody who maybe actually could make you a star. So Reed ended up doing quite well in comparison.

He did even better when he pulled out a business card and handed it to me. In the corner it said FOX NEWS, in shiny raised lettering. In the middle it said REED JAMES, PRODUCER. I guess anybody could go to Kinko's and print up something like that, but it looked real to me.

"What kind of a star are you going to make me?"

"An all-American star. A Fox News star." When he said it, his eyes sparkled. Which was a pretty good trick for somebody with such dark eyes.

"Could you be just a little more specific?" I asked.

"Absolutely," he said. "I can be a lot more specific." He smiled a big smile. "And we can talk about it over dinner."

I thought that was awfully presumptuous of him. In fact he sounded like a crass frat boy, only older. That kind of approach has never worked with me, so my first impulse was to say no.

Then it struck me: Even though I had just met Reed James, I knew quite a lot about him.

Reed was very tall. Whereas Josh Thomas was not.

Reed was dark-haired and dark-eyed and dark-complexioned. Whereas Josh was not.

Reed was presumptuous and forward, having asked me out within about three minutes of meeting me. Whereas Josh was not. He had not asked me out at all, I asked him.

Reed worked for Fox News. And although I never asked Josh his TV news preferences, or his politics for that matter, I was willing to bet he was not a Fox News type of guy.

Reed saw himself as a knight, the cavalry, and the Marines. Whereas I simply could not picture Josh in any context involving armor or weaponry.

Reed said he was going to make me a star. Whereas Josh had never made any such offer.

Reed was blunt, loud, exuberant, and so far seemed pretty uncomplicated. Whereas Josh was subtle, quiet, and thoughtful, with those complicated eyes and probably a complicated soul, too. And he had kissed me so perfectly, in fact had strung together all those perfect moments like a strand of pearls, only then he ruined it all, ripped the pearls right off my neck, all those perfect moments dropping to the floor and scattering and vanishing in a single instant, when he told them to take away my things, and Grandma's dress was lost forever.

I looked up at Reed and realized: he was the un-Josh. "Dinner would be great," I told him.

"Cool," he said. "Excellent." He clapped his hands. "Nine o'clock." He checked his watch. "I'm late for an appointment, but I'll meet you there." He whipped out a fancy cell phone, tapped on the keys, and finally said "Perfect." He jotted down an address and gave it to me, then flipped the phone closed. Then he hailed a cab for me, opened the door, and handed me in. He even kissed my hand—just lightly brushed the back of my hand with his lips. The little hairs on my neck tingled. It was a good tingle. To top it off, he insisted on giving me cab fare home. Whereas Josh Thomas had stuck me with that huge bill at the Bar Hemingway, walked out on me, and left me to wander the streets of Paris all alone in the middle of the night.

"See you tonight," I said to Reed.

As the cab started to pull away, I heard him say, "This is *great.*"

For the first half of the taxi ride back to Celestine's apartment, all I could think about was how Reed's lips felt on my hand. It made me tingle all over again. I reminded myself that Josh had never kissed my hand like that. Although he had licked the tiramisu off my fingers. But I was not thinking about Josh. I wasn't. I wouldn't. I was thinking about Reed.

For the second half of the ride home, I couldn't help but think about what Reed said. It nagged at me. Remember, I had just been fired. Again. And this total stranger thought it was *great.* Something was very odd.

On the other hand, he was not Josh.

Plus Reed was really quite appealing. In an in-your-face sort of way. Also very good-looking, as I have said. And, apparently, he really was a TV news producer who was offering . . . well, I didn't know exactly what. But something. Something involving stardom, I might add.

I have never thought much about stardom. Sure, I watch *Entertainment Tonight* and read *In Style,* but I've never thought much about stardom *for me.* I did not grow up planning to be a star. On the contrary: Except for the couple or three times somebody has remarked that I bear the slightest resemblance to Scarlett Johansson, I can honestly say that I never even remotely considered myself star material.

But Reed was so enthusiastic about me. And he was a professional. So I admit, I found it sort of interesting that he thought he could make me a star. Okay extremely interesting. On balance, I was inclined to give him the benefit of the doubt. Besides, he would explain over dinner what he thought was so great about me. If I didn't like the sound of it, that would be that.

In the meantime, though, I had to get ready. And it takes me a while to prepare for a date.

I don't know exactly how long I spent. I showered. Twice. I worked on my hair for maybe an hour. And a half. I picked an outfit. Eleven different times. Until finally I settled on one: Calvin Klein. Remember, Reed worked for Fox News and was looking for an American voice. So I wanted to wear something, well, American. But still nice. Calvin was one of the only American designers Celestine had in her closet. Sure, the clothes were actually made in France, but Reed wouldn't know that unless he looked at the labels. And no matter how cute he was, he was not going to have a chance to look at my labels. Not on a first date.

"For someone who just got fired, you don't look so sad," Celestine said.

"I'm compensating."

"Don't compensate too hard," she told me.

"It's only a first date."

"No Boilermakers." Okay, point well taken.

Celestine put me in a taxi and told the driver the address. "Behave," she said, and waved.

The cab pulled away. When we turned onto Rue de Rivoli, I started to get a familiar feeling. By the time we were approaching the Place de la Concorde, I was downright queasy. It seemed like the taxi was taking me back to Armani Collezioni. Which was the last place I wanted to go. By now the store was closed, but what if I ran into somebody?

The driver stayed in the right-hand lane—no Indy 500 around the traffic circle for him—and made the soft right turn onto the Champs-Elysées. Just as I actually started to believe he *was* taking me back to the scene of the train wreck, he turned down a side street and pulled up by the curb.

There, waiting for me, was Reed. He opened my door, and again paid for my cab. He looked very nice but a little conservative, fashion-wise: navy blazer, blue button-down shirt, gray slacks, all quality stuff. I was betting Polo by Ralph Lauren. Sure enough, as Reed opened the door to the restaurant, I got a glimpse of the little polo player silhouette on his shirt. I suspect Josh Thomas would not be caught dead with a polo player on his shirt. Which is awfully snobbish of him, don't you think?

The restaurant Reed took me to is called Le Man Ray. "Man Ray was a very famous photographer," Reed explained.

"I know," I said. "He took that picture of Kiki de Montparnasse as a cello."

Reed gave me a funny look, like he didn't expect me to know such things. "That's right."

"Although I don't see what the big deal is. I think he just wanted to get her naked."

Reed shook his head. "First Giorgio Armani, now Man Ray," he said. "You don't care whose sacred cow you gore, do you?"

I didn't exactly know what he meant, so I said, "I just say what I think."

Reed laughed. At first I thought he was laughing at me. Until he said, "You are *perfect!*" Then he hugged me. Both of which I liked quite a lot. Finally he said, "Let's eat."

Once we were seated, I looked around the room. Le Man Ray used to be a theater, which you can tell from its size and shape, the sweeping stairways, and the theater boxes along the balcony. Only I never saw a theater like it. There's an amazing stained-glass ceiling, and enormous round light fixtures that look straight out of Jules Verne. Up in the balcony is a long multicolored bar. And there are big Chinese statues all over. Even with all the different styles, it's fantastic and glamorous. That evening—and I bet every evening—it was buzzing with people in their twenties and thirties who were as fantastic and glamorous as the room.

Reed ordered us martinis—in French, no less. Then he looked at me and blinked those long eyelashes. "What's a real American girl like you doing in Paris?" he asked.

So I told him the story. Not the *whole* story, of course. The *Reader's Digest* version.

Incidentally, the *Reader's Digest* is a very popular publication in Kirland. Still. I kid you not.

Anyway I told him how Grandma left me her fabulous dress, and I wrote a paper about it. How I was drudging at Independence Savings when the phone rang and Elliot Schiffter whisked me off to Paris to find a dress. How I found the dress, only evil bitch slut Nathalie ripped it up. How Gerard Duclos attacked me, then fired me, then they threw away my luggage, including Grandma's dress. How I found a job at Armani Collezioni—although I kind of fudged that part, and left Celestine out of the story altogether. I figured if my best friend had never wanted me to know who her father was, I shouldn't go blabbing it to Fox News. I left out the parts about Josh, too.

"And you know how my Armani job worked out," I concluded.

Reed shook his head, which worried me. Only then he said, "That is fantastic. *You* are fantastic. Your *material* is fantastic."

I wasn't sure what he meant by my *material,* but when a man that handsome is telling you you are fantastic, you can't get hung up on every little word.

At that moment, a brilliant idea occurred to me: Reed was a hotshot news producer. He probably had all kinds of people at his beck and call—TV news reporter types. And remember, he had offered to be my knight in shining armor, the cavalry coming over the hill to save me, and the U.S. Marines, all rolled into one. So he was the perfect person to ask. "Will you help me find my Grandma's dress?"

"Hmmm."

"Hmmm?"

"That's going to be tough."

"I'm sure," I said. "But if anyone can do it, I'll bet Fox News can do it." I smiled as sweetly as I could. "I'll bet *you* can do it."

Okay perhaps that was just slightly manipulative of me. But I really did think that maybe Reed could do it. And I really was starting to like him quite a bit.

"Hmmm," Reed said again. He frowned. Then he smiled. "I'll do it. I'll put my best investigative team on it. If they can't find it, nobody can."

I felt a glimmer of hope. Maybe I wasn't cursed after all. Maybe Grandma's dress wasn't lost forever.

Reed slipped a hand inside his blazer. "Now . . . I have something for you." He handed me a paper folder. Even before I looked inside, I knew it was a plane ticket. To New York.

I took out the ticket. "I've never been to New York," I said. I looked at the seat number: three-B. Which is a First Class seat. Then I looked at the date of the flight. It was the day after tomorrow.

"I didn't want to waste any time," Reed said.

Buying a girl you just met a First Class plane ticket to New York before you've even had dinner with her is certainly not wasting any time.

"Don't you think you're being just a little bit forward?" I asked.

"What?" Reed started to chuckle. "Oh," he said, still chuckling.

"What's so funny?" I asked.

He made himself stop laughing. "Sorry," he said. "I'm offering you a *job* in New York. As a commentator. I want to get you on the air right away." Now he wasn't laughing at all. In fact, he was blushing. The blushing was actually kind of cute. He paused and looked down at the plane ticket in my hand. "So," he finally said, "it isn't . . . what you thought."

"It isn't?" I probably sounded disappointed. I was—at least a little. Sure, if he had bought me that ticket solely because . . . well, you know, that would've been very forward. But it also would've been quite flattering. And did I mention how good-looking he was?

"Well, I guess maybe it is, too. What you thought. A little."

Then he blushed again—a lot. Which was more like it. I wanted him to be at least somewhat interested in me. Because I was at least somewhat interested in him.

In theory, I still wanted to learn more about this whole Fox News star thing before I made up my mind. And I was in no rush to leave Celestine. But remember, I hadn't been paid for either my movie job or Armani. So a job that would actually put money in my bank account seemed like a good idea. Having somebody else pay for my flight home seemed even better. And First Class, better still. Plus Reed was assigning his best investigative team to find Grandma's dress. That made it okay for me to leave Paris, because they would undoubtedly do a better job of searching than I ever could.

I suppose I could've just said I had to go home. But we are talking about *TV.* Reed was going to make me the fresh new voice of Fox News. How could I pass that up?

"Who's in three-A?" I asked.

"I am," said Reed.

So I said, "Okay." And that was that.

Reed ordered wine and dinner, again in French. Even though I don't speak any French beyond *bonjour* and *bonsoir* and *excusez-moi,* I could tell that his accent was not good. Still, he got the order across. I had yummy wok-stirred fish with a sweet curry sauce that I think had coconut milk in it, and Reed had a delicious veal thing in an orange sauce. I know his was delicious because we shared.

I let Reed do most of the talking. First, because I was interested. Second, because he liked that I was interested. Third, because he was going to have his team search for Grandma's dress. And fourth, because he was flying me to New York for some kind of glamorous job as a fresh new American voice, whatever that meant, and I was afraid if I talked too much, he might decide my voice was old or wilted or un-American and change his mind.

I learned several things about him. He was in a fraternity at Dartmouth—yuck—but that was several years ago and I could forgive him some youthful lapses, like the fact that he played varsity lacrosse. He got a Master's in Communication at Columbia. He had been engaged but they broke up six months ago, which meant he wasn't afraid of commitment, and enough time had passed that I wouldn't be a rebound. All in all, I thought everything was going very well.

Until Reed started looking over his shoulder. At first I barely noticed it, but then he picked up speed, until he was doing it like twice a minute.

In my experience, when you're on a date and the man keeps looking over his shoulder, either he's watching for somebody, like an almost-but-not-quite ex-girlfriend, or else he sees a girl he thinks is prettier than you, and he'd rather get whiplash watching her than at least pretend to pay attention to you. "Are you looking for somebody?" I finally asked.

"What?" He turned back to face me.

"You keep turning around. Who are you looking for?"

"Oh." He blushed again. "This is kind of embarrassing," he said. I took that as a bad sign. Then he didn't say anything. So I waited.

My patience won out over his embarrassment. "I'm looking for"—and he lowered his voice—*"Johnny Depp."*

39

"Johnny Depp?"

Reed actually giggled. Which on a big tall shouldery guy like him seemed, I don't know, kind of . . . girlie. "He owns this place, you know. So I thought maybe we would see him."

Since then I have learned a few things. For example, Johnny Depp doesn't exactly *own* Le Man Ray. He is one of the investors. Along with John Malkovich and Sean Penn. Expecting to go to this restaurant and see Johnny Depp is like it's 1996, and I'm going to Planet Hollywood because I want to see Bruce Willis. I actually did that. Just like I'm sure a lot of people did that. Once. Then they found out, just like I found out, that Bruce Willis doesn't actually eat at Planet Hollywood all the time. Or, like, ever. But Reed actually believed he was going to see Johnny Depp.

Even though I did not know an enormous amount about Fox News at the time, I knew enough to understand that Johnny Depp is not exactly a Fox News kind of guy. I said, "It's kind of funny. You. Fox News. And Johnny Depp."

"I know," Reed said, and he blushed again. Still, it didn't stop him from looking over his shoulder and around the room. When he turned back to face me, he said, "Management probably wouldn't approve. What with, well, his . . . views." He lowered his voice. "But *how cool* would it be to see Johnny Depp? Did you see *Pirates of the Caribbean*? How great was he in that?"

I had to admit he was right. Johnny Depp really was just too good in *Pirates of the Caribbean.* But I still had a hard time with Reed getting all girlie about it.

For the rest of dinner, Reed tried to keep from looking over his shoulder quite so much, with only limited success. And no, we did not see Johnny Depp.

When we left the restaurant, the night was lovely, so instead of taking a taxi, we strolled through the Tuileries gardens, the very same ones I'd walked through with Josh Thomas. Right after he kissed me so wonderfully on that bridge and I opened my eyes and saw the Eiffel Tower sparkling in the night.

At that precise moment, Reed took my hand in his. And I completely forgot about what's-his-name. As I have said, Reed has very big hands, and his just kind of swallowed mine up. I wondered what it would feel like if he held me in his arms. If he kissed me. He did not kiss me. I could tell from the way he was holding my hand that he was thinking about it. But he didn't.

"Let's go back to my hotel for a drink," he said. "It's really great. It's called the Hotel d'Aubusson. It's small. Very authentic." He lowered his voice so radically it was as if he was passing on classified information. "Very French. I read about it in"—now he was practically whispering—"the *New York Times.*" Before I could think of reasons not to, he said, "Just downstairs. There's a jazz trio that plays on weekends. And the bartender is the best." When I didn't say anything, he said, "Just for a while. Then I'll put you in a cab."

So I said, "Sure."

We kept walking. Through the courtyard of the Louvre, past the big glass pyramid. Which I guess everybody now thinks is part of some big conspiracy on account of *The Da Vinci Code,* but if you ask me, lit up at night, it looked lovely and romantic. Then we cut over and walked along the Seine. We didn't talk, only walked. It was just us and the river and the lights. In case you are wondering, it is not just good PR: Paris really is the City of Lights.

When we got to the hotel bar, the jazz trio—a piano player,

bass player, and drummer—actually were wonderful. The musicians were all men, but there was also a very fine singer, a Frenchwoman with the most beautiful café-au-lait skin who sang scatty, throaty versions of old American standards, the Gershwins and Cole Porter. She was wonderful, too.

As were the drinks brought to us by the bartender, Flavien. He was sweet and slender and perfectly dressed in a suit, shirt, and tie, and I instantly adored him. You could tell the bar was his kingdom. The jazz music was lovely, but the crowd was there for Flavien.

We sipped extraordinary champagne drinks, Rossinis, which weren't on the menu. What Rossini the composer had to do with a drink made out of champagne and pureed raspberries and some yummy kind of liqueur, I'll never know. Or care. And if you think it sounds like a girlie drink . . . well, I am a girl, but they're not girlie at all. They're perfect and sophisticated. And very easy to drink. In fact, it occurred to me, drinking Rossinis and looking at how long Reed's eyelashes were, that a girl could get used to this.

Reed and I were getting pretty cozy. He ran his fingers through my hair. Then he started to massage my neck with his fingers. His fingers were very strong, but he did not rub too hard, the way a lot of guys do. He rubbed my neck exactly the way you would want a handsome man to just before he kisses you.

That's when Reed excused himself to use the restroom.

I thought, *Okay, well, so my timing is a little off. Or Reed's timing. Anyway somebody's timing is a little off.* But I knew he would be back in a minute. And then he would kiss me.

At that moment, the trio started to play "Bewitched Bothered and Bewildered." Which in case you don't know is by Richard Rodgers and Lorenz Hart.

Let me be clear: I have perfectly normal up-to-date taste in music. I like Green Day and Black Eyed Peas and Evanescence. I listen mostly to WXRT and WZZN, except on Saturday afternoons, when my mom tunes every radio in the house to WBEZ so she will not miss a minute of that Garrison Keillor fellow, who I must admit is pretty amusing. And I only download legally. At least after they started suing people. But "Bewitched Bothered and Bewildered" is my favorite song in the whole world. Grandma used to play it over and over on her old hi-fi. It was her favorite, too, and I guess it just kind of seeped into my pores.

At some point it occurred to me that Grandma had pretty sophisticated musical taste for somebody who grew up and spent her whole life—except for her mysterious Paris escapade, anyway—in Kirland, Indiana. At first, it was hard for me to picture my Grandma young, wearing her dangerous dress, and dancing to all those fabulous old songs. But once I pictured it, it all fit. The songs she played seemed to go with the dress. Now that the dress was gone, there was no point thinking any more about the mystery. But at least I still remembered "Bewitched Bothered and Bewildered."

I was feeling all those things. About Reed. Things were happening awfully quickly—job things, and maybe other things, too. And, even though I hate to admit it, I was also feeling those things about Josh. Who, despite all my best efforts, kept popping into my head at the most inopportune moments. Which was really inconsiderate of him.

The singer's sweet, sad voice washed over me. *"I'm wild again . . . beguiled again . . ."*

At exactly that minute, a man walked up to the bar. He was wearing a Houston Astros baseball cap. My first thought, can you believe it, was *Why are Astros baseball caps suddenly sweeping Paris?* But of course they weren't. Because the man wearing the cap was Josh Thomas.

Before I could even try to hide, Josh saw me. He looked surprised.

"I couldn't sleep, wouldn't sleep, when love came and told me I shouldn't sleep. . . ."

Josh also saw that the seat next to me was empty. In two seconds it wasn't empty anymore, because he was sitting in it. "What are you doing here?" he asked. "I've been looking everywhere for you."

So I was right: He was stalking me. Maybe I should yell for

help. On the other hand, he might know where they had taken my mom's suitcase, with Grandma's dress. If Josh knew where it was, I wouldn't have to sit around and wait for reports from Reed's investigative team. That must have been why, in spite of myself, some part of me was glad to see him.

"Where is it?" I demanded.

"What?"

"I saw what you did. Just tell me, where did they take it?"

"I don't know what you're talking about."

I spotted Reed emerging from the restroom, but he hadn't seen Josh yet. "If you won't tell me where it is, then you have to leave right now."

"Are you kidding? I told you, I've been looking for you. Now that you're here, I'm not going anywhere."

How could I possibly explain to Reed what Josh was doing there? Not only was Josh not going to tell me where they took the suitcase, he was going to stick around for spite and ruin my chances of becoming a star, not to mention my chances with Reed. It was bad enough that Josh had brought down a curse on me for losing Grandma's dress, but now it seemed he was going to magically reappear at the worst possible moments, just to make personally sure that I stayed miserable forever.

"He can laugh, but I love it . . . although the laugh's on me."

I looked right into Josh's complicated, attractive eyes. I felt myself getting warm all over. I thought, *This is the first time I have hated somebody so much that looking them in the eyes makes me warm all over.*

"Is this guy bothering you?" came a deep voice from over my shoulder. Reed was back.

"Why are you still in Paris?" I asked Josh very quietly.

"I'm chasing a lost cause," he said.

Reed put his big hands on my shoulders. "Well?"

"Scram," said Josh. Which he probably should not have done, even though for just a second I thought it was very brave of him.

Then he stood up. Which he definitely should not have done. Because as I have told you, Reed is a very tall man, and Josh is not.

Reed looked down at me. "Is he?"

"Is he what?" I asked, although I felt like I was talking to myself, not to Reed.

"Bothering you," Reed said.

For a second I did not know how to answer. Then all of a sudden the only thing I could think of was Grandma's dress. I remembered how I had watched from across the street while Josh had the desk clerk at the Hotel Jacob toss my luggage into that old trash truck, and how the truck drove Grandma's dress away and into oblivion. Now my face felt so hot, I thought I would burst into flame. "Yes," I said. "He *is* bothering me."

Sometimes real life is like a movie. For example, Josh showing up at that bar at precisely the same time as Reed and me is exactly the kind of thing that would happen in a movie. Then other times, life is not like a movie at all. Because in a movie, there would have been a big brawl spilling into the street and crashing through windows, like the fight between Hugh Grant and Colin Firth in *Bridget Jones's Diary.*

But that's not what happened. Reed only hit Josh once. Boom.

Flavien helped Josh up off the floor. When Josh picked up his Astros cap, his nose bled all over it. He bled copiously on Flavien's shirt, too, but Flavien was so sweet he pretended not to notice.

Then Flavien banished Reed from the bar. And even though this bartender was a complete stranger, and even though I hated Josh, and had very good reasons for hating him, the fact that Flavien was siding with Josh made me wonder if I had done or said the right thing.

Reed wasn't the least bit apologetic. In fact, he was quite proud of himself for sticking up for my honor. What made him think my honor was at stake, I don't know. I just wanted to leave, so he got me a cab and as usual gave me cab fare. Then he leaned over, and I swear, of all times, that was when he thought he was going to kiss me. But I was much too . . . well, bothered, and bewildered, too, for that. So I just gave him a hug. Not even a real cozy one. Then I got in the cab and drove away.

We hadn't even reached the Seine, but as soon as the driver had gone a block and I was sure we were out of sight of the hotel, I told him to pull over. I gave him all the money Reed had given me. It was probably the best tip for the shortest fare that driver ever got.

I looked at my watch. It was past two in the morning. I didn't care. I walked all the way back to Celestine's apartment. Trying to figure out what it all meant.

And, for the first time since I left home, I really, truly wished I was back in Kirland.

40

I called my parents to tell them what was going on. This time they were home. Needless to say, my mom wanted to know all the details I had left out of my answering machine message.

I told them that, with Grandma's dress as my guiding light, I had instantly found the perfect dress, which, of course, the starlet of the movie adored, and now she was my second-best friend in the world, right after Celestine. My third-best friend was now Celestine's father, who it turned out was a world famous director, and who introduced me to the very crème de la crème of French haute society, like for example Johnny Depp, who I assured my mother was even more handsome in person. Not to mention thoughtful, because as soon as my movie job ended, he introduced me to his good friend Mister Giorgio Armani, who immediately hired me to work in his boutique alongside Celestine. Just as my career in high-end retail was taking off, though, I met the very dashing Reed James, TV news producer extraordinaire, who insisted on making me a star as the fresh new voice of Fox News. In fact, he was in such a hurry to get me on the air and boost Fox's ratings, he was flying me to New York—First Class, no less—the very next day.

Well, *some* of it was true.

My parents were very supportive, and agreed it was an excellent opportunity. Then again, they also sounded anxious. Cautious. Parental. "It seems awfully sudden," my dad said.

"It *is* awfully sudden," I said. "My whole life is awfully sudden these days."

"That's what I mean," he said. But if he thought it was a bad idea, he didn't say so. My dad is the least judgmental person I know. Which I really appreciate, even if I don't always tell him. Or ever tell him. Maybe he'll read this eventually. So I'm telling him now: Thank you, Dad.

Then there was an awkward pause. I knew exactly what it was about: My mom was waiting for me to ask her to call Uncle John again.

"I'll call Uncle John," I said.

"You will?" My mom was clearly surprised. Relieved, too.

"I can't ask you to do that twice."

"He won't like it."

"I know. But I'll take care of it."

After we hung up, I actually thought about maybe not calling. But I knew I couldn't do that. So I called. I told Uncle John that Fox News was giving me a job as their fresh new voice.

"You already have a job."

"I'm on vacation."

"You've been gone a week."

"It's a big opportunity."

"You have responsibilities. How do you expect to fulfill them?"

"I don't know. Maybe the Fox News job won't work out." Even though I didn't believe that. I was going to be a star. Reed said so. "If it doesn't work out, then I'll just come back."

"Maybe when you decide to come back, you won't have responsibilities here anymore." Then he hung up. Leaving me wondering, Had I just been fired?

You'd think I would know. Particularly since I had been canned twice within the last week. With so much recent experience, you'd think I'd be an expert on the subject. But both times they actually said, "You're fired." Not, "Maybe you won't have responsibilities here anymore." Who knew what that meant?

Anyway I couldn't dwell on it. I had a plane to catch.

In spite of the fact that she was really upset I was going, Celestine was an angel helping me get ready to leave. "You must come back," she kept saying.

"I will," I kept saying.

"You must promise," she said.

That made me stop and think for a minute. About promises. Here I was, packing my bag to go running off to New York with Reed James. So why was I thinking about stupid Josh Thomas and his stupid promise to himself to wear a stupid Astros cap? I guessed he would have to buy a new one now, since he had bled all over the old one.

Of course, Josh wouldn't have been bleeding if Reed hadn't hit him. Which Reed wouldn't have done if I hadn't practically told him to.

Chasing a lost cause. Just exactly what did Josh mean by that, anyway?

"Well?" Celestine asked. "Do you promise?"

"Yes," I said. "I promise." Then I added, "I'll be such a big star on Fox News, I'll be able to visit as often as I want. I'll even get them to send me to Paris on assignment." We both smiled at that. Then I did my best to concentrate on packing.

Packing made me confront the fact that Grandma's dress was really gone, and that hurt all over again. As long as I stayed in Paris, there was at least a chance I might still find it, although let's face it, the chance was pretty slim, and any hope I'd held that Josh might tell me where to look had been shattered the moment Reed punched him in the nose. I was just going to have to face up to the fact that I was leaving without the dress, and trust in the skills of Reed's investigative team.

I wondered if the curse only applied in Paris, or if it would follow to New York and haunt me forever.

I tried to find a bright side. At least packing was easier this time, since the disposal of my mom's suitcase had left me with almost nothing to pack. In theory, anyway. But Celestine wouldn't let me go with nothing. She kept throwing clothes at me. Literally throwing them. Until there was this huge pile of gorgeous expensive designer clothes on the floor all around me. She would say "Gaultier" and fling a leather bustier at me. We both got such a case of the giggles that we had to sit down on the floor until we could breathe again.

I finally agreed to take a few things. Only things she swore she didn't wear. I didn't really believe her, because the clothes she gave me were absolutely wonderful. Plus she pulled out this classic Louis Vuitton bag and put the things inside. It wasn't an actual suitcase, more like a big carry-on, but still—a bag like that costs a fortune. "I can't take this," I said.

"It's old," she said. Which I guess it was. But if you take care of a Vuitton bag, it will last you pretty much forever. "I can get another one," she said. She probably could. Then she said, "I want you to have it." What could I say to that? So I took it.

The next morning she got up early and made me breakfast. Which is actually quite a big deal, because Celestine is not much of a cook. I should know, having lived with her for a year. Anyway, she ran out early to shop, then cooked the most Midwestern breakfast she could think of. So what if she burned the bacon, and the eggs were a little runny? And the fire she started in her frying pan was only a little one. She is without question the best friend I ever had.

Then it was time for me to go. We hugged each other and cried. I asked her to walk me downstairs, but by the third step down, she was crying so hard I told her good-bye right there and sent her back to the apartment. Before she closed the door, she said, "Remember. You promise to come back?"

"I promise," I said, took a deep breath, ran down the stairs, and went outside.

A black Lincoln Continental sedan was waiting for me. It is not the kind of car you see in Paris every day. In the middle of all the tiny little Peugeots and Citroëns and Renaults, a flying saucer would have been less conspicuous. Do not ask me how Reed found it. He had the driver pop the trunk, even though I only had the carry-on from Celestine and my little duffel baggy. Reed eyed the carry-on disapprovingly. "Louis Vuitton?"

"It's . . . a copy," I said. "I bought it in Chicago. Cheap."

That seemed to satisfy him. He closed the trunk and held the door for me, then climbed in on the other side and sat next to me as the driver pulled the car into traffic.

"I want to say something," Reed immediately began. I waited. "I'm sorry," he said. "I don't know who that guy was. And it's none of my business. But I shouldn't have hit him."

I thought that was pretty grown-up of him. Because I hadn't even asked him to apologize.

"You shouldn't have hit him," I said. I couldn't help it. I was picturing Josh bleeding all over his hat, and all over Flavien.

"I know."

"He did something mean to me." I wasn't saying that for Reed's benefit. I was trying to shake feeling sorry for Josh, and I wasn't entirely succeeding, even though I hated him. "When I got kicked out of my hotel, he was the one who had them throw away my suitcase. My clothes." I almost said *my Grandma's dress,* only I thought that if I said it, I would start to cry. So I didn't. "But you still shouldn't have hit him."

"I know."

Then we rode for a while and didn't say anything. Until a full fifteen minutes later. Out of nowhere, Reed said, "I am really, truly sorry."

"Okay," I said.

41

We were flying American Airlines.

Which kind of figured. You know, what with Fox News and all.

Flying First Class is way better than flying Coach. The seats in First Class are like huge comfy La-Z-Boys that recline all the way back. Plus the minute you sit down, they pour you champagne, and bring you a ceramic bowl full of warm mixed nuts, and hand out little hot washcloths for you to wipe your hands. There is an endless parade of flight attendants, and when they distribute the menus you get to pick real meals, starting with a fresh salad, then yummy elaborate entrées, then hot-fudge sundaes. Not to mention more champagne, and wine, and after-dinner liqueurs. It should have been wonderful.

But it wasn't. For starters, even though Reed had apologized, I was still feeling pretty bad about his punching Josh. Do not get me wrong: I was still just as furious and unforgiving as ever about what Josh did with Mom's suitcase, and specifically Grandma's dress. Although it occurred to me that he couldn't have known Grandma's dress was in it. Not that I would forgive him anyway. But I couldn't help seeing his side of it. His movie didn't happen on account of me. I guess if I were him, I'd have been mad at me too. And we all do stupid things when we're mad.

Feeling bad for Josh made me feel not as good about Reed. Or about myself, since Reed only hit Josh because I said he was bothering me. Maybe that's why everything was a little less fun than it should have been.

Then somewhere in the middle of my third glass of champagne, it struck me: I wasn't just upset about Grandma's dress and Josh. I was upset because I had failed. Over and over again. When I left home eight days earlier, I had thought this was my chance to be a huge success. Instead, I had left a trail of people who didn't want me around. The Movie People. Everybody at Armani. Josh. Uncle John. Okay, in the meantime Mom and Dad still loved me, but they didn't know yet that I had lost Grandma's dress.

Maybe that was why I'd been so quick to say yes to Reed. I didn't care that much specifically about becoming a star on Fox News. I think I just wanted—needed—to prove to myself that I could do something right.

So when the flight attendants started serving lunch, I asked Reed, "Could you be a little more specific? About the job, I mean."

Reed told me how Fox News had picked the anchor from one of their local affiliates, a man named Michael Smith, and was trying him out with his own half-hour format. So far they were only testing him in the Northeast, but his numbers looked good, so they were thinking about rolling him out nationwide. They would introduce me as a commentator during Michael's show, and make it a regular spot if things went well. "Which I know they will," Reed said.

Incidentally, Michael Smith is the man's real name. But don't bother looking for him on Fox News. He no longer works there.

Reed asked me if I have a cell phone. I told him of course. He took the number, and he said that once we started having meetings I should keep it turned on at all times, in case they needed to reach me, twenty-four hours a day. Which made me feel sort of important. They don't need to reach just anybody twenty-four hours a day, right?

The business conversation finished about the same time dessert arrived. Instead of dessert, Reed had a glass of port. Then he adjusted his seat way back and went to sleep.

While Reed slept, the flight attendants gave everybody in First Class their own personal DVD players, with a whole album of movies to choose from. I watched *Ghost World* first, mostly because Scarlett Johansson is in it, and as you know I supposedly bear some very slight resemblance to her. Then I watched *Chicago,* which stars Renée Zellweger, who is quite good in it, although I prefer her in the *Bridget Jones* movies. After the second movie, I napped for a while.

When I woke up, there was still quite a bit of time to kill, because the flight from Paris to New York is very long, since you are going against the jet stream. I opened up my little duffel baggy and pulled out Josh's script. I enjoyed reading it all over again. Only it also made me sad all over again. Because I truly believed it would have been a very good movie, if only I hadn't screwed up. And I truly believed Josh and I could have been happy together, if only I hadn't screwed that up, too.

I was just putting the script away when the pilot announced we were starting our descent. Reed woke up and said "Hi," so I said "Hi." He reached into the seat pocket in front of him and took out this cute little toiletries kit, which is another benefit of First Class. He went to the lavatory, then a minute later came back smiling and smelling like toothpaste and mouthwash. Which was awfully considerate. And he was awfully handsome. Maybe even handsome enough to make me stop thinking about Josh Thomas.

The plane bumped to a landing, and I realized I was scared. Barely a week earlier, I had been ready to conquer Paris, but I was the one who got conquered, and then some. Now I was in New York, and stardom awaited.

Either that, or disaster.

42

Given that Reed is the type of person who can find a Lincoln Continental sedan in Paris, it probably goes without saying that a driver with a luggage cart met us at the gate.

I only had the Louis Vuitton carry-on from Celestine and my duffel baggy. Still, the driver insisted on taking them both, in addition to Reed's briefcase and computer bag. We went down to baggage claim and waited what seemed like forever until Reed's two huge black Tumi suitcases finally made their entrance onto the carousel.

The driver took us and our bags to the Fox News Hummer. Actually it is a Hummer 2. I don't know if Hummer is the official monster SUV of Fox News, or if this was the only one. And it was not red white and blue or anything cheesy. It was black, with a little logo on the door.

By the way, I should mention that Hummers come from Indiana. Hummers and Hoosiers. The Indy 500. And Bobby Knight, but not anymore.

I had never been to New York before, so I stayed very alert on the drive to Manhattan because I didn't want to miss the skyline. Do not get me wrong. As I have told you, Kirland, Indiana is just a twenty- or thirty-minute drive from Chicago. I have been to Chicago I have no idea how many times. And Chicago has plenty of tall buildings. In fact, the Sears Tower, which I know quite a bit about, having written a paper about it during the course of my so-called education, is taller than anything in New York. The point is, even though I have seen plenty of tall buildings, somehow I knew that seeing the tall buildings in New York would be different.

It took a while before I found out if that was true or not. Before you get to Manhattan from JFK airport, first you have to drive through Queens. Queens is a borough. A borough is not a neighborhood, and not a city. Actually, I am not exactly sure what a borough is, but New York has five of them: Manhattan, Queens, Brooklyn, the Bronx, and Staten Island.

I turned to Reed. "Are you a baseball fan?"

"Sure," he said.

"Who do you root for?"

"The Yankees. Who else?"

I turned back to the window and watched Queens blur past. For all I know, Queens may be a fine place to live and work, and it appears that plenty of people live and work there. But Queens is not a tall-building place.

Then finally I saw Manhattan.

I first saw it from a distance, so it was not immediately overwhelming. On the contrary: From far away, even the Empire State Building looks small. But then you get closer, and Manhattan grows, and grows, and grows. Until you are just across the river, and then it strikes you that the whole thing just roars up out of the ground into the sky, and it makes you wonder how it doesn't sink under all those tall buildings.

We crossed the East River. The Seine in Paris is a cozy romantic river with cozy romantic bridges, but the East River is big and serious and all business, and the bridge we crossed was big and serious and all business, too.

The next thing I knew, we arrived at my hotel. I did not immediately recognize it as a hotel, because there was no sign. None whatsoever. Then a young man approached the Hummer. He had cool spiky black hair, and he wore all black clothes. I wondered why he was coming up to us. He opened my door. "Welcome to the Tribeca Grand," he said. Incidentally, Tribeca is a made-up word.

It's short for *tri*angle *be*low *Ca*nal, and it is the name of a neighborhood. I looked at a map. Although Tribeca is below Canal Street, I don't think it's exactly a triangle. But I guess they can call their neighborhood whatever they want.

Reed walked me to the front desk. He carried my bags, even though I just had the two little ones. He checked me in and confirmed that everything was being charged to Fox News. Incidentally, everybody at the front desk was wearing all black, too, just like the man who opened the Hummer door for me. Reed leaned down and whispered, "The suits book people into boring Midtown hotels. I figured you'd like this better."

"This looks great," I said. "Thanks."

"We should have dinner," Reed said.

"Sure," I said. I gave him a little hug. Not a big suggestive hug. A thank-you-for-taking-me-to-New York hug.

He looked down at me. "Tonight?"

I was tired. Very tired. Reed had slept most of the flight back from Paris, and I hadn't. So I was not sure I had the stamina for a romantic dinner. Assuming it was going to be romantic, which was not necessarily a safe assumption, because I could not figure out for the life of me if Reed had romantic intentions or not. On the other hand, Reed *was* smiling that handsome Labrador smile. And let us not forget, he was my knight in shining armor–slash–cavalry officer–slash–Marine who had rescued me from the abyss of Armani-terminated despair. Not to mention that he was going to make me a star.

"What time?" I said.

"Eight o'clock. In the lobby." He gave me a kiss. On the cheek. Not a lot of romance in that kiss.

Then he was gone.

43

Eight didn't give me a lot of time.

As soon as Reed left, I turned to the young woman in black behind the reception desk. She asked how many keys I was going to need.

"Just one," I said. She had seen and heard my whole conversation with Reed, so maybe she was suggesting something. Or maybe not. Either way, she handed me just one plastic room card key. Then she led me back toward the elevator, which rides up and down in an exposed metal-framework shaft. The elevator, like the whole hotel, is a very funky blend of old and new.

My room was modern and sleek and sophisticated. And cool. Funky hip artsy cool. Not your parents' kind of hotel at all. Even if your parents have a lot of money.

The whole place made me feel relaxed. Which was kind of odd, considering that I was either hovering on the verge of stardom in a whole new career or teetering on the brink of homelessness on the mean streets of New York. I should have been a nervous wreck, but I wasn't. Maybe it was the jet lag.

I looked at the Bose Wave clock radio, which was as cool as the room. It was almost five o'clock. I figured my prep time for dinner with Reed was ninety minutes, bare minimum. Which left me an hour and a half to nap. A little risky, because I might wake up feeling worse than before. Then again, falling asleep in the middle of one of Reed's witty stories about Dartmouth or the Republican National Convention would not be socially correct or professionally advantageous. So I called the front desk and ordered not one but two wake-up calls. Then I drew the curtains shut, took off my clothes, crawled under the soft-as-silk Frette sheets, and fell right asleep.

I got lucky. My nap turned out to be a that-was-refreshing kind of sleep, with not a hint of a bad dream about Grandma's lost dress or Josh. I got up with the first wake-up call and canceled the second one. I had to get moving.

I headed straight for the bathroom, where I found myself surrounded by very cool brushed stainless steel. Set into the stainless steel was a tiny little TV set. For a second, I thought about turning on the TV and looking for Fox News so I could do a little research, but I didn't have time to channel surf to find it.

I took a nice hot shower, then brushed my teeth. While I was brushing, I concluded that the hotel was too cool to have a sign outside. If you didn't know what it was without a sign, you didn't deserve to stay there. Then I fixed my hair, rinsed with some lovely mouthwash the hotel was thoughtful enough to provide, and put on a little makeup. Which left about twenty minutes to get dressed. And if you have been paying attention, you know that is not remotely enough time for me.

Ordinarily.

Fortunately, the only clothes I had were the five outfits Celestine had given me. I wondered which one Grandma would have picked, if her mysterious adventure had been in New York in 2006 instead of Paris in 1928. Celestine had not given me any dangerous dresses, but I had a feeling Grandma would tell me that a dangerous dress should only be worn under careless, reckless, gorgeous, sexual circumstances anyway. And dinner with Reed did not seem to meet those criteria, at least not yet. So what to wear?

The Prada.

It was almost as if Grandma had whispered in my ear. Which is unlikely, what with the fact that first, Grandma is deceased, and second, to my knowledge, Grandma never heard of Prada. But

I still felt as if she was helping me pick. Which made me think that just maybe, even though I had lost her dress, Grandma and her power were still with me.

The Prada was perfect. It was all black, which fit right in with the decor. Plus it was very understated, so Reed would probably just assume it was something I got in Chicago. As if.

I finished dressing and looked at the clock. It was eight P.M. on the dot, which meant I had to kill ten minutes, because it's important to always keep men waiting. I admired myself in the mirror. *Definitely* the Prada. Then I went downstairs.

Reed was waiting to escort me into the restaurant. I was pleasantly surprised, because he looked kind of hip. He was wearing a casual suit that fit him nicely. No tie, no button-down shirt, but a black T-shirt under the suit jacket. I bet they don't wear *that* on Fox News.

Not that I had ever watched Fox News, of course.

Our waitress, who needless to say was wearing all black, asked if we wanted anything to drink. "You pick," I said to Reed. Where had I read that if a sophisticated man is buying you dinner, always let him order the drinks? It gives him a chance to feel like James Bond. Although I am still waiting for a man to order martinis, shaken not stirred.

Incidentally, the let-the-man-order rule does not apply in Kirland, Indiana, unless you're satisfied drinking Rock and Rye.

"No, *you* pick," said Reed.

"But—"

"I want to get to know you better," Reed said. "The real you."

Oooh. He wants to get to know me better. The real me.

Then, for just a second, I had a flash of Josh back in that Italian restaurant, asking me to pick the wine until I insisted that he pick. I wondered, is there some guidebook about girls that all these men are reading? Does it say, *Rule 11: Always let the girl order the drinks, because that will make her think you are thoughtful and value her opinion?* I shoved that cynical thought, not to mention Josh, out of my head. Reed *was* thoughtful. He *did* value my opinion.

"What do you drink back home?"

I suddenly was not entirely sure I wanted Reed to get to know the real me. "Nothing special," I said, trying to dodge the bullet.

"C'mon," Reed urged. "Order two of whatever you drink."

"Are you sure?"

"I'm sure," he said.

So to Reed I said, "Okay." And to the waitress I said, "Two Boilermakers."

She did not know what a Boilermaker was. She was too young and hip and downtown. Before I could tell her, she ran to the bartender. Even though he was also young and hip and downtown, not to mention also clad in black, he did know what a Boilermaker was. In a minute the waitress was back with two shots of whiskey and two beers.

"You're kidding," Reed said when he saw the drinks.

"You said you were sure." Before he could say anything else, I picked up the shot glass and tossed back the whiskey like I was some fifty-year-old Slovak steelworker. Then I slapped the little glass back onto the table. *Bang.*

I believe that Reed is overall a fairly smart man. But he is a man, which means that somewhere not very deep inside him he is really a boy. So of course you know what he did: He picked up the shot glass and slammed the shot down just like I had done.

Only I didn't spend the next five minutes coughing and crying, and he did.

I felt kind of bad. Which is not to say I didn't see the funny side of it, too. I did. Still, I patted him on the back and wiped his eyes with the napkin. Which was, you guessed it, black.

Reed skipped his beer, even though I told him it would ease the coughing. I finished mine even before he stopped coughing.

The Boilermaker incident turned out to be a pretty good icebreaker. We were able to relax and not be at all self-conscious, so we just had fun. Reed did not mention the Republican National Convention once. Although he was starting in on Dartmouth when, fortunately, the food showed up. We shared this three-tiered seafood thing that was almost too good to believe. And for dessert I had a raspberry beer float, which was not just ice cream and raspberries, but had ginger beer and alcohol in it too, I think. Odd as it may sound, if you ever have the chance to get one of those, get two.

I have to admit, I was feeling . . . well, cozy. The setting was lovely and dark and velvety, there were a bazillion candles glowing and very seductive electronic music was pulsing in the background. Not to mention that Reed was still a very good-looking man who now seemed very clearly interested in me as a woman. On top of that, he was about to make me into a big TV star. So I was a little dismayed when I realized I had a severe case of déjà vu, as if I had done all this before. Only I had. With Josh. Handsome man. Perfect dinner, perfect setting, drinks . . .

No no no! Reed most certainly was not Josh. Reed was not going to stick me with the check. He was not going to ruin our evening. He was going to seize this romantic opportunity.

I was extremely disappointed when he asked, "Can we talk a little business?"

"Business?"

"Just a little," he said. "Get it out of the way. Then we can get on to"—and then he blushed—"other things." At which my disappointment vanished.

He said we would start with two appearances a week on Michael Smith's program. Assuming the response was what they expected, they'd gradually ramp it up to every day.

"If they like me, you mean." I will be honest with you: I was fishing for compliments.

"Of course they'll like you," Reed said. "Trust me."

"But they might not."

"They will."

"What if they don't?" It is hard to stop asking when a smart, sophisticated, good-looking man is stroking your ego so obligingly.

"They will," he said again. But he could see that I was looking for more. "They *will.* I'm sure. And even if they don't . . ." He smiled. "Even if they don't," he said, "I promise you, no matter what, we won't kick you out of the hotel and throw away your clothes."

We both laughed. *So there, Josh Thomas. From now on, I am sticking with the un-Josh.* To underscore my decision, I gave Reed what I hoped was my very best come-hither look.

He got the check, and as we stood up to go, he took my hand in his.

He was focusing on the hotel door.

Okay, so maybe my come-hither look wasn't obvious enough. I turned toward the elevator and gave him a little tug in that direction.

He looked at me.

I smiled at him. Not just any old smile. And, to be sure I was being quite clear, I winked.

He jumped.

44

I mean he literally jumped. About a foot straight up into the air. Which is not exactly the reaction I was looking for.

"What's wrong?" I asked. Because now he was grabbing rather frantically at his belt.

"Hotline," he said. I am not kidding. Like he thought he was Batman or something.

He found his cell phone. I guess he had the vibrate setting turned up too high. Anyway he flipped the phone open and listened. "Uh-huh," he said. Looking quite grim, I might add. "Uh-huh." Looking grimmer. "Uh-huh." From his expression, I was sure somebody had died. "Okay," Reed said, and snapped the phone shut. He looked at me. At the hotel elevator. Back at me. "I'm sorry," he finally said. "I have to leave. There's a crisis."

"What kind of crisis?" If I'm going to get turned down, I think I'm entitled to know why.

"A news crisis," he said.

"What kind of news crisis?"

"I can't tell you," he said.

Well. Fine. Be that way.

I should not be so harsh. I'm sure there could be a legitimate news crisis he genuinely could not tell me about. Something involving confidential sources and leaks and grand juries and such. Still and all, I did not much like the idea that some news crisis was more important than, well, you know. I was beginning to think that Reed was not only a victim of poor timing, but also poor judgment.

I bet screenwriters don't get news crisis phone calls on the Hotline. I bet Josh would've just let the stupid phone ring, and not even answered it.

I wished I would just make up my mind.

"Oh," said Reed, "I forgot to tell you. You have a meeting tomorrow afternoon at the studio." Great. Now he was *all* business. "I won't be able to be there, but my associate producer will take good care of you. A car will pick you up at two. Unless you want somebody to come by earlier and drive you around. You know, show you the sights."

It sounded like the kind of offer he would make to anybody, as opposed to somebody who had just extended a potentially intimate invitation. Even if the invitation was more implicit than explicit. But if he was going to treat me like just anybody, he was putting at very serious risk his chances of ever getting to the explicit part.

If Reed could instantly turn distant and businesslike, well, so could I. "No thank you," I said. "I'll just walk around by myself. Do some shopping."

"Good idea," Reed said. "Buy American." Then he gave me a little hug. A producer hug. Not a boyfriend hug. He turned, walked through the revolving door, and was gone.

I went back to my room, got out of the Prada outfit, hung it up carefully, and crawled between those lovely sheets. All alone.

I will say this: Notwithstanding my nap, I was so tired that I fell asleep instantly. Which meant I did not have any time to lie there and stew about Reed and his stupid Hotline crisis.

When I woke up, it was ten A.M. And do you know? I did not care about what happened with Reed. Because it hit me: I was in New York City, with nothing to do until two o'clock.

Correction: I did not have nothing to do. If you will forgive the double negative. There were two very important things that I absolutely, positively had to do. First I had to eat. Because I was starved. Then I had to shop.

I have already told you my views about clothes and power. So my corollary theory about shopping will come as no surprise. If clothes confer power and liberty, then by definition, the act of getting clothes—*shopping*—is empowering and liberating. You have probably always enjoyed shopping, but don't you feel even better, now that you know it's good for you?

I looked at the closet, at all the outfits Celestine gave me, to pick clothes for shopping. You cannot wear just anything to go shopping. Especially not to go shopping in New York.

I felt a sudden pang because Grandma's dress was not there in the closet. It should have been. Without it, I never would have gotten to Paris, much less New York.

Although I did write my "A Dangerous Dress" paper all by myself, so I kind of earned Paris. And I actually found the perfect dress, even if evil slut Nathalie had torn it up. And until fashion moron George showed up, I was doing awfully well at Armani Collezioni. And Grandma's dress had nothing to do with me landing my Fox News job, either. So maybe I was selling myself short, and giving the dress too much credit for determining my destiny.

I looked at the closet again. I still got a pang, but it was less sharp this time. And it was pretty much gone once I put on the cute Moschino outfit that Celestine gave me. The pants are just white and cropped, almost plain. But the top is this bright red thing with odd fringes, and there are big numbers printed on it, white numbers on the front and black on the back. It pretty much cried out *European designer.* Which is why I picked that outfit. I suspected I would never wear it around Reed, or anyone else from Fox News, and I didn't want it to go to waste.

I wondered if the Fox News people could be a little flexible on the whole buy-American thing. It hadn't stopped Reed from buying a tie at Armani Collezioni, had it? Although perhaps the policy did not apply outside the territorial boundaries of the United States. I decided I wouldn't ask until after Reed had made me a big star. I would have more bargaining power then.

I turned on my cell phone and took it with me, just like Reed asked me to. In case they needed to reach me. Although I hoped they would not need to reach me in the middle of shopping. Then I had breakfast and headed for Soho, which the concierge with the funky haircut told me was shopping paradise.

The streets were crammed with cars. The sidewalks and crosswalks were jammed with pedestrians. Horns honked. People shouted. Sirens wailed. And despite the chaos I had the strangest realization: I wasn't the slightest bit intimidated. I felt like the city was extending me a big loud invitation to join a club—a club to which, somehow, I already belonged.

Given where I come from, these were very peculiar things for me to be thinking and feeling. I wondered if Grandma had felt just as comfortable in Paris. Maybe it was in my blood. Maybe this was my true inheritance from her—an even greater gift than her dress had been.

I crossed impossibly crowded Canal Street into Soho. The concierge was right: I just couldn't believe the stores. Anna Sui and Betsey Johnson and Cynthia Rowley. And that was just ABC. I bet if I had time I could come up with amazing places for the whole alphabet. Everyone who was anyone. Places with fun, different, dramatic, silly, great clothes. Places that positively radiated the power of shopping.

Surrounded by fabulous shops with famous names, I decided that, oddly enough, I was not looking for a famous name. Needless to say, I wanted someplace fabulous—but a place I never heard of. Nobody had ever heard of me, and in a few days I would be Fox's fresh new American voice. I hoped to find a boutique I had never heard of, that would be my own personal fresh new American shopping mecca.

I looked around, and there she was: Debra Moorefield. I'd never heard of her. For all I knew, this was her one and only store. But the clothes looked awfully sweet. So Debra it was.

As soon as I stepped inside, I knew I had made the right decision. The boutique was filled with clothes that, oh, say, Audrey

Hepburn would wear. Perfect lovely classic never-out-of-style clothes, but with a little magic. Things I could wear to look perfect on the arm of my dashing handsome slightly conservative Fox News producer when he escorted me to timeless but slightly stuffy four-star restaurants . . . and that I could also wear to look perfect while clubbing at three A.M. in neighborhoods that Reed probably didn't even know existed. I just knew the clothes would look good on me. Right away I spotted the most darling little silky lacy black dress—in my size, which you may remember is a six, and since I was in New York I no longer cared what that translated to in centimeters, and neither should you.

The salesperson showed me to a dressing room. Before I pulled the curtain closed, she said, "I love your outfit." Maybe it was just good salesmanship. Salesgirlship. Saleswomanship. Whatever. You know, flatter the customer. On the other hand, the Moschino outfit was pretty marvelous, so she was probably just showing me she had good taste. Which meant that if she liked the way I looked in the darling little black dress, I would have to buy it.

Incidentally, if you find a perfect little black dress, buy it. You can never have too many. Although if you are reading this, you probably already know that.

I slipped out of the Moschino and into the Debra Moorefield, zipped up the dress, flipped back my hair, and looked in the mirror. Not a dangerous dress on the scale of Grandma's, to be sure, but dangerous enough. And I thought, *Oh yes. You are coming home with me.*

When I emerged from the dressing room, the salesperson said, "Let's see." She gave me a long up-and-down look. Finally she said, "That is *perfect* on you." Which was not, in my view, just sales talk. It really did look pretty perfect on me. "Shall I wrap it up?" she asked.

I felt totally invigorated. And empowered. I *deserved* to be a star. I *deserved* to be in New York. I *deserved* to be shopping. I *deserved* this dress.

I looked at the price. Only $358. And I do mean only. With all due respect to the Dolces and Gabannas of the world, if this dress was theirs, I could not have touched it for three times the price. Or four, or more. And let me tell you, this dress showed every penny's worth, which is to say that it concealed me in just the right places, and showed me in just the right places. It was simultaneously modest and dangerous, which is no mean feat. I thought Reed would love it. Depending, that is, on where it was made.

I had not yet had the nerve to look at the tag to see the country of origin. I really was going to have to talk to Fox News about this buy-American thing.

Whether it had been sewn in the USA or China, I was about to say "Yes, I'll take it." Until I remembered I had no room on my credit card. And I still had not resolved my stupid Bank of America Visa ATM card situation. In Paris, Celestine bought everything. Which does not make me a freeloader. The deal was that as soon as I got paid at Armani Collezioni, I was going to cover both our expenses until we were even. Only then I got fired. You know the rest.

So I told the salesperson I left my wallet at the hotel. I was not about to tell her all my credit cards were frozen. I don't think she necessarily believed me. For a split second, I thought about assuring her it was no problem, she could trust me, because after all I was about to be a big TV star on Fox News. I was confident.

But not *that* confident. All I could do was slink out of the store and hope the perfect little black dress would still be there once I cleared up my Visa problem, or got paid, whichever came first.

45

That didn't stop me from window-shopping some more. But it was torture looking at all those fabulous stores without being able to buy anything, and I was getting hungry. It was past noon, so I figured I'd better head back to the hotel, where everything was on Fox News's tab. Especially since I couldn't buy lunch anywhere else. I had nothing in my wallet, because Celestine and I had no reason to get dollars, and I came back to America in a huge hurry and had forgotten the whole spending-money issue. I guess I could have asked Reed for a little money out of petty cash, but I hadn't thought of that either.

The address for the Tribeca Grand Hotel is Two Avenue of the Americas, so I figured the fastest way to walk was straight down Sixth Avenue, which is what real New Yorkers call the Avenue of the Americas. I headed south, which is downtown. At the first cross street, I had to stop and wait for the walk signal. While I was waiting, I looked at the street sign. King Street.

Why did King Street sound familiar?

The light changed, and I started to walk. I was halfway across the street when it hit me, stopping me dead in my tracks. Fortunately it is a small street and there were no cars coming.

Here is why it sounded familiar. On the cover of Josh's screenplay for *The Importance of Beating Ernest,* there was an address. On King Street. In New York, NY.

I was on Josh's street.

What if I saw him? I mean, really, I might. I looked west. King

Street did not look like a very long street. I couldn't remember what number the address was, but I figured you could probably walk the length of it in a few minutes. If I did, I would definitely pass Josh's place. But what if he just happened to step out of his doorway as I passed by? What would I do?

What would I do if he came up to me and said he was sorry? What if he told me he had been impulsive and stupid? What if he said that ever since then, he had not been able to sleep because he felt so guilty? What if he told me he loved me, and begged me to let him spend the rest of his life trying to make it up to me? What if—

My cell phone rang.

Maybe it was Reed. Maybe his crisis was over. Maybe he was calling to tell me he was sorry he had passed up my invitation in favor of a stupid news crisis. Maybe he wanted to come see me right away. Maybe I felt guilty that I had even been thinking about Josh. I answered the phone.

"We've moved your meeting up to two," said a woman's voice I did not recognize. "Be downstairs at one thirty." Before I could say anything, she hung up. So I did not walk down Josh Thomas's street. And I did not see him. And he did not say any of those things to me.

For which I was very grateful to Reed. For saving me from Josh.

Okay it was not Reed himself who called me. Because he was still off dealing with his news crisis. But clearly, whoever called me must have been somebody who worked for Reed. So, in essence, it was Reed who saved me. Just like he saved me when I got fired from Armani.

On the other hand, Reed had not called to tell me I was more important to him than a news crisis. So no matter how grateful I was to him for saving me from Josh, I wasn't one hundred percent thrilled either.

It occurred to me that, given my recent prowess at screwing up relationships with men and landing in strange places without a dime to my name, I should have become a nun.

Okay I am mostly kidding. Fundamentally I am not nun material. You know that and I know that. But if I was a nun I would not have to keep booting horrible Josh Thomas out of my head. And I would not have to keep struggling to decipher Reed James. On the surface Reed seemed uncomplicated enough, but the longer I knew him, the more inscrutable he became. Polo by Ralph Lauren and Fox News on the one hand. Armani and Johnny Depp on the other hand. How did it all fit together? And was he *ever* going to kiss me?

I did not have time to figure any of this out now. I had a meeting to get to, which had just been moved up half an hour.

I rushed back to the hotel, where I had a shrimp salad for lunch because it was the fastest thing the kitchen could make. Then I hurried up to my room. It was already past one. I brushed my teeth again and rinsed with mouthwash. I smiled in the mirror and checked to make sure I didn't have any little pieces of lettuce stuck in unflattering places. I picked out the plainest, most American-looking clothes I had and went downstairs at one thirty. Sure enough, the Fox News Hummer was waiting to take me to the Fox News studios.

I will say one thing about riding in a Hummer: Sitting way up there, you get an extremely good view of the road. It didn't take me long to notice that there are more taxicabs in New York than I'd ever seen anywhere, and they're all yellow, so they resemble a swarm of giant bees weaving everywhere. I might have felt a little insecure if I had been in an ordinary car. But I felt fine. Because I was in a Hummer. Which you will recall is a product of Indiana.

Just because the traffic did not scare me, though, that did not mean I was not scared. I will confess to you. I was. Scared, nervous, excited. After all, the Hummer was not taking me to any old place. It was taking me to Fox News.

Where, I will remind you, I was about to become a star.

46

"I'm Bertie Thorn," said Bertie Thorn.

We were in a conference room at the Fox News complex near Times Square.

Before I tell you about my meeting with Bertie Thorn, I should say a word about Times Square. Which I had only seen on *Dick Clark's New Year's Rockin' Eve.* Judging from those broadcasts, most of the twenty million people on hand appear to be drunk and obnoxious. So that is perhaps not the best representation of Times Square.

I got a very different impression. I thought Times Square was like Disney World. Which is a place I have been, by the way.

Here is what I mean: Even with all the thousands of pedestrians, who are real people going to real jobs in real office buildings, everything is very big, very bright, very colorful. Miles of neon. Huge billboards. Like the enormous one for Calvin Klein underwear. With the very nicely endowed male model. No boxers, thank you. Definitely briefs. Okay, Times Square isn't exactly like Disney World. But you get the idea.

The Fox News Hummer brought me straight to the door of the Fox News studios. Security had my name on their list. They gave me a little badge—a real plastic one with my name printed on it. They told me what floor and what conference room to go to. When I arrived, there was Bertie Thorn.

"Bertie is short for Roberta," said Bertie. "But never call me that." It was a warning.

"You're the one who called me before," I said. Because I recognized her voice.

"That's right."

Bertie Thorne was tall and skinny and pretty. And very severe. She wore a dark gray suit, with a jacket that buttoned all the way up to her neck, sleeves that went all the way to the ends of her thumbs, and pants that scraped the floor. Her shoes were flats. Her short dark hair was gelled flat to her scalp, and her eyes were lined with thick pencil and shadowed in dark brown. It was as if she had spent her whole life getting tired of people telling her how pretty she was, so now she tried as hard as she could to hide it.

Bertie shook my hand. *Ouch.* You'd think she was trying to prove she could shake hands harder than a man. "I'm Reed's associate producer," she explained. "Reed can't be here today."

"I know," I said.

"You do?"

"He told me."

"He did?"

"At dinner," I said.

"Dinner?"

"Last night."

"I see," she said. "Just dinner?"

I wasn't sure what she meant by that. "Well, drinks too," I said.

"Then what?" she asked. Which I'm sorry, I thought was a rather personal question. Except that the way things had happened, I could answer it in a perfectly impersonal way.

"Then he got a call. On the Hotline."

"He told you that?"

"He did. He said he had a crisis."

"I see," she said. "What kind of crisis?" Which struck me as an odd question, coming from Reed's associate producer.

"Don't you know where he is?" I asked.

She flinched. "I know *exactly* where he is. I'm just trying to determine what he told you. And whether he divulged anything he . . . shouldn't have."

Humph. "He said he had a news crisis. And that he couldn't tell me what it was."

"Well," she said. "All right then." And with that, she smiled as if I had just walked into the room. So I smiled back. "Perfect," Bertie said. "Excellent. Let's get you to wardrobe."

I perked up when she said *wardrobe.* Because that meant clothes. And you know how I feel about clothes.

Now I'm afraid I must tell you that wardrobe was quite a letdown. Stop and think about what people on TV news programs wear.

Most of the people you see on TV news are men. Which is fairly obnoxious. But if you just focus on what they wear, let's face it, it's all pretty dull, suit-and-tie stuff. If you can think of a TV anchorman who wears Versace, let me know. Because I can't.

The women are—I'm sorry, ladies—just as dull. I'm not talking about the girl who does the traffic report on your early morning local news, who wears that tight sweater and is it cold in the studio, dear? I'm talking about the network news women. All, like, six of them. Boring. Even the morning shows. I am sorry, Diane Sawyer, I think you and Charlie Gibson are the best, but tell me you aren't much more fashion forward at home. Of course you are.

So I guess I should not have been totally surprised when Bertie and a wardrobe lady named Leila showed me into a dressing room filled with clothes that looked like they all came from Timberland and Lands' End and the Gap. I guess my disappointment showed, because Leila said, "We want you to look natural."

"But this stuff is all so . . . Midwestern," I said.

"Where are you from?"

Bertie answered the question for me. "The Midwest."

"Can't I wear something just a teeny bit more exciting?"

"Listen to me," Bertie said. She put her hand on my shoulder like we were best friends. "Our audience wants a pretty girl from Middle America with a point of view."

"I have a point of view," I said.

"Exactly." Then she took her hand off my shoulder. Which I appreciated, because I am not overly fond of being touched by hostile strangers.

"You'll look great," Leila said. "Plus makeup and hair will do wonders tomorrow."

"Day after tomorrow," Bertie said.

"The schedule says tomorrow," Leila said.

"We're pushing the schedule back a day," Bertie said. "Reed has . . . a crisis."

"Ohhh," said Leila.

I was hoping they would say more about Reed and his crisis, but they didn't. Instead we all turned our attention to the clothes. I tried on a bunch of stuff. You already know that I do not set any land speed records when it comes to picking an outfit. Sometimes having other people there makes it go faster. Like Celestine and I pick outfits about six times faster if we are both together. On the other hand, sometimes having other people there does not make it go faster.

This was one of those times. It took two and a half hours to settle on three possibilities. Not exciting, but not awful either. Oh, and all made in the USA. Leila made sure to point that out.

"Tomorrow, Reed will pick which of the three you'll wear for your debut," Bertie said.

"Does that mean his crisis will be over by then?" I asked.

"Well obviously," Bertie said.

I wondered what kind of news crisis lets you know in advance when it will be over.

"What about the other two outfits?" Leila asked.

"We'll save those for future segments," Bertie said. She looked at her watch. "Oops. Five o'clock. We don't want to keep you too late. Reed feels bad about his crisis delaying your debut."

"He does?"

"Of course he does. He's a very thoughtful man," she said, and I thought I saw a little color spring to her cheeks. "He wants you to go out and do something special tonight."

"He does?"

"Of course he does. And he wants you to charge it to Fox News."

I hesitated. "You're sure?"

"Well of course I'm sure," she said. This time her cheeks definitely got pink. "I know Reed better than anyone. After all, I'm his . . . associate producer." Which somehow I was pretty sure wasn't what she originally intended to say.

"Your car is waiting," Bertie said. "You've got a noon call tomorrow."

And with that, I was dismissed.

47

I did not hesitate a second longer. I ran for the Hummer. And as soon as I got back to the hotel, I ran straight to the concierge desk. It is not every day that somebody offers to treat you to the perfect night out in New York City. Absolutely for free. At least that never happened to me before. Given how long it takes me to pick an outfit, you can imagine how much time I typically need to plan a big night out. But I only had a couple of hours. I needed help. I needed Sasha.

Sasha was the concierge on duty at the desk by the hotel elevator. She had inhumanly red hair and two nose rings. Both through the same nostril, not one on each side.

I told her my situation. And she came up with the perfect idea. Only not immediately. Here are a few of the things she and I discussed, and the reasons we rejected them:

10. A Broadway show in general, and in particular *The Producers.* (Too touristy in general, and in particular because Nathan Lane and Matthew Broderick were not back in the cast.)
9. A Mets game (too outer boroughs) or Yankees game (too out of town, and anyway too Steinbrenner).
8. The New York City Ballet. (Too highbrow.)
7. Bowling at Chelsea Piers. (Too lowbrow.)
6. A taping of *Letterman* (too hip for the room) or *Saturday Night Live* (too Tuesday).

5. A ride on the Staten Island Ferry. (Too cheap, too wet, and too Staten Island.)
4. The observation deck of the Empire State Building. (Too *An Affair to Remember,* too *Sleepless in Seattle,* and, in my case, just too lonely.)
3. Drag divas at Bar d'O. (Too West Village.)
2. The Sex Pistols tribute band at CBGBs. (Too East Village.)

"We're getting close," Sasha said. "What's your favorite song?"

I would not have guessed Sasha was a Rodgers and Hart fan. What with the nose rings and all. But it turned out she also had a grandma who used to stack wonderful old records on the turntable of her old cabinet stereo. Perhaps her grandma was partial to Benny Goodman and mine was partial to Artie Shaw, but they both loved Richard Rodgers and Lorenz Hart. So when I said "Bewitched Bothered and Bewildered," Sasha's face lit up, and her eyes got teary. "There is only one place for you to go," she concluded.

Once I knew where I was going, for a moment I felt overwhelmed with sadness at having lost Grandma's dress, because this would have been the perfect occasion to wear it. But I made myself get over it. I was about to vault from obscurity to stardom, and I was doing it without Grandma's dress. I guessed I wasn't cursed after all. I would find my power in another outfit—and I knew exactly which one.

It was one of my gifts from Celestine, of course, a Narciso Rodriguez stretch cashmere suit, all in black except with a white stripe down each sleeve. The sleeves were three-quarter length and the skirt went to midcalf. The skintight jacket had a long zipper down the front, which was fairly provocative, considering that I was wearing absolutely nothing underneath it, and the skirt fit my hips like there was no skirt there at all, just my hips.

I put on a pair of black Vuitton pumps, also from Celestine, and looked in the mirror. The stylish creature I saw there looked classic, timeless, sophisticated, and very, very sexy. Dangerous, even. And she was me. I looked like a star.

Sasha the concierge almost wept for joy when she saw me. She said it was the perfect outfit for going to see Michael Feinstein, who, according to her, is simply the most wonderful cabaret singer on the planet. She told me the nice people at Fox News were taking care of the sixty-dollar cover charge and my bar tab, then she escorted me out to the Hummer. The driver took me to the very posh-looking Regency Hotel, and told me he would be waiting when the show let out.

I was seated at a perfect little table, all by myself. I didn't have a date, and I didn't care. I was wearing a perfect outfit. I was about to hear the perfect cabaret singer perform the perfect old songs my Grandma and I both always loved. I was in a perfect, expensive setting, surrounded by perfect, expensive people. I ordered myself a perfect martini, even if I don't particularly care for gin, and drank half of it right down as proof of my sophistication.

Then Michael Feinstein sat down at the piano, and started to play and sing. He was handsome and elegant, and when he sang his voice was to your ears what silk feels like against your bare skin.

So this is New York, I thought. *I absolutely, positively belong here.*

I drank the rest of my perfect martini and ordered another one. The perfect waiter brought it out immediately. Michael Feinstein was just segueing from "Embraceable You" to "But Not for Me." Something about the song made me think of Josh Thomas. *Not for me, indeed.* I raised my martini glass, made a silent toast, and drank down half of the second martini.

I still had my glass raised when I noticed a man sitting across the room. He was quite a lot older than me, probably forty. He wore frameless glasses and a very expensive-looking suit. He was looking right at me, smiling, and he had his own glass raised, as if joining in my toast. Which I thought was rather presumptuous of him, since it was my own private toast, not his. I downed the rest of my drink, set my glass on the table, and looked away. Fortunately, Michael

Feinstein started to sing "They Can't Take That Away from Me," so I quickly forgot about the man in the suit.

At least, until the waiter approached and whispered, "The gentleman would like to buy you a drink." The man in the suit gave me a little wave with his fingers.

"No thank you." You would think that in New York, a girl could enjoy Michael Feinstein without having to fend off unwanted advances from much older men. *Yuck.* I turned my attention back to the song, and tried to reconnect with the perfection of the moment.

The perfection only lasted about thirty seconds. That was how long it took the man in the suit to march across the room and park himself in front of me. I guess he thought I was going to ask him to sit down, but I didn't, so he just stood there, blocking my view.

"I bought you a drink," he announced pointlessly. He was holding a tall tropical-drink glass filled with something slushy and red. I wondered, *Who orders frozen fruity drinks in such a sophisticated setting?*

"No thank you." I was repeating myself. I leaned to one side, trying to look past the man, hoping he would figure out quickly that he wasn't wanted. He didn't budge.

"Excuse me, sir," said an elegantly dressed woman at the table behind mine. "We can't see."

"I'm talking to the young lady," he said.

"No he's not," I assured the woman.

"C'mon, buddy," complained a man at the next table.

"Buzz off," said the expensive suit.

"Down in front, asshole," croaked an extremely distinguished-looking older gentleman.

I guess that got my unwelcome suitor's attention. He whipped around to find the source of the insult. Unfortunately for me, he apparently forgot he was holding a big tall fruity frozen drink. When he whipped around, he splashed it all over my perfect sophisticated Narciso Rodriguez outfit.

It was a strawberry margarita, in case you were wondering. Most of it landed in my lap, but enough splattered onto my left arm that what had been a white stripe was now bright berry red.

Needless to say, my perfect moment was shattered. Suddenly my biggest concerns were getting out of my margarita-drenched outfit and getting it into the hands of a cleaning professional before the suit was ruined forever. Both of which meant I had to get back to the hotel as fast as possible. So I got up and headed for the door. On my way there, I swear I saw Michael Feinstein cast me a sympathetic glance.

I wished I didn't have to leave. Because he was wonderful. Better than wonderful: He was perfect. But I was soaked, and sticky, and I could feel the stain setting in with every second that passed.

I reached the door, but the tuxedoed maître d' blocked my way. "Excuse me, miss."

I figured he was going to offer to pay for my ruined outfit. So I said, "I'll just have the hotel send you the dry-cleaning bill."

"Did our waiter spill the drink on you?"

"No."

"Then I hardly see how it's our responsibility." He handed me a black folder. The type that restaurants use to give you the check. "But this is *your* responsibility."

I looked at it. Sixty dollars for the cover charge. Plus the two drinks, which were not as expensive as the Lemon Charlies at the Ritz, but still plenty expensive. Plus tax.

"I guess you haven't heard. Fox News is paying my bill."

He hadn't heard.

At my urging, he called my hotel. Sasha was gone for the night, and nobody there knew anything about it. I thought about calling Reed, but realized I didn't have his number with me, and besides, he was off on a crisis. I didn't have time to think about that, though, because I was having my own crisis. I did a quick inventory in my head: cash, none; Visa ATM card, frozen; MasterCard, credit limit exceeded.

"I guess you're going to have to trust me," I said.

"No, I'm not." The maître d' scowled, then looked over his shoulder, probably searching for the burly enforcer who would haul me off to the kitchen to wash $97.43 worth of dishes.

That is when I made a break for it.

48

I sprinted out of the cabaret, clattered across the stone floor of the lobby, and spun through the revolving door to the sidewalk. I glanced right, then left, but the Fox News Hummer was nowhere to be seen.

"Stop!" I looked behind me and saw the maître d' approaching on the run.

I bolted toward the corner, saw that the light was green, ran across the street as fast as I could, and kept running when I got to the other side. You might not think it is possible to run very fast in Vuitton high heels, but when you are highly motivated, I guess anything is possible. When I looked over my shoulder, I saw that the maître d' had given up chasing me after half a block.

Maybe I shouldn't have been running and looking over my shoulder at the same time. The two martinis probably didn't help, either. Whatever the reason, though, all of a sudden I was falling. I landed on my butt and skidded across the concrete pavement. *Ouch.*

Several people saw me fall. Nobody helped me up. "Thanks a lot," I said to no one in particular. Painfully, I stood up.

And immediately almost fell again. The heel of my right shoe had broken clean off. "Shit." I weighed my options—walk the streets of New York barefoot, or deal with a four-and-a-half-inch height differential. Reluctantly, I took off the other shoe. Then I rubbed the point of impact on my butt, and found that the sidewalk had scuffed a hole in my skirt. A big hole. "Shit fuck." Pardon my French.

I walked to the corner and found myself at the intersection of Lexington Avenue and Sixty-first Street. Which meant absolutely nothing to me. I knew from the Hummer ride to the Regency Hotel that we had traveled quite a distance, probably several miles, but I had no idea how to get back to the Tribeca Grand.

A very old woman walking a very old poodle tottered toward me. "Excuse me," I said. "How do I get to Tribeca?"

"Take the subway!" she shouted, and kept walking. I don't know if she shouted because she was hard of hearing, or just mean.

"Where's the subway?" I called toward the woman's back. She never stopped, just pointed behind her.

I tried to find a bright side to my situation. It wasn't easy. "Could be worse," I finally said out loud. "Could be raining."

That is when it started to rain.

Correction: That is when it started to *pour.*

Just like Paris. Although at least there I had an umbrella. I wondered if I was destined to get poured on in big cities for the rest of my life.

Maybe it's Grandma's dress, I thought. *Maybe I really* am *cursed.*

Cursed or not, I couldn't just stand there, so I started walking. I walked seven blocks, all the way to Sixty-eighth Street. They were short blocks, but by the time I reached the subway station I was utterly soaked. I must have looked like a drowned rat: a bruised, shoeless, margarita-stained, butt-scuffed drowned rat.

I found an entrance marked DOWNTOWN, and hobbled down the stairs. I spotted the token booth, and wondered for an instant what I was going to use to pay for the fare. Maybe, just maybe, my credit card had enough room for a two-dollar charge. I needn't have wondered, though, because the booth was empty.

I think that is when I started to cry.

"Excuse me." I jumped at the voice behind me. I turned around and found myself face-to-face with a very dirty homeless man. Actually, he looked quite a bit like Gerard Duclos had, the first time I saw him. "I think you need this more than I do." The man handed me a yellow plastic card that said METROCARD. He even showed me how to swipe it through the reader and push through the turnstile. When I was through, I tried to hand it back to him between the bars. "Keep it," he said. "You may need it."

Oh God I hope not. "Thank you." I sniffled.

I shivered alone on the platform for fifteen minutes that felt like forever. Finally a train with a big green number six on the front roared into the station. The doors dinged open and I stepped inside. There were only a few riders, but the nearest ones took a look at me and scooted to the farthest reaches of the subway car.

I wasn't at all sure where I was going. Finally, though, the train barreled into a station where CANAL STREET was spelled out on the walls in black-and-white tiles. I remembered that I had crossed Canal Street to get to Soho, so I dashed out of the train and up the stairs.

Needless to say, it was still raining.

After being totally ignored by the first six people I asked for directions, a nice young man with multiple facial piercings told me how to find the Tribeca Grand. I limped to the hotel and dripped my way across the lobby. The black-attired woman behind the front desk looked at me with amazement.

"Do not even ask," I warned, and marched straight to the elevator.

Up in my room, I peeled off the Narciso Rodriguez suit. It was a total loss. I tossed it into the trash. Then I did my best to scrub the scum of New York off my poor feet. I toweled down, bundled myself into the plushy white bathrobe, crawled into bed, and turned off the light.

I thought about everything I had lost in the past week. Grandma's dress, of course, but so much more. The dangerous Narciso Rodriguez suit and Vuitton pumps that Celestine had given me. Two jobs—probably three, if you counted Uncle John. My credit rating. And Josh.

As for Reed, and Fox News, who was I kidding? I was Miss Nobody from nowhere. Bertie Thorn already didn't like me. Once

Reed got to know me, he probably wouldn't like me, either. And plainly, New York *hated* me.

My problem wasn't a curse imposed by the fashion gods. My problem was me. I had been deluding myself. I was never going to be a star. I was never going to be anything.

At that moment, I felt more alone than I ever have in my entire life. I wished I was back in my lumpy old bed in Kirland, Indiana.

I sobbed myself to sleep.

49

That night, while I slept, I was *not* visited by my Grandma's ghost.

I tell you that because the fact is, a lot of people in Kirland actually believe in ghosts. People who are otherwise quite ordinary and sane, even including some members of my immediate family who I will not name to spare them the potential embarrassment. But when people in Kirland dream about a dead person, they inevitably swear it was a ghost.

I harbor no such illusions. I simply dreamed about Grandma.

She was sitting at the foot of my bed, right there in the Tribeca Grand. She looked around and said, "Nice room."

"You can see!" It was a big deal, because as I told you, Grandma was legally blind for years and years before she died.

"Stop changing the subject," Grandma commanded. "The subject is you."

I figured she was talking about what I had done. "I'm sorry I lost your dress."

"Don't worry about the dress. Good dresses take care of themselves. Especially the dangerous ones." She smiled, as if remembering something naughty.

"I just feel like everything is falling apart."

"Oh, no." She shook her head wisely. "Everything is coming together. You just have to let it happen." Then she frowned. "But first you have to stop worrying so much about every little thing. *I found this dress. I lost that dress. Josh kissed me. Reed didn't kiss me.* Those are all *details.* Quit fretting about the details, and get on with living."

"But what if I make a mistake?"

"You've made lots of mistakes."

"Thanks a lot."

"Well, you have. But you're supposed to make mistakes. You're young. You have to take chances. Don't you remember that paper you wrote? All those things you hoped my dangerous dress and I did?"

"Of course."

"Well, we did them all." She laughed out loud. "And then some. Made mistakes, too. Some real doozies. But looking back, the differences between the right choices and the wrong choices don't seem to matter much. The point is that it was all an adventure. *My* adventure. I lived it. And I wouldn't change a thing." She stood up. "Now it's your turn."

"My turn?"

"Why do you think I left you the dress? You've always been raring to go—you just needed a kick in the pants to get you started. And you've done fine so far. Only you can't stop halfway. It's all out there waiting for you. So quit feeling sorry for yourself and get on with it!"

At that moment, a fire truck screamed by on the street outside the hotel, waking me up. And, of course, Grandma wasn't there at all. It was just a dream.

Don't you think?

Even though I had fallen asleep at the very bottom of the pit of despair, I woke up feeling great. My confidence was back. I would win Reed's heart, Bertie's confidence, and Fox's viewers. My butt wasn't even sore where I had landed on it.

So, dream or ghost, thanks, Grandma.

I had room service send up a yummy waffle with fresh strawberries and whipped cream I just knew somebody actually whipped that morning, instead of squirting it out of a can. And a big pot of coffee. While I ate, I turned on the TV and went looking for Fox News. I figured I still had time to do a little quick research. When I switched to the channel the directory told me was Fox News, though, I found a *Simpsons* rerun. Which was actually pretty engaging, and put me in an even better mood.

When I arrived at the studio, I was sent back to the room where I'd met Bertie Thorn the day before. Bertie was alone, without Reed. I thought she was wearing a different suit, but I had to look twice to be sure. And her hair and makeup were exactly the same, like she stamped herself out of a mold every morning.

I was about to ask about Reed when he walked in. He was smiling broadly, and he gave me a hug. An ambiguous hug, somewhere in between a producer hug and a boyfriend hug. Then I noticed Bertie glaring at Reed. He noticed her too, and the hug turned entirely professional. *Thanks a lot, Bertie.*

"How's my star?" Reed asked, still flashing his Labrador grin.

Okay reminding me about that star thing was probably a pretty good move on his part. Because I kind of softened up. I might've even giggled a little when I said, "Fine."

"Good," he said. Then he sat down, and as soon as he was in his chair he was all business. "You've already met Bertie."

"Uh-huh."

"She's my associate producer," he said.

"She told me," I said.

"Bertie is short for Roberta," he said, "but never call her that." He and Bertie laughed like there was some joke I wasn't in on. It hadn't sounded so funny when Bertie said the same thing the day before.

"I won't call her that," I said. "So how's your crisis?"

"What crisis?" Reed asked.

"*Your* crisis."

"Oh," he said. "Fine."

"All resolved?"

"All resolved." Clearly he didn't want to talk about it. Well excuse me. But he did dump me just as we'd been about to become more than associates. I thought it was perfectly fair for me to ask. I guess he didn't agree. "Can we get back to business?" he asked.

"Sure."

"Bertie wants to develop your backstory."

I must have looked puzzled. "It's a movie term," Bertie said. "It means things that happened in a character's life before the start of the film but are still relevant to the story."

"But we're not making a movie," I said.

"Every medium is storytelling," Reed explained. "Whether it's movies or TV news. The audience has to care about you even before they've met you. So we need to tell them your story."

Bertie flipped open a notebook computer that was as thin as a restaurant menu. "What did you do before you went to Europe?"

"I worked at a bank," I said. "Actually, a savings and loan."

Bertie typed. Fast. Her fingers on the keys sounded like hail hitting a car roof.

Reed looked at Bertie. "Savings and loan is better," he said, and she nodded yes.

Without looking up, she asked, "What's the name of the savings and loan?"

"Independence. Independence Savings and Loan Association of Northwest Indiana."

"Can you believe that?" Reed asked Bertie.

"Amazing," Bertie said. They were both smiling. "Job title?"

"Deputy vice president."

"Nice," said Bertie.

In case you're wondering, that really is my title. Uncle John said he felt bad he couldn't pay me a lot, but he could make up for it by giving me a nice title. I don't believe that, though. I don't believe he felt bad about not paying me a lot. But I didn't mention that.

"Current status?"

To which I didn't say anything.

Bertie looked up from her keyboard. "Current job status?"

"I'm . . . on a break."

"What does that mean?" Bertie asked.

"It's complicated," I said.

"Let it go," Reed said.

"We really shouldn't," Bertie said.

"You'll think of some happy way to say it," Reed told her in no uncertain terms.

Then I told Bertie my story. Not in anything like the detail I've given you, but in considerably more detail than the *Reader's Digest* version I told Reed back in Paris. By the way, I told them the real name of Reliable Pictures. Reed said they wouldn't use that name because the conglomerates that own Reliable and Fox News are competitors, and the last thing anybody needed was a lawsuit. Reed giggled when I told how Nathalie took off her clothes in front of everybody, and Bertie blushed, plus she glared at Reed, although she typed it all down.

"That's a future segment for sure," Reed said. "Hollywood's moral cesspool."

"Actually it was kind of a joint-venture thing between the French and Hollywood," I said.

"Hollywood and France's moral cesspool," Reed said. Bertie nodded and typed.

When I started talking about Armani Collezioni, Reed said, "Just call it Giorgio Armani." Finally we got to the part about George, his girlfriend, the dress, and me getting fired. I started to explain that George worked for the State Department, and he wanted to buy his girlfriend a dress for this formal dinner with Jacques Chirac. Only when I said that, Reed frowned. When Bertie saw Reed frowning, she stopped typing.

"Let's leave that part out," Reed said.

"Which part?" I asked.

"The State Department thing," Bertie said. "He was just a

misguided American citizen." She started typing again. "Blinded by the overpriced glitz and flash of Euro-chic."

"Oh, that's good," said Reed.

"He was an asshole," I said.

Bertie stopped typing again. "We don't want to say that."

"We don't?" I couldn't see why not. I mean maybe we couldn't say *asshole* on TV. Although as I recall, they used to say it on *NYPD Blue*. But surely we could convey the concept.

"We don't want your fellow American to come across as the villain," Reed said. "There are much bigger fish to fry." Then he laughed. "But of course you know that."

I laughed too. Even though I had no clue what he meant, or what was so funny. I felt safer acting like I was in on the joke. Plus it made Reed happy that I laughed.

"So get this," he said to Bertie. "Jane tries to tell the man he's making a big mistake; he's going to humiliate himself spending all that money and having his girlfriend wear that dress."

"Fantastic," Bertie said, her fingers flying.

I actually thought Reed did a pretty good job of telling it, considering he wasn't there. Of course, he left out the whole tit thing, but apparently you still have to be quite delicate about what you say on TV.

"So the man spent a fortune, bought the dress—then he and his girlfriend were humiliated, just like Jane tried to tell them they would be. When he came back to Armani to complain, they needed a scapegoat, so poor Jane got fired."

"That's the part Reed saw," I said.

"He did?" asked Bertie.

"He did," I said. "He was in the store."

Bertie turned to Reed. "You were in Giorgio Armani?"

"Armani Collezioni," I said.

"Stick to Giorgio Armani," Reed said to me. "We don't want to confuse people."

"What were you doing in Giorgio Armani?" Bertie asked Reed.

"He was buying a tie," I said.

Bertie recoiled as if somebody had slapped her. Her head snapped around and she looked at me. Then her head snapped back and she looked at Reed. "You weren't," Bertie said to Reed.

"I wasn't," Reed said.

"You wouldn't," Bertie said.

"I wouldn't," Reed said.

"Then what were you doing in the store?" Bertie asked.

"I was . . . location scouting," Reed said.

"You sure looked like you were buying a tie," I said to Reed.

"He was *location scouting,*" Bertie said to me. The way she hissed when she said *scouting,* I could tell that this discussion was over. Then she turned back to Reed, and smiled like her body had suddenly become possessed by a really happy demon. "Where were we?"

"Poor Jane got fired," Reed said.

"You poor girl," the sweet demon inhabiting Bertie Thorn's body said to me. She didn't actually sound all that sympathetic. Then she stopped typing.

"I think we've got it," Reed said.

"Are we done?" I asked. I was tired. I had been talking, Reed had been listening, and Bertie had been typing, for more than three hours.

Reed said he was done, but Bertie and I were not. He told me Bertie was the best, and she would take care of me. "Because you're my star," he said. He smiled, and I smiled. He gave me another hug that was somewhere between professional and personal, and left the room.

Leaving me all alone with Bertie Thorn.

50

Bertie Thorn did not say anything. For quite a while.

It was probably only about thirty seconds. A minute, max. But at the time it felt like we sat there in silence for an hour. She finally said, "So."

"So," I said.

Then she said nothing for a while.

So it was totally out of the blue when she said, "He likes you, you know."

"I'm sorry?"

"Reed," she said. "He likes you. Quite a lot."

"No he doesn't," I lied. Despite Reed's poor judgment, bad timing, and ambiguous hugs, I was pretty confident that he did in fact like me. Quite a lot. Which as I have said was fine with me. But agreeing with Bertie on this issue didn't seem like a good idea.

"Of course he does," Bertie said. "You're perfect." She narrowed her eyes and looked at me. "Aren't you afraid?"

"Of Reed?"

"No, silly. Of going on camera. In front of millions of people." She appeared to shiver slightly before straightening up in her chair. "We're watched by more people than CNN, you know."

I didn't know. And up until that moment, I had not actually focused on how many people might be watching. Now I thought about it. "No, I'm not afraid," I finally said. Which was true. It did not scare me. I don't know why, it just didn't.

"Being on camera scared *me,*" Bertie said.

"You?"

"Me," Bertie said. "You don't know what I'm talking about, do you."

"Know what?"

"About me," she said. "And Reed."

"No."

"I was you," she said. "I mean, I was supposed to be. Reed was grooming me to be Fox News's next big star. A fresh American voice with a point of view."

Hey, I wanted to say, *wait a minute. That's not you, that's me.* But she was still talking.

"The whole time we were getting ready for my debut, Reed and I were . . . together." She blushed. Full-on blushed, like somebody splashed bright red paint across her cheeks. Some people blush attractively. Like Reed, for example. Bertie Thorn does not.

"What happened?" I asked.

"I froze. On camera. I couldn't do it. I knew exactly what I wanted to say. But I couldn't make the words come out of my mouth. On live TV." Her eyes seemed to have sunk back into their sockets. "It was a disaster."

"I won't do that," I said. Meaning *I'm assuring you, associate producer of Fox News, that I will not freeze on your show.* I honestly do not think I was trying to rub my relationship with Reed in his ex-girlfriend's face. But she didn't hear it that way.

"No," she said, "I bet you won't freeze." She thought for a second, as if making some very important decision. Finally she said, "He went fly-fishing."

"What?"

"Reed. That was the crisis. He stood you up to go fly-fishing."

"Fly-fishing?"

"With Dick Cheney. Reed's been expecting the invitation for weeks. You couldn't expect him to pass it up when the call finally came." She looked at me as if she was defying me to question Reed's priorities.

"Fly-fishing," I said.

"Uh-huh," Bertie said.

I just sat there for a minute. I wanted to tell her she was a miserable petty jealous bloodsucker with low self-esteem and no fashion sense. Instead I asked, "Are we done?"

"We're done," Bertie said. "Let's get you back to the hotel. And no late nights," she warned. "You have an early call."

"How early?" I asked.

"Five."

"Five A.M.?"

Bertie nodded yes.

"What time am I going on?"

"Somewhere between ten forty-five and eleven."

"What am I supposed to do for six hours?"

Bertie ticked things off on her fingers. "Hair. Makeup. Teeth whitening. Color check. Sound check. Dressing. Chair fitting." She tilted her head and looked down at me. More than a little condescendingly, I thought. "And a dozen other things that wouldn't occur to you because you've never been in the TV news business."

"But I am now," I said.

"You are now," she said.

51

For the entire Hummer ride downtown, I was more than a little—excuse me—pissed off about having to get up so early. Also puzzled about Reed denying that he bought the Armani tie. Not to mention creeped out by the whole Reed-Bertie thing—how she was supposed to have been Reed's fresh new voice, which seemed to mean that I was now her, at least professionally.

A theory started to form in my head. I tried to stop it, because it wasn't a very pleasant theory, but it moved right in and made itself at home anyway.

Reed was a climber. To be more precise, a dating climber. Most dating climbers are looking for obvious things—always trying to trade up to the prettier girlfriend, the richer boyfriend. But Reed's climb wasn't about looks, or money, or—sigh—even about sex. He was all about, well . . . *Fox News.* How much would it boost his career to find a fresh new American voice? How high would his stock soar if he single-handedly delivered that elusive female eighteen-to-thirty-five demographic? And just how many Bertie Thorns had been his stepping-stones on the way up? Reed's hugs would stay ambiguous until he was sure about me. Sure I was good for his job. Good for The Network.

Falling asleep that night, and waking up grossly early the next morning, I tried to talk myself out of it. Back at the Fox News studios, while we did all those things Bertie had said we would, I worked hard to convince myself. After all, I reasoned, Reed wouldn't go to the trouble of having them whiten my teeth unless he really liked me for me. Right?

Most of all, I reminded myself that Reed had assigned his best investigative team to find Grandma's dress. That counted for a lot. So maybe I was wrong. Maybe he wasn't a dating climber after all.

I wondered if they had found the dress. Forgive me, that question should have occurred to me before, but only a couple of days had passed, during which, as I have described to you, I'd been distracted. Plus, I had started to believe that losing Grandma's dress hadn't cursed me after all, it had set me on my very own path, maybe for the first time in my life. Everything really was coming together, like she said in my dream.

Still, if Reed's team could find the dress, that would make everything just about perfect. So I made a mental note to ask him. Then I turned my mind back to the serious business of preparing for my big debut.

After hair and makeup, I looked in the mirror again. And I thought, *You know, maybe* I do *look a little like Scarlett Johansson.* Okay, a very little. But even wearing the not-so-exciting blue cotton sweater, tan khakis, and brown loafers that Reed chose, I looked nice. And I had to hand it to them: If they wanted Midwestern, they got it. I could've been any girl from Indiana, or Wisconsin, or Ohio, or wherever. Only prettier. If I do say so myself.

Did I mention I had my own dressing room? It was not big, but it was clean, and cozy, and I did not have to share it with anybody. It was all mine.

At around ten thirty, there was a knock on the door. "It's me," Reed said.

I told him to come in. It was the first time I had seen him all morning. He gave me another mixed-message hug and told me I looked great. I almost asked how the fishing was. But I didn't. That would have been unprofessional. And petty. A star should be above such things.

Reed asked me if I was ready. I said I was.

"I really think you're *the one,*" he proclaimed. He said it so solemnly, you'd have thought I was Neo in *The Matrix* or something. He was confirming my theory, but I had to be sure.

I flung my arms around his waist and looked into his eyes as enticingly as I could. "Kiss me," I said.

"Makeup," he said.

"Makeup?"

Gently but firmly, he pushed me away. "You've already been to makeup. Better wait till later." He flashed a killer smile. "Let's see how your debut goes. We can celebrate after." Then he looked at his watch. His smile vanished, and he was all business. "You'd better go to the bathroom."

"I'm fine."

"Once we go to the set, there are no potty breaks."

"I'm really fine."

"Nothing looks worse on TV than a commentator who can't sit still because she needs to pee," Reed said. I went to the ladies' room and peed.

When I came out, Bertie was in my dressing room too, standing next to Reed. I wondered again how many fresh new voices had come before her.

"Once we get on the set, you have to be completely quiet," Bertie said.

"Of course."

"You'll probably go on about ten fifty. Michael will come out of the break at the forty-five and do two short segments. Then there's a sixty-second commercial. We'll move your chair out while that's airing, get you positioned, confirm your sound is on, and then we're ready."

"That's it?"

"That's it."

"Do I have to look anyplace special?"

"We want you to look natural," Bertie said. "Just talk to Michael like you're having a conversation, and one of the cameras will capture it."

"If you're about to make a really dramatic point, you can look straight at the camera where the red light is on," Reed offered.

"Let's not get too advanced our first time out," Bertie said. She was praying so hard I would fail, I'm surprised she didn't cross herself.

"She can handle it," Reed said, and gave my shoulders a little squeeze.

Climber. That's what popped into my head. Still, I gave him a look that I hoped he and Bertie took as affectionate.

"Fine," said Bertie. She gave Reed a look that I am pretty sure she hoped he took as a death ray.

We walked down a long corridor to a large heavy door. A red light was twirling over the door. Bertie put her forefinger to her lips. I nodded. She pulled open the door, and the three of us stepped into a little room that was like an airlock. Bertie closed the door, which was padded around the edges so it wouldn't make any noise. I looked at Reed, then at Bertie. Bertie looked at Reed, then at me. Reed looked at me. Then Bertie. Then me again.

"Did they find it?" I asked Reed in a whisper.

"Who?"

"Your best investigative team. Did they find it?"

Reed looked at Bertie. She didn't have a clue. He looked back at me. He didn't have a clue either. "Find what?"

Reed had never assigned anybody to find Grandma's dress. He had never meant to. It had all been a lie to get me to do what he wanted.

"Never mind," I said.

"It's time," Bertie commanded.

I remembered my dream. *Take chances,* Grandma told me.

I knew what I had to do.

On the other side of the airlock there was another heavy door. Bertie pulled that one open, and we were on the set.

52

TV sets are funny places. There is the part that you see. Which may look like a newsroom, which is what you see on prime-time news, or like somebody's living room, which is what you see on, say, *Good Morning America.* Then there is the part that you don't see, which looks nothing whatsoever like the part you see. It is unfurnished, except for a couple of folding canvas director chairs where people like Reed sit. I got one, too. But that's over on the side. Most of the big space is filled with cameras on wheels, and cameramen, and cables and lights and microphones, and about sixty men and women who I suppose are responsible for all the things you don't see that go into putting a live news show on the air.

The on-camera part of this particular set resembled an old-fashioned office. The oak desk where the host of the segment sat looked like an antique, and there were a couple of framed Norman Rockwell prints on the wall. Sitting behind the desk was a good-looking man who was probably about forty years old, wearing a navy-blue suit, a white shirt, and a red tie. His hair was prematurely gray, but in a very attractive way. Even from across the studio, I could see he had striking blue eyes. He was saying something about taxes, although I must confess to you I really don't recall what. Because I was starting to get nervous.

Reed tapped me on the shoulder and I jumped. Honestly, if they want you to be quiet on the set, they shouldn't sneak up on you like that.

Reed pointed at the good-looking man behind the desk, and

moved his mouth in an exaggerated way. I am not a great lip-reader, and Reed is apparently not a great lip-syncher, but even I could tell he was saying *That's Michael Smith.* Well duh.

Before I knew it, it was ten forty-five. They ran about two minutes' worth of commercials while Michael Smith scooted out from behind his desk and disappeared. Probably to pee. And I thought, *Oh sure, he's the star, he gets to go pee.* Then he was back. He did a segment about a group of parents in Ohio exercising their First Amendment right of free speech by removing objectionable books like *Huckleberry Finn* and *The Princess Diaries* from the public library. Then a segment about a group of teenagers at a public high school in Texas being discriminated against for holding a campus prayer vigil in support of their Second Amendment right to bear arms. He must have used the word *heartland* at least six times in two minutes.

Ohhh, I thought. *So* this *is Fox News.*

Michael Smith talked about The Heartland as if all the issues there were simple and everybody agreed with him on everything. Trust me, I am from Kirland, Indiana, and I can tell you that even when it is not all that exciting, life in The Heartland is as complicated as anyplace else. As for everybody agreeing, let us just say that at Christmas, people in Kirland cannot even see eye-to-eye on what time to hold Midnight Mass. So hearing him go on like that reassured me that I really should carry out the plan I had formulated in the little airlock when I was with Reed and Bertie.

Then Michael Smith stopped talking, and they went to commercial again.

A man carried a chair onto the set and put it next to the oak desk. It was the chair we had picked specially for me that morning. My chair.

Reed puckered his lips and blew me a kiss. I wondered if he blew Bertie Thorn a kiss just before she went on camera and froze. Given that he was a climber *and* a liar, I bet he did. Whether he did or not, though, the kissy-face was the last straw.

I sat in my chair. Hair and makeup people came over to me and looked at my hair and face from about two inches away. "Good," they said. And, "Good." Then they disappeared.

"Sound check," said someone from back behind the cameras.

"Say something," Michael Smith said to me.

"Good morning, America," I said. I was not trying to be a smart-ass. Honest. That is just the first thing that popped into my head.

"Not funny," said Bertie. She really did not sound amused.

"Back in five," said a voice.

Then they actually counted off the seconds the way you imagine they do. The way they did in *Wayne's World*. Which, by the way, is possibly the second-best movie ever. After *Bridget Jones's Diary*. Anyway, you know. Some guy says "Five, four," and then they count down the rest just with their fingers:

three, two, one.

"Now," said Michael Smith to the camera, "we're going to be hearing from a fresh new American voice. In the weeks and months ahead, Jane Stuart is going to share her perspectives on how Hollywood has declared war on American values. On the moral cesspool of the French movie biz. We're going to hear Jane's views on everything from fashion to foreign affairs."

We were? That foreign affairs thing was news to me.

"Before we hear from her, though, let me tell you a little about Jane Stuart. She's a native daughter of Kirland, Indiana, where she's currently on sabbatical from her position as deputy vice president of the Independence Savings and Loan Association."

Sabbatical, huh? That was creative. Chalk one up for Bertie.

"Her scholarly accomplishments at Purdue University led to her being hired as a technical advisor on a big-budget Hollywood epic."

I did not use the words *big-budget, Hollywood,* or *epic.*

"The movie was being filmed on location in Paris, France"—he kind of sneered when he said *Paris, France*—"where Jane was thrown into a sexual snake pit. When she refused to play the obscene bedroom games that France demanded, she was fired."

I was starting to squirm a little. And not because I needed to pee. I really thought they were taking liberties with what I said.

"But Jane wasn't content just to uncover the dirty secrets of the international movie business. Next, she set her sights on high fashion and infiltrated the world of glamour godfather Giorgio Armani, where she attempted to expose Euro-trash corruption and price gouging."

If you ever read this, please, *please* believe me, Mister Armani, I never said any such thing.

"For trying to save an American citizen from being bilked out of his hard-earned dollars, she was summarily fired—an incident witnessed by our own Fox News producer, Reed James."

I looked at Reed. He flashed a smile and gave me a big thumbs-up with both hands. Then he blew me another kiss, and I knew what I had to do.

"Now let's hear from Jane." Michael Smith turned to me. "Hi, Jane," he said.

"Hi, Michael," I said.

"Okay," he said. "Let's set the scene. Where were you?"

"At work," I said.

"At Giorgio Armani," he said.

"Armani Collezioni," I said. Sorry. Force of habit. "In Paris."

"Paris, *France,*" Michael Smith said, sneering into the camera. "And what happened?"

"This man came in. With his girlfriend. They were both American."

"American citizens," Michael Smith said.

"They had a dinner to go to." I remembered to leave out that it was dinner with the State Department and the President of France. "The man wanted to buy his girlfriend a dress."

"Lucky girl," said Michael Smith.

I thought about telling him what I thought of stupid control freak George and how his poor doormat girlfriend wasn't so lucky. But I let it go.

"She tried on a bunch of dresses," I said. "Until finally her boyfriend picked one for her."

"And that's when you came to the rescue," Michael Smith said.

"I tried to."

"You spoke up for American consumers everywhere," Michael Smith said. "You swooped in, trying to rescue Americans blinded by the overpriced glitz and flash of Euro-chic."

"No."

Michael Smith kind of jerked back in his chair, as if somebody had grabbed the cord that connected to his earpiece and given it a good yank. "I beg your pardon?" he asked.

"It was a perfectly nice dress," I said.

"But expensive," Michael Smith said cautiously.

"Oh, yes. Very expensive."

"Exactly!" Michael Smith said. He was back on track again. "You tried to tell the American man that he was making a mistake."

"I did."

"Because he was paying a ridiculous amount for a dress with a fancy Italian name on it, when he should have been buying American, right?"

His question hung in the air like an invitation. It was time for me to set things straight.

"No," I said.

Michael Smith started twitching.

"It was a very expensive dress, but it was lovely. All the clothes there are lovely. And very well made. If you can afford them, they're worth every dollar." The whole episode came back to me, and I got mad all over again. "Although I personally want to know why a man who works for the State Department is shelling out forty-eight hundred bucks to buy his girlfriend a dress for a dinner with the French President. I hope he didn't charge that to Uncle Sam, you know?"

"You were trying to save two American citizens from humiliating themselves." Michael Smith sounded drained. His train had derailed. I could tell he was just hoping it wouldn't crash.

"I was trying to save the *woman* from humiliating herself. Because she had the dress on backward, and her tit was hanging out. Only her stupid State Department boyfriend insisted she wear it like that. On account of stupid George, she spent the whole night flashing her tit at Jacques Chirac." I looked out past the camera and squinted through the lights until I found Reed. Then I looked back at the camera and smiled at the red light. "Can you say 'tit' on TV?" I asked.

Apparently not. Because that is when they pulled the plug.

I don't know if they literally pulled a plug. But that's how it felt. The whole set went dark. I don't just mean the lights went out. I mean the power went off entirely. Microphones, cameras, everything. And there are no windows in that studio, so it was totally black.

Then the lights came back up. Only the red lights on the cameras stayed off. In fact the cameramen had stepped away from the cameras, which were now pointed down at the floor.

Oddly enough, nobody was looking at me. Not Michael Smith, not Bertie Thorn, not the cameramen, not the sixty or so people who fill a TV studio that you never see. They were all looking at Reed. Then Reed did look at me.

"You're fired," he said.

53

I will say this for Reed. He was a gentleman.

He did not yell, or curse, or break things. Most important, he kept his promise. He did not kick me out of my hotel. And he did not throw away my clothes.

He took me to a conference room near the studio. On the way to the conference room I walked past Bertie Thorn. I only caught a glimpse of her, but I could swear she was smiling.

At least *I* didn't freeze up on camera.

In the conference room, Reed didn't even ask me why I hadn't told him before what I was planning to say. Although that is hardly my fault. At least not all my fault. If you go back and look at the things I did tell him, you will see that I was doing my best to explain exactly what happened. He just never asked me certain questions. And I guess he misunderstood some of the things I said. I guess he heard things a certain way because that's how he wanted to hear them.

Plus he was a lying climber, and it served him right.

Anyway, since then, I have had a little time to think about it, and my conclusion is that I am in fact exactly what Reed said I was: a fresh new American voice with a point of view. Okay I don't know about new. But certainly fresh. And absolutely American. And I most certainly had a point of view. I just wasn't the kind of fresh new American voice with a point of view that he wanted. Which is literally what he said in that little office near the studio.

While he talked, everything started to hit me all over again.

I was proud of standing up for myself on camera, but that did not change the facts. I had lost my job three times—four, if you counted Uncle John. I had lost Josh. I had lost Reed, if I'd ever really had him. Not to mention that I had lost Grandma's dress. I wanted to cry like I had the other night, but I didn't. I just sat there and listened. Because that was what a star would do. Even if I wasn't ever going to be one, at least I could act like one for a couple more minutes.

Reed told me that in good conscience, he could not continue to charge my stay to the Fox News Corporation. So would I please go back to the hotel, pack up, and check out? Everything would be paid for by Fox News through today, but not after.

As I said, he was a total gentleman. He gave me cab fare to get to the hotel. He even gave me cab fare to the airport. Out of his own wallet. And I am willing to bet he did not submit an expense report for reimbursement.

When I said good-bye, there were no hugs or kisses. We shook hands. His big hand swallowed mine up, just like it had back in Paris. Only not just like in Paris. Not at all.

I took a taxi back to the hotel. Incidentally, I was right: If you are going to ride around in New York traffic, you will feel much safer in a Hummer than in a yellow taxi.

I went to pack my clothes. I felt another pang when I looked in the closet, where Grandma's dress should have been. Even if she had told me not to worry, I couldn't help it.

Packing only took about five minutes. After that, I knew what I had to do. What, surprisingly, I really truly wanted to do.

I picked up the room phone. I got an outside line, and dialed 0. "I'd like to make a collect call," I said. Even charging this phone call to Fox News would be taking unfair advantage. At least that's how I felt.

I called my dad at work. "I'm okay," I said straight off. Because I knew he would wonder. What with me calling collect and all.

"That's good," he said.

"Things didn't work out so well with the new job."

"Oh." That's all he said. I have no idea what he was thinking. Whatever it was, he kept it to himself. I told you, he is the least judgmental person I know. Thank you, Daddy.

"I think I need to come home," I said.

"Okay," he said. "Can you get to the airport?"

"Uh-huh."

"How soon?"

"Now."

"Okay," he said. "Go to La Guardia. United. Call me back when you get there."

"Thank you, Daddy," I said.

"As long as you're okay," he said.

"I am."

So that's what I did. Only first I took off the clothes I was wearing, because those came from the Fox News wardrobe, and I didn't feel right taking them. And they *were* pretty boring. I left them on the bed.

I put on my own clothes, picked up the Louis Vuitton carry-on and my little duffel baggy, went downstairs, and checked out. The doorman dressed all in black got a taxi for me, and I tipped him, which felt like the right thing to do even if it was with Reed's money. Then I rode to La Guardia Airport. Which is also in Queens, although it is much closer to Manhattan than JFK is. Not that I was paying much attention to Queens. I just wanted to get home.

I got to the United terminal and called my dad collect from a pay phone. He gave me a flight number. He said I was ticketed on the late flight, and wait-listed on an earlier one. I picked up the ticket. Then I went to the gate and waited. I did not get on the earlier flight. I had to wait for the eight P.M. flight. Which was scheduled to arrive at ORD, which is Chicago O'Hare International Airport—do not ask me where ORD comes from—at nine thirty-five. Only we were late pulling away from the gate, and there was a strong jet stream. We did not land at O'Hare until nearly ten thirty.

While the plane was on final descent, they announced that everyone should restow their carry-ons under the seat in front of them. I had never actually unstowed my bags. The Vuitton was in the overhead, and the duffel baggy was under the seat. But I reached down and picked up the duffel. I opened it. Inside was the little First Class toilet kit from American Airlines. Also my box of Tampax, still unopened. Do not ask me why, but I took it as a positive sign that with everything I had been through, I had not needed a tampon.

There were three other things in the duffel baggy.

Josh's script. Josh's note. And Josh's rose.

I zipped the bag and put it back under the seat.

By the way, since I have been telling you about such things in quite a lot of detail, I should mention that my seat was in the next-to-last row. In the very middle.

Which was fine.

As you probably know, in this day and age you are not supposed to be able to get to an airport gate unless you have a ticket. Don't ask me how my dad got there. Probably he found somebody who worked for the airline who was also a dad. Probably he explained how his daughter had just gone through all these traumatic experiences, and he was picking her up and bringing her home. I don't know for sure how he did it. I never asked him. But however he did it, he was there. No limo driver, no uniform, no luggage cart, no sign with my name. Just my dad. Who gave me a huge hug when I got off the plane, and then didn't say anything.

Which was perfect.

54

I got back home on a Thursday night.

Actually it was almost Friday morning, because we didn't walk into the house until a few minutes before midnight. My mom was waiting for me in the living room. After she gave me a hug, she said, "I called Uncle John and told him you wouldn't be in tomorrow."

"Do I still *have* a job?" I asked.

"I don't know," Mom said. "I think you need to ask John yourself."

Incidentally, if you are wondering why I am twenty-five and still living with my parents, the answer is simple: I had never been particularly wild about the idea of spending the rest of my life in Kirland, Indiana. Unfortunately, as I told you, Uncle John does not pay me a great deal. The only way I could save any money and have any options about what else to do and where else to go was by living at home with my parents. After my recent catastrophes, though, it seemed pretty likely that I would be stuck in Kirland forever. Where was there left to go?

I went upstairs to my room. The same room I have lived in my whole life. Except for the first six months, because until I was six months old we lived in the house on Kendall Street.

Oh sure. Now *I remember.*

I climbed into the lumpy old bed. No fancy sheets here. But I fell asleep almost instantly.

I slept late. Depression will do that to you. Then I woke up and just lay in bed for a while. Depression will do that to you, too.

Finally I got up. Mostly because I was hungry. And I smelled the bacon. Not that it takes much, but my mom makes better bacon than Celestine. Better scrambled eggs, too. Still, it wasn't the same as being back in Paris living with my best friend.

The breakfast was really good, though.

After breakfast, I wandered into the living room. My dad was sitting on his recliner. Which was odd, because it was past noon on a Friday. He should have been at work.

He stayed home in case I needed him. He didn't tell me that. But I know that's what he did. So he just reclined and read the papers. And I just sat there and drank Diet Coke.

My mom came out of the kitchen. "Dishes are done," she said.

"Thanks," I said.

Then nobody said anything. I think maybe my folks thought I was going to spill everything that had happened.

Nope.

After we sat around for a while, my mom finally got up and put a movie into the DVD player. It was *The Wizard of Oz.* Do not think for a second that I didn't get the significance. Small-town Dorothy, over the rainbow, blah blah blah, no place like home. So the fact that my mom put that movie on was frankly more than a little annoying.

On the other hand, it's a pretty engaging movie. I love the munchkins. Especially the tough guys from the Lollipop Guild. And I still think the flying monkeys are scary. In spite of myself, I guess I enjoyed watching it. At least it took my mind off things for a while.

Only then came the part near the end, after the Wizard flies away in the balloon. Glinda comes back in her big pink bubble. She says Dorothy has always had the power to go home, only Glinda didn't tell her right at the start because Dorothy wouldn't have believed her. More like if she had told Dorothy at the start, there'd be no movie. But anyway, ruby slippers, *click click click,*

No place like home. And Dorothy wakes up in bed in Kansas. In black-and-white.

"Why does she go back to black-and-white?" I asked. It was the first thing I had said since my mom put the movie in.

"Because . . . that's the movie," my mom said.

"But why would anybody voluntarily go back to black-and-white?" It actually made me quite angry. "After all the beautiful color. After the munchkins, and the yellow brick road, and Oz. Even if that is an awful lot of green. Why would she go back to black-and-white?"

"I don't know," my mom said.

"Plus now the dog dies," I said.

My dad shifted his recliner upright. "No it doesn't."

"Not in the movie," I said. "*After* the movie. Did you ever think about what happens after the movie is over? Before the twister, Auntie Em and Uncle Henry say 'We can't go against the law.' Only the law still has a warrant out to arrest Toto and have him destroyed. Why would you want to come back to a world where everything is black-and-white and they kill your dog?"

I didn't expect an answer. I didn't wait for one, either. I ran upstairs, closed the door to my room, and turned on my rickety old computer. Then I started to type.

I came downstairs for dinner. I didn't stick around, though. As soon as I finished eating, I went back upstairs and typed some more. In fact, I was up quite late typing.

The next day I got up early. I showered and fixed my hair, nothing fancy but neat, and I got dressed for work, even though it was Saturday, and I don't usually work on Saturdays, even though the bank is open. I walked over to Independence Savings. It's only a couple of blocks. Uncle John gets there at seven thirty in the morning, every day, and nobody else comes in until eight. So I knew he would be by himself. I went into his office. "I'm back," I said.

"So I hear," he said.

"I'm sorry," I said.

"So you say," he said.

"Can I have my job back?" I asked.

"I don't know," he said. "Did you lose it?"

"I don't know," I said.

"Do you want it?" he asked.

"That's why I'm here," I said.

"No," he said. "Do you *really* want it?"

"I don't know," I said.

"At least that's honest," he said.

"It is honest," I said. "I don't know. I'm twenty-five. I don't know."

He gave me a long hard look. "You can't just run off on me again," he finally said.

"Okay," I said.

"That doesn't mean I expect you to work here for the rest of your life. Maybe you will, maybe not. But you can't keep running off for some crazy scheme and leave me in the lurch."

"Okay," I said.

"Not okay," he said. "I mean it. I want you to promise."

"I promise," I said.

"Then get to work," he said. So I went back to work. And he didn't mention it again.

I have probably done an extremely imperfect job of replicating that conversation. Even though I have the words down pretty much exactly right. Because first, just the words do not convey how hard it was to walk in there and say those things. Even though he said I might not work there forever, I felt like I had just promised to do exactly that. Which was not my dream. Ever. And second, after that conversation, Uncle John did not talk to me. At all. For weeks.

Which was just as well. I had no time to talk anyway. At work I was busy catching up.

The rest of the time I was at home typing. By now you have

figured out what I was typing. This. This story, or book, or whatever it is.

I never did have that conversation my mom expected—the one where I open my mouth and out spills everything that happened. I spilled everything out here instead. Now I'm done.

Only there doesn't seem to be an ending yet.

55

So now I have this story without an ending. If that's what this is. Now what do I do?

Read it, for starters.

Well. Reading it did not make me feel better. But it did make it quite clear to me that I miss two people. I miss Celestine very much. Even before I went to Paris, I missed having my best friend from college around to share everything with. Now I miss her even more. We *do* e-mail every day. Sometimes I call her, or she calls me, but it's hard with the time difference, not to mention that calling France is expensive and as you know, Uncle John doesn't pay me much.

And I miss Josh. You probably already knew that. But I didn't for the longest time.

I didn't even have it figured out while I was writing this. Now that I've read the whole thing, though, I realize I miss him terribly. Profoundly. And I feel so bad. Even with what he did to me. Even with Grandma's dress. Do not think I have forgiven him. I haven't. How could I? But if he could do something that bad to me and I still miss him the way I do, that must really mean something. Something important.

So I got this crazy idea. I dug out his script. His address was on the cover page. Mind you, it does not say that *the* address is *his* address. But, I mean, who else's address would it be?

I called directory assistance and got the number for the only

Josh Thomas listed in New York, NY. It took me two days, but finally I got up the nerve and called. Only it wasn't Josh. I mean, it was *a* Josh, but not *the* Josh. Not *my* Josh. So all I had was this address.

I printed out a copy of what I wrote. Then I mailed it. To Josh Thomas. At the address on his screenplay.

Let me tell you why I did it. After I finished reading my story, I read Josh's screenplay one more time. How Harold and Catherine managed to find each other again, even if took them till they were ninety years old to do it. I did not know if Josh Thomas was my Harold and I was his Catherine. But I thought just maybe. I knew for sure that I had all these complicated, very intense, very unresolved feelings for him. I did not want to wait till I was ninety to resolve them.

I also took out Josh's rose. By now it was dry and faded, and it had gotten a little crunched along the way. But I was awfully glad I had saved it.

Finally I took out the note Josh wrote when he left me that rose. I read it. It said:

> *You are wonderful. Whereas I am a stupid jerk. I am also very, very sorry. Dinner at La Tour d'Argent? My treat. (I promise.)*
> *Josh.*
> *P.S. I know another spot where the lights are even prettier.*

He promised to treat me to dinner again. He *promised.* And he believes that making a promise has to count for something. And so do I. So I mailed it.

The next day I was sorry I did. Besides my being responsible for Reed's hitting him, Josh's movie didn't get made, would never get made, all on account of me. Which made me think he must hate me. Worse than hate me. I don't know what worse than hate is, but

I was convinced he felt it. And why would you read something written by someone you worse than hated, much less want to discuss it with them? Sorry or not, though, all I could do was hope that I was wrong and I would hear from him. So I waited. And waiting is hard. Very hard.

I guess when you're waiting for something that probably won't ever happen, it helps pass the time if you distract yourself with interesting things. However, because I still live in Kirland, there are not a ton of interesting things to distract me.

In fairness, one interesting thing did happen while I was waiting. Dave Stankowski, the baseball coach at Roger Wells Kent High School for as long as anybody could remember, died. With all due respect to Dave and, more important, to Dave's widow, the fact that Dave died is not the interesting part.

I never really knew Dave. But his wife Rose and my aunt Rose were really good friends, before my aunt Rose died. So I went to the viewing over at Saban Funeral Parlor, which is right across from Independence Savings. I didn't stay long. Just long enough to tell Dave's wife I was sorry. Then I crossed the street to the bank and went back to work.

A bunch of Dave's former baseball players came back for the funeral, and they formed a procession down One Hundred and Nineteenth Street, behind the hearse. When it pulled out of the funeral home, the police held up traffic on Indianapolis Boulevard.

Now here's the interesting part. All the old baseball players had brought black umbrellas with them. Even though it was a bright sunny day. When the hearse pulled out, they all put up their black umbrellas. Like at a funeral in New Orleans. Only instead of singing "When the Saints Go Marching In," they sang "Take Me Out to the Ball Game." I am not kidding.

I stood in the doorway of the bank and watched, since I didn't have to worry about not being at my desk. Dave Stankowski had been a veteran, and Uncle John was part of the American Legion honor guard, so I knew that after the funeral he'd be going to the cemetery.

I will admit the parade was interesting. But it was the *only* interesting thing that happened. So all I had was Kirland, my crummy bank job, and waiting to hear from a man who worse than hated me.

56

Northwest Indiana can get quite hot in June. Humid, too.

When I was growing up, my parents did not have AC. Now they do, which makes life much better. But when the weather turns steamy, the comfort of the house discourages you from going out and doing anything whatsoever unless you absolutely have to.

On Saturdays, I don't absolutely have to do anything.

It was a Saturday in June. It was hot and humid and disgusting outside. I was inside, lying around, watching my dad surf channels on the remote. He may be wonderfully nonjudgmental, but my dad is still a man, and he cannot sit still on a channel for a tenth of a second.

Watching my dad channel surf was not my idea of exciting, but it was better than what I had to do that night. I had to go to Reinhardt's restaurant and chaperone the Roger Wells Kent High School senior prom. Generally speaking, the only people who get stuck chaperoning the senior prom are parents, which I am not, and faculty, which I also am not. Here is how I landed in this particularly unfair position.

My cousin Mary's best friend is Helen Klosek. They grew up together, went to Indiana University together, studied to be teachers together, and moved back to Kirland together. Helen teaches history at Kent High School, so she had to sign up to chaperone the prom. At the last minute, though, Dave Hruska, who is the head of the meat department at Sterk's market, asked Helen to marry him. Helen has only been waiting for Dave to propose for about nine years, so she said yes. He insisted they get married immediately and go on their honeymoon. Nobody knows why all of a sudden Dave was in such a rush, but after nine years Helen was not taking any chances. So she said yes, they got married, and off they went to Aruba.

Before they left, Helen asked if Mary would chaperone the prom for her. Since Helen is her best friend, Mary said okay. Only Friday afternoon, she came home from work with a hundred-and-two fever. So she begged me to take over for her.

I had to say yes. But I hated the idea.

I did not enjoy my own prom, which was also at Reinhardt's. Because that is where the Kent High School senior prom is always held. The boy I wanted to go with did not ask me. The boy who asked me, I did not want to go with. But I went, because it was my high school prom. And how do you not go to your high school prom? Especially in Kirland, where everybody acts like the prom is the biggest event of your life. I now know better.

Enough about my high school prom. My point is, if there is anything less exciting than going to your own Bumfuck prom, it is going to somebody else's.

At about twelve thirty, there was a knock on the door. My dad just kept flicking the remote. My mom didn't move either. Finally I said, "I'll get it."

Kirland is the sort of place where people's front doors do not have little peepholes. Not very long ago, everybody still left their doors unlocked. Nowadays they don't, but there are still no peep-holes. So it should come as no surprise that when somebody knocks, you open the door without saying "Who is it?" Because you pretty much always know who it is. It's cousin Mary and Paris, or Uncle John, or cousin Mikey, and so on. So I just opened the door.

It was Josh.

Josh Thomas.

I think he was about to say something. Only I slammed the door in his face.

I did not slam the door because I was still mad about Grandma's dress. I slammed the door because I had not expected to see him. And I had no clue what to say.

"Who is it?" Mom asked.

I still wasn't sure what I'd say to Josh, but I *was* sure I didn't want to explain the whole thing to my parents. So I opened the door, stepped onto the porch, and shut the door behind me.

"Hi," said Josh.

"You didn't call," I said.

"I thought if I called, you might have told me not to come," he said.

I didn't think that was true, but I liked that he felt insecure about me. I was about to hug him, until I thought, *Maybe he's here to tell me he worse than hates me.* So I just stood there.

Then I noticed he was holding a big shopping bag behind his back. No store logo, plain brown paper. He noticed that I noticed. He said, "I brought you something." He hesitated for a second, then handed me the bag.

Inside was something wrapped in tissue paper. "What is it?" I asked.

"It's for you," he said. Which didn't tell me anything. I unwrapped the paper bundle.

Then I gasped. I mean, literally gasped.

Because wrapped in the tissue paper was my Grandma's dress.

I do not mean a dress that looked like Grandma's. I mean, *my Grandma's dress.*

I could not speak. Which is not a natural condition for me.

"I . . . found it," he said.

I took off all the paper and held the dress up. I looked at the front. The back. The skirt. I even looked at the lining. It was perfect. I don't think there was a single bead missing.

About then is when I started to cry.

"Don't cry," he said.

Men can be so dumb sometimes. Even men who have done

incredibly thoughtful things. Impossible things. Lovely, romantic, perfect things. Sometimes they need to shut up and let a girl cry. I cried. While I was crying, very carefully, I wrapped the dress up again.

"I'm sorry it took me so long to get it to you," he said.

I put the dress back in the bag.

"It was really hard to find," he said.

That is when I kissed him. We are not just talking some little peck on the cheek here. Quite a bit of time passed, in fact. Finally I stopped kissing him. "Ohmygod," I said. Then I hugged him. With my whole body. I wanted every inch of me to touch him, so that all those complicated feelings would pass right through my skin and he would know exactly how I felt.

When I let go, he said, "Wow." I was not sure if my hug had conveyed absolutely everything I wanted it to. But I thought *wow* was a pretty good start.

Then I noticed. Well forgive me for not noticing sooner, but I was distracted. Anyway, Josh was not wearing his Astros cap. "What happened to your hat?" I asked.

"I stopped wearing it."

"The Astros aren't in the World Series," I said. It was only June, and even I know the World Series is in October.

"No," he said.

"I don't understand," I said. "I thought somebody has to stick up for lost causes."

"No matter how lost they are," he said. "I still believe that." He looked down at Grandma's dress, then back at me. "I just decided to pick a lost cause that I really cared about."

I hugged him again. For a long time. Finally I stopped hugging him. I looked at the bag again. I couldn't believe it. Josh Thomas had brought back my Grandma's dress. It was almost too good to be true. But only almost. Because it *was* true.

"How did you find it?" I asked.

We have one of those glider swings on our front porch. What

did you expect? I told you about Kirland. He sat down. I sat next to him. Then he said, "I looked for it."

I said, "Well of course you looked for it. You couldn't have found it without looking for it." That might have sounded a little bit bitchy. Which must have confused him. Especially considering the kiss I just planted on him. And those hugs. But as I said, my feelings for Josh are complicated, and it was then that I realized that some of my unresolved feelings *did* involve my being mad at him. "First you are going to tell me why on earth you told them to throw my suitcase away."

"What?"

"That big pink suitcase. Celestine and I saw you. You talked to the guy at the front desk, and then they tossed the suitcase in that old truck and took it away. Just like you told them to."

"What are you talking about? I told them *not* to."

"You did not."

"I did so."

"You did so what?"

He crinkled his brow as he spoke. "I did so . . . not . . . tell them to get rid of your stuff."

"I saw you," I said again.

"I guess you didn't hear me," he said.

Which was true. "So what? I saw what happened."

"So did I," he said. "But I didn't tell them to do that."

"And why should I believe you?"

"I brought your dress back," he said.

Which was also true. "So what were you doing there?" I asked.

"I came back to the hotel to talk to you. Only Gerard Duclos was in your room."

"He was attacking me."

"I know," Josh said. "I mean, I read what you wrote. You should have asked for help."

"You didn't wait for me to ask. Besides, I've never been attacked before. You just make it up as you go along."

"I'm really sorry," he said.

I kind of shrugged. "I guess it might have looked like something else."

"It did."

I have given that episode a lot of thought. And it has occurred to me that Josh might honestly have thought Gerard and I were . . . well, you know. Yuck.

"Anyway," Josh said, "once I finally cooled off, I decided to come talk to you."

"What were you going to say?"

"That Gerard was an old womanizing pig. That you didn't belong with him."

"Anything else?"

For a few seconds, instead of talking, Josh rocked the glider with his foot. Then he said, "That you belong with me." *Oooooohhh.* "Only I came back and you weren't there. They told me you got fired, you skipped out on your room, and they were going to get rid of your stuff."

"They did not."

"They did," he said. "So I told them that was illegal."

"You did not."

"I did," he said. "I told them I was a lawyer. They asked if I was a French lawyer. When I said no, they laughed at me. That's when I offered to pay your bill."

"You did not."

"I did," he said. "And they said no, they were instructed by Monsieur Duclos himself to dispose of your things. So they did. Right there in front of me. I'm sorry I couldn't stop them."

"Wait a second," I said. "I *did* hear you. After they threw my suitcase in that truck. You thanked the bellman. You said, 'That's great. Thank you very much.' "

"I was being sarcastic," Josh said. "You do have sarcasm here in Kirland, don't you?"

I felt like a dope. Not a total dope. If you had seen what I saw, you probably would have thought what I thought. But it turned out I was wrong. Extremely wrong. Life-alteringly wrong.

"By the way," Josh said. "About all those other Miss Fireworks?"

I think I flinched. I was afraid of what he might tell me.

"There *were* no other Miss Fireworks," he continued. "I knew the Tower sparkled, and I always wished I could find the perfect woman to kiss in the perfect spot. But I never found her. Until you." He smiled. "You were my first. And last. My only."

Searching his eyes, I knew he was telling the truth. I felt so bad for misjudging him. I wondered if he could ever forgive me. I didn't know how to ask. Fortunately, eventually Josh spoke up. "I could not believe," he said, "how many vintage clothing stores there are in Paris."

I just looked at him.

"After I read what you wrote," he said, "I went back to Paris. I found Irene. She told me they didn't throw your stuff away. They gave it to some guy to sell. To pay your room bill. I asked her for the guy's name, but she said it was no use, he had moved to Las Vegas."

"Las Vegas??"

"She said he was a big *CSI* fan." Josh shrugged. "I called directory assistance in Vegas. They never heard of him. Irene felt really bad. So she gave me her list of stores. The same list she gave you. Every store you looked at, I looked at. It took days."

I couldn't believe it. He had taken all that time and trouble. Even more amazing, he had actually found it. "Which store had it?"

"That's the funny thing," Josh said. "None of them did. So I went back to Irene. There was only one other place she could think of." He paused. "She sent me to her mother's store."

"You're kidding," I said. But I knew he wasn't. "Was Françoise still watching that TV?"

"With no sound. Yeah."

"And you had to go up the spiral staircase into that little room."

"That's where the dress was," he said.

"Funny coincidence," I said. Only I don't believe in coincidence.

"I don't think I believe in coincidence," he said. "So," he said. "Can we take a walk?"

"It's gross and disgusting and humid out," I said.

"I noticed," Josh said. "So, can we take a walk?"

I went into the house, ran upstairs, hung Grandma's dress in its spot, and ran back down.

"Is everything all right?" my dad asked.

"Yes," I said. "Everything is definitely all right."

Dad smiled at that. He doesn't say a whole lot. But he doesn't miss a whole lot, either.

57

Josh and I walked to Kirland Park, on the shore of Lake Michigan. It's an okay park, but I don't go there much. In the winter, it can be awfully cold with the wind whipping off the lake, and on a hot disgusting June day, it can be . . . well, hot and disgusting. I didn't care. It seemed even nicer than the Tuileries gardens in Paris.

"I have something else to tell you," Josh said. "And I think you're going to like it. But I'm not sure," he said. "Because it was a little presumptuous of me."

"What is it?"

"It's about what you wrote," he said. "I . . . showed it to some people."

I felt my stomach flip-flop. "That was private."

"You asked somebody to read it."

"I asked *you* to read it. I didn't say to show it to other people." We walked a little way without saying anything. "What sort of people?" I finally asked.

"My agent," he said.

I got this crazy idea. "Does somebody want to publish it?"

"No," he said. I felt . . . disappointed. Rejected, even. "They want to produce it."

"What does that mean?" I asked. I stopped walking. That flip-flop thing in my stomach really started to jump around something fierce. "Produce it, like, make a movie?"

"No," he said. "Produce it, like make a TV show."

"What???" There were no other people in sight. There were squirrels, though. I must've shrieked. Because the squirrels quit chasing one another through the trees. They stopped in their tracks and looked at me. "You're kidding. The whole Paris–New York thing?"

"No," he said. "The Bumfuck thing."

I almost said "You're kidding" again. But I didn't. Because I could tell he wasn't kidding.

Josh had shown my manuscript—which was an awfully serious word for what I had done, but I guess that's how writers talk—to his agent. Who does movies, not TV, although why one agent can't do both is beyond me. Josh's agent did not want to show it to the TV agents at his own agency, because they would take the credit and get the commissions. Which does not sound like a healthy work environment. Anyway, Josh's agent went to his health club, and this new guy started to hit on him. Which Josh's agent was in no mood for, because even though he likes guys not girls, and even though the new guy was attractive, Josh's agent just went through a bad breakup. But the new guy wouldn't leave. He said Josh's agent seemed tense, was anything wrong? Josh's agent said Besides the bad breakup I went through? The new guy said, Besides that. Josh's agent said That's very perceptive of you, Yes, I have this great TV property, only I can't show it to the TV agents at my own agency and I don't know what to do with it. The new guy said Really, can I see it? And it turns out the new guy is a hotshot TV producer.

Josh assured me that in Hollywood, deals get made like this all the time.

So Josh's agent showed my story to the new guy, who loved it, because apparently everyone in TV is desperate for programming that will appeal to Middle America.

Kirland is not the geographical center of the United States. I think that is someplace in Kansas. But trust me. Kirland is as middle as America gets.

The new guy loved the Nick Timko–cousin Mary stuff. Josh's agent set up a meeting, and Josh pitched it as a dramedy, which is a made-up Hollywood word combining *drama* and *comedy.* Like *Northern Exposure* and *Picket Fences,* he said. Neither of which I have ever seen.

And by the way, now Josh's agent and the new guy are dating.

"Can it be a reality show?" I asked Josh.

"I don't think so."

"Reality shows are very popular," I said. Not that I watch reality shows. Although the guy on the last *Bachelor* was awfully cute.

"Reality shows don't have writers," Josh said. "I'm a writer, remember?"

Oh. Well. Anyway, the new guy sold the idea to one of the networks. "As a dramedy," Josh said. "They're ready to commit to a pilot plus six episodes."

"Is that good?"

"It's amazing."

"What did you tell them?"

"I told them you have to get 'Created By' credit. And executive producer credit. And technical advisor credit." He smiled. "I also told them you're my writing partner."

Wow. "Am I?"

He took my hands in his, and it felt like his heart and my heart were beating together at exactly the same time. Maybe that was my imagination. But I hoped not. "Are you?" he asked.

That is when I kissed him again.

On the way back to the house, Josh told me they wanted to film in Kirland. Not all of it. The interiors would mostly be shot on soundstages in LA. But there would be a crew here, working half time. "So you'll still get to spend plenty of time here."

"What do you mean?" I asked.

"All those titles I gave you? Those are real jobs," Josh said. "If you're going to do this, you really have to do it. A lot of it has to be done in California." He looked around. "Not here."

That is when I remembered Uncle John. And how I promised. "I can't," I said.

58

"Because of your uncle?" Josh asked.

"How did you know that?" I hadn't said anything to Josh about Uncle John.

"I read your book, remember?"

Oh, yeah. I could see that this business of writing about myself and actually telling the truth might be complicated. "They'll still do the show without me, right?"

"They'll do it if I want them to," Josh said.

"And you want to, even if I can't, right?"

"I don't know."

We reached the stairs in front of my parents' house. It was three o'clock. Josh and I had walked and talked for two hours. Okay, maybe I kissed him a few more times, too. Okay, a lot.

"You'll get produced. A pilot and six episodes. So you have to do it," I said.

"I don't know."

I stomped up the steps. At the top, I turned around and glared down at him. "No! You cannot make me responsible. Not after what happened with the movie. Not again."

He ran up the steps. And this time, he kissed me. Let me remind you, Josh is a very nice kisser. Better than that. The best. Ever. While he was kissing me, I sort of—how shall I say this?—melted. So, when we stopped kissing, I said, "Okay."

His face lit up. "You'll do it?"

"I don't know."

"But—"

"Okay I'll think about it," I said. "I'm not saying no."

"You're not saying yes," he said.

"But I'm not saying no."

"Okay." Then he got shy, the way some guys get when they are about to ask you out. Which was quite the opposite of Reed. Although not even the tiniest thought of Reed came anywhere near my head at that moment. "Would you have dinner with me?" Josh finally asked.

"Of course," I said.

"Tonight?"

My heart fell. I know that is a cliché, but that's what it felt like. *Plop.* "I can't."

He looked like somebody hit him. "You have a date," he said.

"No," I said. "Are you kidding? I have a prom."

He looked at me like I was a little bit nuts, so I explained to him about the whole Helen Klosek and cousin Mary thing. When I finished, he said, "Oh." Then he said, "Can I come too?"

"Why would anybody in their right mind want to do that?" Perhaps that was not the very smartest thing for me to say, but it was what popped into my head, and out of my mouth.

"Because you'll be there," he said.

"Oh." That was *so* the right answer. "Yes. Absolutely." I had no authority to say that, but if I had to pass up an actual date, and if Josh was actually willing to help me stand guard over a bunch of hyper-hormoned high school seniors, you'd better believe I was going to let him.

"I know you have a dress to wear," he said.

I almost said "What dress?"—but then I knew exactly what dress. "You're kidding."

"It's perfect. Besides, how many occasions will you ever have to wear that dress?"

He had me there. "Okay."

"Wow," he said.

Can you imagine that? Josh Thomas asked if he could help me chaperone the Kirland high school prom, and if I would wear my Grandma's dress, I said yes, and he said "Wow" like I'd just agreed to marry him or something.

Not that I was thinking any such thing.

"Pick you up at seven?" he asked.

"Sure." I guess I might have come up with something more meaningful to say, but I was feeling fairly stunned. So I just gave him another little kiss and waved good-bye.

"Oh," Josh said, "I almost forgot." He reached in his pocket and dug out a small package, wrapped in pink paper and tied with a bow. He handed it to me.

"What's this?"

"I don't know. Françoise gave it to me like that. She said it came with the dress."

I tore the paper open. Fortunately, I saw what was inside before Josh did. I immediately stuffed the package into my pocket.

"What is it?" he asked.

"Nothing," I said. But it was not nothing. It was my little teeny thong, which was in my mom's suitcase when they took it away. I didn't pack it together with Grandma's dress, so don't ask me what somebody was thinking when they sold Françoise the dress and the thong together. All I can say is, if you know who that person is, tell them thank you.

"You're not going to show me?" asked Josh.

I thought carefully before I answered him. "Not right now," I finally said.

"Fine," he said, and smiled. "Seven o'clock." He ran to his rental car and drove away.

When he was out of sight, I went back into the house. Where I immediately panicked. Because I had only three and a half hours to get ready for the prom.

59

That may have been the most confusing and confused three and a half hours of my life. Which, if you take into account all I have been through, is saying quite a lot. Everything was running around and around in my head.

I wanted to be with Josh. Desperately.

I wanted to do the TV show.

I really thought a reality show would be more fun than a dramedy.

I couldn't do the TV show.

I promised Uncle John.

All of which may not sound enormously confused or confusing. But you try to figure those things out while you have only three and a half hours to get ready for the prom.

Of course, I wasn't actually *going* to the prom. I was still just *chaperoning* the prom. Except now I would be chaperoning with Josh. And wearing my Grandma's dress. Which as you know is the most amazing dress I have ever seen. Only now it was even more amazing, because it was the dress that Josh Thomas searched the entire city of Paris to find for me. Grandma had been right in the dream: The dress *had* taken care of itself. And everything really *was* coming together.

All of which made it feel strangely like it was my prom. Not the uninspiring prom I went to, either. The best-night-of-your-life prom that everybody always talks about. Which made it quite a big deal.

Here is the first thing I panicked about: Yes I had a dress. But I didn't know if it fit. Because I had never actually tried it on.

As you know, I have always thought of Grandma's dress as some kind of holy artifact. And also as an incredible source of power—grown-up, sexual, *dangerous* power. Over the years, I think I was afraid that if I actually dared to put it on, I might just melt, like the bad guys at the end of the first *Indiana Jones* movie. And I certainly never felt like I had *earned* the right to wear such a special dress.

Now I felt different, though. Not about the dress. If anything, it felt even holier and more powerful than ever, given the miraculous way it had come back to me. But for the first time, I felt like I had earned it. All on my own. I deserved to wear Grandma's dress. *My* dress.

And so what if a prom—and not even my own prom at that—was arguably a pretty frivolous occasion for wearing such a holy, powerful dress. The more I thought about it, the more it felt to me like the stars and the moon and the planets had all aligned perfectly, all for me, and it was as if they were spelling out a message for me in the sky, and it said WEAR THE DRESS.

So I showered, shaved all the relevant places, put on anti-perspirant, plucked a couple of eyebrow hairs I didn't like the look of, fixed my hair, fixed it again, spent too much time picking makeup, spent even more time picking shoes, brushed my teeth, flossed, mouthwashed, went to the bathroom about six times because I needed to be as skinny as possible, did thirty ab crunches okay twenty, and tried to do ten push-ups to give my arms and shoulders some definition but I'm sorry, push-ups are made for boys not girls. Then I went to the bathroom again, and put on perfume. Then I thought for two or three seconds about putting on panty hose, but no way. First, it was too hot and humid. Second, bare legs would be much more *dangerous,* especially under that skirt which you may remember is extremely sheer. Third and most important, I absolutely positively had to wear my thong, the one that fate had sent back with the dress.

Finally I couldn't think of anything else to do. Nothing else to avoid the moment of truth, when either the dress would fit or it wouldn't fit. I put it on.

It fit. Like it had been made for me. Perfectly. *Thank you Jesus.*

Which was perhaps a little hypocritical of me, because I am not the most devout religious person, notwithstanding all the hard work by my grade school nuns. But thank you anyway.

And thank you Grandma.

And oh, yeah. Thank you, Josh. So very, very much.

I walked down the stairs to the living room. When I came into sight, my mom and dad gasped. So I kind of figured I was doing something right.

Just then there was a knock at the door. "Go back upstairs," said my mom.

"Why?"

"Because you're supposed to keep boys waiting," she said. "Especially for a prom. It's traditional." She was quite right. It is traditional. You may even remember, when I had dinner with Reed at the Tribeca Grand, I kept him waiting. *Always keep men waiting,* I said.

"No," I said. I guess *always* actually means *except when it feels right not to.* I walked to the door and opened it.

Josh gasped. So I definitely figured I was doing something right.

I did not gasp. But almost. He was gorgeous. I mean handsome, sophisticated, sexy. He was wearing the most perfect tuxedo you have ever seen. Black of course. Notch lapels. Three-button jacket. White shirt. Black bow tie—hand-tied, I might add—perfect and classic, and much better in my opinion than one of those trendy straight ties. He looked amazing. I don't know if there is anything more perfect-looking than a man in a tuxedo. Okay Jude Law in a tuxedo. Maybe Josh Thomas was no Jude Law, but right now he was awfully close, let me tell you.

"You look . . . perfect," he said. Which by the way is absolutely the right thing for a man to say to a woman under these circumstances. Or frankly under any circumstances.

"You're wearing Armani," I said. Which was not as good as what he said. But I knew precisely what clothes he was wearing. A month ago I was selling those exact same clothes.

"That's right."

"Why did you have your tuxedo with you?"

"I didn't. I just bought it. In Chicago."

"It fits perfectly," I said. Which it did. Which made no sense. Because a tuxedo off the rack never fits perfectly. Not even an Armani tuxedo. It has to be altered.

"I had it altered," he said.

"That's impossible," I said. Remember, I know how long it takes to do alterations.

"You got a passport in three hours," he said.

"Less."

"Exactly." Then he shrugged. "Okay, I paid extra." I bet he did.

Josh took something out from behind his back. It was a corsage. The wrist kind.

"You're kidding," I said.

"You can't go to the prom without a corsage," he said.

"It's not my prom." Maybe those were the words that came out of my mouth. But that was not how I felt. I felt like this was the most special, most important night of my life.

I almost started to cry. But I willed myself not to. I was not about to ruin my makeup.

He held out his arm. I slipped my hand under his elbow. We walked down the stairs and to the curb. Where he had a stretch waiting. Not a stretch limousine. Not exactly, anyway.

It was a white stretch Hummer.

60

"It's a Hummer," I said.

"All the regular limos are booked up. On account of this being prom season."

"It's a Hummer," I said.

"It was the best I could do on short notice."

The driver unfolded a chrome stepladder. Josh helped me step up into the long back seat. Then he climbed in after me. The driver folded the stepladder and closed the door.

"Besides," Josh said, "they're made in Indiana."

That is when I kissed him. To hell with my makeup.

It is a very short drive from my parents' house to Reinhardt's restaurant. But for the entire length of the drive, we did not talk about Hummers. Or anything else, for that matter.

When we got to Reinhardt's I did my best to fix my makeup. There was a mirror in the back seat. I don't know if all stretch limos have a mirror, but the stretch Hummer did.

We climbed down the stepladder. The parking lot was full. There were a bunch of rented limousines, mostly black, several white, and one that was a hideous shade of pink. Then there were the usual Indiana high school cars, sagging old beater Trans Ams and Mustangs that senior boys had tried and failed to polish into presentable. But at least they had tried.

Josh offered me his arm again. "Shall we?"

"Wait," I said. I had an idea. "Do TV shows have UPMs?" UPM is a unit production manager. You remember that.

"Sure," he said. "I think so."

"Do executive producers get to hire UPMs?"

"I guess," he said. "Why?"

"Because," I said. "We can hire Marty the UPM. He wants to be reborn as a Hoosier. He can move to Kirland. He can work half time on our TV show, and half time for Uncle John. That way I can do the show."

Josh frowned. "It's a crazy idea. I read your book, remember? You said Marty would be reborn as a Hoosier the day Nick Timko came home to Kirland. Meaning never."

"It's the only idea I've got." I tried to smile. "It *might* work."

"What about your uncle?"

"My uncle *might* like Marty."

Josh tried to smile back. I could tell he wanted to be encouraging, even though he didn't believe it. "I should have thought of that," he said.

"But you didn't," I said. "So I guess I cannot trust you to do my show without me."

"I guess not," he said. "Ready for the prom?"

"Wait," I said. I had another idea. "Do TV shows have fashion consultants?"

"Sure," he said. "Costume designers, anyway." Then he figured out where I was going. As I told you, Josh is a pretty smart guy. "But I'm not sure somebody with Celestine's fashion credentials is necessarily the perfect costume designer for a show about Kirland, Indiana."

"Oh." I guess I looked disappointed.

"Although she did spend a year at Purdue," Josh said.

I brightened up. "Plus she always loved wearing my boring Midwestern clothes," I said.

Josh smiled. "Ask her to come for a vacation. We'll see what we can figure out."

I tried to picture Celestine on the loose in Kirland. Boilermaker boys, watch out.

"Thank you," I said to Josh. Then I kissed him again. Only very carefully this time. Because I really didn't want to have to keep fixing my makeup.

When I finished kissing him, he said, "Okay, ready?"

"Wait." If Josh was getting tired of my ideas, it didn't show. He was looking at me like I was the most interesting person on the planet. "*Survivor* doesn't have writers, does it?"

"No," Josh said.

"But somebody created *Survivor,* right?"

"Sure."

"Do you think the person who created *Survivor* is rich?"

Josh laughed. Then he held up both hands. "Okay."

"Okay, it can be a reality show?" I asked.

"Okay, I'll think about it," he said.

"Okay," I said to Josh, and I hooked my hand under his arm. "Let's go."

"Wait," Josh said.

He stepped back and gave me a long look, from the top of my head to the soles of my feet. Which made me instantly self-conscious. "What's wrong?" I asked.

"Nothing," he said. "Absolutely nothing. You're perfect." At which I relaxed. Because a guy cannot do much better than to tell you that you are perfect. "I just had an idea. If we did a reality show—"

Now he had my absolute undivided attention.

"—maybe we could do something about your dress. Like a contest. Whoever can figure out how your Grandma got it wins. It must be a great story."

As I have told you, ever since I inherited it, I have been dying to know how Grandma got the dress. But I couldn't figure it out. "I researched it," I said. "I couldn't find the answer."

"You weren't competing for a million dollars," he said.

Which was true.

"If my Grandma's dress is on the show, does that mean I have to be on it, too?"

Josh shrugged. "I don't know. Probably. You're part of the story."

Hmm. Notwithstanding my brush with TV stardom on Fox News—or perhaps because of it—I was pretty sure I did not want to be part of anybody's primetime lineup.

I think Josh read my mind. Because he immediately said, "Maybe it doesn't have to be about your Grandma's dress. There must be other dangerous dresses out there. And other stories. Maybe we could go looking for the best dangerous-dress story."

Wow. I don't know about you, but *I* would watch a TV show full of dangerous-dress stories. "Will the network buy that kind of show?"

Josh smiled. "We won't know until we ask them." Then he gave me a perfect tiny little kiss on the lips.

"Okay," I said. "Now let's go to the prom."

61

We walked in.

Reinhardt's restaurant is a huge place. If every seat was filled, it would probably hold ten percent of the population of Kirland, Indiana. Do not ask me what made old Mr. Reinhardt such an optimist to think that one in ten Kirlanders (which if you think about it is a much more dignified term than Bumfuckers) would show up at his restaurant every night. Most nights, there are an awful lot of empty seats. But it is the perfect size for high school proms. Which probably explains why the Kent prom is never held anywhere else.

The place was overflowing with color: colored balloons, colored streamers, and miles of colored tissue paper. I suppose the decorations for every prom are colorful, but this was like somebody put a giant Spiral Art in the middle of the floor, turned it on high, then dumped out the entire contents of Joe Vajda's paint store and let everything fly everywhere.

Looking around that vast color-stained room, a new thought occurred to me. New, as in, a thought that I am absolutely sure had never occurred to me, ever, in my entire life. I wondered, *What would the Kent high school prom at Reinhardt's restaurant look like on TV?*

I'm not sure if Josh read my mind, but he looked around, too. "Nice," he said.

A big banner at one end of the room said THE COLORS OF YOUR LIFE, which explained the overstimulated decorations. Obviously that was the theme of the prom. Every prom has a theme. Not just in

Kirland. In America. I believe it is a federal law. I tried to think what song "the colors of your life" is from. Because in Kirland the theme is always a song lyric. And I did not recognize the lyric. Right away I felt old. Only twenty-five, and I was already so out of touch that I didn't know what song the prom theme came from.

As Josh and I walked across the floor, I got a better look at the banner. In the bottom right corner, it said FROM "INVISIBLE," BY CLAY AIKEN. Clay Aiken, as in *American Idol.* I guess Kirland is a very Clay Aiken kind of place. But I didn't feel so bad anymore about not recognizing the lyric. Actually I felt kind of relieved.

Walking across the room made me remember my own prom. Everybody and their dates were color-coordinated. If the boy wore a powder-blue tuxedo, the girl wore a powder-blue dress. If the girl insisted on wearing a magenta gown, well then, her boyfriend was obligated to find magenta formal wear. For reasons I cannot explain, almost nobody wore black or white. I got stuck wearing brown. To match a boy I didn't even like. The brown dress is yet another aspect of my prom that was undistinguished. But that is neither here nor there. Looking around, I saw that color-coordination was still the rule. For some reason, that made me happy.

Then I wondered if prom dates across the country color-coordinate. And if TV audiences would find this interesting. I bet they would. In fact, suddenly, everything about Kirland struck me as considerably more interesting than it had ever been before.

Okay not everything. At that moment, Mrs. Zuback walked up to me. She was my Social Studies teacher in the tenth *and* eleventh grades. She was not interesting in the tenth grade. She was even less interesting in the eleventh grade. And even seen through executive-producer eyes, she was still not interesting.

She recognized me. "Jane?"

"Hello, Mrs. Zuback," I said.

She seemed puzzled. "Not your prom, is it?"

"No."

"Oh." Then she looked at me. "Nice dress," she said, and walked away.

Well, even if she was not interesting, she got credit for noticing my dress. Although how could she not? I looked around at the seniors and their dates. Suffice it to say that among all the lilacs and mauves and taupes and limes and burnt siennas, nobody was wearing a dress like mine.

I wondered how many compliments I would get. A lot, I was sure. I was not being immodest. On the contrary, I think I am a pretty modest person, and ordinarily I do not expect to attract much attention. But this was not ordinarily. I was wearing my Grandma's dress. Which, if I have done my job at all in writing this story, you understand by now is a dress the likes of which no one living in Kirland, Indiana has ever seen, excluding of course my immediate family. It is also, as I hope I have conveyed to you, a grown-up, sexual, dangerous dress. Just like it says in Josh's screenplay. Even Scarlett Johansson dressed up for the Oscars would not look better than I looked in Grandma's dress.

Okay maybe she would look a little prettier. Because I think Scarlett Johansson is prettier than me. But I don't care whose dress she wears to the Oscars, even if it is from Mister Giorgio Armani himself, it could not look any better than the dress I had on.

No offense, Mister Armani.

In any event, I'm quite sure nobody at the Roger Wells Kent senior prom ever saw such a dress. Much less *me* in such a dress. Much less me in such a dress accompanied by very very handsome Josh Thomas, who was wearing, as I said, an incredibly dashing tuxedo (which if you are curious in French is *le smoking*) and shirt (*la chemise*) and bow tie (*le papillon*), all by, as I said, Mister Giorgio Armani. So I was certain we would attract attention.

Only we didn't. Because you are not going to believe who was there, getting all the attention.

Nick Timko.

Nick Timko.

Cousin Mary's Nick Timko. Nick Timko who got all sticky with Tina Kaminski at their senior prom twenty years ago, Nick who broke Mary's heart and ran away and played baseball and never came back. *That* Nick Timko. Only now when people talk obsessively about Nick Timko—which, as I told you in the very first chapter, people still do—they can't say he never came back. Hell has frozen over. Pigs have flown. *Nick Timko has come home.*

Suddenly my idea about Marty the UPM did not seem crazy at all. Suddenly I knew that my uncle really *would* like Marty.

I looked at Josh. "I can do the show. I really can."

He could tell I was serious. He gave me a huge hug.

In the middle of the hug, somebody tapped me on my shoulder. "That'll be enough of that," said a voice I remembered. I unwrapped myself from Josh and turned around. Mr. Demjanich, the high school principal, had his arms crossed and was looking at me disapprovingly. Then he recognized me. "Miss Stuart?"

I said, "Yes."

He said, "Not your prom, is it?"

I said, "No."

He said, "You're chaperoning."

I said, "Yes."

He said, "Nice dress." Then he told me about Nick Timko.

I already told you that Dave Stankowski died. And that Dave was the baseball coach at Kent forever, which means of course that he was Nick's coach. Somehow Nick heard. He came back for the funeral. And I guess twenty minutes in the major leagues and twenty years in the minors is enough for anybody. At least it was enough for Nick. I mean, he's got to be, what, thirty-eight years old? Although I must say, he looks awfully good for thirty-eight.

Even if I didn't tell Josh that.

But anyway, apparently Nick is staying. He's taking Dave Stankowski's job coaching the baseball team. He's also going to teach math. And as his very first official duty as an employee of Roger Wells Kent High School, he is chaperoning the senior prom.

Which is more than a little ironic, if you think about it.

I wonder if my cousin Mary knows yet.

I wonder if my *Uncle John* knows yet.

All of a sudden, because of Nick, things with Josh are just the littlest extra bit more complicated.

Do not get me wrong. Even though Nick is still a very handsome man, my interest in him is purely professional. Nick Timko moving back home is very possibly the single most interesting thing that has happened in Kirland. Not recently. Ever.

Imagine that somebody hired you to make a TV show about Amelia Earhart. Who as you probably know was a famous aviatrix. Which by the way has always sounded like a dirty word to me even though it isn't. Anyway she went off on some historic flight, then she disappeared and was never heard from again.

Now imagine that after all those years, Amelia came flying back into town. You wouldn't leave, right? You'd stick around. You'd want to find out where she had been, and what she had done, and you'd want to see what happens next.

I am not saying Nick Timko is any Amelia Earhart. He's not. Then again, to a town like Kirland, he is. He is our hero and our villain, our Forrest Gump and our Freddy Krueger, all rolled into one. He is our very own prodigal son, and I know my grade school nuns are proud of me for remembering that story and using it appropriately in a modern context. In the Bible, the prodigal son is welcomed back with open arms. In Kirland . . . well, I am not so sure.

If Josh and I are going to create and executive produce and technical-advise and cowrite a whole TV show about Kirland . . . well, we can't leave *yet.* First we have to see what happens. About Nick Timko, of course. But it's not just Nick Timko. I know this is an odd thing for me to say. But all of a sudden, somehow . . . Kirland is a lot more *interesting* than it used to be.

I don't know if our show will be a dramedy like Josh wants, or a reality show like I want. Maybe we'll invent a whole new kind of program. After all, Kirland, Indiana is different from anyplace I've